Merry Christmas
to
Stephanie & David
from
John & Mary Ellen Lundstin
1985

By L. Christian Balling

THE BLACK CHAPEL FILE

THE FOURTH SHOT

MALLORY'S GAMBIT

Mallory's Gambit

L. Christian Balling

Mallory's Gambit

The Atlantic Monthly Press
BOSTON / NEW YORK

FIRST EDITION

LIBRARY OF CONGRESS CATALOGING-IN-PUBLICATION DATA

Balling, L. Christian.
  Mallory's gambit.

  I. Title.
PS3552.A468M34 1984   813'.54   85-47785
ISBN 0-87113-02-6

BP

Published simultaneously in Canada

PRINTED IN THE UNITED STATES OF AMERICA

For
Livia, Christy, and Daria

With appreciation to
Katherine, John, and David Mulhern

My life I never held but as a pawn
To wage against thine enemies.

—SHAKESPEARE

Mallory's Gambit

Prologue

THE microfilm was old. It had been buried in the CIA archives for more than twenty years. Pendleton removed the film spool from its plastic case and slipped it onto the spindle of the film reader. He was probably the first to read the report since it had been transferred to microfilm and filed away. Pendleton switched on the reader and turned off his desk lamp, plunging his office into darkness. Working by feel and the stray light spilling from the projection-lamp housing, he threaded the film through the guide path and onto the take-up spool.

Pendleton liked darkness, and he had an affinity for the night; but because he could not complete all his work at night, his office had been designed to shut out the day. The room was fully sound-proofed, and the windows were sealed with black, lighttight drapes. It had the cloistered, secretive atmosphere of a medieval chamber.

Another man with Pendleton's idiosyncrasies might have been labeled an eccentric, but the more bizarre aspects of Pendleton's character only added to his mystique. Within the CIA, Pendleton, Chief of Counterintelligence, was a legend.

Pendleton pressed the film-advance button, and a series of introductory file codes flashed across the screen. With the sure timing of long practice he released the button precisely at the right moment, freezing the first page of the report on the screen. But he did not begin to read immediately.

He took a pipe from the pocket of his worn tweed jacket, stoked it, and struck a match, the flame glinting on the lenses of his horn-rimmed glasses. He drew steadily on the pipe until the tobacco was well alight, taking his time, savoring a sense of anticipation.

Sometimes, when he was immersed in a particularly deep game, the steps required to thread his way through its intricacies suddenly fell into a logical progression. This was one of those occasions. He did not know precisely what he would find in the report he was about to read, but he was convinced that it would take him a step closer to his goal.

The report had been prepared in 1945 by an OSS staff officer. It was a case history of a British Intelligence operation in World War II. Because OSS training and methods had been patterned on the British model, a study had been commissioned at the close of the war to review British operations and to assess their effectiveness.

Pendleton shifted position so that the smoke from his pipe did not drift across the translucent screen, adjusted the lens focus, and began to read.

CIA Archive No. 75434-R03   OPTRICYCLE
OSS/HIS/EV-44   Page 1

This report summarizes an operation undertaken by the British Special Operations Executive in March, 1944. In the overall context of the current study, it is important to analyze SOE failures as well as successes, and Operation Tricycle was one such failure.

Tricycle is of particular interest because an OSS operative participated in the mission, although no OSS planners were involved in its preparation. In retrospect this circumstance is startling, as the mission — even if it had succeeded — might well have jeopardized the secrecy of significant aspects of American nuclear research . . .

Pendleton smiled sardonically, remembering. The British had nurtured the OSS and had molded it in their image — the better to control it. The Americans had been slow to learn that trust was not always a two-way street, even among friends.

. . . The origins of Operation Tricycle are not entirely clear, as our British colleagues have not been totally forthcoming. The objective of the mission was to assassinate Dr. Hans Damberg, a German nuclear physicist, and it seems safe to assume that the assassination was suggested to SOE by personnel in Tube Alloys, the agency created to coordinate nuclear research in Britain. . . .

Pendleton nodded to himself. That was more than a safe assumption; it was a certainty. Midway through the war, the Tube Alloys Directorate had bowed to the inevitable and had dropped out of the race to build an atomic bomb, sending Britain's nuclear physicists to Los Alamos to work under the Americans. The remaining Tube Alloys personnel had concentrated on espionage — a field in which Britain had been preeminent.

All intelligence relating to German nuclear research had been passed by SIS, the British intelligence service, to Tube Alloys for evaluation, and Tube Alloys had selected its own targets for sabotage. Requests for action were passed to the Special Operations Executive, the paramilitary arm of British Intelligence, where they received top priority. SOE agents assigned to those missions were instructed to press home their attacks without regard to losses.

. . . The record indicates that the SOE was reluctant to carry out this particular operation, which was mounted in haste and without a full complement of properly trained operatives; but apparently Tube Alloys insisted, alarmed by a report SIS had received from a reliable source inside Germany's scientific community.

Throughout the war, the Germans had relied exclusively on heavy water as a moderator for the nuclear reactors they were attempting to build, and SOE sabotage raids on the Norwegian hydroelectric plant which supplied Germany with heavy water had crippled German nuclear development.

The SIS agent had reported that Professor Damberg was planning to reinvestigate the feasibility of graphite as a substitute for heavy water. The Germans had not pursued this possibility because their early experiments had erroneously indicated that graphite was unsuitable. Allied scientists already knew that graphite would work.

The SIS report also stated that Damberg was scheduled to visit the cyclotron laboratory in Paris, which the Germans had staffed with their own physicists. The visit was set for sometime in March, and Tube Alloys, anxious to prevent the Germans from discovering their error, requested the assassination of Damberg in Paris. Apparently Tube Alloys was willing to risk the possibility that the assassination attempt itself would focus attention on Damberg's recent work . . .

And they took the risk without consulting the American liaison group, Pendleton noted sourly. He remembered too well how high-handed the British could be in intelligence matters. They had been the professionals, the Americans the amateurs. The shoe had been on the other foot for decades now, but the memories still smarted.

. . . Even with adequate preparation, the mission would have been desperate, for an attack on Damberg while he was en route between his hotel and the university laboratory was not feasible. Manpower was necessary for an effective ambush — manpower which could only have come from Résistance units in Paris. But by 1944 the Résistance was riddled with German agents, and in Paris the Gestapo was having a field day: arrests were raining down. The danger of betrayal was too great to enlist the Paris Maquis in the assassination attempt.

For this reason, the SOE opted for an attack by a single man who would slip in close for the kill. The cyclotron laboratory was heavily guarded; and wherever Damberg stayed in Paris, he was sure to be within a German security sector. To penetrate the security cordon, the assassin was to pose as a Gestapo agent. A Gestapo ID was not a problem, as SOE forgeries were excellent, but the man had to speak faultless German.

Because of time pressure, the SOE was unable to provide an agent of its own for the job, and it turned to the OSS. A young OSS officer who spoke German like a native was available. He had operated successfully behind enemy lines in Italy, but had had no experience in France and his French was at the schoolbook level. To get the American safely into Paris, the SOE chose one of their own experienced operatives. Recently returned from France, this agent had solid contacts with a reliable Maquis unit northwest of the capital.

The plan might not have been so ill-conceived had it not been for a critical obstacle. The SIS report had not stated the precise dates on which Damberg was to be in Paris, nor where he would stay in the city. In order to locate him, the agents would have to keep watch on the cyclotron laboratory and await his arrival. But the SOE had no photographs of Damberg.

A third man, who could recognize Damberg on sight, had to be recruited for the team. Only days before the deadline for scrubbing the mission, a man was found, a young Cambridge physical chemist who had studied under Damberg in Göttingen before the war. He was completely untrained, and there was not even time to put him through a parachute course.

Neither the civilian nor the two professionals were told why Damberg had to die.

Only the most extreme pressure from Tube Alloys could have forced the SOE to risk one of its most experienced operatives in what must have been viewed as a hopeless mission. To go in without adequate preparation, without reliable support in Paris, and without a detailed plan of action was bad enough, but in addition the SOE agent was required to shepherd an untrained and undoubtedly nervous civilian every step of the way . . .

Pendleton frowned slightly, unwilling to accept the note of censure in the old report. The stakes had been high enough for desperate measures. Pendleton had known some of the men who must have been responsible for Operation Tricycle. He understood the way they had reasoned, the imperatives that had driven them.

But he was not interested in the mission itself, only in the participants. He had spent a lifetime analyzing men's reactions and motives, and he had a rich imagination. As he read on, patiently digesting the report, he fleshed out the narrative in his mind until the people and events became real to him.

1

T HE bomber carrying the assassination team to France took off at dusk. The Halifax climbed to its cruising altitude and lumbered out over the Channel, looking like a giant black insect as it droned into the distance, silhouetted against the dull orange glow lingering in the western sky. Three miles off the coast it picked up its fighter escort. The two Spitfires swept in from the north and swung into position above and behind the Halifax. As the light faded and darkness enveloped the aircraft, the Spitfires closed up on it, the pilots focusing on the flickering blue exhaust flames from its engines.

Inside the bomber, the three-man team sat on narrow benches running along the fuselage walls. The aircraft's dimly lit interior was empty; the three men were the sole cargo. Lieutenant Richard Mallory slouched on his bench, his back pressed against the ribbed aluminum wall. The thrumming vibration of the aircraft helped to ease the tension that always gripped him before a jump. Sitting opposite him were Max Ryder, the team leader, and Roland Stebbings, their spotter.

Watching Stebbings, Mallory knew he was going to be trouble. The bookish, sandy-haired chemist was so frightened he couldn't even begin to hide it. His hands were in constant motion, fiddling with the straps of his parachute harness, plucking at the folds of his jumpsuit.

Ryder was also watching Stebbings. He leaned toward him and poked him jovially in the ribs. "Cheer up, Stebbings!" Ryder shouted over the thunder of the engines. "It won't be so bad."

"But I've never jumped before," Stebbings said, his voice all but lost in the engine noise. Mallory had to read his lips to understand him.

"That doesn't matter," Ryder yelled cheerfully. "There has to be a first time, and this way you only have to jump once."

Stebbings tried to smile, but he didn't quite succeed.

"There's nothing to it," Ryder persisted. "There's only one thing to worry about: be sure you look up as you drop through the hatch. Otherwise you may crack your nose on the rim."

Straightforward encouragement was not working, so Ryder tried gallows humor. "You don't have to worry about the chute not opening. We'll be jumping from eight hundred feet. If it doesn't open, you'll hit the ground before you realize it."

Stebbings turned a shade whiter, and Mallory tried to catch Ryder's eye.

"There's never any blood," Ryder shouted with a grin. "Your insides are smashed to jelly, but there's never any *blood*."

Stebbings looked as if he were about to vomit.

"C-cut it out, Max," Mallory said.

Ryder shrugged and winked at Mallory. "Okay, kid," he said easily. "Bad joke." He settled back, stretched out his long legs, and closed his eyes, his fine-boned, patrician face totally relaxed. Minutes later he was asleep.

Mallory admired his style. Mallory wasn't ashamed of his own fear, for he had learned to control it, but the burden of it was excess baggage he would have preferred to leave behind.

Ryder began to snore, but it was a genteel snoring. Even while he slept there was a touch of the aristocrat in the slim, dark-haired SOE officer, yet there was nothing effete about him. A man had to be tough and resourceful to survive three missions to France.

Colonel Phelps, the officer who had organized the mission, had sent Mallory and Ryder to Scotland to suffer through an SOE refresher course together, while Phelps had scoured the country for a man who could recognize Damberg. Ten days of training side by side was no substitute for working together behind enemy lines, but there had been enough time for the two men to adjust to each other, to feel each other out.

They had gotten along well from the start, partly because Ryder was also an American. He had been living in France when the war broke out, and he had immediately crossed the Channel to join the British army. Within six months the SOE had discovered him and snapped him up. Mallory knew little of Ryder's background beyond the fact that his parents, wealthy and divorced, had educated him in British boarding schools and had then set him adrift on the Continent. What Mallory did know was that Ryder was an experienced, self-assured operative.

Mallory was twenty-three and Ryder was twenty-eight, but in terms of experience, Ryder was even older. Yet he didn't shove his experience down Mallory's throat; he treated him as an equal, assuming without insistence that Mallory would follow his lead when necessary. Ryder's presence was the only thing Mallory liked about the mission.

Stebbings was another matter — the wild card, and a worrisome one. Watching him fidget was fraying Mallory's nerves. Perhaps Stebbings would pull himself together once they were on the ground, but Mallory knew that was a forlorn hope. Stebbings wasn't simply untrained; he was the wrong type of man. They should have scrubbed the damned mission rather than drag Stebbings into it, Mallory thought. The Germans had the right word for this kind of mission: *Himmelfahrtskommando* — a mission straight to heaven . . .

Mallory stood up, wrenching away from his thoughts. Take it a step at a time. Thinking too far ahead was dangerous. He turned and made his way back to where the rear gunner's legs dangled from the overhead gun turret. He tapped one of the gunner's feet and poked his head up into the turret, which was flooded with moonlight.

"Anything to see?"

"Stars and the Channel, mate," the gunner said. "And the two Spits on our tail."

Mallory raised his head until he could see the Channel below them, shimmering silver under the moon. "Is that land over there?" he asked. "That dark patch to the north."

"What you see is cloud cover moving in. That's its shadow on the water."

"But they said —" Mallory bit off his comment. There was no point complaining about bad luck; it only made things worse. "Thanks for the view," he said, withdrawing from the turret.

"Any time, mate, any time," the gunner called down.

Mallory shivered. It was cold in the plane, and his hands were like ice. He unzipped the outer pockets of his jumpsuit and shoved his hands inside, wishing he could get at his cigarettes, which were out of reach in a side pocket of the civilian jacket he wore beneath the jumpsuit.

Restless, he worked his way forward again, balancing against the uneven pitching of the aircraft. Walking was awkward, encumbered as he was by his parachute and thick spine pad. Stebbings did not look up as Mallory passed him; he was staring fixedly at the circular hatch in the floor through which they would drop. Stebbings had too much imagination, Mallory thought, and he was making the mistake of giving it free rein.

Mallory continued forward to the cockpit, where the jumpmaster was hunkered down behind the copilot's seat, talking with the pilots. He was a strapping, flat-faced career sergeant with open, friendly eyes.

"I thought I m-might be able to bum a cigarette from one of you guys," Mallory said.

"Sure, Yank," the copilot said over his shoulder, pulling a pack from his flight jacket.

"Thanks," Mallory said, extracting a cigarette and handing back the pack.

The jumpmaster flicked his lighter and held the flame up for Mallory. "Weather's clouding up," he said. "Sooner than expected. It could be a bad night for a jump. You'll have to watch yourselves."

Mallory nodded, drawing smoke deep into his lungs and holding it there. As he exhaled, some of his tension left him with the smoke. The jumpmaster and the pilots had been deep in conversation as he'd come forward, but now they were silent. Mallory tried a few casual comments, but he lacked the ability to settle into an easy camaraderie with strangers, and conversation died out again. Finally he gave up and returned to his seat.

Ryder still slept, and Stebbings still stared at the exit hatch. He was no longer fidgeting; he sat quite still, his hands clenched in his lap. Mallory reached across and tapped him on the knee.

"Why don't you try to get some sleep, Roland. We have a long way to go yet."

Stebbings managed a weak smile and nodded, but soon he was staring at the hatch again. Mallory dropped his half-smoked cigarette to the floor and ground it under his heel. There was nothing he could do for Stebbings, and Ryder had the right idea. He stretched out his legs, leaned back and closed his eyes.

With his eyes closed, the thunder of the engines and the vibration of the aircraft had a mind-numbing, hypnotic effect, but Mallory doubted that he would be able to sleep. He was too keyed up. He would try, but he didn't think he could drift off . . .

A violent lurch brought Mallory out of his sleep with a start. The Halifax was pitching as if it were caught in a storm, and Mallory felt a sudden pressure on his eardrums as the pilot put the aircraft into a shallow dive. He saw Stebbings seize the bench with both hands, his eyes wide and frightened.

Ryder had also come awake, and he reached out and gripped Stebbings's arm. "We must be passing over the Atlantic Wall," he yelled. "The pilot's taking us down underneath the flak. We'll be through it soon."

Gradually the buffeting diminished and then ceased altogether, but the pilot did not climb for more altitude. They would make the run across France at low level. Ryder glanced at Stebbings and then at Mallory.

"Might as well go through a final check," Ryder said, unzipping the outer pockets of his jumpsuit. Mallory nodded. They had plenty of time yet, but this was for Stebbings's benefit — to give him something to do.

Mallory checked his outer pockets first, drawing out the items one by one and reinserting them. Benzedrine tablets, the regulation compass and knife, the cumbersome revolver. He knew that Ryder intended to dump his as soon as they landed. Ryder refused to carry the prescribed handgun, convinced that it was a psychological crutch of no real value. Mallory agreed with him. A pistol wasn't a substitute for cunning, and if one were captured, the gun would simply provoke an additional Gestapo beating.

The silenced pistol they had brought with them for the job was another matter; it was stowed in the radio pack.

Stebbings had also begun to check his own pockets, and that at least was a good sign. He was still functioning. Mallory stood up and unzipped the front of his jumpsuit so that he could get at the inside breast pocket of his civilian jacket. Inside was his wallet. He drew it out and checked the contents, though he knew everything would be there: French identity papers, ration cards, a thick wad of folding money.

"All right, lads, it won't be long now," the sergeant said. "The Rebecca should pick up the homing signal any time now. Cloud cover has moved in solid, and it's black as bloody pitch down below. You won't be able to see the ground, so you'd better start counting as soon as you drop clear. When you reach thirty get set to hit the ground."

Mallory pulled his rucksack out from beneath his seat and strapped it to his left leg. Ryder strapped his to one leg and the radio pack to the other, and then he leaned over to help Stebbings, who seemed unable to cope with his rucksack bindings.

Mallory, the only one who wore glasses, removed them and placed them in a protective case in his jumpsuit. He carried an extra pair in his rucksack, for he couldn't function without them. He had gotten through the regulation eye tests by memorizing the eye charts.

The three men pulled rubber jump helmets down over their ears, tightened the straps, and stood up to attach their parachute static lines to the cable above them. Stebbings, glassy-eyed, moved like an automaton. Ryder would jump first, Stebbings would follow, and then Mallory. With only three men jumping there should be no problem, but if Stebbings balked, Mallory would have to act quickly to avoid missing the drop zone.

The jumpmaster made a cursory check of their chute packs and hookups and then bent over the hatch and pulled off its canvas cover. Cold air streamed in through the opening and swirled about their legs. Mallory heard a yell from the cockpit, and the red signal light on the fuselage wall above the hatch came on.

"Get set!" the sergeant shouted, and Ryder and Stebbings stepped to the hatch and lowered themselves to the floor on opposite sides of the opening. Mallory closed up behind Stebbings, and he exchanged a quick glance with the jumpmaster. The sergeant could see that Stebbings might give them trouble.

Ryder swung his legs down through the opening, gripping the hatch rim with both hands, and looked up at the sergeant, whose eyes were fixed on the signal lights. The lights flashed from red to green. "Go!" the jumpmaster yelled. Ryder pushed off, stiffened his body, and dropped through the hatch into the black void below.

Immediately Stebbings swung his own legs down through the opening, and for a moment Mallory thought he would be all right. But then Stebbings froze. Mallory bent forward and seized him under the arms, trying to lift him out over the hatch rim, but Mallory was a small man and not very strong, and he couldn't shift him. Precious seconds were ticking way.

With the last of his strength Mallory drove his knee into Stebbings's back and thrust him forward, literally kicking him out of the aircraft. Stebbings's sharp, terrified cry was whipped away by the slipstream as he fell through the hole.

Mallory dropped into position. "Don't jump, sir!" the sergeant yelled, seizing him by the shoulder, and Mallory saw that the red warning light had come back on. "We'll have to come round and make another run in," the sergeant cried, signaling to the copilot, who was looking back from the cockpit.

Mallory hung on as the pilot banked the Halifax around in a 180-degree turn. His legs dangled through the hatch, the wind tearing at them. Again the lights flashed from red to green.

"Go!"

Just in time Mallory remembered to tilt back his head as he pushed off and dropped through the hole. The engine roar rose to deafening intensity for an instant before the slipstream slammed into him, and then he was clear, falling like a stone. A moment later he felt the wrench of the harness as his chute opened. The rumble of the invisible bomber was already fading. Too late, Mallory realized that he'd forgotten to count. Below him a twinkling red necklace of hand-held flashlights marked the drop zone.

2

MALLORY landed badly. He sensed the ground rushing up at him only an instant before he hit. He landed hard on his left foot and it twisted under him. His clumsy roll saved him from breaking his ankle, but he had to grind his teeth to suppress the cry of pain that rose in his throat. Luckily there was no wind to fill his chute, or he would have been dragged across the open field in which he'd landed. Mallory's frustrated instructor at Fort Bragg had sworn that Mallory would never learn to make a clean jump, and the instructor had been right. It took several seconds for Mallory to recover sufficiently to free himself from the harness and begin to pull in the silk canopy.

He unfastened the rucksack from his leg, stood up and swung it onto his shoulder, ignoring the shooting pains in his ankle. He couldn't allow the ankle to stiffen up and cripple him. He was in enemy territory now, and pain had to be endured. Pain wouldn't kill a man, but weakness could.

He heard the crunching footfalls of someone running toward him across the field of dead, brittle grass, and he pulled out his glasses and slipped them on. Two shadows, one large and one small, emerged from the darkness and flitted toward him.

"Welcome to France, monsieur," the smaller shadow greeted him in a stage whisper. It was a girl's voice. As the larger shadow silently gathered up Mallory's parachute, the girl seized his hand to guide him. Her fingers felt feverishly hot against his, which were cold and wet from the dew.

She tugged Mallory in the direction of a wood at the far end of the field, its black outline just discernible in the darkness, and as she broke into a run she released his hand. Gritting his teeth, Mallory tried to keep up with her, but he couldn't, and for a moment he lost sight of her shadowy form. Then, abruptly, she was at his side again.

"Are you hurt, monsieur?"

"My ankle — I twisted it in the landing," Mallory whispered back in halting French, wondering irrelevantly why he never stammered when he spoke a foreign language. "It will be all right."

"Lean on me. We must go quickly."

"Thanks, but I can manage. I'll keep up."

They went on, but the girl stayed beside him and held the pace to a brisk walk. At the edge of the wood the other members of the Maquis reception committee were waiting for them. Mallory couldn't be sure in the darkness, but there seemed to be at least a dozen of them, with Ryder and Stebbings in their midst.

"You're hurt," Ryder said, speaking French.

"Twisted my ankle. It's not too bad."

A tall, commanding figure stepped forward. "I am Lessard," the Frenchman said, grasping Mallory's hand firmly. "Max tells me you are called Richard."

"Yes."

Ryder had contempt for the use of code names in the field, and they had opted to use their own first names.

"Max and I are old friends, and I hope you and I will become friends as well," Lessard said quickly. "We will talk, but not here. A *Boche* patrol passed by minutes ago, and they will return soon."

Mallory heard spades digging into the earth somewhere within the wood. Lessard's men were apparently burying the chutes, and that was a good sign. Ryder had told Mallory that Lessard, a former army officer, ran a disciplined unit, and this was an indication of it. Too often the Maquis preferred to keep the parachutes for the silk.

"We will use a path through the woods that is narrow and difficult to follow," Lessard said to Mallory, "so stay close to the man in front of you."

Silently the group filtered single file through the wood; Ryder and Mallory kept Stebbings between them. Mallory couldn't tell how the chemist was holding up, but Stebbings had survived the jump without injury, which was more than Mallory could say. His ankle was still painful, but he could walk on it.

Mallory found himself wondering where the girl was, and he shook his head in self-derision. What a damned fool he was! A voice and the warm touch of a hand in the darkness — was that all it took to arouse his interest?

But he continued to think about her; it kept his mind off the pain. Not that he would try to do anything about it, if he did see her again. It was too bad he couldn't remain in the dark forever — the heroic mystery man dropped from the sky. In the light she would see him as he was — a short, skinny young man with thick glasses. For that matter, how did he know what she was like? Perhaps she was fat and ugly.

Mallory stumbled over a root and fell headlong against Stebbings. *Christ, Mallory, keep your mind clear. This isn't a Boy Scout hike.* Ahead there was a faint lightening of the darkness; they were coming to the far edge of the wood. Mallory heard a rustling and crunching in the undergrowth to one side of the path as Lessard's men brought out their bicycles from where they had hidden them in the bushes and rolled them out of the wood into a narrow country lane.

Ryder stepped close to Mallory and said softly in English, "How's your ankle holding up, kid?"

"Okay."

"Lessard's taking us to a farm two miles down this road. Can you make it on a bike?"

"Sure," Mallory said, relieved that he wouldn't have to walk the distance.

"How are you doing, Roland?" Ryder said to Stebbings.

"Fine, sir," Stebbings answered cheerfully — too cheerfully, Mallory thought. Stebbings was still buoyed up by his relief at having survived the jump, but that wouldn't last. The jump had been the easy part.

Lessard had gathered his followers in the farmhouse he used as an operational headquarters. Mallory had not bothered to count, but at least thirty Maquisards were crowded into the small living room adjacent to the kitchen. Winter was only reluctantly giving way to spring, and a fire had been lit in the stone hearth. With the windows closed and with the press of bodies in the room, the air had quickly become uncomfortably warm.

Mallory was sweating, and his eyes smarted from the thick coils of tobacco smoke that swirled in the blue-white glare of a carbide lamp hissing on the mantel above the fireplace. He sat at a round oak table with Ryder, Stebbings, and Lessard, in the center of the room and at the center of attention for the men and boys who had come to see the British agents.

Nearly everyone wore the corduroy trousers and jackets of the countryside, and, Mallory concluded from the smell of the room, they all ate a great deal of garlic. Those who had rifles kept them slung on their shoulders or in their hands, prized possessions to be jealously guarded and proudly displayed.

Gatherings like this were a necessary bit of theater. They reinforced the sense of solidarity between the Resistance fighters and the SOE and enhanced the standing of the local commander with his own men. Mallory was glad Ryder was there to carry the conversation, for Mallory's French was not up to it. He had enough difficulty just understanding what was being said.

For the past hour, as the wine had flowed and the laughter had become progressively more raucous, Ryder and Lessard had relived old times together, playing to their appreciative audience. Neither Ryder nor Lessard had anything in common with the rough, unsophisticated men Lessard commanded except the fight against the Germans, but they both understood how to win loyalty and command respect.

Both men could tell a good story. Many of the older Maquisards in the room already knew Ryder and had heard the stories before, but they listened and joined in the laughter with as much enthusiasm as the youngsters who were hearing them for the first time.

Perhaps the Maquisards could detect a foreign accent in Ryder's speech, but Mallory doubted it. There was something of the chameleon in Ryder. He didn't simply speak the language fluently; his mannerisms changed as well. Both his facial expressions and his gestures were undeniably Gallic.

When Ryder spoke English, his words and phrasing were predominantly American, but he spoke with a mid-Atlantic accent. A British upper-class influence was revealed in the economy of his gestures and facial expressions and in a faintly aristocratic reserve, which was lightened by his detached, ironic sense of humor. Now, while speaking French, Ryder's face became more mobile, and the movements of his hands and arms did not simply underline his speech, they became part of it.

Mallory could feel his own energy draining away, and he thirsted for a cup of coffee — black and scalding hot. He had drunk only a single glass of wine, but that had been enough to give him a headache. Sitting beside him, Stebbings looked about to pass out. He had been drinking steadily, and his soft, normally pale face was flushed and his eyes were bleary. Quite suddenly, Stebbings's eyeballs rolled up, and he slumped unconscious in his chair.

Ryder, in the midst of another story, did not notice. Mallory caught Lessard's eye, and gestured toward Stebbings. Lessard leaned across the table and said in cultivated English, "It appears our wine was too much for him."

"I'll p-put him to bed," Mallory said, and Lessard nodded.

"Yes, do that, and then come back. I think it's time to send my men home to bed as well — so that we can talk."

Mallory stood up, trying not to wince as he put weight on his swollen ankle. Now he regretted saying he would put Stebbings to bed; he wasn't sure he could manage. Ryder looked up at him. "Need some help?"

Mallory shook his head, slipped one of Stebbings's limp arms around his neck, and pulled him to his feet. Stebbings groaned and revived enough to partially support his own weight. Mallory dug his fingers into Stebbings's ribs to keep him awake, and to the accompaniment of general laughter, they swayed together across the room and through an open door into the kitchen.

Although Mallory's cigarettes had contributed more than his share to the thick smoke in the living room, it was a relief to breathe the cleaner air of the kitchen. Candles burned on a sideboard and on a small table by a wood stove. A boy was standing with his back to Mallory, grinding coffee — some of the coffee they had brought with them in their packs. Because of the noise, the boy had not heard Mallory bring Stebbings into the kitchen.

In Mallory's imagination he could already smell the coffee, and he unconsciously moistened his lips. "Is that coffee for us?" he asked.

The boy started and turned around. "Oh, it is you, monsieur. Yes, I am making coffee. We have not had real coffee for a long time."

Mallory recognized the voice. It belonged to the girl at the drop zone. The mistake had been an easy one to make. She was dressed in corduroys, and her blond hair was tucked up under a leather cap. But once she had turned, it was obvious that she was a girl, and she was neither fat nor ugly.

Stebbings groaned softly and swayed against Mallory.

"Is your friend ill?" the girl asked, coming toward them, a slip of a girl, not quite as tall as Mallory.

"Just too much to drink. I'm about to put him to bed."

The words had come out all right, but there was a strange tightness in his throat. The strands of the girl's hair were golden in the soft candlelight, and her cheeks were lightly flushed from the heat in the house. Mallory realized that he was staring, and he looked away. Stebbings groaned again.

"I can help you," the girl said. "You shouldn't put too much weight on your ankle."

Mallory shook his head. "I don't want to favor it too much. If I can't walk, we . . ."

Mallory had been about to tell her that they had to get to Paris within the next few days, and he silently cursed his carelessness. The girl had him off balance, as perhaps she knew, for her mouth was turned up at the corners in the impish suggestion of a smile.

He dug Stebbings in the ribs again, and started toward the rear door. They were to sleep in the barn at the back of the house. It would be less comfortable than the farmhouse, but it would be safer: they were less likely to be trapped in the event of a German raid.

The girl went to the door and pulled aside the blackout curtain. "The coffee will be ready soon, monsieur. I will serve it when the others have gone."

"My name is Richard," Mallory said awkwardly.

"Mine is Marie."

Their eyes met for what seemed to Mallory a very long time, and again he felt the curious tightness in his throat. Her eyes were green, highlighted by dark lashes and eyebrows. Mallory was the first to look away.

She opened the door for Mallory and closed it quickly behind him. The darkness was nearly total, and he had to let his eyes adjust before he could see a thing. "Come on, Roland, we don't have far to go," Mallory grunted, steering Stebbings toward the barn. "I want to get back and have some coffee."

But it wasn't really coffee he was thinking about.

Lessard, Ryder, and Mallory were alone at the table in the living room. Lessard's men had left, going back to their own homes, but the smoke of their tobacco and the smell of garlic still hung in the air. The girl had brought the three men bread, bowls of stew, and the coffee, and then she had disappeared into the kitchen. Mallory had ignored the food, but he had drained his cup of coffee at once, and now he could feel the caffeine taking hold. It would keep his fatigue at bay for a while longer.

"So, Max," Lessard said, drawing on one of the Gauloise cigarettes Ryder had brought from London and exhaling twin streams of smoke through his nostrils, "tell me why you have come. The message from London told me nothing."

Although Lessard was dressed in corduroys like his men, Mallory could easily visualize him in uniform. His dark hair was cropped in military fashion. His skin was drawn taut over prominent cheekbones, and although he smiled readily, his thin lips quickly slipped back into a decisive, almost grim line.

"We have a job to do in Paris — a tricky one," Ryder said, "and we'll need a reliable contact in the city. Besides a safe house, we must find a way to keep watch on a certain building at the university."

Lessard did not try to hide his disappointment. "I had hoped you had come to work with us here. It would have been like old times. I also hoped your arrival would mean a supply drop for us; we are badly in need of one."

Ryder looked at his watch. "We have a sked coming up in two hours. I can radio a request for you tonight, but I can't promise you results. The invasion will be coming soon, and they're being more selective in their supply drops."

"I understand."

"What do you need most?"

"Sten ammunition, grenades, and more dynamite. That damned *plastique* makes noise, but it's not effective."

"That's because your men aren't tamping it. Dynamite is a cutting explosive, but plastic isn't. If you tamp it properly, it will do a nice job."

There was no condescension in Ryder's tone; Lessard was a professional.

Lessard nodded. "We will manage," he said, dismissing the subject. "Let us return to the question of your mission. Paris is very dangerous just now. You say your job is tricky, and yet you are going in without prearranged support. That's sloppy, Max. Not like you at all."

"It can't be helped."

Lessard frowned. "Going to the Resistance in Paris for help will be risky," he said worriedly. "Most of the FFI units operating in Paris have been penetrated. Only the Communist cells have proved to be immune."

Ryder shook his head. "Forget the Communists. They'll ask too much in return for their help. There must be some FFI groups that are still reliable."

Lessard did not respond at once, and his hesitation spoke volumes. "I do have contacts with one *réseau* I think you can trust, but one can no longer be absolutely sure. You must understand that, Max."

"We have no choice."

"All right. The group I am thinking of should be able to provide a safe house, and perhaps they can help you in the other matter as well. Will you be watching this building for a man, or for something else?"

"A man, but that is all I can tell you, Jean."

Lessard raised his eyebrows, but all he said was, "When do you intend to leave for Paris?"

"As soon as we can. Tomorrow, if possible."

Lessard looked at Mallory. "Can you walk without limping?"

"If I have to," Mallory said, hoping it was true.

"You will have to," Lessard said with heavy emphasis. "I assume that you are not inexperienced, Richard, but I doubt that you have operated in Paris."

"No, I haven't."

"In the first years of the war it was not so bad, but now it is extremely dangerous. The Gestapo has informers everywhere, and their agents have very sharp eyes. I am not exaggerating when I say that there must be nothing about your appearance or your actions that might attract attention. Nothing."

"We could stay here for another day," Ryder said to Mallory. "It would give the ankle some time to heal, and we do have some leeway."

"I'll be all right, Max."

Ryder looked at Mallory carefully and then nodded and turned back to Lessard. "How do we make contact with this *réseau*?" he asked.

"It would be best to send one of my people with you — someone they know and trust," Lessard said. "I think I will ask Marie."

"The girl who brought us the food?" Ryder said. "A bit young, isn't she?"

"In years only," Lessard replied. "She knows Paris well, and she is very good at this sort of thing — very good."

Ryder was silent for a moment, and then he looked at Mallory. "Does that sound all right to you?" he asked, and Mallory thought he detected a glint of mischief in Ryder's eyes.

"Yes," Mallory replied evenly.

Ryder nodded and turned back to Lessard. "All right, but ask her, Jean; don't order her to go."

"Of course. But I don't think there will be a problem," Lessard said with a slight smile and a glance at Mallory. "I think she will agree readily enough."

Mallory felt his face flush. He had thought he had been careful when the girl had been in the room, but apparently Lessard and Ryder had seen right through him.

"Then that's settled," Ryder said, easing back in his chair. "Now, Jean, I think it's time for you to bring out the good wine. I've had enough rotgut for the evening."

Mallory could see that the two old friends wanted to talk, and fatigue was closing in on him again. He pushed back his chair and stood up. "I'm beat, Max," he said, unconsciously slipping back into English. "I'm going to turn in."

"Sure, kid."

"But you should not go to bed hungry," Lessard protested. "You have not even touched your stew." He grinned suddenly and added, "Perhaps you are afraid it is cat and not rabbit, eh?"

Mallory shook his head quickly. "I'm sure it's very good," he said, stumbling over the French. "I'm just not hungry right now."

"All right," Lessard said with a laugh. He held out his hand to Mallory. "Good night, Richard."

"Good night."

Mallory was hoping the girl would still be in the kitchen, but it was empty when he passed through, and he swallowed his disappointment. Whether the girl came with them or not, he reminded himself roughly, he would have to keep his mind on the job. If he let a pretty girl distract him, they could all end up very dead.

Ryder held his glass of wine up to the light and slowly rotated it by its stem. He sniffed its bouquet, took a sip and nodded with satisfaction. "Very good. Very good, indeed."

Lessard smiled. "You always did have impeccable taste, Max. I've been saving that bottle for you; I knew you'd return one day to share it with me."

Ryder took another sip and looked gravely at Lessard. "I'm sorry, Jean."

"About what?"

"I'm sorry that we're forcing you to move out of this place. It's quite comfortable."

Lessard's smile slipped away. "I didn't want to be the one to say it."

"You didn't have to. We both know this is a half-baked operation. Sloppy, you said, and you were right. And if we're caught, one of us is bound to talk. You'd better clear out of here as soon as we leave for Paris."

Lessard nodded grimly. "You will need much luck this time, my friend — especially since your colleague Roland is bound to give you trouble."

Ryder grimaced. "He shouldn't be here at all. The poor bugger is scared silly. But we need him, so we'll have to cope."

"And Richard?" Lessard asked carefully. "He's very young."

"Young, but not a virgin — at least not in this sense. I've read through his file."

Lessard frowned. "You haven't worked with him before?"

"No, but he doesn't worry me."

"But to operate in Paris requires a very special sort of man, Max. You know that. If he is too brave he will make mistakes, and if he is too frightened he will give himself away. A man must be nervous, but in control; he must be able to sweat on the inside."

"I trust my instincts, and I think he has the makings."

"Perhaps," Lessard said worriedly, "but his French will be a problem. You may be able to cover for Roland, or for Richard, but not for both at once."

"Well," Ryder said, staring at his wineglass, "there's not a thing I can do about it. I don't pick the missions."

There was a silence between them, and then Lessard said diffidently, "I do have a suggestion you might consider. I meant it when I said that the girl is good. She is experienced and very cool, and I trust her implicitly. If you kept her with you in Paris, she could carry part of the load."

"I don't know, Jean," Ryder said slowly. "We wouldn't tell her what we're up to. Would she be willing to work with blinders on?"

"If it is important, yes."

Ryder sipped his wine, swirling it over his palate before he swallowed, as if savoring its flavor, but he was focused on Lessard's suggestion. "We could send her back before the real action begins," he mused aloud. "The risk to her would be limited . . ."

"And she could cover for Richard while you take care of Roland," Lessard prompted.

Ryder still hesitated, but he could not have said why. Finally he nodded. "Ask her, Jean. If she agrees, we might just have a chance after all."

Lessard grinned and poured more wine. "And I think Richard will be a very happy young man."

"He's smitten, all right," Ryder laughed. "I've never seen a boy try so hard not to look at a pretty girl — though I can't say I blame him."

"She is quite beautiful," Lessard agreed, "and it is something to watch her. She moves like a cat. If I were ten years younger, I might be tempted myself. As a matter of fact, I'm surprised you decided to leave the field to Richard."

Ryder shook his head. "Oh, no. I'm afraid she might be more than I could handle. Besides, I saw the way she looked at him. Sometimes women can surprise you; I didn't think Richard was the lady-killer type."

"Well, Max," Lessard said with a smile, "maybe she agrees with you. Perhaps she, too, thinks he has the makings."

CIA Archive No. 75434-R03   OPTRICYCLE
OSS/HIS/EV-44   Page 8

. . . In retrospect, the urgency with which Tube Alloys sought to impede German nuclear research is understandable, but the case of Tricycle underscores the futility of mounting operations without adequate preparation and on the basis of faulty intelligence. Eight days after the Tricycle team was dropped into France, SIS informed Tube Alloys that its original report on Damberg was incorrect: the scientist would not be traveling to Paris after all.

On March 30, a coded recall signal to Tricycle was transmitted by the BBC, but the signal was never acknowledged. When subsequent efforts to reestablish radio contact with the team failed, Tricycle was written off.

3

STEBBINGS was asleep and dreaming when the Gestapo came for him at dawn. He didn't hear the brief squeal of brakes as a black Citroën, rolling down the steep incline of the street outside, slowed and stopped before his apartment building. Had he heard, the sound might have carried a subconscious warning, for only the Germans drove cars in Paris and the Gestapo liked to raid at dawn; but Stebbings slept on.

Although the front window of his ground-floor apartment was slightly open, he didn't hear the thud of doors closing behind the three men in brown leather trench coats who emerged from the Citroën and walked quickly through the wrought-iron gateway of the tiny courtyard in front of the building's entrance. A man with experience and an instinct for survival might have awakened in time to escape through the apartment's rear exit, but Stebbings slept on.

Sleep was Stebbings's escape from fear, and he clung to it, even through the nightmares. He wasn't having a nightmare now; he was dreaming of a raven-haired girl with long legs, who had attended his lectures at Cambridge. He had never had the nerve to venture more than a nod and a smile when their paths had crossed outside the lecture hall, but in his dreams he was more bold. She was smiling at him, and he reached out to take her hand . . .

A muffled bang brought Stebbings awake with a start, his body jackknifing up off the mattress. "Ryder?" he cried hoarsely, not knowing what the sound had been. He blinked, and as his vision cleared he saw that Ryder's bed was empty. "Ryder!" he called, but there was no response.

Stebbings flinched as something struck the front door hard, and an instant later the door flew open with a splintering crash. Three men burst into the apartment, their leather coats slapping against their legs, and Stebbings's mind screamed.

The Gestapo squadleader saw Stebbings's eyes dilate and his mouth open as if to cry out, but no sound emerged. As the squadleader advanced on him, Stebbings's eyes suddenly rolled upward, and he fainted in a tangle of bedclothes. The German turned away, his cold eyes scanning the apartment, and his lips compressed as he spotted the empty bed. "Find the radio," he said curtly to the two thugs behind him.

"*Jawohl*, Herr Scharführer," they answered in unison, two husky young toughs with minds as blank as their faces.

Scharführer Braun was also a big man, with short, bristly hair, but unlike his companions he could think. He had the sour, world-weary look of the metropolitan police detective he had once been. The transition to the Gestapo had not been difficult for him, and it had kept him out of the war. He hunted a different type of fugitive now, but that made no difference to him: an arrest was an arrest.

As Braun's thugs began to tear the apartment apart, he turned his attention back to Stebbings. He approached the bed and stood for a moment, looking down at his catch. The freckles on Stebbings's pudgy face stood out clearly on his milky skin. His thin sandy hair clung wetly to his scalp. This one, Braun thought, would crack like an eggshell.

Braun's belly rumbled, and he grimaced at the hunger pang. "Well, Sleeping Beauty," he said, "you've slept long enough."

Braun struck Stebbings hard in the face, and Stebbings's eyes flew open, his cheek flaring red from the blow.

"Where's your partner?" Braun demanded in French.

"I-I don't understand," Stebbings quavered, cowering back against the wall.

Braun frowned; he hadn't expected a British agent. He repeated the question in guttural English.

"I don't know," Stebbings answered. "I —"

Braun's hand snaked out, seized the front of Stebbings's pajamas, and jerked him up off the bed so forcibly that Stebbings's head snapped back.

"Where-is-he?"

"I don't —"

Stebbings gasped as Braun drove his fist into his stomach, and Braun let him crumple to the floor. Stebbings's mouth worked frantically as he fought for breath, and then he began to retch. Braun kicked him in the ribs.

"I don't know!" Stebbings sobbed, scrabbling away from Braun on his hands and knees.

Braun's lips twitched in disgust; he'd never seen a British agent go to pieces so quickly. He shifted his weight to kick Stebbings again, but he didn't follow through. It was obvious the man didn't know, and Braun never wasted energy.

Braun had seen the rear exit, and he had noted that it was bolted on the inside. The other man hadn't heard them coming; they'd simply missed him by bad luck. Braun accepted the loss philosophically. He would leave one of his men behind in case the agent returned to the apartment. It was a simple trap, but it sometimes worked.

"I've found the radio, Herr Scharführer," cried one of the thugs from the adjoining room. He appeared a moment later, proudly bearing a scuffed, cloth-bound suitcase containing a British-made, battery-operated transmitter.

"Anything else?" Braun snapped. "Equipment? Code pads?"

"No, Herr Scharführer."

"Keep looking."

Moments later the second thug uncovered a single-shot pistol with a silencer hidden in the kitchenette, and he brought it to Braun for inspection. The squadleader's eyes narrowed, and he turned on Stebbings, who still cowered on the floor.

32 —

"And what did you bastards intend to use this for?" Braun growled in genuine anger. "This weapon is good for only one thing: shooting our men in the back on a dark night. Is that what you had in mind, you son of a bitch?"

The thug who had found the pistol heard the anger in Braun's voice, and he took it as a cue. He stepped past Braun and kicked Stebbings in the face, splitting his lips and knocking out two front teeth. Stebbings fell backward, gagging, his bloody mouth agape.

"That's enough!" Braun barked. "They want him delivered in one piece."

It was too soon for Stebbings to die.

As Stebbings gagged on his own blood, Max Ryder was returning from a walk along the Seine. Insomnia had driven him from his bed shortly after the curfew had lifted at five A.M., and he had slipped out of the apartment while it was still dark, hoping that fresh air would clear away the muzzy feeling in his head.

Ryder trudged up the slope of the rue de l'Alboni toward the aboveground Passy Métro station. The walk had not refreshed him, and he felt gritty and on edge. A fine, cold rain was falling, and he had turned up his overcoat collar and pulled his hat brim low over his eyes. Muffled against the weather, he was an anonymous figure, taller than the average Frenchman, but not tall enough to attract attention.

The safe house apartment was located in a U-shaped street off the rue de l'Alboni, opposite the Métro station. One entrance to the street lay below the station, the other above it, and normally Ryder would have walked the extra distance up the hill to the second corner, from which one could see the apartment at the bottom of the U. But this morning Ryder was tired, and fatigue made him careless.

He turned right at the nearest corner. The apartment lay out of sight around the bend in the U a half block away. The six-story apartment buildings on both sides of the narrow street were expensive and well kept, but this section of Paris was too far from the German military command center, and only a few of the buildings housed Wehrmacht officers.

The building Ryder had chosen was one of those few, and the five floors above the safe house apartment were occupied by Germans. The choice had been deliberate, for Ryder believed in hiding in plain sight.

It was still quite early, and Ryder took no notice of the absolute silence behind the shuttered windows of the buildings he passed. The street was deserted, and there was nothing to warn him of the danger before he rounded the bend in the U and saw the sedan parked in front of the apartment — a black Citroën, the car preferred by the Gestapo.

Ryder's breath caught in his throat as he saw it, but he was too experienced to reverse course, and only a keen observer would have noticed the momentary break in his stride. If the Gestapo had the street covered, a false step could finish him. So he kept going at the same pace, though the hair rose on the back of his neck. Ryder didn't ask himself how they had been betrayed; he concentrated on surviving.

As he passed his apartment on the opposite side of the street, he resisted the urge to look toward it. Out of the corner of his eye he thought he detected a movement of a window curtain. If they had his description, if they were watching for him . . . *Don't think; keep walking. Don't hurry!*

As he followed the bend back toward the rue de l'Alboni, he half expected to hear a shout and to see a Gestapo man break from cover to block his escape. He didn't think about Stebbings; Stebbings was finished. Ryder's muscles were so tense that it took conscious effort to keep his stride and bearing natural, but mingling with the fear was a strange exhilaration. He had experienced it before in similar moments of danger, and it was a part of himself that he didn't understand.

He was halfway back to the rue de l'Alboni now, and no one had sounded an alarm. Were they playing with him? His heart skipped a beat as a shutter opened with a bang above him. The street was coming to life. A moment later a woman emerged from the entrance of a building on the corner, carrying an empty basket. Even the rich had to get out early and wait in line for hours in front of food stores. Still no one made a move to stop him, and Ryder realized he was going to make it. He was really going to make it!

As Ryder reached the corner he heard a muffled cry behind him, and he turned to look back down the street toward his apartment. Two men in leather trench coats were dragging Stebbings across the sidewalk toward the Citroën. Even from a distance Ryder could see the blood on Stebbings's face and on the front of his pajamas. Stebbings was trembling like a terrified puppy, and Ryder knew he would talk soon — if he hadn't talked already.

Ryder swung away from the sight and headed up the rue de l'Alboni toward the Trocadéro. He was in the clear now, and he lengthened his stride, anxious to get to a telephone to warn Mallory and the girl.

"Are you awake, *chéri?*"

Mallory murmured unintelligibly and rolled onto his back. Hovering between sleep and wakefulness, he felt Marie's lips brush his cheek. "It's still early," he said drowsily in English.

"What? I didn't understand."

"It's too early," Mallory repeated in French, the effort of switching languages bringing him fully awake. He opened his eyes and saw Marie smiling down at him, her face close enough for him to see clearly even without his glasses.

Her short, straw-blond hair was tousled, and her cheeks were still flushed from sleep. Her coloring was Nordic, but to Mallory there was something undeniably French in her features — a hint of feminine willfulness in the delicate curve of her lips, a feline cast to the dark eyebrows. She had a wide, full-lipped mouth and high, clearly defined cheekbones.

Mallory doubted he would ever know a girl more beautiful.

He slipped his arm around her and gently pulled her closer, marveling at his luck, and not quite believing in it. He had not

— 35

yet put his bitter adolescence behind him, and part of him was still the skinny, acne-ridden teenager with thick glasses whom girls had ignored.

"I must get up now, Richard," Marie said, pronouncing his name with a soft *ch*.

"Why? It can't be much past six."

"I have a small job to do this morning — for the *réseau*."

"What! Why should —"

Marie cut him off by pressing her fingers over his lips. "I didn't tell you before, because I didn't want you to worry — or to argue," she said, taking her hand away.

"What job? Let them do their own dirty work," Mallory said, his voice rising.

Marie bit her lower lip, as she did sometimes when she was worried or unsure of herself. It was a disarmingly childlike mannerism in such a sophisticated young woman. "You see? I knew you would argue. It's just a small favor — in return for the help they've given us."

"I thought there weren't any strings attached," Mallory said. At least that's what he intended to say, and Marie understood him well enough.

Marie shook her head. "I could hardly refuse them," she said patiently. "Not only did they provide us with two apartments, but they made the arrangements with the custodian of the building from which Max and Roland keep watch."

"I don't need reminding," Mallory said tightly, groping with his free hand for his glasses on the nightstand. The right or wrong of it didn't interest him; he didn't want her taking unnecessary risks.

"Then you know I must go," Marie said, slipping lithely out of his arms and off the bed. "There will not be much risk; it's a simple courier job."

"Have you cleared this with Max?" Mallory said, grasping at straws.

"Yes. I told him yesterday."

Marie turned away and walked to the large wooden wardrobe

36 –

that held their few clothes. She opened the door and stepped behind it before removing her nightdress. Despite their intimacy, there was still a reserve of shyness between them.

"I assume your FFI friends want you to smuggle something through a security check," Mallory said, mangling French grammar as he fumbled for the right words. "They think your blond hair will make the Germans less suspicious, is that it?"

Marie continued to dress without answering.

"The Germans aren't that stupid!" Mallory said heatedly.

Marie stepped out from behind the door, tugging her comb through a tangle in her hair. She wore a faded print dress of the type that had become the uniform of the wartime Parisienne, and it fitted loosely, making her appear even thinner and frailer than she was, just a slip of a girl.

"Were you listening to me?" Mallory demanded, his anxiety coming out as anger.

She approached the bed, smiled, and shook her head, like a mother trying to deal with a sulky child. "Yes, I was listening. You said the Germans are not stupid. And now, monsieur, it is time for you to get up."

With that she reached down and pulled off Mallory's covers before he could stop her. He was wearing only shorts, and he winced as the cold air in the room hit him. "Jesus!" he yelped in English, scrambling off the bed. "Is Paris always this cold in March?"

"It's the *Boches*," Marie sniffed. "They ruin everything."

She disappeared into the apartment's tiny bathroom, and Mallory hurriedly began to dress. The cold bothered him more than it did Marie, but in one respect he was grateful for it. In warmer weather, the gray woolen suit they had provided him in London would have been conspicuous as well as uncomfortable.

Each piece of Mallory's wardrobe had been manufactured in London by SOE tailors, but it was indistinguishable from genuine French clothing. Only his shoes, which had articulated wooden soles, had been made in France. Leather-soled shoes had become rare enough to attract notice.

Marie reappeared and went to the alcove where they did their cooking. "They've turned on the electricity already!" she exclaimed happily. "Shall I heat some water for you to shave?"

"It will take too long," Mallory said, knowing she was anxious to be off. He didn't want her to go, but he wouldn't delay her. "Just heat up some coffee water."

But in the bathroom Mallory regretted his decision as soon as he plunged his hands into the icy tap water. At least, he consoled himself, they still had real soap. They used the bar he'd brought with him from England sparingly, for when it was gone there would only be ersatz soap — ineffective lumps of grit and chemical cleanser. He could hear Marie humming to herself in the other room, as if the prospect of carrying contraband past the Germans was nothing to be concerned about.

Mallory had washed and shaved, and he was running a comb through his dark, wiry hair when it hit him. For no particular reason, and without warning, the fear he kept bottled up in a corner of his mind spilled out, and he began to tremble. It began in his hands and worked its way up his arms and into his shoulders, until he had to grip the basin with both hands to steady himself. He gritted his teeth and waited for it to pass, grateful that Marie could not see him.

He had heard of men getting the shakes, but this was the first time it had happened to him. Behind enemy lines in Italy there had been little time to think beyond the moment. He had been on the move constantly, and action, when it came, had been sharp and quick. This was different; the waiting was tearing at his nerves.

Gradually the shaking subsided, and his fear retreated into its corner, leaving him with a strange sense of unreality. He stared at his own reflection in the cracked, yellowed mirror above the washbasin, as if to verify that it was really he who stood there, living on borrowed time, waiting to kill a man he had never seen.

Was this what enabled other men to risk their lives again and again, Mallory wondered — this sensation that nothing was quite real? His reflection stared back at him unfeelingly, mocking his weakness. His was a homely face, he thought — narrow, pale, with skin scarred by the acne that had ravaged it, and masked by thick-lensed glasses that gave his brown eyes an opaque, beady look. Was that how Marie saw him?

He looked away from the mirror and shook his head. To him, her love seemed the most unreal thing of all.

They ate their meager breakfast at an oilcloth-covered table next to a window overlooking the street. Their room was on the top floor of a shabby, three-story, white stucco house that had been converted to apartments. It was one of a row of similar rundown houses along the rue de l'Armée d'Orient, a narrow little street in Montmartre. The houses' stucco facades were chipped and cracked, and the tiny wrought-iron balconies before the narrow shuttered windows were streaked red with rust.

Normally a safe-house apartment was on the ground floor to facilitate escape, but the room Marie and Mallory occupied had an excellent rear exit. The rue de l'Armée d'Orient was a short, L-shaped side street joined at both ends to the rue Lepic, which curved to climb a steep hill leading to the Sacré-Coeur. The safe house stood on the inside corner of the right-angle bend in the rue de l'Armée d'Orient.

The apartment's rear door opened onto a flight of stairs leading down to a courtyard behind the house, through which one could reach the rue Lepic. Alternatively, using the same stairs, one could reach a second-floor window at the side of the building from which one could drop onto the courtyard's outer wall, and from there to the street — out of sight of the front entrance around the corner.

Marie had set out some bread and saccharin-sweetened jam and two steaming cups of ersatz coffee. Mallory tore off a chunk of bread, but ignored the jam, for he detested its sickly sweet aftertaste. He sipped the acorn brew that passed for coffee and grimaced. "Damn Max," he growled.

Marie had heard the complaint before, and she smiled patiently. "He might not have gotten the radio into Paris otherwise," she reminded Mallory.

"We don't need the transmitter here," Mallory said. "We could have left the damned thing with Lessard. We're on receive only now, and if London should scrub the mission, we could wait until we return to Lyons-la-Forêt to acknowledge the signal. We don't need the transmitter, but what *I* could use is coffee."

The coffee had been lost on the train to Paris. As was standard SOE practice, they had traveled first class in a car filled with Germans. Ryder, in his practiced cover role of black market operator, had spent the last two hours of the halting journey over bombed and sabotaged rail lines working on a homesick, overaged Wehrmacht corporal who was in charge of the officers' baggage.

Ryder had commiserated with the corporal, had admired his family snapshots, and had persuaded the man to swallow considerable quantities of cognac in the intervals when the car corridor was clear of officers. By the time the train had pulled into the Gare Saint-Lazare, Ryder and the corporal had become bosom friends. With a final gift of their entire stock of real coffee, Ryder had induced the soldier to slip the suitcase containing the radio transmitter in among the officers' luggage — to spare the soldier's newfound friend "needless delay" at the baggage control.

Mallory admitted that it had been neatly done, but in his mind, carrying the radio with them had been a needless risk. Ryder, as the team leader, had overriden his objections. Mallory pushed the mug of ersatz aside and took out a tin of tobacco and a packet of cigarette papers to roll himself a smoke. Drinking the bitter, muddy liquid only intensified his thirst for real coffee.

Without being asked, Marie reached across the table and took the paper and tobacco. Mallory was clumsy with his fingers, and he had still not gotten the knack of rolling a well-packed cigarette. Ryder's cover allowed him to carry factory-made cigarettes, but Mallory was posing as a commercial traveler, too low on the economic ladder to afford such a luxury.

Attention to such details had to be made habitual, for Mallory could not risk a slip in public. The Gestapo documents in his possession were reserved for the assassination attempt, and although his French identity papers were perfect, his command of the language was not sufficient to survive interrogation by a French policeman.

Marie smoothed the finished cigarette and handed it to him, wishing she could get him to eat more and smoke less; he seemed to live on cigarettes. She sipped her coffee and watched him in silence as he lit up and drew in his first lungful of smoke. His addiction to caffeine and nicotine seemed to her an odd weakness, for she knew he was capable of iron self-control. She could imagine the pain his ankle had caused him the day they had left for Paris, but he had hidden it completely. And he used the same rigid self-control to suppress his fear.

Marie knew the fear was there; she had seen the signs in other men she had worked with. There were moments when Mallory would fall silent, his gaze fixed on some random object, the muscles of his jaw knotting with tension. But he never spoke of it, and Marie pretended that she did not know.

Max, the leader — suave and confident — was a different type. It was all a game to him, and Marie suspected he found danger a stimulant. The Resistance had men like Max, and they were much admired, but Marie preferred the men who were afraid. The team leader was certainly handsome. His features were well proportioned, and his dark eyes, eyebrows, and hair contrasted effectively with his smooth, lightly tanned skin. He would have been a natural for the silent films of the twenties, Marie thought. Yet it was Mallory, not Max, to whom she was attracted.

She had felt herself drawn to him the very first night she had seen him, and she had seen him react to her — though he had tried to hide it. His expression when he looked at her that night at the farmhouse had been remote — almost cold — but his eyes had given him away . . .

"What are you smiling to yourself about?" Mallory asked.

"Nothing important," Marie replied, reaching out to touch his hand.

Marie wondered what had made him so afraid to show his feelings — so determined to rely on himself, alone, and not to reach out to others. She knew he was in love with her, but even after she had taken him to her bed, she had sensed that there was a hard core inside him that she could not soften.

She squeezed his hand. "I must go now, Richard."

Mallory looked away from her and ground out his half-smoked cigarette.

"Don't be angry," she said, biting her lower lip.

"I'm not — I'm just worried."

"Yes, you *are* angry. You want to keep me from taking risks, no matter how small, and I won't let you. So you are angry."

Mallory said nothing, and Marie sighed. "You have no right to be, you know. I have my job to do, just as you have yours."

Marie waited for him to respond, and when he did not, she pushed back her chair abruptly and stood up. "Do you think I do not worry about the danger for you?" she said angrily. "I do not even know why you have come to Paris. I have not asked why Max watches at the university — or for whom or for what you wait. I understand that it may be better that I do not know, but it makes it very hard for me. Yet I do not complain. I ask the same consideration from you, Richard. I am not a British agent, and I have my own work to do, my own duty. You must respect that."

"I know — it's just that . . ." Mallory just wanted to hold her, to protect her, and to hell with the war, or with duty. "I love you," he said hoarsely. "I guess that's all there is to it."

He saw her start to smile, and then her eyes glistened suddenly with tears and her teeth dug into her lower lip. "I know, *chéri*," she said softly. "I know."

She bent down, kissed him quickly, and pulled away. "I'll be back at noon," she said, going to the wardrobe for her coat. "I know you will get restless, but don't go out. Please! There is not much risk in this neighborhood, but your French —" She smiled again and shook her head. "It really is atrocious."

Mallory got up and started toward her. "You're sure you'll be back at noon?"

"Yes," she said, going quickly to the door, as if she were afraid

42 —

he might try to stop her. She blew him a kiss over her shoulder and was gone.

Mallory listened to Marie's footsteps descending the spiral staircase to the ground floor, followed a moment later by the muffled thump of the front door closing behind her, and depression settled over him like a shroud.

Outside it was raining in earnest now, and water ran down over the skylight above him in rivulets, drawing ragged lines in the sooty glass. He walked back to the breakfast table and sat down to fashion a crude cigarette. Through the window he saw a scrawny cat creep around the corner on the opposite side of the street, its black fur plastered to its emaciated body. It was searching the gutter for food. The cat, too, Mallory reflected morosely, was living on borrowed time; sooner or later it would end up in someone's stew pot.

Mallory watched the cat until it moved out of sight. Then he lit his cigarette, brushed the tobacco he'd spilled back into the tin, and turned again to stare out of the window. There was nothing to see outside, but he knew every inch of the studio apartment, and he was sick of it. For nearly a week he had been cooped up, while Ryder and Stebbings had watched in vain for Damberg's arrival at the cyclotron laboratory. Each day they monitored the BBC broadcasts, hoping to receive a coded signal indicating that SIS had confirmed Damberg's departure to Paris.

When Ryder had learned that the *réseau* Marie had contacted on their behalf could provide two apartments, he had suggested that they split up to minimize the chance of their being caught in the same trap if something went wrong. Ryder had kept Stebbings with him, and he took a chance every time he went out on the street with Stebbings in tow, for Stebbings was frightened to the core and never far from panic.

Still, if Mallory had had the choice, he would have traded places with Ryder. When Marie was absent, the apartment became a prison. At first he had tried reading the newspapers Marie brought home for him each day, but he found it impossible to concentrate long enough to follow the articles. Several times during the past week he had been reduced to counting the flowers on the apartment's yellowed, peeling wallpaper.

Damberg was days overdue, and the waiting was eroding Mallory's resolve. He had begun to hope that Damberg would never come, that London would send a recall signal. It was a dangerous frame of mind, and he wondered if Ryder knew.

When Marie was with him, Mallory could keep his mind off what lay ahead, but when he was alone he couldn't stop himself from thinking ahead to the moment when he would have to go in alone for the kill — and the odds against him making it out again . . . *Think about something else, damn it! Think about Marie.*

Why was it so difficult for him to conjure up her image? It was as if she had been gone for years instead of minutes. Why did the details of her face elude him? Only the look in her eyes stayed with him always, a look tinged with sadness even when she smiled. Once, late at night, he had awakened to hear her crying softly in the darkness. He had never asked her why . . .

The shrill ring of the telephone on the nightstand shattered the silence in the room, jolting Mallory like an electric shock. The telephone was strictly reserved for an emergency, and it had never rung. Mallory was halfway to the phone before the chair in which he'd been sitting clattered to the floor.

4

"GET out now!" Ryder said the instant Mallory answered the phone. "Meet me at nine."

"*D'accord*," Mallory responded automatically. He heard the click as Ryder hung up.

Mallory had to suppress the urge to dash from the apartment, for Ryder's warning meant that the safe house had become a trap. His heart pounded and his breathing quickened as adrenaline flooded into his bloodstream. Like Ryder, he didn't waste time wondering what had happened; his only thought was to get out fast.

He checked to be sure that his wallet was in the inside pocket of his jacket, but he didn't need to check its contents. What he needed would be there: the forged *carte d'identité* bearing his photograph and valid stamps, his French demobilization certificate, and ration cards. His Gestapo identification was sewn into the jacket's lining.

He went into the bathroom to retrieve the pocket radio receiver and battery pack that were hidden in waterproof bags in the toilet's overhead water tank. He discarded the bags and half walked, half ran to the wardrobe to get his overcoat and hat. He stuffed the battery pack into one overcoat pocket and the radio into the other. As he pulled on the coat, he swept his eyes over the room in a final check, though he knew there was nothing incriminating. The transmitter and the pistol were with Ryder, and neither he nor Marie had left telltale scraps of paper to be found.

Only ninety seconds had passed since Ryder had called, but to Mallory it seemed much longer. He started for the rear exit, caught himself, turned quickly and left the apartment by the front door; he had to leave a warning for Marie.

Mallory pounded down the tight, dizzying spiral of stairs to the ground floor, missing a step in the semidarkness of the stairwell and nearly falling. At the bottom of the stairs, he ducked under the low ceiling beam and walked quickly across the vestibule, his shoes scraping on traces of sand on the tile floor. He told himself it was the sound of the scraping that raised gooseflesh on his arms. He took a deep breath and opened the front door, half expecting to come face to face with the Gestapo.

A cold trickle of sweat ran down over his ribs as he stepped out onto the sidewalk, but the street was clear. He went down on one knee as if to tighten a shoelace, slipped out a piece of chalk from his overcoat pocket, made a heavy mark on the drainpipe beside the doorway, and straightened up. No one but Marie would notice it.

As rapidly as he dared, he walked down to the rue Lepic and paused beside the corner streetlamp to make a second warning chalk mark on the post. Across the street a line of women had formed in front of a bakery, but no one took any notice of him. The women huddled together in the rain, clutching their breadbaskets and ration cards. In their black, shapeless coats and with their faces muffled by drab scarves, they were without individuality. Young or old, their pinched faces held the same look of resignation laced with desperation. Hunger was tightening its grip on Paris.

Mallory turned to his right and walked quickly uphill in the direction of the Sacré-Coeur. At the second corner where the rue de l'Armée d'Orient met the rue Lepic, he left a final chalk mark. Now both directions from which Marie might approach the safe house were covered. For the moment he had done all he could for her.

He continued up the slope toward the Sacré-Coeur, and his

breathing became more regular as he put more distance between himself and the apartment. The approach to the rear of the basilica was a tangle of narrow, winding streets, and Mallory paused frequently in front of shop windows to observe the street behind him. By the time he walked out onto the broad, open terrace before the Sacré-Coeur, he was sure no one was following him.

He walked to the edge of the hilltop terrace to look out over the city, heedless of the rain soaking his shoulders. It was good to be standing in the open, feeling his heartbeat slow, knowing that for the moment he was safe. On a sunny day, the terrace would have swarmed with German soldiers playing the role of tourists, but now it was deserted, silent. The distant outline of the city stretching out before him merged with a gray mist, and low-lying clouds shrouded the Eiffel Tower, hiding the Nazi banner flying over Paris.

Mallory did not linger long, and he took shelter from the rain at the deserted entrance to the basilica. He glanced at his watch. A BBC broadcast would be coming up soon, and the hilltop made for good reception. He uncoiled the earphone lead from the pocket radio receiver and ran it through a slit inside his overcoat pocket and up under the coat. He inserted the earphone in his ear, connected the battery pack in one pocket to the radio in the other with wires running under his coat, and switched the radio on.

Adjusting the tuning capacitor, he threaded his way through the soft crackle of static and the whistle of overlapping transmissions until he found the correct frequency and heard the staid voice of a BBC announcer reading the news of the day. The transmission of coded messages to the Resistance groups would follow. There was no longer any point in listening, of course; the mission was blown. But Mallory's sense of irony demanded that he listen in. Now that it was too late, he was certain there would be a signal from London.

Mallory met Ryder at eight. Ryder believed in simple codes, and the time of their rendezvous was one hour earlier than the time specified over the phone. He also believed in simple procedures, so there was only one prearranged emergency meeting place: the Café de la Paix, situated on a corner of the place de l'Opéra. Mallory entered the café at precisely eight o'clock.

Before the war, the Café de la Paix had been the most fashionable of the large cafés. Its interior was graced with gilt-ribbed columns, and original oil murals covered the high ceiling. The café's glass-enclosed terrace allowed one to sit alongside the boulevard des Capucines, as in a sidewalk café, regardless of the season, and the café still enjoyed a brisk business. Now, however, the clientele was mostly German. The café still retained much of its prewar elegance, but its famous green and gold decor had a faded, neglected look and the ambience that the cream of Paris society had once provided was gone.

Mallory came in through the corner entrance, where he could view both sections of the terrace at once. Already the café was crowded with green-uniformed Wehrmacht officers, SS officers in field gray, and a sprinkling of affluent Frenchmen who didn't mind eating with the enemy. Some of the Germans had their French mistresses with them, and the girls' too-shrill laughter punctuated the garble of chatter filling the air.

Because the Germans had made the café one of their own, there was plenty of coal for the braziers set up along the outer glass wall, and the air was overheated and stuffy. Mallory removed his hat and opened his overcoat as he looked out over the crowded tables for Ryder.

The SOE agent was seated in a far corner at a table beside the floor-to-ceiling window overlooking the sidewalk. Ryder caught Mallory's eye and raised his hand in casual greeting. Despite his tension, Mallory smiled. Ryder was a class act.

He sat sideways to his table, his back to the street, legs crossed and apparently completely at ease. The polish on the shoes he displayed, as well as the Gauloise he was smoking, advertised his supposed black market connections. Ryder's fine-boned face with its straight, narrow nose was suited to airs of superiority, but the expression he affected was shifty as well as arrogant. His dark hair was combed straight back from his high forehead, and he had slicked it down with hair oil. The suit he wore, though tailored to his tall, slim frame, suggested a crude, albeit expensive, taste.

Seeing him, no one would doubt that he was a black market operator — a Frenchman Germans could trust.

Mallory picked his way through the closely packed tables, wary of the waiters, who darted through the aisles like taxis in rush-hour traffic. A waiter with a fully loaded tray on his shoulder cut across Mallory's path, and Mallory stepped back to make way for him. At that moment, an SS major seated behind Mallory decided to push his chair farther into the aisle, and Mallory backed into him and nearly fell into the burly man's lap.

Mallory managed to recover his balance, but not before he had jostled the cup in the SS man's hand, spilling ersatz coffee down the front of the major's spotless tunic.

"*Verdammt nochmal!*" the officer thundered, his fleshy face reddening.

The girl sitting with the major took hold of his arm and tried to restrain him, but he shook her off and pushed himself to his feet, cursing Mallory in a mixture of French and German.

"I beg your pardon, monsieur!" Mallory said in his best French, hurriedly producing a clean handkerchief and proffering it to the enraged major. "If you will permit me, I will pay for the . . ."

Mallory's voice trailed off as his French failed him, and he had to complete the sentence with a gesture at the stain. His voice was no more unsteady than might have been expected in such a situation, but his heart was pounding wildly. Heads were turning their way. More experienced men than he had been caught as a result of just such an unforeseen incident.

The major, puffed up and self-important, had also noticed the attention they were drawing, and Mallory was afraid it would only spur the German's show of anger. He wasn't sure whether to humble himself further or to look the SS man in the eye.

The girl, clearly upset by the scene, reached up and took hold of the major's arm again. "It was an accident, Putzi!" the girl said, just loudly enough for the major to hear. She was French, but if she had detected Mallory's accent, she gave no sign of it. The major, glaring at Mallory, tried to pull his arm free, but the girl held fast and continued to implore him to sit down.

Abruptly the major yielded. He snatched Mallory's handkerchief, pressed it against the stain, and sat down again. Mallory repeated his offer to pay, but the officer brusquely waved him off. With an inward sigh of relief, Mallory nodded gratefully to the girl and moved away. The girl's clothes were flashy and expensive, and she was clearly the SS man's mistress. In French eyes, she was a traitor, but Mallory would have gladly kissed her hand.

Ryder had shifted around in his seat and was gazing with apparent interest at the passersby in the street. He drew on his Gauloise and exhaled the smoke slowly through his nostrils in his own sigh of relief. The kid had done all right, he thought. There had been no sign of fear in Mallory's expression, only apparent embarrassment at having caused the incident. The glasses had helped, of course; they tended to mask his eyes. But Mallory had handled himself well; the kid had nerve.

Mallory smiled for the benefit of anyone who might be watching as he approached the table, but the smile vanished as he took off his wet overcoat and sat down. He was surprised his hands weren't shaking.

"I'm glad you made it," Ryder said. "I wasn't sure my call would reach you in time. Was Marie already gone?"

Mallory nodded. "What happened?"

They spoke in French, but there was no need to talk softly. The babble of a hundred voices drowned out individual conversations.

"The Gestapo raided our apartment early this morning. I couldn't sleep, and I was out for a walk when they hit us. Stebbings wasn't as lucky, poor bastard. I saw them drag him away. He'll be talking soon, if he hasn't already."

"Were we betrayed by someone in the *réseau*?"

Ryder shrugged. "What else? That's the risk we took when we asked for their help, but we didn't have any choice — not on this bloody, cocked-up operation."

Ryder raised his hand and signaled a waiter, who came to their table immediately. No one commanded more respect from waiters than the men of the black market. "A coffee for my friend."

"Certainly, monsieur," the waiter said unctuously and hurried away.

50 –

"Why didn't they hit our place?" Mallory asked.

"Maybe the informer didn't know about the second apartment, or perhaps the Gestapo is slowing down. In any event, you can't go back there. Did you leave a warning for Marie?"

"Yes."

"She'll be all right then. Even if they do stake out the apartment, she's too smart to walk into their arms."

"I picked up the latest BBC transmission," Mallory said. "Nothing for us."

"You mean you still have the receiver with you?" Ryder snapped. "Get rid of the damned thing! Don't you understand? We're blown!"

"Take it easy, M-Max," Mallory said softly in English. "I get the point. How about giving me one of those f-fancy cigarettes of yours. I still can't roll a decent smoke."

In spite of himself Ryder smiled. "Sorry, kid," Ryder said, handing Mallory the pack of cigarettes. Ryder wondered suddenly if he was slipping; Mallory was calming him down, when it should have been the other way around.

The strange exhilaration Ryder had felt earlier had worn off quickly, leaving him on edge. Maybe his experience was beginning to work against him, he thought morosely. He had seen it happen to other men — men who had learned that the odds of survival grew shorter with every mission. It was only that strange need for walking close to the edge that had kept him coming back, pushing his luck. Maybe now it was time for him to quit.

The waiter returned with the coffee and placed it in front of Mallory. When the waiter left, Mallory said, "How much time do you think we have before Stebbings gives them our descriptions?"

"I don't know. We can only hope he holds out until we get clear," Ryder said. His lapse had been brief, and he was once again the cool professional. "I've got first-class tickets for us on a train out of the Gare Saint-Lazare that leaves in forty-five minutes for Rouen. We'll wait here for a while longer and then go straight to the train. We'll make contact with Marston's group in Louvier. He should be able to whistle up a Lizzie for us, and with any luck we'll be back in London within forty-eight hours."

Mallory tried a sip of coffee, but it was worse than the ersatz he'd had at breakfast, and he pushed the cup aside. "What about Marie?" he said, knowing already what Ryder's answer would be.

"When is she due back at the apartment?"

"Noon."

"That was definite?"

Mallory nodded.

Ryder compressed his lips. "We can't wait that long. Even if Stebbings has already talked, there's bound to be some delay before they can get the descriptions circulated to all the checkpoints, but we can't risk staying in Paris one more minute than necessary. Marie wouldn't expect us to wait for her; you know that. She can take better care of herself than we can. When she spots your warning, she'll find her own way of of Paris. Frankly, I fancy her chances more than ours."

"*If* she sees the mark I left," Mallory said. "Once Stebbings talks, the Gestapo will stake out our apartment for sure — and they'll be looking for a girl of her description. I won't let her walk into a trap, Max."

Ryder expelled his breath in a hiss of frustration. He had already lost one man; he didn't want to lose another. He leaned toward Mallory and switched to English. "Look, Rich, only one thing is certain: the clock is ticking away. We have to play the percentages or they'll bag the lot of us. I don't like leaving her any more than you do, but you won't do her any good sitting in a Gestapo cell."

Mallory nodded, and for a moment Ryder thought he had convinced him, but then Mallory said softly, "Catch your train, Max. I'm going back for her."

Ryder looked at Mallory for a long moment in silence. "There's no future in it, kid."

"In what?"

"You and the girl."

Mallory did not respond, and after a moment Ryder sighed and shook his head. "Well — what the hell. Maybe I'd do the same in your place."

There was another silence between them, and then Ryder

52 –

glanced at his watch. Time was slipping away; he would have to go soon.

"Once you've picked up Marie, you have a choice to make," Ryder said, still speaking English to be sure Mallory understood him. "Either you gamble that Stebbings hasn't talked yet and take the first train out of Paris you can catch, or you go to ground and try to wait them out.

"If you do go to ground, use a *maison de passe*. They're strictly for one-night stands, and having a girl with you will explain why you're there. No one will ask questions and no one will check your I.D. If you stay in a different place each night, you should be able to stay under cover till your money runs out. By that time some of the heat will be off, and if you make a few changes in your appearance you may be able to get through the checkpoints."

"Maybe," Mallory said, "and m-maybe not. We'll take the train out today. Waiting only guarantees that the men at the checkpoints will have our descriptions."

Ryder nodded. "All right, but the girl may have other ideas. Whatever you do, don't let her talk you into contacting the FFI. If she has a way to get out of Paris without their help, fine; but stay clear of that *réseau* she contacted. Once you clear Paris, head for Louvier. I'll see to it that Marston has the station covered. They'll be on the lookout for you. And don't go near Lyons-la-Forêt."

"What about Lessard?"

"He vacated that farmhouse the day we left for Paris, but I'll have Marston pass along a warning to him anyway," Ryder looked again at his watch. "You're sure you won't come with me now?"

Mallory nodded. "I'm sure."

Ryder sighed in resignation, took two first-class railway tickets from his pocket and gave them to Mallory. "I was hoping Marie would be with you, so I bought three. There's another train to Rouen out of Saint-Lazare at one-thirty this afternoon. The seat reservations won't be good, but you'll be able to use these in the second-class cars."

"Thanks, Max."

Ryder smiled slightly. "You know, kid, it's a shame Damberg never showed. I think you just might have pulled it off."

"To tell you the truth, I'm not s-sorry I didn't get the chance to try. Not one bit."

Ryder's smile broadened into a grin. "Well, I knew right off you weren't stupid."

"Time for you to get going, Max."

"Okay," Ryder said. "You might as well stay put. As I said, this is as safe a place as any to kill the morning. There'll never be an I.D. check in here."

Mallory shook his head. "I'll go out with you. Sitting will just make me m-more nervous than I am already. I need to walk."

Mallory and Ryder left the café by its side entrance on the boulevard des Capucines. The rain had stopped, and a freshening wind signaled a weather change. Pedestrians hurried past, their wooden-soled shoes clattering on the pavement. On the street, bicycle traffic streamed silently by, the skirts of the women cyclists billowing out behind them like sails in the wind.

Ryder turned to Mallory and they shook hands.

"There is one last thing," Ryder said quickly. "If you should get caught, you might consider using your L-pill. The Gestapo is going to want to know why we came after Damberg, and they'll never believe we don't know."

Mallory nodded, but his mind shied away from the thought of the cyanide capsule hidden in his signet ring. "Good luck, Max."

"Good luck, kid. See you in London."

As Mallory watched Ryder walk away, a chill passed over his spine, and he felt a sudden urge to run after him, but the feeling passed as quickly as it had come. Unconsciously he squared his shoulders as he turned and walked out across the place de l'Opéra. He was alone now, but that was nothing new. Sometimes it seemed to Mallory that he had always been alone.

5

STEBBINGS died at eleven forty-five that morning. The rain-storm was moving way toward the coast, pushed aside by a warmer air mass drifting in from central Europe, and a momentary break in the clouds permitted the sun to shine on Stebbings one last time. He did not see the sunlight, for his eyes were squeezed shut during the long two seconds it took his tormented body to fall from the fifth floor of Gestapo headquarters onto the cobblestones of the dark, narrow rue des Saussaises. Stebbings didn't scream as he fell, for he had already suffered more than he could stand; death was his release.

A man leaned out of the fifth-floor window through which Stebbings had plunged and looked down at the body spread-eagled on the street below. A crimson stain, brilliant in the brief sunlight, was spreading out from beneath Stebbings's head. It flowed over the cobblestones and into the gutter and was washed away by the rainwater streaming into the drains.

"Now we're in for it," the man grunted to his companion standing behind him, and he pulled his head back inside.

"How were we to know that he still had some strength left?" the other Gestapo man said. "God, he got me right where it hurts."

"Mueller won't give a damn about your balls, Bruno. I'm telling you, we're in for it."

"But why? He talked; Mueller got what he wanted."

"Why? Because Mueller is Mueller, that's why. Come on, let's go back to his office and get it over with."

Mallory had been standing in a doorway in the rue Lepic for five minutes, watching the street, with fear lodged in his stomach like a stone. There was no sign of the Gestapo, but they could still be there, waiting. Mallory's tension was overlaid with fatigue. He had been on his feet for more than two hours, and a week of inactivity had sapped his endurance.

He had kept moving, skirting the roadblocks the Germans set up throughout Paris at different locations each day. The Paris through which he'd walked was a city devoid of life or color. Civilians in their shapeless gray or black coats moved listlessly through the streets against a drab background of somber, age-blackened buildings. Only the scarlet banners of the enemy, draped before official buildings, provided splashes of color.

Yet it was the lifeless silence, rather than the drabness of the city, that had oppressed Mallory. Absent were the blare of horns and rumble of traffic. Parisians bicycled or made their way on foot, and the quiet was only occasionally broken by a German car or truck. There was nothing peaceful in the quiet; it was sullen and bitter.

Looking down the slope of the rue Lepic toward the corner where he had left one of his warning marks, Mallory could see nothing out of the ordinary; the people in the street were behaving naturally. If the Gestapo had laid a trap, they had done so quietly. Mallory drew a breath and left the doorway; there was no point in delaying any longer.

He walked slowly down the street, his eyes sweeping the windows and doorways ahead. His gait was casual, but he was tensed to turn and run. He wouldn't have a chance if they were waiting for him, but it was better to be shot than to be forced to use the L-pill. He reached the corner of the rue de l'Armée d'Orient and stopped. A half block away, in the bend of the rue Lepic, was a small local bar.

He could wait in the bar for Marie. If he took a table by the window he would be able to see in both of the directions from which she might come, and he would be off the street. But now that he'd come this far, he had to know if Stebbings had talked. If he had, it would be suicide to try for a train today. Mallory felt gooseflesh rise on his arms; he would have to check the apartment.

He stepped around the corner and walked across the mouth of the rue de l'Armée d'Orient. The street was clear. Moving quickly now, he walked down the steep incline toward the safe house on the corner, keeping close to the high wall of the courtyard behind the house. He stopped beside a rough wooden door in the wall and tested the latch. As usual, the door was unlocked, and he put his weight against it. The door hung askew on rusted hinges, and they squealed sharply as he forced it open.

Mallory slipped through the doorway and made his way through the overgrown bushes behind the house, grateful that his apartment had no window overlooking the courtyard. He reached the stairwell that ran up the rear of the house, took out a key and unlocked the door. He stepped inside and paused to listen and to allow his eyes to adjust to the gloom.

He could hear the couple in the second-floor apartment yelling at each other, and the familiar sounds had a calming effect; his breathing became more regular. Slowly he began to climb the stairs, placing each foot carefully to minimize the creaking of the warped wooden steps. He heard a dry scrabbling of rats beneath the stairs, and he could smell the musty odor of their nests.

Mallory paused on the second-floor landing to listen again, but the argument raging in the apartment was too loud. He continued to climb, slowly and as silently as he could. He reached the third-floor landing, crept to the doorway, and put his ear against the door. Nothing.

The temptation to leave it at that was almost irresistible, but he had to be sure. He slipped a key into the doorlock and turned it a degree at a time. The lock opened with a soft click, and Mallory took a deep breath. Then he depressed the door handle and eased the door open a crack. The apartment was empty.

Relief flooded through him. Either they had not yet interrogated Stebbings, or he was still holding out. Mallory started to close the door, but he hesitated, thinking of the suit and the pair of leather-soled shoes in the wardrobe. The suit jacket had the heavily padded shoulders and drape lapels favored by the Gestapo, and the costume had been provided for his Gestapo impersonation.

Marie didn't know he carried Gestapo identification or that he spoke German, and she had never asked about the suit and shoes. Not telling her had been a simple, cold-blooded precaution. The less she knew, the less she could reveal under torture if she were caught.

Now, Mallory toyed with the idea of changing clothes and using the Gestapo I.D. to get them both through the railway checkpoint and onto the train, but he quickly discarded it. If Stebbings talked and their descriptions were circulated before they reached the railway control, Mallory doubted that the Gestapo I.D. would save them; and if Stebbings held out, the impersonation might simply draw needless attention to them. He closed the apartment door and slipped out of the building the way he had come.

"*Vin ordinaire,*" Mallory said, indicating by his manner that he was in no mood for conversation.

He waited in silence as the bartender poured him a large glass of red wine and then took the glass to one of the three tiny round tables at the window of the cramped little barroom and sat down. He was grateful that this was a *jour avec.* The Germans had decreed that wine could be served only every other day, and on a *jour sans,* the bartender would have had no one to talk to but Mallory.

As it was, only one other customer was present, a swarthy, sad-eyed laborer with powerful arms too long for his short-legged body, who was draped on a stool in front of the miniature brass-topped bar listening to the bartender's marital woes. The bartender, a big-bellied, garrulous man with thinning hair on his scalp and thick, matted hair on his forearms, evidently didn't like his wife, but he enjoyed discussing her defects.

No one in Paris bars discussed politics, or the war, or the

Germans. The *Boches* were a fact of life warranting far less interest than the weather.

Ryder would be clear of Paris now, Mallory thought — if his luck had held. At least Stebbings hadn't talked yet, but how much longer would he hold out? Mallory could almost feel the time running out. But no one had forced him to come back. Ryder undoubtedly thought him a fool, even if he'd had the grace not to say it. Ryder had acquiesced, but he hadn't really understood.

How could he? How could he begin to understand the intensity of a homely young man's feeling for the first woman to return his love? For that was it, Mallory acknowledged to himself, his lips twitching in self-derision. That was it exactly.

In the Ohio town in which he had grown up, physical appearance and athletic prowess had been everything, and Mallory's body had betrayed him. He had waited in vain for his skinny frame to fill out, for his muscles to gain in strength and coordination. Instead, acne had ravaged his narrow, sharp-nosed face, and his eyes had required ever-thicker lenses.

Some high-school wag had dubbed him "Ferret," and the sobriquet had stuck. If Mallory had been more self-assured he might have laughed it off, but instead he had withdrawn from his classmates, immersing himself in schoolwork and adjusting to an unnecessarily lonely existence. College should have allowed him to make a new beginning, but he had been slow to come out of his shell. He had been twenty before he had had his first date.

Mallory had graduated with an engineering degree in 1942 and had immediately enlisted in the army. He might have washed out of basic training had not his drill sergeant taken pity on him, and his application to join the paratroops, following basic training, had been rejected with a smile.

For six months he had languished at Fort Dix as a file clerk in the Quartermaster Corps, but at the beginning of 1943, his service record had passed across the desk of an officer in Washington who recruited for the OSS.

Mallory's parents had died in an auto accident when he was five, and he had been raised in a foster home by German immigrants, who had brought him up bilingually. The army had ignored this, as they had ignored his qualifications as an engineer — and his application for hazardous service. The OSS had not . . .

Mallory glanced at his watch. Marie would be coming soon. She knew that if she was late, Mallory would have to take it as a danger signal. But how much time did they have left? Stebbings could be talking right now. Mallory shifted his chair, moving closer to the window to see farther up the street in the direction from which she would probably come. But again his thoughts began to drift, as if seeking refuge from the tension . . .

In his own mind, Mallory's life had begun the day he had joined the OSS. The men and women who found their way into the OSS were from all walks of life, many of them misfits. What they had in common was a romantic streak and an unorthodox sense of adventure. Among them Mallory found what had so long eluded him — acceptance.

OSS training was loosely based on the SOE model, but in the early years it had been haphazard and improvised. Parachute school, radio school, demolitions, small arms, silent killing: the accelerated courses had followed one upon the other in random order.

In the summer of 1943, Mallory had been sent to England for final training in SOE schools set up in English country estates and in the Scottish Highlands. Mixed in with the trainees were SOE veterans who had been sent back to school between missions — ostensibly to sharpen their skills, but in reality to keep them from brooding on their dwindling chances of survival.

At times, during a lecture, the veterans would nod in agreement with the instructor, but sometimes they would shake their heads with ill-concealed scorn. Mallory had watched for their reactions and had listened to their occasional, offhand comments; and he had learned an unpleasant truth, which the instructors preferred to gloss over: training was no defense against betrayal, and in the end, survival depended as much on luck as on tradecraft.

It had been a sobering realization, but Mallory had shelved it

60 –

in the back of his mind, as young men do with thoughts of death. The allure of secret operations had been too seductive, and the danger not yet real. But in Italy, death had become real enough — and now so had betrayal . . .

Marie was coming. He recognized her even before she was close enough to see clearly.

The bartender had switched from complaining about his wife to disparaging his mother-in-law. He looked over as Mallory stood up casually and fished in his pocket for some money. Mallory laid a bill on the bar as he strolled out and received a brief smile and an *au 'voir* in return.

Overhead the clouds were breaking up, and the wind had lightened to a breeze, warmer and carrying a hint of spring. Normally the shift in the weather would have cheered Mallory, but now he barely registered the change. Marie was walking up the rue Lepic from the direction of the Blanche Métro station, sunlight glinting intermittently on her hair.

As he watched her coming toward him, he realized that it didn't matter if his decision to come back had been foolhardy or not; he had never really had a choice.

Marie, on the opposite side of the street, had not yet noticed him, but as he crossed the road he saw the break in her stride when she caught sight of him and realized that something was amiss. She smiled at his approach, but as he came near he could see the concern in her eyes. She asked no questions as he took her arm and turned her to walk back the way she had come. She fell into step with him, and as they walked he told her what had happened.

"If Roland talks," Marie said, squeezing Mallory's arm. "We will never get through the control at the railway station."

"I know."

"Perhaps we should go into hiding."

"And then what?" Mallory said, unable to keep his voice from rising. "We can't trust your FFI friends any longer. If we wait, we guarantee that the police at the checkpoints will have our descriptions, and we don't have enough money to stay under cover indefinitely."

"Then let me try to get out alone. I'll be able to find Lessard, and he can arrange to smuggle you out of Paris."

It was a reasonable suggestion, but Mallory's instinct urged him to get out now. He shook his head. "If Roland had talked, they would have staked out our apartment, and I'm willing to gamble that he can hang on a little longer."

Mallory saw that Marie was about to say something more, but she changed her mind. "We'll head for the Gare Saint-Lazare," he said. "I have tickets for a train out of there at one-thirty."

Marie looked at him for a moment and then nodded in agreement, but he noticed that she was biting her lower lip. As they headed for the Blanche Métro station, Mallory prayed that he had made the right decision.

Five minutes after Mallory had left the bar, the bartender's lone customer decided to go back to work. He paid his bill and ambled outside, but as he stepped out onto the sidewalk, he abruptly turned on his heel and reentered the bar. The lips of his downturned mouth were compressed, and his sad eyes had lost some of their listlessness.

Outside a teenaged boy flashed by on his bicycle, and the bartender heard his shout, *"Rafle! Rafle!"*

"Merde," the bartender muttered sourly as the workman settled onto his stool again. He poured the man a fresh glass of wine and then eased his bulk out from behind the bar, lumbered to the door, and went outside to satisfy his curiosity.

From up the hill to his left came the rising whine of an engine as the driver of a gray, canvas-covered Wehrmacht truck downshifted on the steep grade. Brakes squealed, and the truck slewed to a halt, blocking the street two hundred feet from where the bartender stood watching with open disgust. Troops spilled from the rear of the truck in a clatter of boots and weapons, as a second truck, coming up the rue Lepic from the opposite direction braked to a stop around the bend to the bartender's right.

"Merde," the bartender growled again and walked back inside, closing the door firmly behind him.

To the accompaniment of whistles and shouted orders, soldiers were fanning out, blocking off the street. A flying squad, weapons at the ready, charged into the rue de l'Armée d'Orient, running toward the deserted safe-house apartment.

Marie stood close beside Mallory on the subway platform, holding his arm tightly. He looked at her and tried to smile reassuringly, but she could feel the tension in his muscles, and her answering smile was no more convincing than his.

They had been waiting less than five minutes, but it seemed much longer to Mallory and the subdued, depressing atmosphere in the Métro station weighed on him. The handful of passengers scattered over the platform stood alone or in pairs. No one laughed or raised his voice, and what little conversation there was seemed as morose as it was hushed.

A lone Wehrmacht officer paced restlessly up and down in the platform area designated for first-class passengers, where the car marked *Nur für Wehrmacht* would stop. The heels of his polished boots beat a monotonous tattoo on the concrete. No one gave him as much as a glance; he was ignored as if he didn't exist.

Mallory didn't like using the Métro, for he knew the Gestapo frequently set up temporary checkpoints at the subway exits; but time was important, and if they couldn't make it through a subway checkpoint, they had no hope of getting through the railway control.

A rumble from the black tunnel mouth signaled the approach of the train, and Marie tightened her grip on Mallory's arm possessively, as if she were afraid for him, alone, rather than for them both. "You should not have come back for me, Richard," she said, but her voice was lost in the rattling roar of the train as it swept into the station.

6

MALLORY knew they were in trouble even before they entered the outer hall of the Gare Saint-Lazare. He and Marie had come through an underground passage from the Métro to an arcade beneath the station, and as they ascended the stairs to the upper level, he heard the crowd noise spilling from the hall above them. At the top of the stairs they stopped, momentarily taken aback by the milling mass of civilians and German soldiers thronging the station's concourse.

"What's happening?" Marie gasped.

"They must be loading troop trains," Mallory said grimly, leaning close to her to be understood over the noise in the cavernous hall. The barked commands of Wehrmacht noncoms and the intermittent blaring of a loudspeaker issuing unintelligible announcements in French and German punctuated a rushing noise like the amplified sound of a seashell held close to the ear.

"I know," Marie said, "but I've never seen so many troops moving out at once."

Mallory shook his head. "They must be intending to reinforce the Channel ports. Maybe there's an invasion alarm."

The muscles along Mallory's jaw knotted as he looked at the jam of civilians in front of the two security control gates leading to the station hall adjacent to the boarding platforms. Military police at the gates were holding back the civilians to make way for the troops being marched out to the platform area, and it was impossible to estimate how long it would take them to reach their train. Units were marched through the gates at irregular intervals, and throughout the hall new units were constantly forming as knots of green-uniformed soldiers coalesced around their non-coms.

"Jesus Christ," Mallory said in English, and Marie squeezed his arm in alarm. She had never seen him drop his guard before.

"Be careful, *chéri!*"

"We'll miss the damned train," Mallory said tightly.

"It will probably be delayed as well," Marie said quickly. She saw the indecision in his eyes, and it worried her as much as his momentary lapse into English. "Wait here," she said quickly. "I will check the schedule."

"Wait! Marie —"

But she had gone, disappearing into the crowd swirling around them. Mallory was jostled from behind, and a moment later he cried out sharply as the tip of an umbrella was driven into his ribs.

"*Pardon, monsieur,*" said a frail, white-haired lady who carried a suitcase in one hand and an umbrella in the other. She was holding the umbrella in front of her like a spear, and there was no real apology in her tone. She brushed by him and marched on, clearing her path through the crowd with the point of her umbrella.

A pair of Wehrmacht privates stopped beside him, arguing about what they should do if they couldn't find their unit. Mallory gathered that they'd returned late from leave and had missed the transport to the station. Neither boy looked older than sixteen, and Mallory doubted they had ever heard a shot fired in anger. They were obviously more afraid of their sergeant than of the prospect of meeting the Allied invasion. Out of habit, Mallory automatically noted their unit patches and the condition of their equipment, but he had no real interest.

It was time that mattered — time that continued to slip away. They must have gone to work on Stebbings by now. How long could he hold out? Minutes seemed like hours as Mallory stood there, waiting for Marie. He didn't dare move for fear that they might not find each other again.

Suddenly she appeared at his side. "It's all right, Richard," she said, sounding out of breath. "Our train has been delayed and it won't depart until it's loaded. We'll just have to try to get through the control as quickly as possible."

The confusion in the station did not deter the Germans from carefully checking the papers and luggage of each passenger passing through the railway control. Mallory and Marie had been waiting for forty-five minutes in one of the long, ragged lines, and now they were close enough to observe the procedure.

Because of the crush of people, a temporary wooden barricade surrounded the control area, and at intervals civilians were admitted in groups of fifty. Normally, Germans and French gendarmes worked together in pairs at security checkpoints, but now the security men on duty were being aided by additional German military police. Hovering close behind the security police were men in civilian clothes with restless, alert eyes.

Occasionally one of the Gestapo agents would step forward and check the identity papers of a civilian, but so far no one had been detained. The Gestapo never detained civilians at random; they knew for whom they were looking.

Marie said something to Mallory that he didn't hear clearly, and he leaned closer. In addition to the general noise, her voice was masked by the howls of a five-year-old boy belonging to a couple standing in front of them. The parents had given up trying to comfort him and were staring ahead with long-suffering expressions on their stolid faces. The boy's knees were blackened from kneeling on the grimy floor and more dirt was smeared on his tear-streaked face. Mallory thought the boy should have exhausted himself by now, but he continued to wail and to pull in frustration on his mother's skirt.

"Richard, I don't think we should go through together," Marie repeated. "It should be possible for you to have your papers checked by a German and avoid the gendarmes, and that means I won't have to cover for you."

66 –

"I was thinking the same thing," Mallory said.

"I will go through first," Marie said. "If I am not detained, you will know that Roland has not given them our descriptions."

"No. It was my decision to try for the train, and we promised Lessard that we would keep you in the clear. I'm going through ahead of you."

"But I have a better chance of talking my way out if they do stop me," Marie said quickly. "You would have no chance at all."

"No!" Mallory snapped, startling the five-year-old, who abruptly stopped crying. In spite of himself, Mallory had to smile, and he winked at the child. Immediately the boy began to cry again.

Marie did not argue further, but she released his arm, which Mallory took as a protest. He ignored it; he had not returned for Marie to have her risk her life for him.

The German MPs in front of the barricade were pushing back the crowd and removing a section of the barricade to allow a large Wehrmacht contingent through, and Mallory wondered why the Germans had not opened up a separate gateway to the platforms for their troops. As the last of the soldiers marched through the opening in the barricade, the crowd of civilians pushed forward restlessly. Arguments and some angry shoving broke out as tempers flared. Fatigue, frustration, and the heat generated by the press of bodies were taking their toll.

Mallory could see from the faces of the people around him that these Frenchmen were unafraid of the control. To them it was simply an inconvenience, not a gauntlet to be run. He looked anxiously at his watch. An hour and a quarter had passed since he had picked up Marie.

The MPs were preparing to admit a fresh batch of civilians to the security area, and Mallory was jostled from behind as more people pressed forward. He reached out to take Marie's arm and discovered she was no longer at his side. In the momentary confusion she had slipped away, and he saw her darting forward, skirting the crowd as she made directly for the opening in the barrier.

Mallory realized immediately what she intended to do, but it was too late to stop her without attracting attention. A Frenchman near the front of the line angrily snared her arm as she tried to slip past him, but the MPs had already begun to let people through the barrier and she pulled free and pushed her way ahead. No one else tried to stop her for fear of delaying themselves, and she made it into the security area just before the German guards sealed the barrier once again.

Mallory craned his neck to see past the heads of the people in front of him to the security area. The civilians had formed into three lines, and Mallory saw Marie standing with the passengers who were carrying no baggage. Anxiously he followed her slow progress toward the security check, catching intermittent glimpses of her blond hair, and although he did not believe in God, he found himself praying — praying that he had gambled correctly on Stebbings.

He saw her step forward to hand her papers to the nearest German MP and then lost sight of her as two French laborers moved up behind her. The German had smiled as he had looked at her, and that at least was a good sign. He would be more interested in making an impression on Marie than in her papers. Mallory realized that he was holding his breath, and he expelled it and tried to breathe normally. He would be able to see her when she moved on. The seconds ticked by . . .

Suddenly the laborers standing close behind Marie backed away from her, as if from a leper, and Mallory's breath caught in his throat as he saw a man in a civilian suit standing beside the MP. Marie's identity card was in his hand, and he was staring at her coldly. The smile on the MP's face was gone. For Mallory time seemed to stand still, the figures he was watching frozen in a tableau.

Then Mallory saw the Gestapo agent say something, and Marie moved backward, recoiling involuntarily. The soldier stepped forward quickly and seized her arm, and Mallory lost sight of her again in a momentary swirl of confusion around her. He saw her once more, head erect, as two Gestapo agents led her away. Holding her firmly between them, they took her through the gate leading to the platform area, and she was gone.

The arrest produced barely a ripple of response in the crowd of onlookers. Some exchanged glances, and Mallory heard someone say, "Resistance," softly, but there was no protest or even an indication of anger among these careful Parisians.

Suddenly the crowd noise in the station seemed to fade, and Mallory's vision blurred. Blindly he pushed his way out of the crowd in front of the barrier, in a daze, barely aware of what he was doing. He had made his way out into the middle of the concourse before he recovered from his shock. It left him abruptly, as if someone had switched on the sound again and restarted the clock, and anguish hit him like physical pain. He should have known Stebbings couldn't hold out. He had gambled and lost, and Marie was to pay the price. They would do to her what they'd done to Stebbings. Mallory groaned aloud.

He saw a woman nearby staring at him curiously, and automatically he turned and moved away from her. Training still retained a partial hold on him. He knew what he was expected to do — what Marie would want him to do. He should leave the station at once, before Marie's arrest triggered a response and the Germans sealed off the exits. He should leave and find a *maison de passe* in which to hide.

He turned and started toward the exit leading to the street, moving like an automaton, but his steps slowed and then he stopped, oblivious to the people moving past him. He was thinking again, and an idea born of desperation began to take form.

The Gestapo had not taken Marie directly from the station, and Mallory was sure they would interrogate her first, in the hope of catching him as well. They, too, would expect him to try to escape; they couldn't know that escape meant nothing to him now. Mallory took a deep breath and then another, grimly determined to clear his mind. He still had one last card to play.

The floor of the railway station's men's room was slick with water and urine, and the stench was overpowering, which suited Mallory. No one would be inclined to loiter. The two soldiers urinating into the trough against the wall ignored him as he walked directly to one of the rusted metal stalls at the rear. He went inside and flushed the toilet to cover the sound of tearing cloth as he ripped open the lining of his overcoat to remove the leather-bound Gestapo identity card bearing his photograph.

He slipped the I.D. into his jacket pocket, cocked his hat at an intentionally casual angle, and left the men's room. He was still tense, but there was no visceral fear in him; he felt only a cold, desperate determination. "It's all a matter of bluff, old man," the SOE instructor in London had said to him before the mission. "Keep Jerry off balance; bully him, and he'll lick your boots." With the clothes Mallory was wearing — particularly the wooden-soled shoes — it didn't seem possible that the bluff would work, for they were alerted and looking for a man of Mallory's description, but he would try anyway. He felt he had nothing left to lose.

As Mallory approached the barrier surrounding the railway control, another contingent of infantry was marching through the gap in the barricade. Mallory didn't hesitate; he swung in behind the soldiers and strode into the security area in their wake, flashing his I.D. at the nearest MP.

Three groups of German MPs and French gendarmes were occupied with processing the twenty-odd civilians inside the barrier, and Mallory allowed himself a moment to size up the situation. Only two Gestapo agents were present, one young and the other middle-aged, and neither man had looked his way yet. Mallory chose the older man, assuming he would have the higher rank, and walked quickly toward him, shouldering aside the civilians in his path. Mallory had to establish himself as a German in the Gestapo agent's mind before the man had time to connect Mallory's appearance with the description he had been given.

An MP stepped forward to block Mallory's path, but Mallory scowled, flashed his I.D. and swept past him, forcing the young soldier to step back or be bowled over. The Gestapo agent turned toward him. He was a short, square-jawed man with a pock-marked, sallow face, and he looked sharply at Mallory.

"I'm Strauss," Mallory barked, as if he expected the man to snap to attention at the mention of his name. "Where's the girl?"

"Girl, Herr . . . ?" the Gestapo agent said coolly.

70 –

"Sturmbannführer Strauss," Mallory growled, holding up his I.D. for inspection two seconds longer than necessary, and Mallory saw the man stiffen slightly. Mallory was unusually young to hold the SS rank equivalent to a major, but instead of arousing the Gestapo agent's suspicions, Mallory's youth implied that he had solid Party connections. "What's your name?" Mallory demanded.

"Dorn, Herr Sturmbannführer."

Mallory's foster parents had come from Swabia, and he spoke German with a pronounced Swabian accent, and that accent worked for him now. That Mallory might be a foreigner simply didn't occur to a German who heard him speak. Adrenaline was driving Mallory's pulse at an accelerated rate, but still there was no fear; he could see the bluff was working, and exhilaration swelled within him, propelling him forward as if he were riding the crest of a wave.

"Where is the French girl who was just apprehended?" Mallory said. "The fools haven't taken her away yet, have they?"

"No, Herr Sturmbannführer. She is being questioned in the stationmaster's office," the agent replied with careful respect, but then he noticed Mallory's shoes and he frowned.

"What the hell are you staring at?" Mallory snapped, and the man blinked. Out of the corner of his eye, Mallory saw the ghost of a smile appear on the lips of the nearest MP; there was no love lost between the military and the Gestapo. Mallory shot a sharp glance at the soldier, and the smile vanished.

"I wasn't staring, Herr Sturmbannführer," the Gestapo agent said defensively.

Mallory was the focus of attention in the security area now, but that didn't bother him. *Hide in plain sight.*

"Where is the stationmaster's office?"

"Through the arch and to your left, Herr Sturmbannführer."

"Well?" Mallory demanded impatiently.

"Herr Sturmbannführer?"

"Take me there. I haven't got all day!"

"But my post is here —"

"Take me there. Now!"

"Yes, certainly, Herr Sturmbannführer."

Mallory wanted to keep the man with him, close and off balance, with no chance to think, and he also wanted the Gestapo agent to run interference for him. Agent Dorn believed in Sturmbannführer Strauss, and he would transfer that belief to the Gestapo men in the stationmaster's office.

He followed the Gestapo man through the arch leading into the hall adjacent to the platforms. Overhead a huge skylight ran the six-hundred-foot length of the hall, and Mallory had to squint as the sun once again broke through the clouds and sunlight flooded down through the glass. Behind them, through the second gateway, came another three squads of infantry, forty men in marching order, their nailed boots pounding the concrete in unison. Mallory thought he had never heard a more ominous sound.

He walked close behind the Gestapo agent, pushing the pace, hoping he could keep him from making the connection: a short, thin man with dark, wiry hair, thick glasses, narrow face . . .

Mallory had no definite plan; when he reached the stationmaster's office he would have to play it by ear. But somehow he would get Marie out; he was sure of that now. *It's all a matter of bluff, old man.*

A military policeman armed with a machine pistol stood at the entrance to a narrow staircase ascending to the stationmaster's office, but the Gestapo man ignored the guard and led the way up the steep stairs. Mallory made the mistake of using the railing, and his hand came away covered with sooty grime. He wiped off the dirt with his handkerchief as he continued to climb, amazed that he could still be distracted by trivia.

On the landing at the top of the stairs was a single door with the words *Chef de Gare* stenciled in flaking gold paint on its frosted-glass window. The Gestapo man entered without knocking, and Mallory followed him into a stuffy anteroom, in which the stale odor of tobacco smoke mingled nauseatingly with the cloying scent of cheap cologne.

Two men in gray suits cut exactly like the suit Mallory should have been wearing lounged in chairs by a desk beside the door, cigarettes dangling carelessly from their slack lips. The cologne fancier was playing solitaire, and his companion was fondly stroking the barrel of a machine pistol with an oiled cloth. Both men shot to their feet when Mallory's rank was announced.

Mallory heard muffled voices from beyond the door that led to the main office, and his pulse quickened. One of the voices was a woman's. Mallory looked at the man who had brought him and indicated with a curt nod that he should return to his post. The man gave his comrades a warning glance and left quickly.

Mallory noted the wary look in the Gestapo hoods' eyes. They were a hulking, rawboned pair, but he could see that they were prepared to jump at his command. If there would be trouble, it would come from the officer in charge — the man in the next room.

"Is the girl in there?" Mallory said.

"Yes, Herr Sturmbannführer," the gun lover said.

Mallory nodded and went to the door, wondering what he was going to say, but there was no time to compose a speech. He opened the door and marched in as if he owned the place.

Mallory had expected to see the room's occupants as soon as he opened the door, but instead he was confronted with a huge diagram of the Gare Saint-Lazare's switching network, which covered the wall opposite him. The desk in front of the plate-glass window overlooking the station platforms was unoccupied. Mallory turned to his left and saw Marie.

She was sitting on a sagging divan against the wall, her hands clasped tightly around her knees, her face drawn and deathly pale. Marie's lips parted in shock as she looked up and recognized him, and he heard her sharp intake of breath, but Mallory was sure the man standing over her would mistake her reaction for fear. Mallory turned deliberately and closed the office door.

"Strauss," Mallory said curtly to the man. "Sturmbannführer Strauss."

"Indeed," the man replied, making no move toward Mallory. "My name is Mueller," he said in a soft, cultivated voice that contrasted sharply with his crude, blunt-featured face.

Mueller was a stocky man in his late forties, with a broad,

fleshy face. A shock of coarse black hair fell across his forehead, and with a mustache, he could have given a fair imitation of the Führer. His dark eyes glittered coldly.

"I'm afraid I've never heard of you, Sturmbannführer Strauss," he said, and a faint smile touched his heavy lips. "Your business here?"

Marie was staring at Mallory with wide, disbelieving eyes, the look of shock still frozen on her face.

"That is my affair," Mallory snapped, hoping that his fictitious rank exceeded Mueller's. "What have you gotten out of the bitch?"

Mueller did not reply immediately, and Mallory felt his momentum slipping away. Mueller was too cool by half.

"I'm sure she hasn't told me everything she knows," Mueller said, "but we've made a beginning. May I see your identification, please, Herr Sturmbannführer. Just a matter of form, you understand."

It wasn't working. Mallory's I.D. was good enough, but he could see that he'd never bluff Mueller into handing over Marie. Mallory took out his I.D. and stepped toward Mueller. He would have to take him first and then sucker the two hoods into the room one at a time. His first judo chop would have to be sharp and sure; there could be no noise. He hoped Mueller was carrying a pistol, for he wasn't sure he could handle the hoods with his bare hands.

But Mueller had read his mind.

Before Mallory could reach him, he took a quick step backward. "Schmidt!" he bellowed.

Mallory spun back toward the door, tensing to spring, but he never had a chance. The door burst open and the gun lover appeared, his machine pistol leveled at Mallory's stomach. Close behind him was the second hood, a Walther automatic in his hand.

Mallory heard Mueller produce a theatrical sigh. "You see, Lieutenant Mallory," Mueller said in stilted English, "panache is not always enough."

Mallory looked toward Marie and started to speak, but the gun lover, Schmidt, stepped forward and drove the gun barrel into Mallory's stomach, doubling him over.

"Easy on that trigger!" Mueller barked, as Schmidt forced Mallory backward and pinned him hard against the wall.

Gasping for breath, Mallory looked again toward Marie, knowing they might never see each other again, but she had averted her face, her features set like stone. Mueller walked to the divan, bent down, and said something to her that Mallory couldn't hear. Without looking at Mallory, she stood up and walked quickly across the office and out the door, as Mallory stared after her in stunned disbelief. He heard the outer door open and close behind her, and then she was gone. No one had made a move to stop her.

Mueller laughed softly, obviously amused by the look on Mallory's face. "Ah, women," he said, shaking his head. "You can never trust them."

CIA Archive No. 75434-R03   OPTRICYCLE
OSS/HIS/EV-44   Page 15

. . . Tricycle was set in motion by faulty intelligence and was doomed to failure from the start, but mistakes were also made in the field, and these highlight shortcomings in the training of OSS operatives. Instructors concentrated on methods of avoiding detection, and too little attention was paid to procedures to be followed once an agent or his network was exposed.

Ryder's escape was more a credit to his own judgment than to specific training, and instructions covering such situations might have prevented Mallory's rash action. Stebbings's capture was perhaps unavoidable, but Mallory's was not.

In another respect, SOE and OSS training was woefully inadequate. Agents were routinely issued cyanide tablets to be used in the event of capture, but in only a very few instances were they used. Had they been, fewer agents would have been betrayed and those who were captured would have spared themselves prolonged physical torment.

Beyond the warning implicit in the issuance of the capsules, the subject of Gestapo treatment of captured agents was largely ignored in the training schools. Given the quite natural instinct for survival, it is not surprising that few agents chose suicide, for they were not properly indoctrinated. Yet Gestapo methods were well known to the SOE command and unvarying: captured agents were routinely beaten and tortured, and ultimately put to death ...

7

THEY began by breaking Mallory's nose. Mallory saw the first blow coming, but he couldn't protect himself. Mueller's two hoods had him pinned between them in the backseat of a Citroën, as they rode across town to Gestapo headquarters in the rue des Saussaies. He had made a fool of them, and they now took their revenge.

Schmidt twisted around in the narrow seat and drove his fist straight into Mallory's face. The force of the blow snapped Mallory's head back, and he heard the crunch as his nose broke. Pain tears spurted into his eyes, and he sucked in air in a ragged gasp only to have it driven out of him as Schmidt's partner, the cologne fancier, rammed his elbow into Mallory's solar plexus.

Mallory doubled up, and his glasses, which had been knocked askew by the first blow, fell to the floor of the car. Schmidt bent forward and caught Mallory in the left eye with a short, choppy uppercut, and when Mallory brought up one free arm to shield his head, Schmidt's partner hammered his kidneys.

Mallory could hear himself gagging and gasping, and his mind reeled, drunk with shock and pain as the two men continued to drive their fists and elbows into his body. A blow behind his ear stunned him momentarily, and though he was still conscious as the beating went on remorselessly, his response to the jolts of pain was dulled. The part of his mind that still functioned wondered vaguely whether they were beating him to death.

Perhaps they would have, despite their orders, if they'd had more room; but it was hot, frustrating work in the cramped confines of the Citroën, and the muscles of the two big men were slack and overlaid with fat. Soon their red, angry faces were slimy with sweat, and they were panting heavily. Finally, Schmidt had had enough, and he struck Mallory across the back of the neck with the heel of his hand, knocking him unconscious.

Chests heaving, the two men loosened their ties and shirt collars and leaned back in their seats to spend the remainder of the short ride listening to their own labored breathing and to the steady drip of blood from Mallory's nose and mouth onto the floor.

Mallory came to as they dragged him from the car and pulled him to his feet, and he cried out in agony as a dagger of pain stabbed the right side of his chest. Ribs broken, he thought dully. It didn't seem to matter; nothing mattered now. He tried to stay on his feet, but his rubbery legs gave way and he sank to his knees. Dizziness rolled over him in waves. His entire upper body throbbed in time to his pulse.

Someone had set his glasses back in place, but Mallory could only open his left eye and its vision was blurred. As the two men pulled him to his feet, he stared dazedly up at the surrounding buildings, not realizing that he was in a narrow courtyard of the Gestapo headquarters complex. They half dragged, half carried him to a rear entrance of the nearest office building.

Beside the entrance was a gray pile of wet, rotting straw, on which were sprawled the bodies of two men and a woman. Mallory looked at them as he was dragged past, but he couldn't tell if they were dead or just too weak to move. As the Gestapo hoods hauled him through the doorway into the dimly lit interior, nausea convulsed him and he vomited onto Schmidt's shoes. The man's furious curse was the last thing Mallory remembered before everything went black.

"I see that you have no wish to die, Lieutenant," Mueller said in English in his peculiarly soft voice, pretending to inspect the

L-pill he had found in Mallory's signet ring. "You might have tried to swallow it, but you chose not to."

Mallory did not respond. Technically he had been conscious for at least five minutes, but only now were his thoughts and sensory impressions forming coherent patterns. He had been stripped to his underwear and propped up in an armless wooden chair in front of Mueller's desk. For his interrogations, Mueller used a bleak, unheated storeroom close under the eaves of the building. Empty packing cases had been pushed aside to make room for Mueller's military-issue desk and the prisoner's chair.

"Is it fear that makes you shiver, or are you cold?" Mueller asked contemptuously.

Again Mallory did not respond, and the slack-jawed giant who stood behind him shifted restlessly on his feet; but Mueller was in no hurry. He returned to his inspection of Mallory's effects, which were spread out on the desk. "Excellent forgeries," Mueller said, holding Mallory's identification papers up to the light streaming in from the narrow dormer window behind him. "Excellent."

The afternoon sun had not warmed the room, and Mallory's skinny body, still partly in shock, had no resistance to the damp chill in the air. He hugged himself with his arms, trying to minimize the stress his shivering was putting on his broken ribs. Adding to his misery was an excruciating pressure on his bladder; he urgently needed to relieve himself. His swollen nose was blocked with clotted blood, and he breathed shallowly through his mouth, drawing in the air through clenched teeth.

But Mallory almost welcomed the pain that racked him; it blotted out thoughts of Marie.

Mueller laid the identification papers aside and looked coldly at Mallory. There was little imagination in his dark, opaque eyes, only a peasant shrewdness, and Mallory realized he would use only one tool in his interrogation: the strong-arm man.

"I asked you if you are cold," Mueller said.

"Yes —"

Mallory gasped as the giant behind him struck him across his right ear. The stinging, open-handed blow nearly knocked him off the chair. Through the ringing in his ear he heard Mueller correct him: "Yes, *sir*."

"Yes, sir," Mallory repeated hoarsely.

Mueller's thick lips twitched into the semblance of a smile, and he nodded in mocking approval. "Your code name was Richard. What is your real name?"

"Richard Mallory — sir."

"You see how simple it is, Lieutenant. Answer my questions promptly, truthfully, and with respect, and Horst will not be obliged to hurt you. You are a spy and an assassin, Lieutenant, sent to kill a noncombatant, and I could have you shot right now."

Mueller paused and leaned back in his chair to give his words time to sink in. The stick had been applied, Mallory thought; next would come the carrot. Mueller did not disappoint him.

"I *could* have you shot," Mueller said, "but we are not barbarians. If you cooperate, I can use my influence on your behalf. You would be sent to a detention camp in Germany as a prisoner of war."

"Would I have your w-word on that? — your word as a gentleman."

"Of course."

Mueller was an unconvincing liar, but Mallory tried to look as if hope had been rekindled within him. They would still kill him in the end, but he might be able to spare himself some pain.

"And why should you not cooperate?" Mueller continued. "You've done your best, and you've given your masters a good run for their money. But now it's over — finished. No one can possibly hold it against you if you choose to act sensibly. Do you agree?"

Mallory nodded slowly.

"Excellent," Mueller said. "What is Max's real name?"

"Captain M-Maxwell Ryder."

"How did he leave Paris?"

"By train."

"And his destination?"

Mallory tried to remember if Marie had known. What had he told the bitch? "The girl m-m-must have given you that information," Mallory said, stalling for time to think.

The goon behind him struck him again, this time across the left ear. The blow caught his glasses and drove them against the bridge of his broken nose, and blood spurted afresh from his nostrils. Now both ears were ringing, and Mallory could barely hear Mueller's soft voice.

"That was f-f-for impertinence, Lieutenant M-M-Mallory," Mueller mocked. "Answer the question."

"The Vercors," Mallory gasped, hoping that he had not told Marie where Ryder was headed. His mind was simply too sluggish to remember. His answer was a plausible lie, for he had heard Lessard mention that Maquis forces were massing in the Vercors.

"And how was he to make contact with the terrorists?"

"The FFI? I don't know. He didn't —"

Mallory shrieked involuntarily as the goon hit his right ear again with a cupped palm and the sudden overpressure ruptured his eardrum.

"He didn't tell me!" Mallory cried, his words tumbling out. "That was how we worked. The girl can v-v-verify that. He told me they would have someone watch the railroad station at Valence so that I c-could follow him."

"And who was your terrorist contact here in Paris?"

Pain had filled Mallory's eyes with tears, and he squeezed them now so that the tears rolled down his cheek for effect. "I don't know, sir! We worked through the girl."

"What was your communication arrangement with London?"

"One-way only, sir, until the mission was completed. M-messages for us were to be sent out by the BBC, p-prefaced by the code words, apple orchard."

"You had no transmission schedule?"

"Yes, but Max had the sked."

The goon standing behind Mallory shifted his weight, and Mallory flinched, but nothing happened. Mallory had tried in vain to detect the signal Mueller gave the man, and he was unable to anticipate the blows.

"Surely you, yourself, could transmit if the need arose — in an emergency."

"Yes, sir," Mallory said quickly. "Twenty-two hundred hours was a f-fixed emergency transmission time."

"What was your security code?"

" 'Rich.' It must p-preface the transmission and appear once more in the text, or London will assume I am sending under duress."

That was one lie Mueller wouldn't bother to check out. Mueller wouldn't try to play back the captured transmitter, because he knew Ryder would warn London that the team had been blown.

"And now," Mueller said, leaning back in his chair and steepling his blunt fingers, "we come to the heart of the matter, Lieutenant. Your colleague, Stebbings, insisted that he didn't know why you were sent to kill our countryman, Professor Damberg. I hope, for your sake, that you will be more forthcoming."

There it was, the question Mallory had been dreading. If he didn't answer it effectively, the real torture would begin. They wouldn't accept the truth — that he didn't know why Damberg had been marked for death — and the only lie he could think of was hopelessly thin. On impulse he decided to invite more punishment in the hope of making it less obvious that he was lying.

"You p-promised me leniency if I c-cooperated, sir," he whined. "If I tell you, how do I know you will keep your prom —"

Mallory was cut off as the goon seized him by his hair and yanked him to his feet. The giant's huge fist slammed into Mallory's back, over his right kidney, and Mallory collapsed like a sack of meal.

"You don't bargain with me," Mueller snarled as Mallory groaned in agony on the floor.

"I'll tell you!" Mallory choked out. Nausea convulsed him again, and pain lanced his chest from the dry heaving of his stomach. He rolled onto his side and found himself staring at the giant's boot.

"Well?" Mueller demanded.

"Radar," Mallory gasped, knowing the lie wouldn't stand up. At best it would only delay the inevitable. "Damberg is designing a new radar device for night f-fighters. The British are afraid it will increase their bomber losses."

The floor creaked as the goon shifted his weight, and the boot Mallory was staring at moved . . . The man kicked Mallory in the stomach, lifting him off the floor and flipping him onto his back. Mallory's eyes were open, but he couldn't see through the red mist. He couldn't breathe, and he didn't care. The burning in his lungs was just there, without significance. The light and the ringing in his ears faded, and he fell away into darkness.

The blackout did not last long enough. Mallory came to in agony. A wet warmth was spreading out over his upper thighs, and he realized dully that he had lost control of his bladder.

"Don't lie to me," he heard Mueller say from what seemed to be a great distance. "Damberg is a nuclear physicist."

The words meant nothing to Mallory, and he shook his head feebly — or thought he did. "I don't know what you're talking about," he tried to say, but only garbled mumbling emerged from his mouth. He lay helplessly on his back, staring blankly up at the dark slope of the roof, his chest encased in pain. He would have welcomed execution; it was better than being beaten to death by inches.

"Give him a bath," Mueller snapped.

A bath? Someone inside Mallory's head began to laugh hysterically. A bath! That's what he needed, all right. Christ, these Germans were hygienic. *Yes, by all means, give me a bath.*

"*Jawohl,* Herr Hauptsturmführer," the goon said, and the voice in Mallory's head giggled. The giant had a little boy's voice.

Mallory felt the man pulling off his underwear, and then he cried out against the pain in his chest as the giant seized him under the arms and lifted him. He was a foot taller than Mallory and one hundred pounds heavier. The fingers of one great hand closed around Mallory's upper arm, holding him up, and the giant carried him from the room, one-handed, like a child carrying a rag doll.

Mallory blacked out again, and when he revived, he was at one end of a long, dim hallway lined with offices. Above the clatter of typewriters Mallory heard the quick, sharp footsteps of a woman, but she was too far down the hall for him to see without his glasses. The giant called out to the woman, and Mallory heard her laugh in response.

The goon seemed to be waiting for something. He stood there at the end of the hallway, holding Mallory up. Mallory heard doors opening and a swell of female laughter and chatter. The Gestapo clerks were coming out into the hall to jeer at the naked prisoner.

Apparently satisfied with the crowd, the giant dragged Mallory down the hall, past the catcalls and cackling laughter of the women. The floor seemed to pitch and roll beneath Mallory's feet, but even in his dazed condition, Mallory could still feel astonishment at the stupidity of the bizarre parade. They were beating him to death, and yet they still expected him to be humiliated by women laughing at his naked body.

At the far end of the corridor the giant opened a door and shoved Mallory across the threshold. Mallory stumbled forward and fell full length on the gray tile floor. His head struck the side of an antique metal bathtub, but he barely registered the new pain. The giant shut the door, and the sound of laughter in the hall died away. Mallory lay as he had fallen, and the giant stepped over him to reach the bath's water taps. Dimly Mallory heard the squeak of the handles and the rush of water into the tub.

Mallory felt himself being lifted up, and in the instant before he was plunged into the tub of icy water he realized what was about to happen. The water closed over his face, blotting out all sound, save for the ever-present ringing in his ears, and his face contorted at the searing pain in his right ear as the water penetrated to his ruptured eardrum.

He tried to push himself up out of the water, but the giant's hand was at his throat, holding him under. Mallory kicked spastically with his legs, and his arms thrashed, but his tormentor's viselike grip never slackened. As the burning in Mallory's lungs became unbearable, he exhaled slightly, but the relief was only momentary and his lungs screamed for air. Mallory could feel consciousness slipping away, and his reflexes took control. His diaphragm heaved, and as water entered his bronchial tubes his cough reflex drove the last of the air from his lungs. His chest heaved again, but Mallory could no longer feel.

When he came to, he was face down on the tile floor, retching. The sledgehammer pounding in his head and the hideous pain in his ribs blotted out all thought.

"Are you ready to talk?" a voice shouted in his ear, but he couldn't tell if it was Mueller or the giant.

Mallory gurgled, and before he could make a more coherent sound, hands seized him again and dragged him up over the bathtub rim. The agony of drowning began immediately, and Mallory was no longer a human being with a mind — just a tortured organism thrashing desperately in its death throes.

But the giant wouldn't let him die. He pulled Mallory out and revived him, only to drown him once again — and again. And again . . .

Marie was smiling at Mallory as he walked toward her. It was a languid smile that sculptured her lips and almost banished the hint of sadness in her green eyes. He could see her face quite clearly, but though he walked ever faster he could not close the distance between them. He reached out to her and called her name, but she silently shook her head and turned away. Behind him he heard cackling laughter and the rush of water. Marie was receding from him and he tried to run after her, but something was holding him back, pressing into his chest, hurting him . . .

Mallory stirred in his sleep and rolled off the arm that had been pressing into his ribs. Slowly he came awake to the dull, insistent ache that throbbed through his upper body. Water had flushed the clotted blood and mucus from his nostrils, and his first sensory impression, aside from pain, was the pungent smell of disinfectant. As the dregs of sleep drained away, he opened his eyes to a muted, gray light.

He was lying on his back on a steel-framed cot bolted to the wall of a narrow cell no more than eight feet wide. The swelling that had closed one eye had diminished enough for him to use it. The light came from a small barred window set high up in the stone wall that formed the end of the cell, and Mallory guessed that he was confined in the cellar of Gestapo headquarters. The window, he assumed, was slightly above ground level and looked out onto the courtyard. It would have to remain an assumption, for the window was too high to reach without jumping, and Mallory found it difficult to move at all.

He was naked beneath a coarse blanket, and through the thin, straw-filled mattress he could feel the individual cords of the sagging rope mesh supporting him. The stink of disinfectant came from the mattress as well as the blanket.

His breathing was constricted, and when he brought up his hand to explore his chest he discovered that his ribs had been bound with adhesive tape. There was also tape across the bridge of his nose, and cotton in his right ear.

Why had they given him medical attention? Was Mueller through with him? Did some bizarre German sense of order demand that he be patched up before execution? Or was it meant to give him false hope — to set him up for the next round of torture, for another session in the tiled bathroom . . . Mallory's mind recoiled, but the memories pressed in on him. Again he felt the giant's hand like an iron band around his throat, the burning in his lungs.

He wrenched his thoughts away from the horror of that endless drowning, only to be confronted by the image of Marie as he had last seen her — in profile, her face cold and remote, like a sculpture in ivory. It was this image that ultimately crowded out all others . . .

Mallory awoke again hours later, having drifted into a dream-filled, restless sleep. He was desperately thirsty. His nostrils were again clogged with mucus, and his throat burned from breathing through his mouth. Although he dreaded moving, his thirst demanded it.

Gritting his teeth, he raised himself up on one elbow and eased his legs over the edge of the bunk. He felt as if every muscle in his body had been either bruised or strained. With a final effort he pushed himself into a sitting position on the edge of the bunk and waited for the dizziness that assaulted him to pass.

The light filtering through the dirty glass of the window was brighter now, more yellow than gray, and Mallory guessed that it had been early morning when he had first awoken. The time between his last, confused memories of the tiled bathroom and his first awakening was a blank, but more than twelve hours must have elapsed. Perhaps the doctor who had worked on him had given him an injection. Why had they bothered?

On the floor beside the heavy oak cell door was a mess tin in which a moldy chunk of black bread floated in a gray, greasy liquid. Beside the tin was a cup of water. There was no toilet in the cell, not even a bucket, but for the moment Mallory's only need was water. He licked his dry, swollen lips, girded himself for the effort, and lurched to his feet. Swaying drunkenly, he tottered to the door, leaned against it and lowered himself to his knees on the cold stone floor. The water in the cup was stale and musty, but he drank it down in three greedy gulps.

The cup of water was not enough to slake his thirst, and he looked hopefully at the liquid in the mess tin. He raised it to his lips, but the smell of the unidentifiable soup nauseated him, and he put the tin down again and crawled back to his bunk.

The side walls of Mallory's cell were of rough, unpainted wood, and names and dates had been scratched into the wood above the bunk: Pierre Dupré, Dec. 1943; Robert Simmons, June 1943; Jean Dumont, July 1942.

Why, Mallory wondered. Had these men simply wanted to leave something of themselves behind? Had they wanted to give courage to those who would follow them down the same lonely road? Or was it a forlorn attempt to relieve their own terrible loneliness as they awaited death, by reaching out to strangers who would one day occupy the same cell?

Loneliness was not something Mallory feared; he knew it too well. He had always felt alone — until he had met Marie — but that had been nothing but illusion. Mallory's spasm of self-pity had passed; she could not have betrayed him, he thought with cold self-contempt, if he'd not been such a willing fool.

Mallory's chest was hurting, but he didn't want to lie down. He pulled the blanket around his shoulders and settled himself as comfortably as he could in a sitting position with his back against the wall. He was sure they would not leave him in peace much longer, and he didn't want to be asleep when they came for him.

Mingling now with his dread of what was to come was a bitter, corrosive anger that simmered within him — gradually displacing his fear. They had tormented him beyond endurance, but his mind had not snapped. The torture had wrought a different, but equally irreversible change in him. Mallory had learned to hate.

It was late afternoon and the shifting angle of the sun's rays had dimmed the light in Mallory's cell when he heard the muffled tread of boots approaching down the corridor. He tensed as the footsteps halted before his door.

The bolt was slammed back and the door flung open, and Mallory saw a prison guard in a gray SD uniform silhouetted in the doorway against the weak electric light from the corridor. Without his glasses Mallory could not see the guard's face clearly, but he saw the machine pistol in the man's hands and knew that Mueller was finished with him. Weapons weren't necessary inside Gestapo headquarters.

"Get dressed," the man growled in guttural French and tossed Mallory's bundled clothes into the cell.

Mallory's suit and shirt had been wrapped around his shoes and tied with a length of cord. He shivered slightly and stood up, wincing at the stab of pain in his ribs. At least, he thought grimly, they were allowing him the dignity of dying with his clothes on. Despite the pain and the dizziness that washed over him in waves, he dressed as quickly as he could; he had no wish to drag out the last few minutes of his life.

The shirt and jacket were easy enough, but the effort of pulling on his trousers forced from him a grunt of pain. He lost his balance, staggered and nearly fell to the floor.

"*Mach schnell!*" the guard snapped.

Mallory looked at the guard, the hatred bubbling up inside him plain in his eyes, and the SD man took a half step backward and raised his weapon. The expression on Mallory's face wasn't civilized; Mallory wanted to kill.

" '*Raus!*" snarled the guard, stepping farther back into the corridor.

Mallory slipped his bare feet into his shoes, left the laces untied and walked unsteadily out of the cell. He was still dizzy and every step he took jarred his ribs, but he was determined to stay on his feet. He didn't want to be dragged to his execution. But he was moving too slowly for the guard. As Mallory stepped into the corridor, the man seized him by the shoulder and shoved him forward, not bothering to close the door to the cell.

Mallory gritted his teeth as the SD man jabbed him repeatedly in the spine with the muzzle of his machine pistol, driving him down the long, narrow corridor. If Mallory had not been so weak, he would have made a try for the weapon. His finger itched to pull a trigger. God, how he wanted to take one of the bastards with him! But he would be too slow, and if he tried he would only be giving the guard an excuse to kick him to death.

Their footsteps were the only sound in the dimly lit corridor, but Mallory sensed the presence of other prisoners behind the dark green cell doors they passed. The misery that filled the cellar prison was almost palpable. Mallory felt the urge to call out to them, to make contact, but what was there to say? This was the end station for all of them, the last stop before oblivion. Of what use were words?

A steel-barred gate blocked the end of the corridor, and a second guard emerged from a small office beyond the door and came forward to unlock it. The miasma of the man's unwashed body drifted into Mallory's nostrils. From inside the office came the clatter of a typewriter. For the Gestapo and SD, murder was acceptable, but the neglect of paperwork was a sin.

The door slid open, and Mallory's guard once again drove his gun barrel into Mallory's back, propelling him toward a narrow staircase that led up from the cellar. Mallory trudged up the stairs. Movement was becoming easier as his muscles loosened up, and he was steadier on his feet. Now, perhaps, if the guard got careless . . .

"*Halte!*"

Mallory had reached the ground-floor landing of the stairwell. The guard came up behind him, pushed him against the wall, and opened a door leading to the courtyard. The guard backed through the doorway and motioned Mallory to follow him outside. For the first time, Mallory saw the guard's face clearly. Instead of the grizzled, cold-eyed veteran he had imagined, the guard was a moon-faced youngster not old enough to shave.

Mallory's eyes dropped to the machine pistol in the boy's hands, visualizing the flaring muzzle flash as he would see it. Would he hear the gun's sharp, staccato rattle, or would he be dead before the sound reached his brain? Raw, animal fear rose suddenly in his throat. *Don't give way now. Fight it down!*

" '*Raus!*" the guard demanded impatiently.

Mallory stepped into the courtyard and walked slowly out of the shadow of the building into the sun, squinting against the unaccustomed light. The patch of afternoon sky bracketed by the tall buildings surrounding the cobblestoned courtyard was blue and cloudless. The air was warm, and Mallory felt the sun soaking into his shoulders, helping to keep him from shivering. He could hear the clatter of typewriters drifting down from the open windows of the surrounding buildings. It was such an innocuous, peaceful sound.

How many men had made this walk before him? What had they done to hold their fear at bay? *Just don't think about it.* He squared his shoulders, took as deep a breath as the binding around his chest allowed, and walked past the guard toward a brick wall on the opposite side of the courtyard. It was the logical place. He was steady now, and it would be over soon.

"*Halte!*" the guard yelled angrily. "Not that way, you idiot!"

Mallory stopped and spun around, his hatred and helpless anger spilling out. "Kiss my ass!" he snarled in gutter German. "You can shoot me right here, you son of a bitch."

Startled, the SD man retreated a step, but then he brought up his weapon and Mallory heard the snick-snick of the gun's bolt, sharp and clear in the still air. Mallory gritted his teeth and held his breath, waiting for the bullets to tear into his chest.

8

"No one is going to shoot you just yet, Lieutenant," called an unfamiliar voice in German.

Mallory was transfixed by anticipation of death, and for the space of three heartbeats his eyes remained fixed on the gun in the guard's hands; his body held its rigid pose. Abruptly the words that had been shouted to him from across the courtyard penetrated his consciousness, and he expelled his breath in an involuntary, shuddering gasp. But as he looked to his left in the direction of the voice, he angrily suppressed the reflexive relief flooding through him. This was one of Mueller's tricks, it had to be. The bastards had mastered the art of making a man die more than once.

One hundred feet away two men stood beside a car parked near the gateway to the street. To Mallory, it seemed impossible that they had been there all the time. One of the figures came toward him with a brisk, clipped, military step, and Mallory saw that the man wore a uniform — not the gray or black of the SS, but Wehrmacht green.

The Wehrmacht officer stopped before Mallory and nodded formally. "You were not brought out here to be shot, Lieutenant," he said. He wore the insignia of a captain. "I regret the misunderstanding. I can imagine how you felt."

Mallory swallowed to relieve the dryness in his throat, wishing that he could control the trembling in his hands. "Can you?" he said icily.

"Yes, I think I can," the captain replied evenly.

He was a small, wiry man no taller than Mallory, with dark, close-cropped hair and dark, flinty eyes, which were narrowed against the sun. Exposure, either in the Arctic or in the desert, had weathered his face, and the skin was creased and leathery, so it was difficult to judge his age. He appeared to be in his mid-thirties, but he might have been ten years younger. He had a straight, thin-lipped mouth and a short, straight nose. His was a hard face, the face of a tough, self-reliant man without illusions, but there was no bitterness or cruelty in it.

"My name is Steiner," he said. "Abwehr Counterintelligence. We have taken charge of your case."

"Is that supposed to make a difference to me?" Mallory said with undisguised bitterness. The hatred he felt made no distinctions between German uniforms.

"Perhaps," Steiner said. He reached into his jacket pocket. "I have your glasses. Judging from the lenses, you must need them badly."

Mallory took the glasses from Steiner and slipped them on, and the world beyond a radius of fifteen feet snapped into focus. Across the courtyard was the same pile of gray straw he had seen the day before, but the bodies were gone. For those three it was already over. Perhaps they were the lucky ones, he thought.

"Come with me, please," Steiner said, gesturing toward the gate. Mechanically, Mallory set his legs in motion and accompanied Steiner to the waiting car. He was still emotionally off balance. Only minutes before he had been sure he was going to die. Now he had no idea what was happening. If this was one of Mueller's games, he didn't understand it.

"It will be a very short ride," Steiner said, as they reached the car, "but it will be more pleasant if you will give me your word as an officer that you will not attempt to escape."

"You have it," Mallory said, just a little too quickly.

Steiner looked at Mallory for a long moment and then nodded

tiredly. "Yes, I see," he said, taking his service automatic from its holster and slipping off the safety. "I will ride in the back, and you will ride in front beside the driver. Please do not jump from the car if we are slowed down by bicycle traffic. I am an excellent shot, and I will shoot to cripple, not to kill."

As they drove in silence through the city, Mallory stared out the car window with uncaring eyes. The fleeting relief he had felt at the stay of execution was gone. Mallory knew it would only delay the inevitable. The driver headed up the Champs-Elysées toward the Étoile. When he circled the Arc de Triomphe and entered the avenue Foch, Mallory realized where they were going; the headquarters of Gestapo Counterintelligence was on the avenue Foch.

"I was not lying to you," Steiner said, reading Mallory's thoughts. "You are no longer under Gestapo control. The Abwehr merely shares the office building."

Mallory made no response. What difference did it make?

The broad avenue was lined on both sides with luxury apartment houses, and two minutes later the driver pulled up in front of 82–84, avenue Foch. Mallory looked up at the three adjoining six-story town houses, which were discreetly set back from the sidewalk, their entrances screened by thick hedges and a high, wrought-iron fence. The apartments' facades were of clean white cement, with wide, floor-to-ceiling windows opening onto ornate balconies. The elegance of the Gestapo CI headquarters was grotesque.

Steiner got out of the car, opened Mallory's door, and gestured with his pistol for Mallory to precede him. "Before we begin the interrogation, you will be given the chance to clean up and to eat a decent meal," Steiner said as they walked toward the entrance. "You can consider it part of the technique," he added dryly — "what your instructors no doubt referred to as 'softening you up.' "

Captain Rolf Steiner sat alone in the sixth-floor room he called his office, waiting for Berlin to return his call. He smoked and stared at the bare walls. The cream-colored paint was old and faded, and rectangles and squares of darker, unbleached paint showed where photographs and paintings had once hung.

The room had been stripped of most of its original furnishings for the benefit of Gestapo offices in other parts of the town house. Variations in the wear on the beige carpet indicated the positions of chairs and tables that were no longer there. Even the drapes were gone from the two stately windows overlooking the avenue Foch.

The Abwehr had been officially merged with the SD, the intelligence arm of the SS, for barely two months, and Steiner was viewed as an unwelcome interloper. Canaris, chief of the Abwehr, was under house arrest, and now every Abwehr officer was viewed with suspicion. Besides the desk and two chairs, Steiner had been given only a file cabinet and a safe. The sparse furnishings had been intended as a snub, but he couldn't have cared less.

Steiner sighed as he heard a distinctive knock on the office door. He straightened up in his chair and put out his cigarette. Sergeant Merz's knock was unmistakable. The man was a stickler for military correctness.

"Come in, Merz."

The door opened, and Merz stepped in. He was a balding, pear-shaped retread from World War I, whom the Second War had rescued from a nagging wife and a dull civil service job. He loved the war.

Merz closed the door carefully behind him, marched to the desk, cracked his heels together, and stiffened to attention. "Feldwebel Merz, reporting, Herr Hauptmann!"

"Yes, Sergeant, I can see that." Steiner said. "I've told you before, you needn't be so formal when we're alone."

"*Jawohl*, Herr Hauptmann," Merz said, and clicked his heels again.

Steiner shook his head in exasperation. "Stand at ease, Sergeant. Good. Now, what is it you have to report?"

Merz smiled involuntarily, caught himself, and resumed a sober expression. "We have succeeded again, Herr Hauptmann," he announced proudly. "Yesterday the prisoner, Brixton, transmitted our request for supplies and for two more agents, and this morning and again this afternoon the BBC broadcasted the coded affirmative reply. The British will make the drop tonight."

"Has it occurred to you, Sergeant, that Brixton agreed to send for us a bit too easily? Quite probably he omitted the security code in his transmission."

"Possibly, Herr Hauptmann," Merz answered with undampened enthusiasm, "but apparently London chose to overlook it. They have ignored such warnings before. As I said, they are sending a plane tonight — two more agents dropped into our laps."

Steiner looked away and shook his head slowly. "How can they be so stupid!"

Bewildered by the sharpness of Steiner's tone, Merz shrugged uneasily. "It is the same in Belgium and in Holland, Herr Hauptmann. In Brussels, Beckmann has been playing back three separate radios, and in the last year he has captured seventy-five parachute agents."

Steiner didn't need to be told; he knew the statistics. Yet the carelessness of the British controllers in London continued to amaze him. It was incredible — almost criminal. But he didn't voice his thoughts a second time; Merz already thought him an odd fish.

"All right, Sergeant," Steiner said tonelessly. "You've baited the trap, so you can spring it. Select the men you want to take along tonight; I'll initial the orders."

Merz beamed, "*Jawohl,* Herr Hauptmann."

"Dismissed."

Merz snapped to attention again, executed a perfect about-face, and went to the door.

"And Sergeant —"

"Yes, Herr Hauptmann?"

"Congratulations," Steiner said belatedly.

"Thank you, Herr Hauptmann."

As Merz closed the door behind him, Steiner got up and went to the window to look out over the city. If one stood quietly, one could almost feel the hostility rising up from the silent streets, invisible but there, like heat waves shimmering above a sunbaked pavement. Out in the countryside when darkness fell, men would gather in deserted farmhouses to talk and to plan, and perhaps to make a furtive attack on a railway or telephone line.

Toward midnight the British planes would come, flying low to drop supplies and agents. At isolated fields in Belgium, in the Netherlands, and in France, men would be waiting to receive the drops — and some of the reception committees would be sent by the Abwehr. Steiner grimaced, as if at a bad taste in his mouth. He did his job, but it gave him no satisfaction. Too often it was like shooting fish in a barrel.

The phone rang on Steiner's desk, and he turned to his chair and lifted the receiver.

"Berlin calling, Herr Hauptmann," said an operator. "Major Heinrich."

"Put him through."

There was a click and then a man's voice came over the line. "Rolf? How are things in the City of Light?"

"Hello, Karl," Steiner said. "It's blacked out at night and even more depressing by day."

"Cheer up, for God's sake. It's better than the eastern front."

"Any place would be," Steiner said, absently rubbing the frost-bite scars on his ear.

"Are you connected into a secure line?" Major Heinrich asked.

"More or less."

Steiner heard Major Heinrich laugh softly. Now that the SD had been merged with the Abwehr, the Abwehr's secure A-network was no longer immune to Gestapo taps.

"Do you have the American?" Heinrich asked.

"Yes. Luckily he was still in one piece. I haven't interrogated him yet."

"The powers-that-be are very interested in what he has to say. Very interested."

"If he didn't talk to the Gestapo, with their more persuasive methods, he isn't likely to open up to me."

"Did they work him over?"

"Yes. Pretty thoroughly."

"Bastards."

Steiner winced. Heinrich had never cared who might be listening to him, but with Canaris gone it was no time to be careless.

"If you can't get anything out of him," Heinrich said, "you're to ship him to us in Berlin. The psychological boys will want to have a go at him."

"Damberg still hasn't talked?"

"No. He continues to insist that he has no idea why the British wanted to kill him. He refuses to discuss his work, and we're not able to force the issue."

Not without calling in the SD, Steiner thought. The Abwehr itself had no authority to conduct investigations on German soil, and no one in Berlin would call in the SD except as a last resort.

"Why the hell won't Damberg talk to us?" Steiner said. The situation was bizarre; the British had sent in a team to kill a German scientist, and Germany's principal intelligence service couldn't even find out why.

"No one here knows," Heinrich replied, "but he seems terribly afraid of attracting attention to his work. He is part of a loosely knit team of scientists working on some new type of weapon, but it's all very odd. The work is ultra hush-hush, yet it seems to have a very low priority — and the scientists working on the project appear to want to keep it that way."

"Are you sure he's playing with a full deck?"

"The British obviously think so."

"Well, you can thank the Gestapo for this mess," Steiner said, giving vent to his frustration. "I had a textbook operation going, and given a little more time, we might have found out what this is all about; but their damned raid queered it."

"How did they know about the assassination team?"

"They didn't; the raid was a fluke."

"Well, do the best you can with the Ami. Call me when you've talked to him," Heinrich said. "*Wiederhören,* Rolf."

"*Wiederhören.*"

Steiner heard the click as the line to Berlin went dead, and then a second, fainter click a moment later. He nodded grimly to himself and hung up. He lit a fresh cigarette and opened the folder lying on his desk, intending to read the girl's report one more time. Steiner had not yet adjusted to his transfer to counterintelligence, and he wasn't looking forward to interrogating the captured American agent. Perhaps, he thought, he had simply worked the other side of the fence too long.

He was remembering his last night with the 292nd Division, dug in on the river Narva. They had known an attack was coming, and they had known they couldn't hold. Steiner had stayed up all night in a forward observation post, waiting for his Ukrainians to slip back through the Russian lines. He remembered the bitter, Arctic cold that had sucked the heat from his body. He remembered the stars shining in the black sky and how they had dimmed as the Russian artillery and rocket launchers had lit up the horizon. But most clearly he remembered the faces of those Ukrainians he had trained. Not one of them had made it back.

The sun was setting when Mallory was brought before Steiner for interrogation, and its last rays, slanting in through the windows, cast two oblong rectangles of orange light onto the opposite wall. Mallory's guard left him alone with Steiner, who gestured for Mallory to sit in an armchair in front of his desk. The chair's upholstery was worn thin, as was the varnish on the armrests, and looking around the room, Mallory could see that Steiner's standing in the CI headquarters was not very high.

Mallory eased himself carefully into the chair, but he couldn't quite suppress a grunt of pain as he sat down. Steiner shoved a pack of cigarettes and matches across the desk toward him. Mallory itched to take one, but he hesitated, automatically suspicious of any kindness from a German. "It's all right, Lieutenant,"   . Steiner said in German when Mallory hesitated. "Forget your instructors. I know you're a chain-smoker. So am I, and I don't want to have to watch you fidget while I smoke."

Mallory slipped a cigarette from the pack. His hand shook as he lit it, but not from fear; he was simply exhausted. At least, he thought bleakly, Steiner didn't intend to try to beat answers out of him — not yet, at any rate. He dragged hungrily on the cigarette and immediately began to cough. Daggers of pain drove into his chest.

"Maybe you shouldn't smoke, after all," Steiner said.

Mallory, still coughing, shook his head. "It's worth it," he said when the spasm had passed.

For several seconds the two men studied each other in silence, and Mallory wondered what Steiner was doing behind a desk. The German had the unmistakable look of a combat officer. The lines around his mouth and in the corners of his habitually narrowed eyes were deeply etched for a young man, and his eyes had the world-weary, distant look of one who had seen too much.

"Your colleague, Ryder, has apparently made a clean escape," Steiner said, breaking the silence.

"And Stebbings?" Mallory asked, and to his chagrin he realized that this was the first time since his arrest that he'd thought of Stebbings.

"He threw himself out a window," Steiner replied without inflection.

"You bastards!"

Steiner's face remained impassive. "This is not some game, Lieutenant. Captured agents die — ours as well as yours."

"We don't drown men in bathtubs."

"You are in Abwehr custody now, and we don't make a habit of torturing prisoners."

"Good for you," Mallory said with bitter sarcasm, and this time he provoked a reaction.

Steiner's expression hardened. The change was slight, but for a man like Steiner, who did not augment his speech with gestures or frequent changes in expression, it was significant. "I don't control the Gestapo any more than you control the generals who bomb our cities indiscriminately," he said coldly. "How many women and children will die tonight in Bremen, or Munich, or in Berlin? — torn apart, roasted, crushed, suffocated. You yourself came to kill a noncombatant, and you were caught. Don't cry on my shoulder."

"I won't," Mallory said listlessly, finding it impossible to sustain his anger. He felt infinitely weary. "Let's just get this over with."

"That is my intention. You are on your own, Lieutenant; nothing you say can harm your colleagues now, and if you cooperate with us there is a chance you may survive. Otherwise I'm afraid a firing squad is the best I can offer you."

"I'm willing to cooperate," Mallory said, knowing it would make no difference. He didn't have the information Steiner wanted. In the end, he was sure, there would be a bullet-scarred wall somewhere and a man with a gun.

"My agent was not aware you spoke fluent German," Steiner said. "Where did you learn?"

"From my parents."

"But Mallory is an English name."

"Foster parents."

"You are an officer in the OSS?"

"Yes."

"How long did you train for this mission?"

"Six weeks."

Steiner shook his head. "You will have to learn to lie more adeptly. The girl was my agent, not the Gestapo's, and I know a great deal about you."

But not about the mission, Mallory thought. He dragged again on his cigarette and stifled another cough. "I wouldn't bring her into the discussion if I were you," he said tightly. "It's poor salesmanship."

"I'm not trying to sell anything."

"Then why don't we skip the charade," Mallory said, his voice rising. "Call in your boys and put me up against the wall. Agents die, you said. All right, finish it!"

Steiner ignored Mallory's outburst. "You were dropped into France with virtually no preparation and with no established support on the ground. Why the rush?"

"I don't know."

"Don't you? It seems rather obvious. Apparently your intelligence people received a report that Professor Damberg would be in Paris, and that report arrived too late for adequate preparation.

Luckily for Damberg, the information was incorrect. Why were you sent to kill him?"

"You seem to have all the answers. You tell me."

"I am asking *you,* Lieutenant."

"I don't know."

"Then why did you tell the Gestapo that fairy tale about radar?"

"I didn't think Mueller would accept the truth, and I was tired of being slapped around."

"Good," Steiner said, pausing to light a cigarette. "That much I'm prepared to believe. Now, according to Stebbings, his only job was to identify Damberg, and we know that Ryder spoke little German. That leaves you — a man who speaks our language fluently. It seems clear to me that you were the man who was to slip in for the kill."

Mallory said nothing.

"Do you expect me to believe that your superiors would ask you to take that kind of risk without giving you at least a hint of the mission's purpose?"

"I don't give a damn whether you believe me or not," Mallory said tiredly. "If you want to know the reason for the mission, why don't you ask Damberg?"

"There!" Steiner said sharply, rapping on his desk for emphasis. "You've made my point. We know why Damberg's work is important, so there is no secret to be kept. Why would your superiors leave you, of all people, in the dark? It makes no sense."

Strangely, Mallory had never thought about it before. It *didn't* make sense — but neither did Steiner's questioning. If the Germans knew why Damberg was so important, why were they asking? What the hell was Steiner after?

Mallory was too tired to think straight. He shifted in his seat, trying to ease the pressure on his chest. "I don't know," he said.

Steiner looked thoughtfully at Mallory, but he said nothing. Mallory's eyelids began to droop. If only they would let him sleep. Steiner was still watching him, and Mallory shifted his gaze out the window. Dusk was settling over the city. Soon Steiner would have to switch on a light or they would be sitting in the dark.

"All right, Lieutenant," Steiner said abruptly. "I'll let you get some rest now."

Mallory looked at Steiner with unconcealed surprise. "That's it?"

Steiner smiled slightly. "I can ask you the same question again, if you wish, but I don't see the point — do you?"

"What happens now?" Mallory asked. He sensed that from Steiner he would at least get a straight answer.

"I will be sending you to Berlin tomorrow. There are professionals there who want a crack at you."

"It's a waste of time; I can't tell them a thing."

"They will want to make sure of that themselves. There are questions that must be answered — one way or another."

What questions, Mallory wondered. What were they trying to find out? And why had Steiner given up on him so quickly?

"I can assure you that there will be no more torture," Steiner said. "Your escort to Berlin will be Gestapo, but you remain under Abwehr control."

"And afterward?"

Mallory thought he saw Steiner's eyes flicker, but in the dim light he could not be sure. "I'm afraid the options are limited," Steiner said tonelessly. "You are a saboteur, not a prisoner of war. You will be sent to a concentration camp."

"And a firing squad?"

"Possibly."

Steiner picked up his phone, dialed an inside line, and requested a man to escort Mallory to the room where he was to be kept overnight. Steiner replaced the receiver and drew on his cigarette. "I will state in my report that you cooperated willingly, Lieutenant. That may be grounds for leniency."

"Am I supposed to thank you?" Mallory demanded, his voice grating.

Steiner was silent for a moment, and then he shrugged slightly. "I imagine that depends on whether or not you survive."

Steiner had to wait twenty minutes before his call was finally put through to Berlin, and when Major Heinrich came on the line, his voice was muffled in static. Either sabotage or delayed-action bombs had played havoc with the trunk lines.

"The American doesn't know why they were sent after Damberg," Steiner said without preliminaries.

"Are you sure?"

"If he's lying, he's one hell of an actor. When a man is as physically and emotionally exhausted as he is, you can look right through him. He didn't care what I asked about Damberg; he just didn't give a damn. It was the indifference of a man who doesn't know the answers, and it's hard to fake."

"Section Three will still want a crack at him," Heinrich said.

"I know. I'm sending him to Berlin tomorrow."

"Jesus, the British send in a team to assassinate one of our scientists, and we can't even find out why. It's absurd!"

"My advice is to put the screws to Damberg; the American doesn't have the answers."

"I'll pass your advice along," Heinrich said dryly. "I'm sure it will be appreciated."

"What will happen to the American when Section Three is finished with him?" Steiner said, and there was a short silence at the other end of the line.

"That's not up to us, Rolf," Heinrich said stiffly. "A KZ, probably."

"Yes, but which one?"

"Does it make a difference?"

"They sent Stevens and Best to Flossenbürg, and they're still alive. Talk to Bentivegni for me, Karl. He may have enough pull to make it Flossenbürg."

"What reason can I give him?" Heinrich said, and Steiner could hear the reluctance in his voice.

"The American cooperated; it's not his fault he has nothing to tell."

"I don't get it," Heinrich said, still balking. "What's this guy to you?"

"Nothing. Maybe I'm just tired of shooting fish in a barrel."

"What? I didn't catch that. The damned static."

"Listen, Karl, get him into Flossenbürg, and one of these days I'll buy you a beer. Okay?"

There was a long pause filled with the crackle of static. Finally Heinrich said, "Okay, I'll do what I can, but no promises."

"Thanks, Karl."

Again there was a pause. "If anything develops, I'll give you a flash," Heinrich said, placing a very slight emphasis on the last word.

"It's not necessary," Steiner said quickly. "I'm out of it now."

"Are you sure?"

"I'm sure."

"All right, Rolf. I understand. *Ende,*" Heinrich said, and Steiner heard the line go dead.

He hung up the phone. "Good luck," he said into the silence.

So *flash* was still the code word. Steiner shook his head. So careless, he thought — and so typical. Probably they'd use the same damned bomb that had failed to detonate a year ago. Maybe it would go off this time and snuff out Hitler's life, but it could make no difference now. It was too late. Too damned late.

9

THE night train carrying Mallory to Germany never made it out of France. British bombers stopped it twenty miles from the German border. Mallory was dozing on the damp wooden floor of the prison car when the train's brakes squealed and it came to a stop with a rattling jerk. The train had already made countless stops during the last six hours of its halting journey across France, and Mallory did not come awake until the crack of antiaircraft guns split the night.

Moments later the floorboards vibrated in response to the first ground wave from a thousand-pound bomb, and in an instant the air was filled with the thunder of detonations as British Lancasters unloaded over a marshaling yard in the train's path. From the intensity of the shock waves Mallory knew that the train had stopped too close to the target for safety. A jittery bombardier could toggle his bombs too soon, or the pilot of a crippled aircraft turning away from the target might jettison his load. The train carried troops returning home on leave, and outside, shrill whistles and shouted commands cut through the din as noncoms and officers emptied the train to disperse the men.

Mallory got to his feet and stood tensely in the middle of his cell, wondering if they would let him out. A small square window covered with a steel mesh had been cut in the car's wall, just below the roof, and Mallory considered trying to reach it; but he knew his broken ribs would prevent him from pulling himself up to see outside. From the sounds alone, he could imagine the confusion in the darkness outside.

For the first time since his capture, Mallory thought of escape. Following his interrogation in the avenue Foch, he had been allowed to sleep around the clock, and he had slept more on the train. Although movement was still painful, he had recovered much of his strength, and he was prepared to fight for his life. If he was important enough to the Germans to protect, his Gestapo escort might come to take him off the train. And once outside, in the confusion . . .

Mallory heard the rattle of the chain on the cell door, and exhilaration surged through him. *That's right, my friend, come for me.* He flexed his fingers. His wrists were tightly manacled together, but the circulation had not been cut off entirely. Somehow he would have to get the key.

The door slid open, and an SS guard directed the feeble beam of his hooded flashlight into Mallory's eyes. Mallory couldn't see the guard's machine pistol, but he knew he would be carrying one. *Not here, not yet.* A leather-coated figure brushed by the guard and came into the cell. It was Mallory's Gestapo escort — a tall, thin man with a pasty, cadaverous face. Mallory could smell the alcohol on the man's breath as he came close.

"Come on, you, we're getting off the train," the Gestapo man said in English. It was the longest speech he had made since he had collected Mallory in the avenue Foch.

"The Brits are making it too hot for you, is that it?" Mallory responded in German.

"If I get it, runt, so will you," the Gestapo man growled, seizing Mallory's wrists.

He unlocked one cuff and closed it around his own wrist, manacling Mallory's right hand to his left, leaving Mallory's left arm free. The SS guard lowered the beam of his flashlight, and Mallory smiled to himself in the darkness; he was left-handed. The German slipped the key to the handcuffs into his overcoat pocket, drew out a Beretta automatic and leveled it at Mallory. "Outside," he said curtly.

As the Gestapo agent hustled Mallory down the narrow corridor toward one end of the car, the SS guard turned and went in the opposite direction, and Mallory's stomach muscles tensed with suppressed excitement. Outside, he and his captor would be one on one.

The thunder of bombs seemed to be rolling closer, punctuated by the deafening crack-crack-crack of antiaircraft fire from an additional flak battery opening up close by. The Gestapo agent opened the car door, and Mallory saw that the train had stopped beside a small railroad station. The platform swarmed with troops pouring off the train. The scene was suffused with the ghostly light of a half moon hanging in a starlit sky, blending with the orange glow of fires and the bright flashes of explosions on the target a mile up the track.

The Gestapo man shoved Mallory forward onto the platform, but manacled together as they were, he could not walk behind Mallory. He was too confident, Mallory realized, too accustomed to cowering victims. He had produced the pistol as a matter of form, but he obviously had no thought that Mallory might turn on him. Mallory saw a sign above the station house, and it verified that they were still in France. He didn't care what the odds were; this was his chance.

A soldier brushing past them looked up at the sky. "*Scheisse!*" he cried, and Mallory caught the barely detectable drone of aircraft flying directly over them. Instead of following the flow of men off the platform, the Gestapo agent inexplicably headed for the station house. "Let's get away from the train!" Mallory shouted, but the man paid no attention as he shouldered his way through the crowd, pulling Mallory after him.

Fifteen thousand feet above them, an errant British bombardier toggled his bombs.

They reached the small brick building and the Gestapo man tore open the door to the dark, deserted waiting room. At that moment they heard the shrieking whistle of falling bombs, and every man on the platform knew that time had run out.

It was a stick of eight, and it bracketed the station. The three or four seconds they had to react was too little time. Discipline on the platform dissolved as some soldiers made a last, futile rush to get away, stumbling and falling over those who had thrown themselves flat and had started to pray.

As the whistle of approaching death rose in a nerve-tearing crescendo, the Gestapo man backed out of the doorway, whirled, looked wildly around him, and then plunged back into the waiting room, dragging Mallory after him. He didn't see Mallory bare his teeth and raise his left arm. Mallory was not a strong man, but his blow carried the force of desperation and pent-up hatred. The Gestapo agent never felt the vicious judo chop that caught him below the occipital bone, snuffing out his life.

As Mallory struck, the first bomb in the stick exploded beside the train's locomotive fifty yards away, tossing it onto its side like a toy. Steam shrieked from the gash in the locomotive's boiler, but the sound was lost in the deafening explosions that marched up the track and through the station, tearing and twisting steel, pulverizing concrete, and vaporizing men.

Mallory was reaching out to catch the Gestapo agent's body when a brilliant white flash lit the waiting room, casting their shadows on the far wall. A sudden, massive pressure on Mallory's chest drove the air from his lungs, and he was lifted and hurled across the room as if swept up by a giant broom. There was no sound, only light. Infinitely slowly, the wall rushed toward him.

At first Mallory thought the darkness was total, but when he turned his head he saw the moonlight reflecting off the remains of the station house's rear wall above him, its jagged outline showing clearly against the sky where the roof should have been. A lone searchlight still probed that patch of sky, but the bombing had ceased and the last of the flak batteries had fallen silent. The acrid stench of cordite mingled with the smell of plaster dust that still hung suspended in the air. From all directions came cries for medics and the insane howling of men in agony.

Blood trickled down over Mallory's temple from a wound in his scalp. He was dazed, but he didn't think he'd been unconscious for long. Incredibly, his glasses were unbroken and still in place. He was lying on his back on the waiting-room floor. A heavy wooden bench had shielded his upper body from the rubble that had fallen in on him, but from the waist down he was buried beneath a heap of masonry.

A wooden beam, its jagged end jutting out from the rubble, lay across his legs, pinning him to the floor. He raised himself up on his elbows and tried to pull himself free, but the effort only set him to coughing painfully from the dust in the air. The beam was cutting into his thigh muscles, but the pain was bearable and he didn't call out for help. He needed time.

Behind him sprawled the Gestapo agent's body, facedown and partially buried under loose brick and plaster. Mallory groped for the man's wrist and felt for his pulse. There was none, and something like a sigh of satisfaction escaped Mallory. He reached back with his free arm, seized the dead man's arm with both hands, and, ignoring the pain in his ribs, pulled with all his strength. He had to get the key.

Slowly, inch by agonizing inch, he dragged the body closer to him, and sweat mingled with the blood running down the side of his face. Outside men still cried and screamed and died as medics moved among them, bandaging those who could be saved, injecting the dying with morphine and carrying off the dead. Mallory could hear the metallic clang of steel on steel and the hiss of cutting torches as rescue teams began to fight their way into the tangled wreckage of the train.

As fearful as Mallory was that someone would discover him before he had freed himself of the handcuffs, he could not continue pulling on the body without pause. Again and again he had to rest until the pain in his chest subsided. At last the body was close enough for him to reach the dead man's coat pockets.

He grasped the key, twisted onto his side, and after some desperate, awkward fumbling managed to unlock the handcuff, wincing as the blood rushed into his swollen right hand. He heard voices just outside the ruins of the station house, and he hurriedly slipped his hand under the chest of the corpse, probing the dead man's inside pockets. His fingers closed on the Gestapo agent's leather I.D. case and he pulled it free. He slipped it into his own pocket and lay back, gasping with exhaustion and relief. Whatever happened now, he vowed to himself, they wouldn't take him again — at least not alive.

"There's not going to be anyone in there," Mallory heard a man say just on the other side of the heap of brick that had been the front wall of the station house.

"We'll check anyway," said a second voice, and two soldiers carrying a stretcher between them climbed over the rubble pile into what was left of the building. As they set down the stretcher, one man's flashlight beam flitted over the corpse lying on it. The dead soldier's face had the ghastly red flush of a man killed by a bomb's pressure wave.

"I'm in here," Mallory croaked. Startled, both men swung their flashlights in his direction and hurried over to him, slipping and stumbling over the loose brick.

One of the soldiers was a medic. He knelt at Mallory's side without giving the dead Gestapo agent a second glance. "Why didn't you call for help?" he said, examining Mallory's head wound with a professional air. He was a gawky teenager who looked too young to be in the army.

"I've been unconscious," Mallory said, intentionally slurring his words.

"It's not a bad wound," the medic said, "and it's stopped bleeding. They'll clean it up at the aid station. Can you tell if you're injured anywhere else?"

"I don't think so, but my legs are pinned and I can't pull them free."

"We'll get you out, don't worry," the medic said. "You sound like you could use some water."

"Yes. I'm parched."

The medic opened his canteen and handed it to Mallory, who put it to his lips immediately. The medic looked again at the Gestapo agent's body. "What the hell —" he said as he saw the handcuffs.

"He was my prisoner," Mallory said between swallows of water. "I can forget about him now."

"I guess so," the medic replied with a nervous laugh. "Are you —?"

"Gestapo. You said you'd get me out."

"Sure, we'll —"

"Not so fast, Hans," said the medic's companion. He was shining his flashlight at the top of the mound of rubble beneath which Mallory was pinned.

"Jesus," the medic murmured.

"What's the matter?" Mallory asked. The bench that had shielded his head and chest also blocked his view of the rubble pile above him. Whatever they were staring at was just out of his line of vision. He could see nothing but masonry, small sections of roofing, and jagged beam ends.

The two soldiers looked at each other and then at Mallory. "We'll have to leave you here for the moment, sir," said the medic.

"Why? What's the problem?"

"No problem. We just can't handle this ourselves."

"What can't you handle?"

"The five-hundred-pound bomb sitting right on top of you," said the medic's companion bluntly. "If we disturb it, we could all get an express ride to heaven."

Mallory swallowed. "A dud?"

The medic shook his head and stood up, leaving the canteen beside Mallory. "Delayed-action fuse more likely. They've already found two more like this one farther up the track, and a bomb-disposal team is on its way. They should be here soon. Don't worry, they can handle this, and we'll be sure that they come here first."

Mallory tried to smile. "I'd appreciate it."

"Come on, Hans!" the medic's companion said nervously and turned away.

The medic stooped down, seized the Gestapo agent's body, and started to drag it away.

"Leave it!" his companion said. "One's enough to carry for now."

"Yes, clear out," Mallory said. He didn't ask if they knew what the bomb's time delay was likely to be; he didn't want to know.

Seconds after the two men had left, Mallory heard officers shouting to their men to stay clear of the station house. His throat was dry again, and he took another drink from the canteen, suppressing the urge to try once more to free his legs. He sipped the water slowly, trying to keep a grip on himself. He wondered if British time bombs ticked. Even if they did, he couldn't hear the sound above the noise of the work crews cutting through the wreckage of the train. It was just as well, he thought grimly. The ticking might have been too much for him.

The fires in the marshaling yard had died away, and only moonlight illuminated the dark mound of debris pressing down on his legs. Mallory put the canteen aside, lay back, and began to breathe slowly and deeply, trying to force his body to relax. He was trapped, and there was nothing he could do but wait and hope. If the bomb detonates, he thought, I won't know a thing. I'll die still hoping.

Hoping, but not praying. Mallory's lips twitched into a twisted, bitter smile at the thought. He had prayed for Marie, and in a way his prayer had been answered. Perhaps God did exist, after all; perhaps He liked to play tricks.

Mallory heard the scuffle of footsteps on the platform outside, and a moment later a flashlight beam probed the station-house ruins. "Over here," Mallory called quickly.

He saw three men climbing over the rubble near the entrance. One of the men advanced alone, his companions illuminating his path. The man briefly directed his flashlight at Mallory and then flicked the beam up toward the top of the rubble pile.

"Are you men the bomb-disposal squad?" Mallory asked.

"Bergmann. Lieutenant Bergmann, Luftwaffe ordnance," the man replied, but his attention was focused on the bomb. Mallory shifted his upper body as far to the right as possible, and when he propped himself up he found he could see the bomb's exposed tail fins.

Bergmann set down the bulky tool kit he was carrying and slowly walked around the mound of debris, studying the positioning of the bomb. He was dressed like a street workman, with thick woolen trousers stuffed into knee-high rubber boots. Over a woolen shirt he wore an apron-length, sleeveless, leather tunic.

The only piece of military clothing he wore was a forage cap, but it bore no insignia.

His movements were slow and deliberate, but there was nothing phlegmatic about him. Bergmann radiated tension. As he turned toward Mallory again, his face caught the light of his companion's flashlights, and Mallory saw how pale he was. His dark eyes were sunk deep in their sockets — wary, alert eyes that glinted like a hawk's.

"That's an MC five-hundred-pounder on top of you," he said, coming over to Mallory. "It's positioned nearly vertically, with its tail exposed. It looks secure enough, so we won't waste time right now shoring it up. Are you all right?"

"I'm okay."

"Right," Bergmann said, kneeling to open his tool kit. "The Tommies use a chemical fuse in their time-delay bombs. Inside that bomb is a puddle of acetone eating its way through a celluloid disk. When the disk disintegrates, it will release the spring-loaded bolt of the detonator. The time delay is determined by the thickness of the disk, and the sooner we get at it the better."

Bergmann removed a heavy pipe wrench from the tool kit and a smaller, specialized wrench Mallory didn't recognize. Then he turned and directed his flashlight at the two men waiting for his orders, and Mallory saw with surprise that they wore striped, pajamalike uniforms under their coats. They were convicts.

"Meyer," Bergmann said, "I'll need you on the pipe wrench, but you can clear off, Linz."

"*Jawohl,* Herr Leutnant," one of the convicts said and scrambled back over the rubble and disappeared without looking back.

Meyer came over and picked up the pipe wrench. He was a big, broken-nosed man with a scar cutting through his close-cropped gray hair above his ear. Meyer handed Bergmann a miner's lamp. Bergmann switched it on and set it in place over his forage cap.

Slowly, and with infinite care, Bergmann and Meyer climbed up to the top of the rubble mound and began to clear away some of the debris from around the bomb.

"Do you want to know what we're doing?" Bergmann asked

Mallory, "or would you prefer to remain in blissful ignorance?"

"I'd like to know."

"This is a standard Type Thirty-seven fuse, and we know how to handle it. You can see the bomb's tail, and that's what we'll be working on. Meyer is tightening the pipe wrench onto the fuse body to keep it from twisting when I unscrew this housing here," Bergmann said. "The bomb is activated as it falls. The airstream spins a propeller that turns a threaded spindle. The spindle moves down into the fuse body to crush a glass ampoule containing the acetone, and the propeller flies off. That acetone is eating through the celluloid now, but once I get the spindle housing off, I can stop the chemical reaction."

Bergmann nodded to Meyer, who tightened his grip on the pipe wrench and braced his legs. Carefully, Bergmann fitted his special wrench into place around the spindle housing and pulled on the wrench handle, his face tensing as he gradually increased the torque on the wrench.

"Damn!" Bergmann burst out, easing his grip. "The bastard's frozen." He rested a moment, took a deep breath and tried again. Mallory could hear his gasping as he strained against the frozen threads.

The threads suddenly gave way with a shrill metallic squeal, and as Bergmann lurched sideways, Mallory heard Meyer's sharp intake of breath. The convict's eyes, illuminated by Bergmann's miner's lamp, were wide with fright, but he had maintained his grip on the pipe wrench.

"Sorry about that, Meyer," Bergmann said, panting from his exertion. "Didn't mean to scare you." He shifted position on the rubble pile and gripped the knurled surface of the housing with his fingers. "Ah, that's better. It's loose. We'll take her out now, slow and easy."

Slowly — a quarter turn at a time — Bergmann unscrewed the cylindrical housing. The brass threads squeaked in protest, but the cylinder continued to turn. With a sigh of satisfaction, Bergmann lifted the housing free and set it down beside the bomb.

Meyer removed the pipe wrench and handed Bergmann a magnifying glass and a syringe.

"Take off," Bergmann said, bending over the tail of the bomb.

"I'll stay, Herr Leutnant."

"No," Bergmann said, adjusting the angle of the miner's lamp and peering through the magnifying glass into the fuse opening. Bergmann looked up as Meyer still hesitated. "Clear out!" he said sharply. "You know the drill."

"*Jawohl,* Herr Leutnant," Meyer said and turned away and left.

Bergmann shifted his position and readjusted the lamp to see farther into the fuse's interior. "I'll be damned," he exclaimed, more to himself than to Mallory. "Some silly bugger forgot to put in the sieve and the cotton wad. I can see all the way down to —"

Bergmann broke off and quickly inserted the syringe into the fuse opening. Mallory could see his jaw muscles working.

"What did you see?" Mallory asked.

"I'm injecting ether into the fuse," Bergmann said, ignoring the question. "The ether counteracts the acetone reaction and resolidifies the dissolved celluloid, but it must go in a drop at a time. You can't rush it."

Bergmann straightened up into a more comfortable position, but he continued to depress the syringe's plunger, millimeter by millimeter, feeding the ether into the fuse. With his free hand he pulled out a handkerchief and wiped his forehead. He hadn't been sweating earlier.

Mallory could smell the acetone fumes emanating from the fuse opening. "Could you see the celluloid?" he asked hoarsely. "Can you tell how much time —"

"Shut up, will you!" Bergmann snapped, his voice brittle with tension, and Mallory realized that they were hanging by a thread. He tried to swallow, but his throat was suddenly too dry, and he could feel beads of sweat break out on his own forehead.

Mallory winced as a brilliant white flash outside turned the night into day, followed instantly by a shock wave that battered his eardrums and brought down a rain of dirt from the remains of the roof. Mallory opened his eyes and looked up at Bergmann. The lieutenant hadn't moved; he still crouched beside the bomb. Dust stirred up by the blast swirled in the beam of his headlamp.

"There's your answer," Bergmann said tensely. "This one has the same time delay."

10

"WHY hasn't it gone off?" Mallory said, his voice barely above a whisper.

Bergmann didn't answer. He continued to depress the plunger, feeding in the ether drop by drop, his breath hissing softly through his clenched teeth.

Mallory's own breathing had quickened, and he could feel his heart pumping, but as frightened as he was, he was awed by Bergmann. Where did he find the courage to stay with the bomb?

Ten seconds passed. Twenty seconds. Forty. Sixty.

"I think we're winning," Bergmann said. "If we weren't, she would have gone up by now. The celluloid must be resolidifying."

Another minute dragged by in silence, and then Bergmann straightened up with a heavy sigh and slipped the syringe into a pocket. He backed away from the bomb and climbed stiffly down to the floor. He shook his head and gave a low whistle. "We were lucky, my friend. I wasn't sure we'd make it."

"Lieutenant, I . . ."

"You don't owe me a thing," Bergmann said brusquely. "I didn't stay because of you. That disk was so far gone, I thought I had as good a chance sticking with it as trying to run."

Mallory nodded, but he didn't believe him. "Just the same," he said, "Thanks."

Suddenly Bergmann began to shake. The trembling swept over

him in a convulsive wave and then died away as quickly as it had come. Bergmann laughed hollowly. "Aftershock. It happens to me sometimes," he said in a bemused tone, as if he were describing some unaccountable eccentricity. "How are you doing? They told me your legs are pinned by a beam."

"I'm all right," Mallory said, but his thighs were throbbing, and he was losing feeling in his toes. "Can the bomb be moved now?"

The light beam from Bergmann's headlamp danced crazily as the lieutenant shook his head. "Not yet. That was just the beginning — the easy part. First I'll have to cut open the tail fuse and remove the detonator, and then we'll have to deactivate the trembler fuse I'm sure we're going to find in this baby's nose. If we try to shift her now — bang."

"How long will that take?"

"An hour — maybe less. We'll shore up the bomb and dig away enough of the debris to expose the nose. Then, while I'm working on the tail, Meyer will cool the bomb's nose with dry ice — to freeze the battery in the trembler circuit. Then we'll be able to get you out of there."

Bergmann shouted for Meyer, and a moment later the convict came scrambling over the rubble at the entrance.

"Get some support beams and tackle from the truck," Bergmann ordered. "When you've got it fixed so that bastard can't shift on us, dig down to the nose. I'm betting we'll find an Eight Forty-five waiting for us."

"*Jawohl,* Herr Leutnant," Meyer said and hurried away.

"I'm going out for a smoke," Bergmann said to Mallory. "My zebras know what to do. Want a butt?"

"Yes. I could use a smoke."

Bergmann knelt beside Mallory, gave him a cigarette, and lit it, the flame illuminating Bergmann's face. He looked exhausted, and his eyes were too bright. "Don't worry," he said. "I'll get you out."

"I'm not worried, Lieutenant."

"It should be straightforward enough," Bergmann said, as if

he had not heard Mallory. "It's called the 'Düsseldorf procedure.' Works every time."

Under Meyer's direction, the convicts had braced the bomb in position with heavy wooden beams and wound hemp cable around its tail. A block and tackle had been rigged to lift the bomb clear once the trembler fuse was deactivated. After the bomb had been secured, Meyer had slowly dug away at the debris to expose the nose, as his companions had looked on nervously. Now much of the bomb was visible, a dark, malevolent steel cylinder three feet high and a foot in diameter. Two bright stripes of paint, one blue-green, the other red, circled the bomb's nose, indicating its type.

The convicts were gathering up their tools, preparing to leave, and Meyer was relieving the pressure on Mallory's legs by clearing away the masonry he could move without disturbing the bomb.

"They told me you're Gestapo," Meyer said to Mallory. His voice sounded permanently hoarse, as if his larynx had been damaged by a blow to the throat. "They also told me that the stiff over there was your prisoner."

"That's right."

Meyer smiled and nodded. "Poor bastard," he said and turned to the other convicts. "Get a move on, boys, the lieutenant will be waiting by the truck. Tell him I've got his baby ready for him."

As the convicts left, Meyer laughed softly. "Have you got his I.D.?" he asked Mallory when the others were out of earshot.

Mallory tensed. "What are you talking about?"

Meyer bent down, and Mallory felt the convict pull off his shoes. "I'm talking about these," he said and laughed again. "My, my, wooden-soled shoes — and no socks! The Gestapo must have fallen on hard times. Attention to detail, son — attention to detail. Wooden-soled shoes simply won't do."

Before Mallory could think of a response, the convict darted away, carrying Mallory's shoes with him, and Mallory forgot about the bomb gleaming dully in the light above him. The goddamned shoes! If Meyer turned him in, he was finished; the I.D. in his pocket had the other man's photograph. He raised himself on his elbows and tried again to pull himself free, but the beam was still wedged firmly in place. Mallory pounded the stone floor in frustration. He had come so close. So close!

He heard the rattle of brick and twisted his head to look toward the entrance. Meyer was returning. The convict slipped back over the rubble, moving surprisingly swiftly and silently for a big man.

"You're a lucky son of a bitch," the convict said, going to the Gestapo agent's body. "They moved the truck, so we have some time. Everyone else is standing clear until old Bergmann spikes this baby."

Mallory watched tensely as Meyer pulled off the dead man's coat and shoes. He came across to Mallory, knelt down, and jammed the Gestapo agent's shoes onto Mallory's bare feet; and Mallory, with a flush of relief, at last understood that the convict was intent on helping him.

"You'll have to try to pick up some socks at the aid station," Meyer said. "You can think of something to tell them. How do the shoes feel?"

"Fine," Mallory said gratefully. First Bergmann and now this convict: two strangers to whom he owed his life. "Meyer, I . . ."

"Save it," Meyer said. "Now for the coat. We'll make the switch for effect. These Gestapo types love leather."

Mallory raised his upper body as high as he could and slipped out of his overcoat. Meyer pulled it out from under him and tossed it into a dark corner. "Bergmann will never notice the switch," Meyer said, helping Mallory into the leather trench coat. "When he's working, he only sees his baby."

Mallory started again to thank the convict, but he didn't get the chance. At that moment Bergmann appeared, carrying a bucket in one hand and what looked like a large electric hand drill in the other.

Meyer straightened up. "All set, Herr Leutnant. You were right. There's an Eight Forty-five in the nose."

"Have you got the clay for the mold? I couldn't find it in the truck."

"Yes, Herr Leutnant."

"Good. Here's the dry ice and turpentine," Bergmann said, handing the bucket to Meyer. He looked carefully at the supports holding the bomb in place and nodded, satisfied. "Get to work on the nose," he said to Meyer. "I want that battery frozen by the time I'm finished with the Thirty-seven."

As Meyer set about building a clay mold beneath the bomb's nose to hold the mixture that would cool down the fuse battery, Bergmann attached the cord of his power tool to a storage battery the men had brought in earlier. The tool was in fact an electric hand drill, but in place of a drill bit there was a circular cutting disk on the end of a long steel rod. Bergmann looked over at Mallory.

"I'm not going to want to talk while I'm working this time," he said, "so I'll explain now what I'll be doing. It's a straightforward procedure, as I said before, but it requires concentration."

"I'll keep my mouth shut," Mallory said.

"Right. The Tommies don't want us unscrewing their fuses, so they've rigged them with booby traps. The Düsseldorf procedure gets around that. The booby trap's release mechanism is in the lower part of the fuse cylinder, and it is designed to trip the detonator if the cylinder is twisted in a counterclockwise direction, as one would normally try to do.

"I will insert the cutting tool into the fuse and cut the cylinder in two, from the inside out, just beyond the depth of the threaded portion of the cylinder. Then I'll be able to unscrew the upper part of the cylinder without twisting the lower part, which contains the booby trap. Once that's done, I can reach in and pull the lower part straight out, detonator and all. So hang on, and we'll have our baby disarmed and ready to haul away in about fifteen minutes. Okay?"

"Okay," Mallory said, but he knew it wasn't as simple as Bergmann wanted him to believe.

Bergmann went up to the bomb and settled himself into position, switched on the miner's lamp to illuminate the interior of the fuse, and inspected the celluloid disk again with his magnifying glass. Satisfied, he began to remove pieces of the crushed acetone ampoule from the fuse with a long pair of tweezers.

When the interior of the fuse was clear, he shifted position again and delicately inserted the shaft of the cutting tool. He hesitated for a moment and then pressed the switch, and Mallory heard a high-pitched, whistling whine as the cutting edge bit into the brass cylinder wall. He could see the muscles in Bergmann's jaw working as he painstakingly moved the disk around the inside of the fuse.

Meyer, crouched on the rubble pile below Bergmann, had fashioned his clay mold beneath the bomb's nose, and he was pouring in the dry ice–turpentine slurry, producing a white, swirling cloud of condensation vapor. Meyer swore vividly when he discovered a leak in the mold. He repaired it, filled the mold, and sat back on his heels to wait. Above him, Bergmann continued to cut through the fuse cylinder.

Mallory had been craning his neck, and the strain forced him to lie back and rest. The minutes dragged by. Bergmann hadn't needed to explain what would happen if he slipped.

Outside, the work of clearing the wreckage from the track was still in full swing, accompanied by the roar of diesel motors and the bang of sledgehammers, but Mallory heard only the high-pitched whine of Bergmann's power tool.

It seemed to go on forever, the maddening sound rising and falling as Bergmann varied the pressure on the cutting edge, and with each variation in pitch Mallory's stomach muscles tensed. Abruptly the whine died away. Mallory raised his head again and saw Bergmann withdraw the cutting tool from the fuse. Bergmann inspected the interior again and then straightened up, arching his back to relieve the stiffness. "That's it, gentlemen," he said.

"I think the battery should be cold by now, Herr Leutnant," Meyer said. "There's plenty of frost on the nose cone."

"Good. You can take off, Meyer."

"I'll stay, Herr Leutnant."

This time Bergmann did not object. "Suit yourself," he said, drawing another specialized wrench from his tool kit. "It's time to find out if I still have the touch."

He inserted the wrench, took a deep breath, and slowly began to turn the threaded half of the severed fuse cylinder. A quarter turn; half a turn; three-quarters of a turn. Bergmann stopped and expelled his breath. "So far, so good," he muttered and began to turn the cylinder again. After two more complete turns he carefully removed the wrench and unscrewed the cylinder the rest of the way with his fingers, lifted it free, and examined the marking stamp on its side.

"I was right," he announced. "A thirty-minute fuse." He dropped the harmless piece onto the rubble pile. "We're right on schedule," he called down to Mallory. "The last bit is coming up."

He took from his kit yet another tool, and painstakingly pulled the remainder of the fuse from the tail of the bomb.

Bergmann grinned in triumph and looked down at Meyer. "Well, my faithful zebra, it seems we've survived one more time."

A first-aid station had been set up in a pasture beside the railroad track to tend the lightly wounded, and Mallory stood outside the tent, watching dawn break in a cloudless sky. The last of the dead had been extracted from the train wreckage, and the twisted, blackened hulks of the cars lay beside the rail bed, where they had been dumped by a crane that had been brought up to clear the track. The train's locomotive lay on its side like a slain prehistoric beast. Silence had once again descended on the surrounding farmland and the smoke had drifted away, but the residual odor of charred wood still lingered in the air, mingling with the scent of wet grass. Somewhere not far away, a cock crowed.

A frail, teenaged medic in an oversized uniform emerged from the tent and handed Mallory a tin cup of steaming ersatz coffee. "The coffee's lousy," the medic said, "but the Schnapps I put in it will pick you up."

"Thanks," Mallory said, taking a sip, and he nodded appreciatively as he felt the alcohol burn its way down his throat into his stomach.

"Perhaps you should let us take you to a hospital, sir — for a real examination. I didn't like the look of those ribs."

"I'll be okay. You patched me up just fine."

The medic shook his head. "To be injured in one raid only to be caught in another a few days later is what I call bad luck."

"I survived. That's luck enough for me."

The medic had cleaned the cuts on Mallory's head and legs and had rebandaged his ribs, and despite the aching stiffness that permeated his body, Mallory was sure he could travel. He had been given food, and someone had even found him a pair of socks.

"You said you have to get back to Paris," the medic said. "Corporal Schultz will be driving over to Metz in a few minutes, and you can hitch a ride with him. You'll be able to catch a train to Paris from there."

"Good, I'll do that. Where do I find him?"

"You just stay put, sir. I'll tell him you want the ride."

"Thanks. Thanks very much."

The medic left, and Mallory allowed himself a smile. It was going to work. It was really going to work! He had seen how strangers reacted to him: they treated him politely, but they kept their distance, their responses edged with wariness. He slipped out the dead man's identification wallet to look at it again. Kolb. Special Agent Kolb. Mallory bore no resemblance to the man in the photograph, but if he held the wallet in his left hand when he flashed the I.D., he could quite naturally block the photograph with his forefinger. No one would look past the word *Gestapo*, boldly lettered in the center of the card.

Mallory wished he had obtained Kolb's billfold, for he had no money. He had no travel permit either. But he could get by without food, and he was sure the Gestapo I.D. would take him anywhere in France. The injuries on his head and face were easily explained, and thanks to the foxy Meyer, he looked the part. The leather trench coat hid the French cut of his suit, as well as the rents in his trousers. He had wiped the grime and mortar dust from the coat and from his shoes, and although the coat was an inch too wide at the shoulders and his feet were swimming in the dead man's shoes, it was already clear that no one would notice.

He had perhaps twenty-four hours' grace before Kolb and he

were missed and the alarm went out. It was too late to try to follow Ryder; Marston's men would no longer be looking for him. No, he would return to Lyons-la-Forêt. Lessard would be in hiding, but Mallory was sure he could contact him somehow. Mallory had a good memory for faces, and many men had been at the farmhouse that night. He thought he had a good chance of recognizing someone in the village — or of being recognized once he started asking questions.

But Mallory had a more compelling reason for returning to Lyons-la-Forêt. He was the only one who knew Marie was working for the Germans, and Steiner might send her back to Lessard. She could be there already. Mallory's fingers tightened around the cup in his hand till the knuckles turned white. He hoped Lessard would let him pull the trigger.

"You wanted a lift into Metz, sir?" called a voice behind him.

Mallory turned and waved in acknowledgement to a soldier standing on the edge of the pasture beside the railroad track. As he walked toward the tracks, the rays of the rising sun cast his shadow before him, sharp and clear on the meadow grass; it was going to be a bright spring day.

"Are you Corporal Schultz?" Mallory asked as he came up to the young soldier.

"Yes, sir. I'm taking one of our ambulances back now," he said, pointing. "That one over there by the station platform."

But Mallory was looking up the track, where the bomb-disposal squad's truck was now parked, two hundred yards away. The convicts were unloading gear from the rear of the truck, and Mallory recognized the figure of Bergmann standing off to one side, beside the hulking Meyer.

"Those poor bastards must still have another bomb to defuse," the ambulance driver said. "Christ, I wouldn't want to have their job. You never know when the damned thing is set to go off. It's like playing Russian roulette."

The soldier turned away and started toward the ambulance. Mallory watched the distant figures for a moment longer as they turned and trudged off down the track toward the waiting bomb. He wanted to remember them.

The springs of the clapped-out, mud-spattered ambulance groaned in protest as the soldier climbed into the cab. Mallory went around to the other side and got in beside him. The starter emitted a low, whimpering whine as it cranked the engine, which finally coughed and sputtered into life. The driver ground the gears and popped the clutch, and the ambulance lurched forward, throwing Mallory back against the seat.

Mallory grunted in pain. "I hope you don't have wounded back there."

The driver flashed a grin. "No, we're empty. They won't let me drive when we have wounded to carry."

"I can see why. Take it easy, will you? I'm not in such great shape myself."

"Sorry. Say, you wouldn't happen to have some smokes with you?"

"No," Mallory said. "I was hoping I could bum some from you."

With another grinding of gears, the driver turned the ambulance onto the main road passing through the middle of the village beyond the station and headed west. Purely by chance, no bombs had fallen into the cluster of white, red-tiled cottages nestled beside the railway. The civilians had been very lucky, Mallory reflected. That one stick of bombs could have obliterated half the town.

Outside the hamlet the dirt road narrowed as it ran in a straight line across the flat countryside, a patchwork of green fields and freshly cultivated squares of reddish earth dotted with small stands of trees. Mallory rolled down his window, rested his elbow on the door, and stretched out his legs. He felt relaxed and charged with confidence. He had only begun his run, but he was on his way — thanks to Bergmann and to Meyer.

Silently he wished them luck.

The ambulance had traveled three miles down the road when the sound of the bomb blast reached it, like a single, great clap of thunder from the cloudless sky.

Mallory lay on his stomach in the wet grass on the edge of the landing field. The feel of the dew on his palms reminded him of that other field and the sound of the girl's light, running footsteps coming toward him in the darkness. How long had it been? Three weeks? No, not even that long, yet the gulf between then and now seemed too great to measure in weeks.

The Maquisards were spread out along the tree line, and the soft breeze drifting over them picked up their garlic scent. Mallory grinned in the darkness, thinking that the Germans should patrol the roads at night with hunting dogs.

"What's funny?" whispered Lessard, who lay beside him.

"Nothing," Mallory whispered back. "Just a wild thought." He was surprised that Lessard had seen his smile. Clouds had blotted out the moon, and the darkness was nearly total. Lessard's profile was a blurred black silhouette, recognizable only by the outline of his large nose.

"That is the first time you have smiled in the three days you have been with us," Lessard said. "I am glad to see it."

Mallory nodded but remained silent.

"I think we should turn on the homing transmitter," Lessard said softly, looking at the radium dial of his watch.

"Leave it for a few more minutes. Even if the Lizzie is on time, it will just be coming into range now."

"The batteries are good; we can turn it on now."

"I'm not worried about the batteries. I don't want to give the *Boches* any extra time to get a radio fix on us."

"But they have no DF trucks in this area."

"As far as we know, Jean. As far as we know."

Lessard acquiesced. He wouldn't argue against caution, and he considered Mallory his equal, for this was not the same boy who had jumped into France. It was a pity he could not keep him. The invasion would be coming soon, and he could use a man like Mallory. The American had gone through the fire and had survived. Such a thing always changed a man, Lessard thought, but the result was unpredictable. Some men were consumed, but others, like Mallory, emerged like diamond — harder than steel and impervious to flame.

The day of Mallory's return, Lessard had seen the change in his eyes — eyes from which youth was gone. They were cool, calculating eyes, which saw more than they gave away, the eyes of a man determined to make no more mistakes. And there had been another change as well. Mallory had been trained to kill, as had so many others, but for most it did not become a part of them. But in Mallory, Lessard now sensed a quiet deadliness.

Yes, it was a pity he could not keep him.

"Max will be waiting for you in London," Lessard said. "To celebrate. It came through on the BBC when they sent the code for the Lysander's ETA."

"Good. We'll tie on a big one."

But Lessard saw no smile.

"I didn't tell you earlier," Lessard said, "because it might have been bad luck."

"I didn't think you were superstitious."

Lessard shrugged. "A man needs luck."

"Yes, but you can't trust to it. You can only trust yourself, and you have to make your own luck."

Yes, like a diamond, Lessard thought, hard and clear — but cold to the touch.

"We'll find the girl, Richard. Wherever she hides, we'll find her."

"You can switch on the Eureka now."

Lessard pulled a metal box toward him, removed the cover, and flipped the toggle switch. Silently the electromagnetic pulses from the homing transmitter raced upward into the night sky, invisible bubbles of energy expanding at the speed of light. Mallory turned his head to the southeast, waiting for the sound of the approaching Lysander.

Two minutes later, Lessard touched Mallory's arm. "Here it comes. Right on schedule."

Mallory heard nothing but the sound of his own breathing, and for the first time he realized how badly his hearing had been damaged. Lessard gave a low whistle, and his men scrambled to their feet and ran out into the field to mark the landing zone. Then Mallory heard the aircraft, too, its small engine sounding like a far-off motorcycle.

At both ends of the field, kerosene-soaked bonfires burst into flame, and Lessard's men spread out in a line. They switched on their flashlights and pointed the beams skyward. Mallory and Lessard got to their feet, and Lessard raised his flashlight and began to signal M-M-M. To the southeast, above the tree line a winking light appeared, flashing R-R-R in acknowledgment, and a moment later the black silhouette of the high-wing monoplane swept over them.

The pilot swung the plane in a tight arc, throttled back the engine, and settled the aircraft onto the field as lightly as a feather. The plane ran the length of the field and swung around, engine idling, ready for takeoff, the flames of the bonfire reflecting dully off its black-painted fuselage. Lessard ran beside Mallory toward the Lysander. The Frenchman ran awkwardly, trying not to shake the bottles of champagne he held in each hand.

As Mallory and Lessard reached the plane, the pilot opened the narrow cabin door. "Bloody sweet landing, if I do say so myself," he shouted with a grin.

"Great," Mallory laughed, scrambling in behind the pilot's seat. "Now let's get the hell out of here."

Lessard shoved one bottle into the pilot's lap and reached into the cockpit to give the other one to Mallory. "Share it with Max!" he cried in English.

"Will do," Mallory replied, gripping Lessard's hand. "Thanks, and good luck!"

"Au 'voir, mon ami."

The pilot tossed a heavy parcel into Lessard's arms. "Coffee and cigarettes," he shouted, revving the engine.

Lessard slammed the cockpit door shut and stepped back as the plane started forward.

"Fasten your seat belt if you can find it back there," the pilot yelled to Mallory as the Lysander gathered speed. At the very end of the field the pilot pulled back the stick, and the plane rose steeply into the night. As the pilot banked above the trees and turned toward England, Mallory looked down and saw a single flashlight swinging in farewell.

The pilot brought the wings level, and the glowing red dot of Lessard's flashlight slipped out of sight behind them. Mallory settled back and let the thrumming engine noise wash over him, cutting his thoughts adrift. A hot bath and clean sheets, coffee and cigarettes . . . Then old Max and he would raise some hell together. The bottle of champagne Lessard had given him would be just for starters.

And after he recovered from their binge, he'd take a long walk by himself through London. It would be good to walk through the streets without having to look over his shoulder, to pass a policeman without that twinge of dread. It would be good to feel like a normal man again, if only for a time.

They might not want to send him back again immediately, but he would fight that. He was coming back. Even if he had to wait until the war was over, he was coming back — to France, or to Germany — wherever he had to go to find Mueller. Lessard would take care of the girl, but Mueller was his. He only hoped no one would get to the Nazi first.

Beyond that, the future was a blank, and Mallory wondered how he could ever settle into the routine of ordinary life again.

11

PENDLETON reached out, switched off the microfilm reader, and sat for a moment in total darkness. The whir of the machine's cooling fan fell to a whisper and died. The counter-intellgience chief pushed up his glasses and rubbed his weary eyes. The afterimage of the last page of the OSS file lingered on his retinas, the words turning from white to red, and then to green, before they finally faded away entirely. He was tired, and it was difficult to resist the seductive darkness, to resist the need for sleep.

He turned on his desk lamp and squinted irritably at his watch. One A.M. Ten years ago he could have worked until dawn. His pipe had gone out and he relit it, though his tongue was raw from hours of continuous smoking.

Pendleton hated growing old. The corners of his mouth turned down as he gazed at his hands. His long, bony fingers looked much the same as they always had, but the skin on the back of his hands was tight and shiny and dotted with the freckles of age, a constant, visible reminder that his body was wearing out. His job required the energy of a younger man, and he knew it was time to think of retirement. But who was there to replace him?

He could not go home just yet. He had to think while the contents of the file were still fresh in his mind. He was sure his ability to analyze had not abated, but he no longer trusted his memory — not completely.

He removed the microfilm spool from the machine, slipped it into its plastic case, and placed it on top of the file folder labeled MARTIN, which lay on his desk. The old OSS report had told him little that he didn't already know about Ryder, but it had helped to explain some of the curious aspects of Mallory's history with the Company. As the report merged in Pendleton's mind with Mallory's personnel file, the missing pieces fell neatly into place, forming a coherent picture of the maverick case officer.

Pendleton had hoped Mallory would be the key to unlocking MARTIN, but he had known that using him would require precisely correct opening moves. Now he was sure that it made sense to draw in Ryder, and that Ryder, in turn, would understand Pendleton's need for his help. Tomorrow he would approach Ryder, and as soon as that was settled he would have Mallory recalled to Langley.

With a grunt of fatigue, which he would only allow himself in private, Pendleton got to his feet and undertook the nightly ritual of clearing his desk. He opened two of the five safes in his office and shifted the piles of folders to the safes, an armful at a time. Then he locked those two safes and opened the other three. In one of them he placed the microfilm spool, and he divided the contents of the MARTIN file between the last two. The division was a needless precaution — perhaps even a sign of incipient paranoia, but no one would know, so he could afford the self-indulgence.

As he was closing the last safe he heard a knock on the office door. He locked the safe and started toward his desk to release the door's electronic lock, but a buzz from the door indicated that the lock and warning sensors were being overriden from the outside. The door opened and a young, black security guard came in.

"Sorry, sir. I didn't realize you were still here," the guard said. "Security sweep," he added unnecessarily.

"I'm just leaving. It's all clear in here," Pendleton said, walking past the guard to the door.

The guard nodded and walked to the nearest safe to begin his check anyway. Pendleton would have had the guard fired if the man had taken his word that the office was secure.

"What kind of night is it out there?" Pendleton asked.

"Muggy, sir. Hot and muggy."

Pendleton walked down the long corridor toward the nearest bank of elevators, his footsteps on the asphalt tile echoing hollowly in the deserted hallway — deserted, save for the ever-present building guards. The silence of inactivity in the huge building depressed him. He wondered if KGB headquarters was also deserted at night. Possibly, but that made no difference. An intelligence service shouldn't sleep, he thought. Never.

He blinked tiredly. Why did so few men in the Company understand the cunning — no, the tenacity — of the Soviet service? If he did retire, who was there to replace him?

Two foreign spies engaged each other across a chessboard in a café in downtown Buenos Aires. They had chosen a window table to catch the winter sun, but it was a poor substitute for the sidewalk table they had taken in the summer months, enjoying the life and color of the crowds streaming up and down the Avenida de Mayo. The American was drinking coffee; the Russian drank *maté,* the local brew that Argentinian laborers prefer to tea or coffee.

The American, playing White, moved his queen's bishop across the board to attack Black's king's knight, pinning it to the Black queen. The Russian nodded thoughtfully, his oversized head rocking ponderously on a neck so short that his head seemed to rest directly on his thick shoulders. He had black, bushy eyebrows, which grew together over the bridge of his nose. His coarse, black hair was combed straight back from his forehead, and shorter, recalcitrant gray bristles stuck out over his ears. Had it not been for his eyes, V. A. Kurov would have looked dull-witted.

Kurov wore an expensive, gray tweed suit with a West European cut, hand-tailored to fit his bearlike frame, but the understated elegance intended by the tailor misfired. Kurov looked like a heavyweight wrestler masquerading as a banker. If Kurov was aware of the incongruity in his appearance, it did not embarrass him; embarrassment was an emotion that had little meaning for Kurov.

There was not even a pretense of elegance in the American's dress. His off-the-rack blue suit hung limply on his thin, narrow-chested body, and it needed pressing. His shoes were scuffed. Cognoscenti of the intelligence world could have immediately identified Kurov as KGB, but they would not have guessed that Richard Mallory was a CIA officer; he simply didn't look the part.

Mallory saw the telltale glint in Kurov's eye and knew the game would soon be over. He sighed inwardly in resignation, shifted around in his seat, and stretched out his legs to the sunlight streaming in through the window. He missed the summer; he missed the crowds that strolled the streets in warm weather, with their unique Argentinian mix of European nationalities. He missed the pervasive scent of broiling steaks in the summer air as workers at construction sites prepared their midday meals. In summer one did not notice the dreariness of the nondescript European architecture along the avenues, and the task of driving in a city without traffic lights seemed an amusing challenge rather than a day-to-day annoyance.

"I did not think you would come today," Kurov said, his voice a gravelly rumble.

"I came to say good-bye."

"Are you not impressed?" Kurov asked with a sly grin, revealing a set of chipped, tobacco-stained teeth.

"With what? That you knew I'm being recalled?"

Kurov nodded, and he gazed again at the chessboard.

"Sure I'm impressed," Mallory said, lighting a Lucky Strike.

Kurov smiled to himself. Perhaps Mallory was impressed by his little demonstration of penetration, and perhaps not. As always, it was impossible to read him with certainty.

"When do you leave?" Kurov asked.

"Tonight."

Kurov moved up a pawn, attacking Mallory's bishop and revealing a check on White's king. "Check," he said.

"Shit," Mallory muttered. He studied the board for a few seconds, saw that the loss of his bishop was just the beginning of a disaster, and tipped over his king.

"You are right to resign; you were finished."

Kurov was glad that this was their day for chess, and not poker. Mallory invariably beat him at poker, and Kurov hated losing. He took out a thin cigarette case and extracted a black, gold-tipped Turkish cigarette. "You really should switch to my brand," he said. "These will kill you much more quickly."

"I'm q-quitting when I get back to the States."

"Would you like to make a wager on that?"

"How much?"

Kurov shook his head. "No, I've changed my mind. I don't steal candy from children."

"While we're on the subject of unhealthy habits, how can you drink that rotgut?"

"The *maté*? It's invigorating. It puts hair on the chest."

"You don't need any more hair."

"The more the better," Kurov laughed. "The women love it."

Mallory smiled and shook his head. Kurov talked women and wine like a debauched White Russian count, but he was too careful to overindulge in either.

"I shall miss you," Kurov said. "There is little enjoyment in intrigue without a competent opponent."

"You just don't like the idea of being left behind in this b-backwater."

"It may be a backwater, but it is a pleasant one. Consider the women — blondes, brunettes, redheads — a variety one might expect to find only in New York. And in the summer this *avenida* could be a boulevard in Paris, don't you think?"

Mallory shrugged. "I wouldn't know. I haven't seen Paris since the war, and it was a bit grim in those days."

"But you were five years in Berlin. In all that time you never made a little trip to Paris?"

"I never found the time," Mallory said, sipping his coffee. It was no longer hot enough for him, but it was certainly strong.

"You should have made time. It is a pity our paths did not cross in Berlin. When did you leave — 1955? I came there shortly afterward."

And you cut a wide swath, Mallory thought, for a time. What happened, Viktor? Whose toes did you step on? The file on Kurov had a large gap in it, from the time he had left Berlin in 1963 to his arrival in Buenos Aires two years ago, in 1968.

"Professionally, of course, Berlin is exhilarating," Kurov said expansively, leaning back in his chair, "but I much prefer the people here — their vitality and sophistication. As for the Germans — I saw enough of them in the war. I'm sure you know what I mean."

Mallory nodded noncommittally, and once again he wondered how much Kurov really knew about him.

Kurov drew on his cigarette and exhaled a long stream of smoke. "Do you know who is coming down to replace you?"

Mallory shook his head. "I don't think even the COS knows yet."

"Well, you wouldn't want to hand over your string of agents to a stranger. Why not give them to me?"

Mallory laughed softly. "Most of them already work for you."

"Only part-time," Kurov protested. "You know that I can't compete with the exorbitant rates you people pay. Why don't you let your replacement find his own agents?"

"You're too late, Viktor. The COS already has my payoff list."

"What about Magda, then," Kurov said, raising his bushy eyebrows. "You know I've always admired her. Perhaps you could put in a word for me."

Again Mallory laughed. "She's a broad-minded lady, but not that broad-minded. I don't think she'd like the idea of being passed on like a basket of fruit. You'll have to make your own pitch — after a decent interval."

"But you're not taking her with you."

"No. Neither one of us is the marrying kind, so . . ."

Mallory signaled the waiter, who came over and refilled his coffee cup. Mallory drank it immediately, before it could cool.

"Perhaps your recall will mean a promotion," Kurov said casually.

"I doubt it."

"One is overdue, I would think."

Mallory shrugged. It was overdue, all right, he thought. Terminally overdue. His career was at a dead end.

"I hope you're not thinking of resigning," Kurov said, and for once Mallory allowed his surprise to show.

"No inside information," Kurov said, holding up his blunt hands, palms outward. "Just a guess. I thought I recognized the signs, that's all."

"What signs?"

"Signs of ennui, my friend. The ennui that comes with time and too much experience. The challenge is gone; operations seem routine — and unappreciated."

Mallory looked at Kurov curiously. "Are you making a pitch, Viktor?"

"No, of course not," Kurov said, putting on a pained expression. "One of the reasons I like you, Richard, is that you have never tried to recruit me. Naturally I exercise the same restraint."

"If you wanted to be turned, you'd tell me," Mallory said.

"Precisely. But not everyone perceives the obvious — certainly not our superiors. Still, I think you would have been happier with us. The KGB values its operations men, appreciates their skill and effort, but the CIA does so only up to a point. Then a man must leave the field in order to move up. The ascendancy of Mr. Helms is a celebration of the rise of the efficient administrator."

Mallory sighed. "All right, Viktor, what are you leading up to? Why the psychoanalysis?"

Kurov ground out his cigarette, taking his time about it, as if he were choosing his words, but Mallory knew it was an act. Kurov was never at a loss for words.

"I have a proposition for you," Kurov said finally. "You may consider it a small parting gift. I suggest that you tell your station chief that you've finally made some progress with me after all these months — that I've agreed to be turned, in exchange for a guarantee of an eventual safe and comfortable retirement in the United States.

"I understand that the men at Langley who run your Hard

Target Program are getting desperate for results. With nothing to show for their efforts, they're having a difficult time justifying their budget. I expect that my recruitment would guarantee your promotion."

"N-not if you don't deliver."

Kurov smiled and laid his forefinger alongside his nose. "Oh, I could play along with your replacement for a while — until your promotion came through."

Mallory realized to his surprise that Kurov was serious. It was even possible that Kurov was really acting out of friendship.

Mallory shook his head. "Thanks, anyway."

"Scruples?" Kurov said with an exaggerated look of disappointment.

"Maybe."

"What a pity. I would have enjoyed my role."

Mallory turned to look out the window, and for a time the two men sat together in silence.

Still gazing out the window, Mallory said, "Tell me something, Viktor. Haven't you ever felt like packing it in?"

Kurov laughed and shook his great head. "And settle into a modest *dacha* on the Black Sea?"

"Something like that."

"No. I only dream when I'm asleep, and when I dream, I dream of recruiting your Mr. Helms."

"That would be a waste of time. I doubt that he knows the details of a single operation."

"Then someone lower down on the ladder — someone in a position like Philby's. *That* is something to dream about."

"Dream is the right word," Mallory said disparagingly. "The only significant thing Philby ever did for you people was after he fled to Moscow — when he persuaded the KGB to let you guys wear those ritzy suits."

Kurov sighed. "You are *too* cyncial. How old are you, Richard — forty-nine? You look much younger, but inside you are even older than I am. Too much cynicism ages you, and it makes you vulnerable. One day you may find yourself caring again, and then you may care too much — and make mistakes."

"Christ, Viktor, you should have taken up psychiatry."

Kurov leaned across the table and tapped Mallory's forearm. "But I am quite serious, and you should listen. We have both seen real war, and we have both been in the field a very long time. We have watched our services change and grow toward each other until they are practically indistinguishable — modernized, homogenized, computerized, and dominated by technocrats who —"

"Now who's being cynical," Mallory cut in.

Kurov shrugged. "I am simply stating facts, but unlike you I accept them and ignore them as unimportant. The game itself is what is important, the game we play so well. It does not matter that it seems stale and even pointless at times. We have no choice but to continue."

"You may have no ch-choice, but I sure as hell do," Mallory said. "I know when it's time to get out."

Kurov shook his head, "No," he said with heavy emphasis, "it would be a great mistake to walk away from your work."

"Why?"

"Because it is what you do. It is what you are."

Mallory shook his head and grinned. "Is that supposed to be profound?"

And suddenly both men were laughing, their outburst loud enough to startle the young family of four seated at the next table.

Late that afternoon, Viktor Kurov sat at his desk by a third-floor window in the Russian embassy. The window, which overlooked the embassy courtyard, faced west, and there was still enough red-tinged twilight to read by. Kurov, who had an old European's distaste for wasting electricity, held the decoded cable up to the fading light to read it a second time.

Kurov could find nothing in the terse message summoning him back to Moscow that could connect it with the recall Mallory had received twenty-four hours earlier. It could be coincidence, of course — two shopworn operatives recalled from the same backwater at the same time; but Kurov felt in his bones that it was not. The very brevity of the message from Moscow signaled that something was brewing.

He heard the far-off rumble of a jet high in the sky and thought of Mallory, but then he realized that the American would not be flying out of Ezeiza for another few hours. He swiveled around in his chair and gazed out the window at the dying day. He looked forward to seeing Moscow again; it would be summertime there, and it would be good to be home, if only for a short time.

If he was right, he would be briefed and sent out again. It made no difference where they would send him. The important thing was that they needed him again, that once more he was to play the game in earnest. *And if I'm right, Mallory, my friend, you will be playing on the other side — whether you want to or not.*

12

MALLORY might as well have worn a CIA badge on his lapel. He still carried an old passport that listed him as a civilian employee of the Department of Defense, and that overused cover was known to immigration officials the world over. The U.S. Immigration officer at Dulles International Airport was no exception, and he winked conspiratorially as he handed back the passport.

Mallory was not amused, and his eyes said so. He slipped the passport into his pocket, picked up his overnight bag, and moved on. Watching Mallory walk away, the Immigration officer reconsidered and decided he'd been wrong after all. Mallory lacked the spiffy, cosmopolitan polish of a CIA officer.

Mallory paused at the door to the terminal lobby and lit a cigarette. Thirty minutes had passed since his last smoke, and that was too long. He sighed wearily and pushed through the door to the lobby. The overnight flight from Buenos Aires had been crowded, and he had been wedged between two restless passengers, who had kept him awake half the night. He started for the exit, intending to catch a few more hours' sleep at the airport hotel before reporting in, when he heard a man call his name. He turned and saw Max Ryder striding toward him.

Mallory grinned. "Max! How the hell are you?" he said, shaking hands.

"I can't complain."

Ryder was elegantly turned out in a lightweight gray suit hand-tailored to his tall, slim frame, a silk tie, and expensive Italian shoes. His dark, straight hair, graying at the temples, had receded somewhat from his forehead, and his fine-boned facial features had thickened somewhat with age; he was still a handsome man, tan and fit, but, at fifty-four, his dashing, film-star good looks had given way to a more mature, dignified appearance. And as ever, despite the leveling influence of his postwar residence in the United States on his speech and gestures, there was still a touch of the aristocrat in Ryder.

"How long has it been, Max? Two years?"

"Closer to three. When you came back from Cairo, I was off on a TDY, and by the time I got back you'd already gone PCS to Buenos Aires. It's good to see you again, Rich, but if you don't mind my saying so, you look a little beat."

"Yeah, well, I could use some sleep. I was hoping to crash for a few hours at the airport hotel before checking in."

Ryder shook his head. "I'm afraid that's out. You're wanted at Langley."

"What's the flap, Max? There I was, m-minding my own business in a cushy PCS, and suddenly I get a back-channel, hush-hush, rush-rush signal to come back to Washington. And to top it off, you meet me at the airport."

"So? I came out to meet an old friend."

"Bullshit. Since when does a supergrader have the time to pick up old friends at the airport? What's going on?"

"You'll find out soon enough. Come on, we'll talk in the car."

"At least let me go to the john."

"Okay. I'll bring my car around to the front entrance. Is that all you've got with you? One suitcase, after two years?"

"That's it."

"Then I'll meet you outside in a few minutes."

Watching Ryder stride away, his movements charged with youthful energy, Mallory became even more aware of his own deep-seated weariness, a weariness sleep could not cure.

Mallory took his time in the men's room, trying to wash away some of his fatigue with tap water, but when he was finished he still felt tired and gritty. He adjusted his tie in the mirror and perfunctorily ran a comb through his hair.

For a moment he stared impassively at his reflection. Seeing Ryder had made him aware of his own faintly seedy appearance. In his wrinkled trench coat, he thought, he looked like a down-at-the-heels private investigator. He now wore contact lenses, and without the distortion of his eyes by thick-lensed glasses, he was perhaps no longer as homely as he had once been. His narrow, acne-scarred face, he decided, could best be characterized as nondescript, its mediocrity unrelieved by the mustache he had affected for the past year.

Outwardly, he wore his forty-nine years lightly. He still had all of his dark, wiry hair, which was only lightly flecked with gray, and he was still as thin as he had been at twenty. But inside he felt old.

Remembering that it would be hot outside, he slipped off the trench coat and stuffed it into his suitcase. Then he went out to meet Ryder.

Once, he reflected, an urgent summons to headquarters would have intrigued and excited him, but now he only felt a vague, detached curiosity. He could not remember when he had first missed the sense of excitement and purpose that had suffused his early years with the Company; the change in him had been too gradual.

Ryder was waiting for him in a Mercedes 280SE. The car was so new that the factory scent still lingered in its interior. Ryder didn't ask Mallory what he thought of the car, and Mallory made no comment. Ryder lived as his means allowed and his taste required, not for show; it was one of the reasons Mallory liked him.

Mallory settled into the rich leather seat and relaxed as the Mercedes swept them away from the airport in air-conditioned comfort. Ryder turned onto a beltway that circled southward around Washington.

"How are Karen and the kids?" Mallory asked dutifully.

"Fine. Karen wants you to come to dinner, if time allows. She's missed you."

"Sure. I'd like that. You lucked out with her, Max."

"I know. With the kids, too. Margie is seventeen now, and Tom's twenty. He'll enter Harvard Law next year."

"Great."

Ryder kept the small talk going for a while, but Mallory had difficulty feigning interest. After they had driven for a time in silence, Ryder said, "What's the problem, Rich?"

"No problem."

"Then why so subdued? And don't tell me it's because you're tired."

"I've decided to quit, Max. I'm opting for early retirement."

Ryder nodded, and Mallory cocked an eyebrow. "You don't seem very surprised."

Ryder glanced in his sideview mirror, swung into the passing lane, and swept past a line of slower-moving cars. "Your letter of resignation is lying in my desk drawer."

"*Your* drawer? What's going on, Max?"

"Pendleton doesn't want you to resign just yet."

"Pendleton!" Mallory said incredulously, shifting in his seat to face Ryder. "What the hell does he have to do with it? I've n- never even laid eyes on the guy. And where do you come in? I thought you were in SR."

"I am," Ryder said calmly, but Mallory detected a hint of tension below the surface — or was it eagerness? "I'm doing a little moon- lighting for Pendleton. He wants you to run an op for him, and he wants me to act as your backstop at this end — and to help persuade you to take the job."

"What do you mean, he wants me to run an op for him? CI doesn't run operations."

"Officially, no. This one is strictly off the record."

Mallory frowned. "I repeat my question, Max. What the hell is going on?"

"I can't tell you a thing until Pendleton okays it, and first he's going to want to put you on the box."

"Oh, Christ," Mallory snorted. "That's a waste of time. I was on it two months ago. A team came down and checked out all the Station personnel."

"This is Pendleton's show, and he says to put you on the box."

Mallory shook his head. "You seem to have forgotten that I'm quitting."

Ryder compressed his lips in annoyance as a car swung into their lane in front of him and he had to brake sharply. "Look, Rich, this is something big. I kid you not. Don't quit until you've heard what Pendleton has to say."

"Let me get this straight," Mallory said. "Pendleton is about to set up an unauthorized operation, he's pulled you off your desk at SR, and he's intercepted my official letter of resignation. Just how does he expect to get away with it?"

"Pendleton can do whatever he pleases. You should know that. Even the DDO's writ doesn't extend to Pendleton's domain."

"He can even use a supergrader like you as an errand boy?"

"Rich — I'm interested. This could really be big, and it could make all the difference in the world to you. I know you think you want to quit, but that's because you've been stuck in the field too damned long. It's time you moved up, and this could do it for you. Play your cards right, and you'll come out of this with at least a GS-Fifteen."

"Wow."

"Can the crap, damn it," Ryder snapped. "You should have moved up long ago, and you would have, if you hadn't made a habit of saying the right thing to the wrong people at the wrong time."

"I know, I know. Be a team player and nice things will happen to you. Look, Max, you've been trying to look out for me ever since I've known you, and I appreciate it; but you can't make a silk purse out of a sow's ear. When you rescued me from that engineering job back in '47 and brought me into the Company, I was grateful — I still am. I wasn't ready to settle down then, but maybe I am now."

"That's what I'm saying! You can leave the field and move up. You can lead a settled life without leaving the Company. What the hell is the point in throwing away a whole career? What would you do on the outside, anyway?"

"I thought I'd try my hand at teaching, and I've got a temporary one-year appointment lined up at a prep school in Pennsylvania. Money's no problem in any event; I'll have my pension, and I've saved a fair amount over the years."

Ryder shook his head. "I can't see you as a teacher, Rich."

Mallory shrugged. "I can. What are you now, Max, a Sixteen?"

"Seventeen."

Mallory whistled softly. "Not bad."

Ryder had always played his cards right, Mallory thought, but he didn't begrudge Ryder his ambition or his success. He was the only administrator Mallory knew who had gotten his feet wet — who knew what it was all about. But Mallory had never understood how Ryder had resisted the urge to stay in the field. In the war, he had seemed almost addicted to danger. The answer, Mallory reflected, probably lay in Ryder's natural adaptability.

Mallory, in contrast, had never developed a tolerance for desk work or for the politics of advancement. He could guess what was written in his own 201 File: "a good operations man" — with the implication that he was unsuited for administrative duties.

"Do me a favor, Rich," Ryder said. "Don't ask me to forward your letter until you've talked to Pendleton. It won't kill you to listen."

Mallory sighed and settled back in his seat. "Okay," he said. Ryder was right; it wouldn't hurt to listen. In spite of himself, Mallory felt the tug of curiosity.

Ryder smiled and visibly relaxed. "You won't be sorry."

"I don't promise I won't quit afterward."

"Fair enough, but I'm going to work on you. Case officers never see the whole picture, only a small part of it. That's why you're jaded. Once you move up, you'll get the perspective you've been missing all these years."

"The big picture?"

"Exactly," Ryder said, not hearing the sarcasm in Mallory's voice.

Mallory smiled wearily. Ryder would never understand; he was a hard driver who never looked back. There was no point in telling Ryder that he no longer believed in the big picture.

Ryder turned off the highway onto an access road that cut through a small wood. As they came around a bend their way was blocked by an elaborate security gate.

"I love those flashing red lights," Mallory said. "You'd think the gate and the guards would suffice to make the point."

Ryder slowed the car, rolled down the window, and came to a stop beside a blue-uniformed guard. "Maxwell Ryder and Richard Mallory," he said, showing his pass and the one he'd brought along for Mallory. The guard nodded, wrote their names on a clipboard log, and waved them on. The gate opened, and Ryder drove through onto the campuslike grounds of Langley Headquarters and headed for the parking lot nearest the front entrance to the main building.

Mallory raised his eyebrows as Ryder pulled into a reserved parking slot marked with his name. "I thought only division chiefs rated reserved parking," Mallory remarked.

"I was made Deputy Chief of SR six months ago," Ryder said casually, handing Mallory a photo I.D. badge to pin to his lapel.

"In line for chief?"

"I think so."

Mallory digested the information as they got out of the car. If Pendleton had dragooned a man with Ryder's status, one thing was certain: the operation, whatever it was, had to be important.

Stepping out of the car was like stepping into a Turkish bath, and instantly Mallory felt himself begin to wilt in the humid Virginia heat. "Ah, home base," Mallory said, looking up at the massive, seven-story headquarters building that towered over them. "You supergraders must feel very close to heaven here."

The sprawling building had been built with a bureaucratic pecking order firmly in mind, and the space and amenities within it had been apportioned according to rank. The top floor was ringed by a ribbon of glass that formed the floor-to-ceiling win-

dows of the director's suite, the executive dining room, and the
offices for the Men at the Top.

Division chiefs were accorded comfortable offices on the lower
floors with leather easy chairs and sofas, and they were given
reserved parking near the main entrance. Branch chiefs received
smaller offices, and deputy branch chiefs were accorded cubicles
that they called offices. Section chiefs had to work in the open,
but their desks were positioned at windows and they were permitted to park in the south parking lot. Lowest on the totem pole
were the junior career officers, whose desks were jammed into
whatever space was available.

Langley Headquarters was a bureaucrat's dream.

"Have you ever had a homosexual experience, Mr. Mallory?"

"Well, I lay with a whore once who had a m-mustache. Down
in Juárez. But I was just a kid."

"Please don't be facetious," said the technician administering
the lie-detector test. He pursed his lips and penciled a notation
on the chart paper flowing out of the multichannel recorder on
his desk.

Mallory slouched in a padded leather chair beside the desk,
facing away from the chart recorder. A pressure cuff around his
left arm monitored his pulse, electrodes attached to his palms by
springs running across the backs of his hands measured his skin
resistance, and a rubber tube bound across his chest registered
changes in his breathing.

"Let's try that question again," the technician said with the
maddening patience of a telephone company employee handling
complaints. "Have you ever had a homosexual experience?"

"No."

"What was your mother's maiden name?"

"My real mother?"

"Yes."

"Marjorie Barnes."

"Where were you born?"

"Cleveland."

It was too warm in the soundproofed testing room and the

fluorescent lighting was too bright, and the dry, inflectionless voice of the technician running the test was too monotonous.

"How old are you?"

"Forty-nine."

"Have you been approached recently by an agent of a foreign power?"

"Yes."

"By whom?"

"Viktor Kurov. He runs the *residentura* in Buenos Aires."

"Did he try to recruit you?"

"No."

"Never?"

"No. He knew it would be a waste of time."

"Did you meet him more than once?"

"Yes. We met often."

"What was the basis of your association?"

Mallory shrugged. "I was —"

"Please don't make unnecessary movement! You're an old hand, Mr. Mallory; you should know the drill by now. Answer the question."

"I was just doing my job — trying to recruit him."

"And were you successful?"

"Up to a point."

"What point?"

"I was building rapport."

In a darkened, soundproofed office adjoining the windowless testing room, Ryder and Pendleton observed the interrogation through a panel of one-way glass. Mallory's bored voice carried clearly to them over a small loudspeaker in the wall beside the glass panel.

"It sounds like he has a cold," Pendleton remarked.

"His nose was badly broken, and it never healed properly," Ryder said, shifting restlessly in his seat. "Is this really necessary? I feel like a damned Peeping Tom."

"Don't. He knows he's being watched. He spotted the glass the moment he entered the room."

"Then what's the point?"

Pendleton ignored the question and continued to study Mallory. Ryder felt strangely ill at ease in the CI chief's presence. He couldn't decide if the feeling derived from Pendleton's mystique, or if it sprang from the man himself. Certainly in the semidarkness he was an eerie figure, gaunt and stoop-shouldered. The blue-gray light filtering through the one-way glass reflected off the tinted lenses of his owlish horn-rimmed glasses, effectively hiding his eyes.

"That puffiness around Mallory's eyes," Pendleton said. "Is that scar tissue or the result of too much drinking?"

"Scar tissue."

Pendleton nodded and refocused his attention on Mallory.

"I'd like to return to a question that seemed to give you some difficulty," the interrogator was saying, and Ryder shook his head. Mallory had been on the box too many times to be rattled by that shopworn ploy.

"I'll repeat the question now," said the interrogator. "Are you absolutely loyal to the United States Government?"

"More or less."

"What is that supposed to mean?"

"I'm a Democrat."

Pendleton smiled thinly. "He doesn't give a damn, does he?"

"He did once," Ryder said.

"But can we count on him now?"

Ryder hesitated for only a fraction of a second before he answered. "He's the best ops man I know."

"Don't hedge," Pendleton said, swiveling his head to look at Ryder.

"I don't really know," Ryder responded coolly.

"Why not? You used to be close friends."

"We've been out of touch for a long time."

Pendleton returned his gaze to Mallory in the interrogation room. Ryder expected Pendleton to say something more, to ask if he still trusted Mallory, but Pendleton remained silent. The silence stretched out, broken only by the droning of questions and answers drifting over the loudspeaker, and it drew from Ryder the answer to the unasked question.

"It's not a matter of loyalty," Ryder said. "If Mallory agrees to do the job, he'll do it well. The question is, will he agree?"

"You're referring to his letter of resignation."

"Yes."

"Well, you've asked him to cooperate, and I assume you have explained to him the rewards he can expect. As a friend, your advice should carry weight. You've done your part; the rest is up to me."

The box man turned Mallory loose shortly after eleven A.M. Mallory rolled down his sleeve, slipped on his suit jacket, and left the testing room. Ryder was waiting for him in the hall.

"We have some time to kill before Pendleton can see you," Ryder said. "How about some coffee?"

"I could use it," Mallory said, carefully rubbing his eyes and wishing that he'd removed his contact lenses. The need for sleep was dragging him down, and the long lie-detector test had left him with a dull, throbbing headache.

"We'll get some in my office. I still hang my hat in SR."

They walked down the long corridor. The hallway was lined on both sides with color-coded office doors. The bright red, yellow, and blue doors invariably reminded Mallory of a child's nursery. Several of the staffers who passed them nodded and smiled to Ryder. A number of the building guards monitoring the traffic in the corridors obviously also recognized Ryder, but they did not smile, and they scrutinized his badge as closely as they did Mallory's.

Ryder and Mallory took an elevator to the floor below and walked down another long corridor to the Soviet Russia Division. Ryder led Mallory into one of the division's office complexes. In the common room, surrounded by a dozen small offices, junior officers sat hunched at desks squeezed in between filing cabinets and safes, trying to compose reports and replies to routine cables amidst the clatter of secretaries' typewriters and general office chatter.

A group of staffers had gathered in front of a bulletin board on which a flash cable had just been posted. The cable board was one of the attractions of working at Langley. It gave all staffers immediate access to secret information flashed from the far corners of the world, and for many it became addictive. For Mallory, the thrill had long since worn off. The feeling of being in the know was largely illusory; sooner or later, he knew, anything of real importance could be found in the back pages of the *New York Times*.

"Two black coffees, when you get the chance, Merle," Ryder said to a comely clerk-typist at a desk just inside the door to the corridor. "On second thought, make that three."

"Certainly, Mr. Ryder," the girl said, getting up immediately.

Ryder turned and led Mallory across the hall to the yellow door of his private office. He turned the dials on the combination lock, opened the door, and ushered Mallory inside, leaving the door open. The large desk, padded leather chairs, drapes, and carpet were sufficiently expensive to match Ryder's status, but they were also sufficiently tasteless to indicate that he had had no part in their selection.

Ryder took his seat behind the desk and gestured to Mallory to sit down. Instead, Mallory walked to the large, tinted, plate-glass window and looked out. "Gee," he said. "A view of the loading dock."

"Nothing but the best," Ryder replied with an easy grin. "Pull up a chair. Here's the coffee."

The secretary had appeared with three cups of coffee on a tray, which she set on the desk. "Shall I close the door on the way out, Mr. Ryder?"

"Yes, please. And thanks for the coffee."

The secretary left, and Mallory sat down, immediately reaching for the coffee. "I assume that the two cups are for me."

"Naturally. I'll say one thing for SR: we have the best coffee in the whole damned place."

"You should have let me get some s-sleep, Max," Mallory said, balancing his coffee on the arm of the chair as he took out his cigarettes. "I feel like hell." He lit up and tossed the pack to Ryder.

"No, thanks. I've quit."

"Oh, for Christ's sake!" Mallory snorted and retrieved the pack. He drank the coffee down in four quick gulps and reached for the second cup.

"I can get more coffee if you want," Ryder said.

Mallory shook his head and settled back in his chair. "Okay, Max. I've been on the b-box, and Pendleton has had a good look at me. Now, what's the scoop?"

"Pendleton wants to lay it out for you personally."

Mallory frowned and rubbed his eyes. Games and more games. How they loved them at Langley — like kids in a sandbox. The games went with the nursery-school doors. But he wasn't in the mood for games; he was sleepy and his head hurt.

"Does Pendleton know that I don't have a spooky clearance?"

"He knows."

"Then isn't this a waste of time? I thought anyone coming near CI country had to have a Staff D."

"Only for access to Comint, and that won't be necessary in this case. Besides, this is a special, one-shot deal. The red tape is being cut."

Mallory looked hard at Ryder. "Don't tell me," he said suspiciously, "that Pendleton is running this op out of his pocket."

Ryder did not respond immediately, but finally he nodded.

"Terrific," Mallory groaned. "That's just terrific. Whatever it is, count me out."

"You said you'd hear him out."

"So, I changed my mind. I'm not interested in acting out a role in one of Pendleton's fantasies. I don't want to get sucked into his convoluted world. I just want early retirement."

Ryder sighed, took a sip of coffee, and said quietly, "Okay, Rich."

Mallory raised his eyebrows in surprise. "Okay? Just like that?"

Ryder shrugged. "If that's the way you want it, that's it. I'll forward your letter of resignation today, and you'll be processed out by the end of the week."

"And how will that affect you?"

"It won't affect my career, if that's what you mean. No problem. It just cuts me out of this little business."

Mallory frowned. "I don't get it. First you give me the hard sell, and now, suddenly, you ease off. Why?"

"Give me one of those butts of yours, will you?" Ryder said.

Mallory grinned wickedly and tossed Ryder the pack. He struck a match and leaned across the desk to give Ryder a light. Ryder inhaled and sighed with satisfaction. "You're worse than Eve with the apple."

"I prefer the image of the serpent," Mallory said.

"I'm easing off," Ryder said, "because we're friends, and I've had some second thoughts. Pendleton hasn't said so explicitly, but once he fills you in I don't think he'll let you take a walk until this business is finished. If you're sure you want to quit, do it now."

"I don't understand why my quitting cuts you out."

"I'm not absolutely sure it would," Ryder said, "but the principal reason I'm in at all is because of you. He wants you, Rich, and he wants me to hook you. He also knows that we've worked together, and that we trust each other, so I'm a natural choice to backstop your action from this end. He hasn't given me the whole story yet — just the punch line — but I'm interested. Real interested. This has the makings, Rich — not career stuff, the real thing."

"But why the hell does he want me?"

"Why not? He needs a good operations man, and you're one of the best we have."

Mallory grimaced. "Sure," he said sarcastically. "That's why I've been on the shelf for two years."

"Look, it's your choice. I'm through twisting your arm."

"Why do I feel I'm being had, Max?" he said.

"Because you're a suspicious son of a bitch, that's why."

"Yeah, well, that comes from a rich and varied experience."

"That may be," Ryder said, "but you know I wouldn't con you."

"And Pendleton? He's straight as an arrow, I suppose."

"If you listen to what he has to say, you can judge for yourself. There's no other way."

"Will I get the Lecture?"

Ryder laughed. "I don't know. I've never heard it myself."

154 -

"Too bad. I'd like to talk to someone who's actually heard it. My guess is that it compares favorably with Sterling Hayden's m-monologue in *Dr. Strangelove* — the one about the world-wide conspiracy to pollute our precious bodily fluids."

Ryder shook his head. "Pendleton isn't crazy. He may be too intense, but he's also brilliant."

"Intense! That must be the understatement of the decade. I've run afoul of his acolytes often enough to know that much. They think the only reasonable way to deal with a man is to b-bug his room, tap his phone, read his mail, and put him on the box. Then, when they've exposed the intimate details of his private life, they *really* distrust him."

"But we've never been penetrated," Ryder said pointedly, "not deeply, at any rate. And that we owe to Pendleton."

"And I'd like a dollar for every operation that's been needlessly paralyzed because of CI's suspicions. Pendleton plays with a stacked deck, Max; he can't lose. He simply suspects everyone indiscriminately. Whenever a rotten apple does turn up, people say, 'That Pendleton is brilliant. He had the guy pegged from the beginning.' And they ignore the countless times his suspicions are unfounded. Those wild swings just add to his m-mystique: 'Wow, Pendleton is so tough-minded he even suspects the DCI.'"

"Maybe it takes a man like that to keep the house clean. Otherwise we might have our own Philby sitting in an office on the seventh floor."

"I don't think so," Mallory said. "I think it's the other way around; the job shapes the man. Pendleton has spent a lifetime hunting for a mole, and he's never found one. But he can't stop hunting, because he can't prove the mole doesn't exist. What does that do to a man? He's condemned to go on and on, forever searching, never satisfied —"

Mallory broke off suddenly and stared at Ryder, who returned his gaze impassively. "Is that what this is all about, Max? A mole hunt?"

Ryder's eyes remained carefully neutral. "I can't discuss the op, Rich. This is Pendleton's game, and you play it by his rules or not at all."

In the silence Mallory heard the ticking of a miniature pendulum clock on a shelf behind Ryder's desk. Mallory had given him the clock as a wedding present.

"When am I slated to see him?" Mallory asked.

"In fifteen minutes. Are you in or out?"

Mallory picked up his coffee cup and drained the last of the coffee. It was cold and bitter-tasting.

13

THE black, lighttight drapes were drawn across the windows of Pendleton's office when Mallory entered, and the room was lit only by the reading lamp on Pendleton's cluttered desk. Although the room was large, it was crammed with safes, filing cabinets, and tables sagging under the weight of unfamiliar apparatus, some of which appeared to Mallory to be photographic equipment. The room was more inner sanctum than office, Mallory thought, and despite the modern paraphernalia, the atmosphere was somehow medieval.

Yet the man who rose from behind his desk to greet Mallory with a somewhat shy smile seemed disarmingly normal. Mallory judged him to be about sixty. He was a lanky man, and he had the stoop-shouldered posture of one who is not comfortable with his height. Age had loosened the skin on his mobile face, and the lines in his forehead were deeply furrowed. With his drooping, worn tweed jacket and horn-rimmed glasses, he looked very much like a college professor, which was precisely what he would have been, had it not been for the war and the OSS.

"I'm Tom Pendleton," he said, brushing back a shock of thick, gray hair from his forehead and leaning across the desk to shake hands.

"Richard Mallory."

"Have a seat," Pendleton said, sitting down. He picked up a

briar pipe and began stoking it with tobacco from a worn leather pouch. Mallory settled himself in a lumpy, ancient armchair in front of the desk. For several seconds Pendleton was fully occupied with the ritual of tamping and lighting his pipe.

Mallory looked in amazement at the clutter on Pendleton's desk. The desk was covered with vertically stacked In and Out trays filled to overflowing with documents and folders, which were festooned with bright red Top Secret tabs. Mallory had never seen so many highly classified papers outside of a safe at one time.

Mallory sniffed audibly as the pungent smoke from Pendleton's pipe drifted across the desk.

"Balkan Sobranie," Pendleton said. "It helps to keep the bugs away — real bugs, I mean — when I'm out fishing. Are you an angler?"

Mallory shook his head, though he was sure Pendleton already knew the answer. Pendleton would know everything there was to know about him.

"Has Max filled you in?" Pendleton asked conversationally.

"No, sir."

Pendleton peered at Mallory through the large, round lenses of his glasses, as if he expected to hear more, but Mallory just let the silence stretch out.

"I understand that you want to resign," Pendleton said at last.

"That was my intention."

"May I ask why?"

Mallory shrugged. "A man named Kurov diagnoses it as a case of ennui. That sums it up pretty well, I suppose."

"But you've had a change of heart?"

Mallory crossed his legs and looked steadily at Pendleton. "I'm here to listen," he said noncommittally.

"Why?"

"Max told me it's important, and he's not given to exaggeration."

Pendleton swiveled around in his chair to free his legs, crossed them and leaned back, puffing on his pipe, no longer looking at

Mallory. "Kurov was your KGB counterpart in Buenos Aires. What sort of man is he?"

"Smart, old guard, a survivor — but out of favor at the moment," Mallory said. He couldn't decide if Pendleton was really probing, or if delay was just part of his style. "Kurov wasn't my counterpart, though. He was the *resident* in Buenos Aires — more the COS's speed."

"Why did he cultivate you?"

Mallory shrugged. "I always looked at it the other way around: that I was c-cultivating him."

"And why did you consider him to be out of favor in Moscow?"

"He's a pro, and he's wasted down there."

"Like yourself?"

Mallory didn't bite, and again there was a silence.

"You say you were cultivating him," Pendleton said. "Did you think he might be susceptible to an offer?"

"Not really. You can't turn a man like Kurov."

"Then why did you persist in meeting with him?"

"I liked him."

"And what did your COS think of the arrangement?"

"He loved it. Burgess is a great believer in the Hard Target Program."

"And you're not, I take it."

Mallory shook his head.

"I would have to agree with you," Pendleton said to Mallory's surprise. "Our CE staff lacks the single-minded dedication and patience of their KGB counterparts, and the problem of recruiting potential penetration agents is hardly a symmetrical one. Since our offense is weak, we must have the stronger defense. That's my job."

Pendleton's pipe had died on him, and he paused to relight it. "By the way, you can smoke if you wish," he said, waving his burning match in the air to extinguish it.

"Are we through with the preliminaries, sir?"

Pendleton smiled and turned back to face Mallory. "You're not exactly overawed by rank, are you, Mallory?" he said mildly. "Very well, we'll get down to business. Three weeks ago, I received information that a well-placed officer in the East German SSD wants to defect. He can get himself out, but apparently not his wife. He won't come over unless we agree to extract her at the same time. He has given himself the cryptonym, Martin."

"What's the exchange commodity?" Mallory asked, looking for the punch line. An SSD defector was nothing to get excited about.

"The identity of a Soviet penetration agent here at Langley."

Pendleton peered at Mallory, awaiting his reaction, and Mallory wondered how Pendleton expected him to react. A KGB mole at Langley was the stuff of legend, always rumored but never found. Yet any excitement Mallory might have felt was canceled by skepticism. Had it not been for Ryder's interest and Pendleton's reputation, he would have smiled in derision.

"And you're buying that?" Mallory asked without inflection.

"Shouldn't I?"

"My quick answer would be no," Mallory said, realizing full well that Pendleton needed no instruction from him. "Even if there is a KGB plant in the Company, it's hardly plausible that an SSD officer would have the goods on him."

"It's implausible, perhaps," Pendleton said, "but not absolutely impossible. Whenever there is cooperation between intelligence services, there is the chance of a security breach. Martin may have run across the information purely by chance . . ." Pendleton arched his eyebrows, rippling his forehead, over which a shock of gray hair had again fallen, and the corners of his mouth turned upward in a suggestion of amusement. "I take it you're not impressed."

"I think this Martin is pulling your leg — sir."

"Then he is doing it with sophistication and a surprising expenditure of effort," Pendleton said. "Last month, an agent working in the Zone narrowly escaped being picked up in an SSD raid. He escaped because of a telephone warning, and with that warning came our defector's initial message — to be passed directly to me, and not to anyone else in the Company. Martin's choice of courier was clever; it virtually guaranteed the transmission of the message to me, and to me alone."

"Then the agent who was blown wasn't ours."

"No."

Israeli, Mallory decided. Liaison between the CIA and the Mossad was Pendleton's personal fiefdom — an anomaly in the CIA's organizational structure that Pendleton had preserved for twenty years. Passing a message to Pendleton via the Israelis was as secure a means of bypassing CIA channels as any Mallory could think of.

"If Martin is a fake," Pendleton continued, "he is playing his part carefully — as if he is a man who remembers the fate of the would-be defectors who tried to warn the British about Philby. He took great care to ensure that his message would not be intercepted by the man he seeks to expose."

"I take it that you don't know Martin's identity, nor the identity of the supposed sleeper," Mallory said tiredly. He was still willing to hear Pendleton out, but it was with a growing sense of anticlimax that he listened; the idea that an SSD officer could hand them a KGB mole on a platter was incredible. Mallory felt fatigue closing in on him again.

"No, we don't know who Martin is," Pendleton said. "Not yet. Martin is playing his cards very close to his vest. His initial message only stated that he wished to defect and that he needed our help. There was no mention of a Soviet agent. He specified a dead drop in the Zone that we could use to make further contact. I do have access to certain limited operational resources, and I used them to open the dead-drop channel — bypassing Berlin Station. Through the dead drop I learned what Martin is offering. He is not yet ready to reveal himself or the identity of the agent-in-place."

"I wouldn't touch it with a ten-foot pole, if I were you," Mallory said, surprised at the disappointment he felt. "Either you're dealing with some shlub who thinks he can con us into pulling his wife out of the Zone, or this is a second-rate SSD setup."

"I'm not stupid, Mallory," Pendleton said too quietly, and the softness of his voice had a more chilling effect than if he had spoken in open anger. "And I can assure you that this is neither a one-man con nor an SSD setup."

Mallory blinked and straightened in his chair, trying to shake off the tightening coils of fatigue. Pendleton might be paranoid, but, as he had just sharply reminded Mallory, he was no fool.

Satisfied that he had made his point, Pendleton continued. "Martin has agreed to reveal himself, and to provide absolute proof of the value of his information, but not until the last possible moment — and not to a courier or a contract agent. He insists on meeting with a Company case officer. The meeting will take place once we've set up the extraction and are prepared to go through with it immediately upon confirmation of his bona fides. The meeting will be in East Berlin, on his terms, and we must be in a position to extract his wife that same day. That rules out a one-man con. If he can't deliver proof of value, he gains nothing."

"A case officer, you said. Me?"

Pendleton sucked noisily on his pipe, spit gurgling in the stem. "That's what I had in mind."

Mallory frowned. Asking to meet with a case officer was an odd wrinkle. CIA case officers worked their agents at arm's length; they never did the dirty work themselves. Unlike the KGB, the CIA didn't send its officers in close under real cover. If they ran an operation from inside foreign territory, they worked under diplomatic cover — and diplomatic immunity.

"Why demand a case officer?" Mallory said. "If he is an SSD officer, he knows that cuts against the grain."

"It makes sense from his point of view. If we risk sending a case officer into the Zone to meet him, it guarantees that we're serious. We match his risk with our own, and we're unlikely to take half measures to extract his wife."

"That assumes this is a genuine defection. It could equally well be a simple SSD setup. Now that they've destroyed poor old Gehlen's networks and driven him into retirement, they must be fairly cocky. And with no more BND agents to put on television, they may be getting restless. I could walk into East Berlin in the morning and find myself on DDR television that evening. It's a hell of a simple way to burn a Company man, and it would make great copy."

"An SSD trap is out of the question," Pendleton said flatly.

"The East Germans can play in their own backyard, but they wouldn't dare stir up our nest without KGB approval."

"Why should the KGB disapprove? If we get burned, we'll be slower to respond to genuine defectors."

"That may be the way our own dirty-tricksters would play it," Pendleton said disparagingly. "They're fond of simple ploys. But the Soviets are not."

Pendleton tapped the ashes from his pipe and laid it aside. His glasses had slipped down on the bridge of his nose, and he tilted back in his chair to look at Mallory through the lenses.

"Defection is the principal weakness in the Soviet intelligence service," he said, "and the KGB does its best to stop defectors before they cross over. Yet the KGB has turned its own weakness to an advantage — by slipping us the occasional poisoned pawn. A well-trained, determined agent posing as a defector can feed us twisted information that will tie us in knots for years. That is why this is not an SSD trap. The KGB would never permit such an operation. To discourage us from welcoming defectors with open arms would be to ruin their own game."

Pendleton paused and pushed his glasses back into place. He looked steadily at Mallory, his eyes insisting that Mallory accept his argument. Perhaps it was Pendleton himself, or the strange atmosphere in his office, but Mallory was drawn by the convoluted logic, and he gave a slight, involuntary nod of tentative agreement. As if that were a cue, Pendleton began speaking again.

"It is an obvious trick, but it works — again and again. It works because too few of us are willing to accept the patient deviousness of the Russian mind. And I deliberately say Russian, not Soviet. Oh, we give lip service to the Russian penchant for secrecy, to their congenital distrust, but it is lip service only. The KGB continues to succeed because Westerners cling to the belief that, deep down, the Russians are like us. *They are not.*"

Mallory wondered briefly if this was the beginning of the legendary Lecture, but the thought was only fleeting as Pendleton continued to speak, compelling his attention — patiently, seductively urging him to follow his reasoning.

"There is a school of thought within the Soviet intelligence community — primarily in the GRU — that emphasizes straight-forward intelligence gathering. The GRU relies heavily on open sources and on Comint from their own version of NSA, but it is the KGB that truly reflects the Russian mind. KGB analysts fundamentally distrust open sources; they believe nothing unless it is obtained secretly. The determination to extract all information, however trivial, by secret means is difficult for Westerners to accept.

"For years we've laughed about the KGB agent who spent eighteen months developing an agent in the Washington Weather Bureau to obtain meteorological data he could have gotten by simply asking to be placed on the bureau's mailing list. You must have heard the story. What you may not realize is that it's true. And it's not funny. That apparently ludicrous story reveals a single-minded dedication to intelligence by penetration that permeates every fiber of the KGB. Those who laugh simply lack the imagination to visualize what such an organization, working over decades, can accomplish.

"We cannot take the measure of the KGB as long as we dismiss Russian deviousness as an understandable quirk — a temporary societal aberration. We must accept it as a permanent fact of life. It is what gives the enemy its limitless potential, its love for the long, deep game.

"There is not one major Western government that the KGB is not continually attempting to penetrate. That is hardly a secret, yet each time a new penetration is uncovered, the reaction is shock. And each time the fundamental lesson goes unlearned.

"We refuse to draw the obvious inference from the agents who are occasionally exposed: that there are others who have not been detected. By what stretch of the imagination can one assume that every KGB penetration ends in exposure? Is it reasonable to suppose that every KGB agent will recklessly betray himself like Felfe in the BND, or risk entanglement with degenerate acquaintances as Philby did? And if it is unreasonable to make this supposition, one *must* acknowledge the probability that KGB agents are still in place and active.

"The danger of these agents is not merely in the intelligence

they provide, but also in their ability to facilitate further penetrations — to help new agents filter through our security screens.
Until we root out the agents already in place, our attempts
to bar the door to future penetrations can only be partially
effective.

"The *primary* mission of Western counterintelligence," Pendleton concluded, rapping on his desk for emphasis, "should be
the exposure of Soviet penetration agents. To do this, we must
rely on method; but always, Mallory — always — we hope for
luck."

"Luck, I presume, in the person of a man called Martin," Mallory said.

"Perhaps."

"Do you really think that Martin is genuine?"

Pendleton shook his head. "I said we hope for luck. We don't
necessarily believe in it. Still," he added, selecting another pipe
from the rack on his desk and stoking it with tobacco, "it is a
possibility we cannot ignore."

"And *you* are willing to take the risk."

Pendleton smiled disarmingly. "I take your point, but if it is a
trap, you are not the target."

"Who, then?"

Pendleton struck a match and put it to the pipe. "Me."

"You think Martin is one of the poisoned pawns?"

"Quite probably."

"But you won't consider passing him by."

"No. Even if Martin is a plant, we can hope to learn something
from him. We can't defeat the opposition unless we're willing to
engage."

"And if I don't choose to play?"

"Let me be plain. If I knew for certain that Martin is a KGB
plant, I would not ask for your help. It is because Martin just
might be genuine that I want you to go in. We have good, young
operations men, but they only know how to *run* agents. If they
had to go in themselves without diplomatic cover, they'd wet their
pants. You're a relic, Mallory — a man who's worked as an agent
as well as a case officer."

"That was a long time ago," Mallory said quietly. "I'm not the kid who saluted and jumped into France."

"Still, you've been there. *If* Martin is genuine, I don't want to lose him. If something should go sour, you have the best chance of getting Martin through. You speak the language like a native, and you know this game inside out."

"I know this much: if something goes wrong, I won't know it until they put the cuffs on me."

Pendleton shook his head impatiently. "You're still thinking the SSD is out to burn you. Forget that. There are only two possibilities: either this is a KGB ploy to plant a ringer on us, in which case you'll have no trouble at all, or Martin is genuine. If he is, there is risk for you, but I think you'll agree it's worth it."

"Maybe I would now," Mallory remarked dryly, "but I'm not sure I'd feel the same way about it in an East German jail."

"I would have you out in less than three months."

"An exchange? The SSD is perverse, you know — as was Gehlen. The Germans are not always willing to make a civilized deal."

"I won't be trading SSD agents; it will be a KGB man we already have cold. He was blown six months ago, but we've been letting him run. The SSD will spring you whether they like it or not; Moscow will see to that."

"Even three months can be a long time," Mallory said, "if they want you to talk."

"Then talk," Pendleton said calmly.

Mallory stared at Pendleton for a moment, and then he nodded slowly. At last he understood why Pendleton had dragged him out of mothballs for this operation. He had one attribute of crucial importance to Pendleton: he was expendable. He had been out of the mainstream of Company operations for so long he didn't know anything worth the telling. Suddenly he wanted to get out in the open, out of Pendleton's cryptlike office.

"I'll have to think it over," Mallory said, standing up.

Pendleton looked at his watch. "Be back by two. I can give you that much time. We'll go over the details then."

Mallory cocked his eyebrow. "Are you so sure of me then?"

Pendleton was looking up at Mallory, but the oversized lenses of his glasses caught the light from the desk lamp at an angle that rendered them opaque. His pipe was clenched firmly in the corner of his mouth, and neither the set of his lips nor his permanently furrowed brow held any definitive expression. "You are a logical man," he said, "and the logic is clear. If this *is* a setup, it is a KGB operation with no danger for you. If, on the other hand, Martin is genuine, getting him out would be worth the risk."

"Worth it to you," Mallory said.

Pendleton nodded. "And to you, as well, I think. In any event, we'll soon know, won't we."

14

MALLORY watched a group of fresh recruits on their orientation tour file into the domed auditorium that had been erected beside the main building. He had eaten a quick, indifferent lunch in the cafeteria and then had gone outside for a walk around the grounds. He had hoped the walk would make it easier to think, but the oppressive heat and humidity had only intensified his headache. Now his body demanded a respite, and on impulse he headed for the auditorium, following a circuitous route from shade tree to shade tree across the well-kept lawns. In the auditorium he could cool off without having to talk to anyone. He had made his decision; now he needed to come to terms with it.

He sighed with relief as he came into the auditorium's lobby and cool air washed over him. He paused inside the entrance to wipe the sweat from his forehead and neck. The door to the auditorium was open, and he could hear the voice of the recruits' orientation officer. The man had already swung into his upbeat, Dale Carnegie spiel.

As Mallory walked quietly into the auditorium and slipped into a seat in the last row, the orientation officer glanced up at him briefly, decided he was harmless, and rattled on without missing a beat. Mallory loosened his tie and settled back to listen. At least, he thought wryly, the talk might provide some comic relief.

"In the next few weeks you will be working harder than you have ever worked before," the orientation officer was saying in a carefully modulated baritone, "learning the basic skills the Company requires of its case officers — skills that you will continue to perfect as you grow and develop in the course of your career.

"At times you may feel that you cannot master all that we demand of you, but I assure you that you would not have been selected for career training if you did not possess the dedication, intelligence, imagination, and integrity necessary to achieve the goals we set for you — and the goals you will set for yourselves. We ask you to aim high, ladies and gentlemen, aim high . . ."

Mallory couldn't see the faces of the recruits, who were listening with rapt attention, but he could have profiled the group of thirty-three men and six women without seeing them at all. Gone were the days of haphazard, seat-of-the-pants recruitment.

The men would be in their mid to late twenties, and most of them would have served as military officers. The women would be somewhat younger. All would be college graduates, and at least half of them would have higher degrees. One or two would be black. The officer candidates might not represent the best and the brightest in the land, but they would all be above the average for government service. Their physical appearance and psychological profiles — thoroughly tested — would fall within the narrow limits the Agency considered optimum: not too short, not too tall, clean-cut, not too aggressive, not too passive, and with no detectable eccentricities. And all would be Loyal Americans.

Mallory had once suggested to a recruitment specialist that the elaborate psychological examinations the Company used to screen applicants could be eliminated and replaced by a simple, twenty-second test: if the applicant could recite the Boy Scout motto with obvious sincerity, he was Company material.

This orientation officer was good, Mallory thought as he watched the man's slick performance. He was personable, sincere, and smooth as glass.

". . . and it is part of my job to give you an overview of what you can expect from your career — an overview you may find useful in the hectic weeks ahead, when the course load may seem too heavy and you find it hard to see the forest for the trees. Down on the Farm they will feed it to you fast and heavy: tailing a rabbit, agent radio communication, Flaps and Seals, use of the Identikit, SW, unarmed combat, codes and ciphers, the use of cutouts and dead drops — in short, all the elements of tradecraft . . ."

That's it, Mallory thought, give them a quick jolt of the jargon right off the bat — a heady whiff of espionage. That's why they're here; that's why we're all here.

"But, ladies and gentlemen, tradecraft alone does not make a good case officer. Many personal qualities are necessary, and perhaps the most important is morality. *Yes,* I said morality. The most moral individuals make the best case officers, because the agents with whom you must build rapport can sense this. The CIA never lets its agents down, and that is why so many people, in so many dangerous areas of the world, agree to work for us. We do not cynically use people; we look after our own. Our case officers are caring individuals . . ."

Maybe so, Mallory thought bitterly, but what about the supergraders who pull the strings from Washington. One thing was certain: this bright, smooth young man had never sat up all night in Germany, drinking with a cold-eyed ethnic who would be jumping into oblivion the next day. *How many men did I lose on those useless Black Ops into Russia? Three? Four? There was Majek, and the blond kid, Karule . . . Christ, I can't remember the others. Why can't I remember the names?*

". . . and despite what you may have heard, we do not bribe agents. The people who work for CIA do so out of a thirst for freedom. Often it is necessary to alleviate an agent's financial difficulties — to eliminate a possible distraction that might interfere with his work on behalf of the Free World — but when we pay an agent, we do so on the basis of a contract. Contractual remuneration is not a bribe . . ."

Does he believe this crap he's handing out? These kids will get the straight scoop soon enough down on the Farm: buy the agent, not his information. Gear the payments to his standard of living — just enough to keep him dependent.

"Oh, there may be times when you are forced to engage in activities you may find distasteful," the orientation officer said with a deprecating smile, "The development of a special-access agent, for example . . ."

Mallory saw a girl in the row of seats farthest from the orientation officer turn to a young man seated next to her and whisper to him. The recruit shrugged and shook his head in ignorance.

Mallory smiled. *Hookers, young lady. Special-access agents are hookers.*

"There will be times when you are in the field in a part of the world that seems unimportant," the orientation officer said, "but remember, wherever you are sent you will be developing as a case officer — adding to your experience, perfecting your tradecraft . . ."

Pendleton was right, Mallory thought, I am a relic — one of the few operations men still working who had learned tradecraft the hard way. Mallory doubted that the Company would even consider an application from a kid like him now. Too insecure, too small, too nearsighted, too big a chip on his shoulder. The computer would process the data and spit out the card.

Very few of the old OSS hands were left — not the foot soldiers, at any rate, most of whom had failed to adapt to changing times. In contrast, OSS administrative types like Helms, who had sat out the war in London, learning to say, "Let's get on with it," had flourished. Some OSS analysts had also survived, chief among them Pendleton.

Now the orientation officer was blithely assuring the recruits that the quality of their reports from the field would be what counted, not the quantity, and Mallory knew it was time to leave. In another minute he would be shouting, "Bullshit!" He looked at his watch. He had stalled long enough; Pendleton would be waiting for him.

As Mallory got up and turned away from the group of recruits, he smiled wryly. Was he so different from these wide-eyed youngsters? For all his cynicism, he could not shake off Pendleton's hook: the possibility that Martin was genuine. Pendleton was offering him a chance, however slim, at a counterintelligence coup, and after so many years in which his energies, training, and experience had been wasted, Mallory couldn't resist making a try for it.

The elevator door opened with a sigh, and Mallory stepped out and headed for D Corridor. As he walked into CI territory the number of doors that were closed and "vaulted" with combination locks and electronic sensors increased dramatically. Pendleton's world was as hermetically sealed as humanly possible.

As Mallory passed one of those doors, it opened and a thin, middle-aged woman emerged, locked it behind her, and scurried past Mallory, a sheaf of papers clutched to her chest. She flitted by a watchful building guard, moving as quickly as she could without actually breaking into a run. Running in the corridors was strictly forbidden, and an unwary trainee could make the guard's day by giving him an excuse to blow his police whistle.

Mallory stopped before the door to Pendleton's office and knocked, wondering if Pendleton had deliberately chosen red for his door. He heard the double click of the electronic latches disengaging, and as he opened the door to the inner sanctum, it occurred to him that someone should jimmy the hinges so that they would creak — for effect.

"Sit down, Mallory," Pendleton said. "I take it you're ready to hear the details."

"I'm ready."

Pendleton nodded. He had known Mallory was hooked as soon as two o'clock had passed and he had not arrived. Had Mallory intended to refuse, he would have come on time.

"Martin has set the meeting for three P.M. on August second, at Alexanderplatz," Pendleton said.

"That's this coming Saturday. You're cutting it a bit fine, aren't you? What if I'd said no and you had to find another boy?"

"You didn't say no," Pendleton replied, puffing contentedly on his pipe. "Martin will make contact at the fountain in the center of the square. You are to approach the fountain and stand or sit beside it on the north side precisely at three P.M. As soon as you have reached the fountain, you are to tighten the shoelace of one shoe and then walk around to the south side and await contact. He will introduce himself as Martin, and you will respond by giving your name as Simon. You are to wait no more than five minutes. If, for any reason, the meeting is a washout, a second rendezvous is set for the next day, at the same time and place."

"I'm going to need men for the extraction."

"Berlin Station has already lined up a team. If you don't like their plan for the extraction, there will be time to change it."

"Who's the COS?"

"Avery Hollis."

"I don't know him."

"Five years your junior. A trifle unimaginative, perhaps, but reliable. He'll do what he's asked to do."

"How much does he know?"

"Only what Ryder has told him: that SR is about to extract an agent escaping via the Zone. There was no mention of the SSD or of a defector. Ryder is my cutout in this, and he will be your sole contact here at Langley. As far as Berlin Station is concerned — or anyone else, for that matter — this is an SR op."

"I get the impression that you're running this out of your pocket."

"Yes," Pendleton said. "Any objections?"

Mallory smiled slightly. Pendleton knew the answer to that question. Without official Agency backing, Mallory was solely dependent on Pendleton to get him out if things went sour. If Ryder had not been there to watch his back, he would have turned Pendleton down cold.

"You will be given full support," Pendleton said, "just as you would if this were a top-priority SR op. The operation cryptonym is QLRAIN. Your cryptonym is Simon; Ryder's is Sam. You'll have a flash commo channel between Sam and Berlin Station open to you at all times."

"Has Max been fully briefed?" Mallory asked, but he had already guessed the answer.

"Not completely," Pendleton said evenly.

"You mean you didn't tell him that I'd be going into East Berlin m-myself."

"No."

No, Mallory thought sourly, you're too smart for that. Had Ryder known, he might not have been so willing to play along.

"How much clout will I have in Berlin?"

"Hollis will give you anything you ask for."

"You told me that you didn't use Hollis's men to contact Martin. I want to know who serviced the dead drop."

Pendleton was silent for a moment, but then he nodded. "The Israelis."

"Mossad?"

"Yes."

"Okay," Mallory said, satisfied. It was what he had assumed, but he'd wanted to be sure. The Israelis, at least, could be counted on not to trip over their own feet. If the SSD knew about Martin, it would not be because of clumsy service of the dead drop. "I don't know what Hollis has in mind, but I intend to use a diplomatic car for the extraction."

"I'll leave that up to you. Martin has supplied us with a physical description of his wife for passport purposes."

"What did your computers make of it?"

"Nothing definitive. Our files on SSD personnel and their families are not that complete, and one can't trust the age and hair color Martin gave us. Wigs are easy enough to come by."

Mallory had put off smoking for as long as he could, and he took out his cigarettes. "Why is Martin intent on coming across on his own instead of coming out with his wife?"

Pendleton shook his head. "I don't know. His dead-drop messages have been terse, to say the least."

"If I can persuade him to come out with his wife, would you have any objection?"

"No."

"All right," Mallory said, lighting a cigarette. "Now we come to the sixty-four-dollar question. I'm going to have to decide on the spot whether or not he's worth extracting. How choosy do you want me to be?"

"If he's an obvious plant, forget him and get out. Anything less than a full-dress KGB ploy isn't worth our time. But we'll have to rely on your judgment."

174 −

"If we do extract them, what then?"

"They both go straight into the deep freeze. After that it's not your problem anymore."

"Then there's only one last thing I want to be sure of before Max and I work out the details," Mallory said, rubbing his eyes. He was running on nervous energy, and he wasn't sure how much he had left. "You *do* want me to go in under a deep Action Cover."

"Yes."

"Then I'll need a new passport — a tourist passport. I'll use it for Status Cover as well. When I go into the Station, I'll walk in through the consulate."

"When do you want the passport?"

"Right now. I'll take off tonight. I'm tired enough to sleep on the plane, and I'd just as soon spend the next two days fidgeting in Berlin. It's a good place for it."

An accident still out of sight beyond a curve had slowed the traffic to a bumper-to-bumper crawl on the highway leading to the airport. Cloud cover had hastened the coming of dusk and heat lightning flashed on the horizon, but the thermometer had not yet dropped below ninety degrees and Ryder kept his eyes on the car's temperature gauge.

"Don't tell me you're afraid this new car is going to overheat," Mallory said, stifling a yawn. "I'll never buy a Mercedes." His eyes were red and gritty, and his need for sleep was becoming desperate.

Ryder's fingers drummed restlessly on the steering wheel as he slipped the clutch and eased the car forward another few feet. "You'll miss the damned flight at this rate!"

"It doesn't matter. Flying out tonight was probably a dumb idea anyway. Relax, you're making me nervous."

"You should be nervous."

"I'll be nervous enough later. Right now I wouldn't mind dozing off."

"Why the hell couldn't you tell Pendleton to shove it?" Ryder said.

"Let it rest, Max. We've been around the same course ten times at least."

When Ryder had learned that Mallory was to go into East Berlin without diplomatic cover, Mallory had barely been able to restrain him from charging into Pendleton's office. Only grudgingly had Ryder settled down to work out the operational details, and his misgivings had not gone away.

"This is an SSD setup," Ryder said tensely. "A blind man could see it."

"Pendleton rules that out, and he makes a pretty good case."

"Pendleton is obviously a nut!"

"A nut? This morning he was brilliant."

"That was this morning. The son of a bitch conned me."

Mallory smiled. "You really did think he wanted me b-because I'm a good operations man, didn't you. I appreciate that, Max."

"I thought you were to *run* an op, not stick your head in the noose to see if someone springs the trap — and I didn't know the defector was SSD. There's no way in hell an SSD officer would know about a KGB sleeper in the Company."

The traffic in their lane began to move forward at a steadier pace. Ryder let out the clutch and kept his foot off the gas, letting the idling engine drag the car forward in low gear.

"Even if Pendleton is right and this is a KGB ploy, sending you in is stupid," Ryder went on heatedly. "They'd settle for a meeting on our terms."

"And what if Martin is the genuine article? Stranger things have happened, and we might lose him."

"Maybe. And maybe there's a Santa Claus. I don't get you, Rich. This morning, you were ready to quit, and now you're willing to be Pendleton's cat's-paw."

Mallory sighed tiredly and closed his eyes. "You know the song. 'Baby, the QLRAIN must fall; Baby, the wind must blow . . .' "

"Cut it out," Ryder snapped.

Mallory turned his head and looked at Ryder. "You don't have to mother me anymore. I know that this smells like an SSD setup; but if it didn't, Pendleton wouldn't have pulled me out of Buenos Aires. Expendability is my ticket to the game. If I could explain why I'm going in, I would. M-maybe I just want one last shot at the brass ring before I quit — even if it is a long shot. If Martin is for real, he deserves a good operations man. That's what I am, Max, and not much else."

Mallory closed his eyes again, too tired to think or to worry. He half heard, half felt his breath rattle in the back of his throat as sleep closed in on him. Ryder said something he didn't catch. His last conscious thought was that Kurov had been right: *I couldn't walk away from it; it's what I do.*

15

"THE American consulate, sir," said the Berlin taxi driver in English, slowing the Mercedes cab and pulling over to the curb on the broad, tree-shaded Clayallee. German elevator music swirled softly from twin speakers behind the rear seat.

"Thanks. Keep the change," Mallory said, handing over a twenty-mark bill as if he were a tourist unfamiliar with the currency. The driver smiled politely and accepted the overpayment.

Mallory slid across the seat, opened the door, and stepped out of the air-conditioned cab into the midafternoon heat. Overhead the sun shone brightly in a clear blue sky. The taxi pulled away from the curb and slipped into the light traffic zipping along the divided highway, leaving Mallory standing on the wide, deserted sidewalk in front of the U.S. Military Command Center. The Berlin Mission's solidly built, three-story stucco buildings stretched for hundreds of yards along the Clayallee. They were set far back from the sidewalk behind a ten-foot concrete wall surmounted by barbed wire.

The marble facade of the consulate jutted out through a gap in the wall toward the sidewalk, a diplomatic appendage grafted onto the military complex. The heavy steel bars on the consulate's ground-floor windows negated the stately affectation of the marble-veneered facade and columns of the portico.

The short, broad flight of steps leading up to the consulate entrance and the guarded military gateway one hundred yards down the street were the only breaks in the protective wall. Behind the nearest buildings, rising high above the roofline, were the antenna masts and microwave dishes shared by the military and the CIA's Berlin Station. This part of Berlin, at least, was as Mallory remembered it.

The glass door at the consulate entrance slid aside automatically as Mallory approached, and he walked into a small vestibule. A West German policeman stood just inside the door, blocking Mallory's path to a steep, narrow staircase leading up into the consulate. At the top of the steps, the staircase was flanked by two glass guard booths.

"I have an appointment to see someone in the consulate," Mallory said in English to the German, and the policeman nodded and stepped aside. Only one of the guard booths was manned, and Mallory trudged up the steps and stopped in front of it.

"Your business, sir?" said a bored young civil-service type.

"My name is Ralph Peck," Mallory said. "I have an appointment to see Mr. Goode."

The young man consulted a list on his clipboard and nodded. "May I see your passport, please."

Mallory produced his passport and slipped it through the opening in the glass. "Nice, friendly place you're running here," he said.

"This isn't New York or London, sir."

"So I've noticed."

The young man checked the passport, handed it back, lifted his telephone receiver, and punched one of the intercom buttons. "Mr. Peck to see Mr. Goode," he said and replaced the receiver. "Go through that door, sir, and down the hall to the waiting room. Mr. Goode will be right there."

"Okay," Mallory said, removing his wrinkled suit jacket and slinging it over his shoulder. The German architects of the complex had designed solid buildings, but they had not included central air conditioning.

Mallory opened the door leading to the consulate's interior and walked down a short, cheerless corridor to a drab waiting room, where President Nixon's image smiled at him from a photograph on the wall above a tired-looking sofa. Beside the sofa, a rubber plant was expiring from lack of water. Mallory did not feel much better than the dying plant looked; the six hours of sleep he had gotten on the flight from Washington to Frankfurt had not been enough.

Mallory heard the staccato tap of a woman's heels in the corridor, and intuition told him that it would be the station chief's secretary. *Brunette, about thirty, sharp mind and an even better body — within Company limits.* He turned as a stylish, attractive woman in her early thirties appeared in the doorway.

"Mr. Peck?"

"Yes."

"I'm Mr. Goode's secretary. Follow me, please; he's expecting you," she said, looking right through him.

Mallory sighed inwardly. What was the use of being a tough-as-nails secret agent if you didn't look like Sean Connery?

Hollis's secretary led him through a maze of corridors, some of them underground, and he quickly lost his sense of direction. The Station was no longer housed in the same building Mallory had worked in. As they approached the steel gate barring the underground entry, the secretary clipped on her badge and handed one to Mallory. A guard seated at his closed-circuit TV console pushed a button and the gate slid open.

Berlin Station was larger than most, but it was still overcrowded and only the corridors provided breathing space. Hollis, the COS, apparently liked a station to hum with activity, and even while holding coffee cups, the Station's earnest young staff officers contrived to look busy. It was a pity, Mallory thought, that no one would ever have the time to separate the wheat from the chaff in the information flowing in. In a station that hummed, everything was grist for the report mill.

Hollis had taken an office directly across the hall from the steel door sealing off the Commo Room from the rest of the Station. The secretary knocked on Hollis's door, opened it, and ushered Mallory inside.

"Ah, Mr. Peck," Hollis said with a welcoming smile as he rose from his seat behind his desk. The secretary left the room, closing the door softly behind her.

Hollis came forward and extended his hand. "Avery Hollis. I've been looking forward to meeting the mysterious Simon," he said in a mellow baritone.

"Richard Mallory."

Mallory had to look up as he shook hands. Hollis was a tall, athletic man with a smooth, carefully tanned face. His brown hair was graying nicely at the temples, saving him from looking too young for his job. His lightweight sport coat and slacks had an expensive Ivy League look.

"Would you care for a sherry?" Hollis asked, guiding Mallory to a leather armchair in front of his desk. "The sun's over the yardarm, and I think we can bend the Company rules a bit."

"No, thanks." Mallory could have used a stiff shot of bourbon, but he doubted that Hollis stocked it. FBI men drank bourbon.

Hollis seated himself behind his desk and flipped the single folder lying on the desk into the Out tray. "So, Max Ryder has a special job for us. We have a trim, efficient Station here, and we'll help you in any way we can. Max tells me you're a first-rate operator, and coming from him that's high praise. I have a lot of respect for Max."

Mallory nodded and fished in his pockets for his cigarettes.

"Believe me," Hollis said, "I envy you — a senior man still working in the field. That's the one thing I dislike about my job: being forced into the role of a bystander."

"Mmmh," Mallory said, flicking his lighter.

"Of course, someone has to do it," Hollis continued. "Goals have to be set and priorities determined. Someone has to be willing to make the hard decisions."

Mallory nodded and dragged on his cigarette.

"If it weren't for the load of paperwork, I'd like to take on a case myself now and then, just to keep my hand in."

Mallory glanced at Hollis's orderly desk. Papers did not appear to be piling up on it.

"Do you know Max well?" Hollis asked.

"We've been friends a long time."

"I see," Hollis said, but Mallory guessed that he didn't. Mallory didn't look the type to be a friend of Max Ryder.

"I take it that you've got yourself a place to stay."

"Yes," Mallory said, and Hollis waited in vain for him to say where. Mallory couldn't blame him for trying. It would gall any station chief to have a man operating in his own backyard and to be unable to keep tabs on him.

If Hollis chose, he could find out in a matter of hours where Mallory was staying and follow his movements every minute of the day or night. Berlin Station's City Eye was one of the best, a network of low-grade informers that blanketed West Berlin: bellhops, taxi drivers, newsstand operators, bartenders, policemen, and hookers.

But Hollis wouldn't try, for his instructions had been clear. He was to know only what Simon or Sam told him, nothing more, and Hollis was obviously a careful man. He would do as he was told. Hollis had not come so far so fast by showing initiative.

"Exactly what do you know about QLRAIN?" Mallory asked.

"Precious little. We've been told that its purpose is to aid the escape of one of SR's deep-cover agents, who is coming out via Berlin. We have the responsibility of extracting the agent's wife. You, I understand, will have full local control of the operation. We have set up the commo channels Max requested, and our Black Ops Section has a team on standby for the extraction. Nick Bradford runs Black Ops, and he is first-rate; he has, as they say, a black mind."

"I assume that Bradford and you are the only Station personnel outside the Commo room who know about this op."

"Yes. As a matter of fact, my secretary believes you are from NSA."

Mallory nodded. "Good. Let's keep it that way. I probably won't be coming back to the Station after today, so I'll need a twenty-four-hour phone channel direct to you."

"I've already set it up," Hollis said. He produced a slip of paper and handed it to Mallory. "Call that number. An operator will tell you that the number is out of service, but if you respond with

'Simon,' she will put you through. We have a scrambled patch set up to reach me if I'm outside the Station at the time. Of course the incoming Berlin telephone line is not secure."

"It doesn't matter."

Hollis nodded as if he understood, and then he cleared his throat. "You know, we could be of much more use to you if we knew a little more about the operation. That way we could be sure we have all our ducks in a row."

"I thought you said the extraction team was ready."

"It is, but I was thinking of unforeseen contingencies."

"I'm afraid that's my responsibility."

Hollis smiled with a practiced, easy charm. "I understand that, and I wasn't suggesting any dilution of your control. I'm simply pointing out that our talent and resources cannot be fully exploited if we don't have the full picture. I have a good team here, and my men know the turf."

"I appreciate that, but SR wants Berlin Station cut out of this to the maximum extent possible. You have a right to be sore, but those are my orders."

Hollis flashed a quick, deprecating smile. "I'm not upset — not in the least." Again he cleared his throat. "Am I to assume that you have your own resources to draw on — a courier, for instance, for contact with SR's agent?"

"Yes," Mallory said with a private, ironic smile. "I have my own resources. Your responsibility is strictly limited. Pick up the woman in East Berlin, and pick up the agent when he crosses into West Berlin. Slap them both in the deep freeze and draw the wagons in a circle. That's it."

"Very well," Hollis said smoothly. "You can rely on us. You'll want to talk with Bradford, of course."

"Yes. Let's call him in now. We can settle the details, and I'll be on my way."

Mallory had to admire Hollis's stiff upper lip; the COS had to be feeling more than he showed. It wasn't just that his authority was being short-circuited; he was being tied to an operation over which he had no control, and if it didn't succeed, he might be tied to its failure. Pendleton's hand was clearly discernible, Mallory thought. Ryder alone didn't have the clout to make Hollis swallow that kind of pill.

Bradford with the black mind was cast in Hollis's Ivy League mold, but he was ten years younger. He was fit and tanned, and his straight blond hair was bleached by the sun. His blue eyes were charged with energy and confidence.

"As you know," Mallory said to Bradford, "an SR agent, code-named Martin, intends to cross into West Berlin day after tomorrow, and he has asked us to extract his wife before he comes over."

"Right," Bradford said crisply. "We're all set for the East Berlin pickup. I'll be sending in two men in a diplomatic car. Why don't we pick up Martin at the same time? It would be cleaner."

"I agree, but Martin may not. Nevertheless I want your men prepared to bring both of them out."

"Will he be carrying a U.S. passport?"

"No, and neither will she. I know you have a blank prepared for her, but if you want her to have it, you'll have to bring it in the pickup car." Mallory had no intention of carrying anything across into East Berlin.

"No sweat," Bradford said. "TS has given us a portable, self-contained machine that we can use to fill in a passport in five minutes, including the picture. Fits in a suitcase. We'll bring an additional blank along in case we have to bring out Martin. Passports are just a bit of added insurance, anyway; unless we're blown, the Vopos will just wave my boys through the checkpoint."

Mallory nodded. "What kind of car, and what's the number on those diplomatic plates?"

"Black Cadillac, and the number is four double-oh three. I would have preferred to go with a military car. No chance at all of being stopped, but the chief nixed it."

"Mr. Hollis is right. As you pointed out, the Vopos won't interfere with a diplomatic car unless they've been tipped off, and if that happens they just might stop a military vehicle. If we get caught using U.S. military equipment and uniforms, the Russians could use it as an excuse to interfere with our military traffic through the Zone. We're not going to risk a war for this op."

Bradford shrugged. "Diplomatic plates, then." He seemed unimpressed by the possibility of a full-scale Berlin crisis, and Mallory had to suppress a flash of irritation.

"The pickup will be at eighteen hundred," Mallory said, "unless I call to cancel or to change the time. If it's a washout, you should stand by to go in the next day with the same arrangement. I want the rendezvous to be somewhere in the center of town."

"Okay," Bradford said, walking to a large wall map of Berlin. "I suggest we make the pickup here, at the entrance to the Hotel Stadt Berlin. Diplomatic cars pull up there all the time. How do we recognize the lady?"

"Your men won't have to; she'll know what to look for, and she will be told to approach the car and ask for Simon. She'll expect the car at eighteen hundred, and your men are to wait for her no more than five minutes. If she doesn't show, they are to cruise around the city and make a second pass a half hour later."

Bradford frowned and glanced at Hollis.

"I want your men to cross into East Berlin at least a half hour ahead of time, but if they're late for any reason, they are to make their pass at eighteen-hundred thirty."

"Why so sloppy?" Bradford said, shooting Hollis a who-is-this-guy look.

"Forget your tradecraft primer," Mallory snapped. "This isn't a rendezvous exercise in Baltimore. If your men and the woman hit the hotel at eighteen hundred on the dot, great; but this is too important to screw up because of a flat tire."

Faint red patches appeared on Bradford's cheeks. "My boys will be on time," he said stiffly.

"Good. I'm glad to hear it," Mallory said, and then he deliberately softened his tone. Like it or not, he had to depend on Bradford. "Look, this is a very dicey setup, and I'm being forced to play some of it by ear. That's why the book rules don't apply. If I could explain the situation fully, I think you'd understand. Unfortunately I can't. I don't like asking you to work with blinders on, but I can tell you that if we didn't have full confidence in this

Station's capabilities, you people would have been cut out of this altogether."

Bradford's checks started to return to their normal shade, and Mallory hoped that he had mollifed him.

"Who are you sending in?" Mallory asked.

"Two contract agents. Americans. One to drive and the other to slip the lady a needle if she needs quieting."

"Have they operated in the Zone before?"

"Of course."

"Any chance that their descriptions are on an SSD checklist?"

"No way."

Bad answer, Mallory thought. There was always a chance.

"We'll also need a team to pick up Martin if he does cross on his own," Mallory said.

"I've already lined up two of my staffers for that."

"Okay. You'll have to keep them on standby day after tomorrow, because I won't know in advance where or when Martin will cross. If I call for a pickup, I want them to park in plain view of the checkpoint and wait for Martin to approach them and ask for Simon. Can you use the same type of car?"

"Sure. We can even use the same diplomatic plates with the next number in the series: four double-oh four."

"Good. That will save wear and tear on my memory. Tell them to stay put outside that checkpoint until Martin shows or they're recalled. Once they've got him, they are to bring him directly to the Station; they are not to stop for *anything*, not even the Berlin police. The same goes for the team bringing out the woman once they're in West Berlin."

Mallory turned to Hollis. "I think that about covers it."

"Any questions, Nick?" Hollis asked.

Bradford shrugged and shook his head. "I think I've got the picture." It was clear that Bradford was neither enthusiastic about the operation nor impressed by the ringer Washington had sent out to run it.

"All right, Nick, thanks," Hollis said. "I'll touch base with you later today."

Mallory lit a fresh cigarette and waited until the office door

186 –

closed behind Bradford. "Has Bradford's outfit ever actually executed an extraction?" he asked Hollis.

"Just six months ago, as a matter of fact," Hollis said. "One of our networks in the Zone was rolled up, and Bradford's men pulled out two agents in one day. It was very slick. I have to put a rein on some of his wilder ideas, but he's a solid team player and he delivers. For the last three years, Bradford has controlled all our black traffic across the border, and we haven't had as much as a close call."

Mallory's eyebrows rose fractionally. "No slipups at all?"

"Not one," Hollis said proudly.

16

It was dusk, but the gathering darkness was held at bay by the blaze of streetlamps and the light from the window displays and neon signs of the four hundred stores, cafés, restaurants, and bars crammed into the two-mile stretch of the Kurfürstendamm. The housewives and businessmen who crowded the thoroughfare by day had gone home to supper, leaving the Ku'damm to the teenagers who, with the coming of darkness, swarmed onto the boulevard like brightly colored insects.

Mallory watched them parading past each other from his window table in a cheap restaurant across the street from the Hotel Kempinski. There was no breeze through the open window, and he was sweating in the steamy air of the crowded, noisy restaurant. He had taken a room in the Kempinski, and he would have been more comfortable in the Kempinski's café, but the hotel's menu was homogenized Continental, rather than German, and they did not serve the *Berliner Eisbein* he had been looking forward to.

He stretched out his legs and sipped the last of his beer, wishing that he had not eaten quite such a heavy meal. The taste of the old-style cooking was a tangible link to the past, but Mallory still felt out of synch with time. Berlin of the mid-fifties had remained frozen in his memory, while the city itself had changed radically in the fifteen years he had been away.

When he had last seen Berlin, there had still been isolated, neatly stacked piles of rubble and vacant lots where buildings had once stood. Now, even the pockmarks left by bullets and shrapnel on old monuments and buildings had been filled in, and trees grew on the grassy mountain in the suburbs where the rubble of an entire city had been dumped.

More than its appearance, the feel of the city had changed. Gone was the need for struggle and the sense of purpose that had come with it. Pride and determination had given way to languid satisfaction and to a generation of youngsters for whom a comfortable life was as unremarkable as the air they breathed. The boys and girls strolling along the Ku'damm and collecting at the street corners to watch the sidewalk artists or to listen to impromptu, radical political harangues had a bored, vacant-eyed look. After years of exodus, youths were returning to Berlin, but not out of patriotism or a love of the city; young men residing in Berlin were exempt from the draft.

Gone, too, was the submerged tension that had once pervaded the city, the subliminal fear that one day the Russians might send their tanks into West Berlin. It was as if the building of the Wall had crystallized the status quo, as if the Wall shielded West Germans as effectively as it imprisoned their countrymen in the East. American armed forces were still tolerated, but the belief in their necessity was slipping away.

Mallory signaled the waiter for the check. He had seen how West Berlin had changed; now it was time for him to have a look at enemy territory.

Rain clouds were blacking out the stars as Mallory emerged from the Kochstrasse U-Bahn station close to the sector border. A breeze was stirring, its coolness a welcome relief after the fetid air in the subway. Checkpoint Charlie was a half block away, and this was another part of Berlin that had not changed. The area near the sector border was a dead zone — dark, deserted, silent.

Mallory could hear footsteps coming toward him from the direction of the border, and as he crossed the street three young women came into the circle of light of the corner streetlamp and stopped uncertainly. They looked like American college students. As Mallory came near, one of the three stepped forward and asked in halting German for directions to the nearest bus stop.

"I'm afraid I don't know," Mallory replied in English. "I always use the subway."

"Oh, you're American! Your leather jacket fooled me — the European cut."

"Why don't you take the subway? The station's right over there."

"We know the bus routes, but we haven't figured out the subway," one coed said.

"And we lost the damned map when we were in East Berlin," another said.

"What did you think of East Berlin?" Mallory asked.

"It didn't look so bad to us; it was interesting."

"Well, I'll have to try it sometime," Mallory said. "If you'll tell me where you want to go, I can tell you how to get there on the subway."

"Thanks, anyway," the first girl said, "but we'll find the bus."

Mallory watched in bemusement as they drifted away, wondering how they could blithely spend a day on the wrong side of the Wall and still worry about getting lost in the subway. He turned and continued up the street toward the checkpoint, where the darkness ended in a flood of light. Twice he turned and checked behind him, but no one was following. Nerves, he thought in self-disgust. Nerves already.

At night the sector border at Checkpoint Charlie was marked in color; the Western side was lit by blue-white mercury lamps, and the Eastern side was bathed in the orange-tinted glare of cadmium lamps. Checkpoint Charlie straddled the Friedrichstrasse, and in the center of the street stood three guard booths in a row, manned by American, British, and French MPs. Opposite the booths, in a building on the left side of the street, was the American ready room. Above its open entrance was a large, painted-glass sign, illuminated from within, spelling out CHECKPOINT CHARLIE in glowing white letters on a black background. It looked like a sign over a seedy New York bar.

As Mallory approached the checkpoint he felt the tug of the past drawing out long-buried memories. He crossed to the left side of the street and walked past the open door to the ready room, a bleak haven from the weather in which he had spent long nights sweating out the return of contract agents on the run.

Inside, the sagging vinyl-covered couch against the rear wall was green now instead of black, but otherwise it looked just like the one on which he had sat for hours, drinking black coffee from paper cups. The faded, yellowing wall chart of Soviet military shoulder boards was probably the same one he had stared at fifteen years ago, but the posters illustrating East German uniforms looked relatively new.

A car approaching from the East slowed as it neared the Allied Control booths, but one of the bored youngsters in the American booth leaned out and waved it through without ceremony.

Now that Mallory was here, his coming suddenly seemed pointless. Still, he thought, he might as well have a look at what he had come to see. He crossed the street again and walked around behind the small, one-story building that housed the West German guard post. Two Berlin border guards sat in wooden chairs on the sidewalk in front of the building, talking together in low tones. Compared to the Allied MPs, they were old men.

Behind the building was a high, wooden observation platform built up against the Wall for the benefit of tourists. Mallory climbed the steps and walked across the platform to look out over the Wall into the East. Fifty yards away, a square, twenty-foot guard tower dominated the checkpoint. Behind the plate-glass observation windows atop the tower, the watching East German border guards were hidden in darkness.

The guard tower stood in the middle of the roadway, and beside it an electronically operated boom blocked the exit from East Berlin. Beyond the gate, a maze of massive concrete barriers prevented a high-speed run at the boom. Vehicles passing through the East German Control were forced to follow a narrow, zigzag path between the barriers before reaching the gate to the West.

In a futile attempt to disguise the grim purpose of the maze, the concrete barrier nearest the West had been adorned with a bed of flowers planted on its upper surface.

The Wall, stretching into the distance on either side of the checkpoint, was actually two walls. Each reinforced concrete wall was thirteen feet high and surmounted by a smooth concrete tube to prevent firm handholds. The two walls were separated by a fifty-yard death strip filled with tank traps and patrolled by armed guards and dogs. As additional insurance, the approach to the wall on the East German side was blocked by a lethal electrified fence.

The wind was picking up, and gusts of cool, moisture-laden air swept across the platform. Mallory tightened the waist belt of his jacket and turned up the collar. He leaned forward to rest his arms on the wooden rail and stared across into East Berlin. The nearest buildings were dimly lit by the glare of the floodlights high above the inner wall. Overhanging the border strip was an unnatural silence, oppressive and ominous.

Mallory heard the footsteps of someone climbing the stairs. The footsteps reached the platform and came toward Mallory, but he didn't bother to look around; it was a tourist, probably, whose Kodak Instamatic would soon be flashing away.

"So, an old spook returns to old haunts," said a man's voice behind him in German, and Mallory turned in surprise.

The German's hard, flinty-eyed face was much as Mallory remembered it. The lines around the eyes and mouth were more deeply etched, perhaps, and the set of the straight, thin-lipped mouth a little grimmer.

"Hello, Rolf."

Rolf Steiner smiled and came forward to shake hands. "Welcome back to Berlin, Richard."

"Thanks."

The handshake was warm but very brief, and Steiner shoved his hands back into the pockets of his raincoat. "I would not have recognized you," he said. "With a mustache and with contact lenses, you look quite different."

"It's good to see you."

"Yes, we were friends, were we not? But still alarm bells are sounding in your head."

The alarm bells *were* ringing. West German Intelligence was no longer under the thumb of the CIA, and security barriers had grown up between the two services. How had Steiner discovered that Mallory was in Berlin?

"I must be getting old," Mallory said. "I didn't make the surveillance."

Steiner shook his head. "I didn't need to keep you in sight; I knew where you would go."

"Am I that predictable?"

"Only to your friends," Steiner said. "In the old days, when you were nervous about an operation, you would come here. I see you are even wearing the old jacket. You reminded me of a Channel swimmer coming to the water's edge before the swim — to look out over the water, to get the feel of it." Steiner gestured at the Wall. "How does it look to you now?"

"Colder and darker" Mallory said, leaning back against the railing. Being told of a habit of which he had not been explicitly aware was vaguely unsettling, but Mallory shook off the feeling. It was no surprise that Steiner knew him so well, for they had worked in close collaboration for much of Mallory's tenure in Berlin.

The BND, West Germany's intelligence service, had begun life as the Gehlen Organization, a private intelligence service funded by the CIA. Soon after Mallory had come to Berlin, he had been assigned to look into ex-Wehrmacht General Gehlen's recruitment policy. The increasing numbers of former SD and Gestapo officers finding employment under Gehlen had begun to attract notice. Mallory had found Steiner's name on a list of rejected applicants.

Following the abortive attempt on Hitler's life in July 1944, Steiner had been forced to flee to Switzerland, a half step ahead of the Gestapo. When he had returned to Germany four years later, he had been unable to find suitable employment, and in 1950 he had applied to the Gehlen Organization. Mallory, who had not forgotten the civilized treatment he had received in Steiner's custody, had intervened, and Steiner's application had been belatedly accepted.

At the time, the CIA had only begun to develop its own operational capability in Germany and was still heavily dependent on the Gehlen Organization. When Steiner had joined one of Gehlen's numerous field stations in Berlin, Mallory had sought him out. At first, theirs had been an uneasy alliance, based solely on mutual interest and a respect for each other's abilities, for they were quite different men.

Steiner, who had a cool, inborn toughness, had not been scarred inside by the war, and he had been wary of the bitterness that Mallory hid behind a mask of cynicism. Gradually, however, they had learned that they could trust each other, and respect had developed into friendship.

But that, Mallory reflected, had been a long time ago. "Why did you follow me out here, Rolf?" he said.

Steiner took out a pack of cigarettes, took one for himself and gave one to Mallory. "I wanted to talk to you in private," he said, flicking his lighter. "This seems as good a place as any; only the Vopos are watching."

Mallory leaned forward to accept the light, and their eyes met over the flame. "Am I talking to an old friend, or to the Org's COS in Berlin?"

"What do you think?"

Mallory drew on his cigarette and exhaled a stream of smoke, which disappeared into the night. "Is there a leak in our Station? I need to know."

Steiner shook his head. "No leak. I knew that someone was coming from Washington for a special job, but my information didn't come from your people. I put out the word to watch for that man, and you're not the first operative to use the consulate entrance to get to your Station."

"And I thought I was being original," Mallory said, his offhand tone masking his worry. "A special job, you said. What, exactly?"

"I was hoping you'd tell me."

"I can't."

"Can't, or won't?"

"Won't."

"So Pendleton is keeping you on a short leash."

Mallory failed to react, and Steiner smiled. "You always were a good poker player, but I happen to know that Pendleton sent you."

"Even Hollis doesn't know that. How do you?"

"Trade?"

Mallory shook his head. "No deal. Just tell me how you know."

Steiner smoked in silence for several seconds, but finally he nodded. "All right. Last month, a contract agent working for the Israelis was warned that he'd been blown, and he got out just in time. The warning came with a request for the Israelis to pass on a message to Pendleton. What the Israelis don't know is that they pay only part of the agent's bills. I pay the rest."

"And you got curious."

"Naturally. It *is* our city, after all. I thought that Pendleton might send in a new man if anything important was to happen, but I assumed there would be at least minimal contact with your Berlin Station. So I put out the word and distributed a fair amount of cash. Then I sat back and waited to see who might turn up."

"Me."

"Yes. A short, skinny American who sounded like he had a cold — in the middle of the summer."

It could have been the taxi driver, Mallory thought, but the Berlin cop at the consulate entrance was a better bet.

"*Scheisse,*" Mallory muttered, turning back to look out over the strip slicing the city in two.

"Don't worry, Richard; the opposition hasn't got wind of this. I'd bet my own life that the Israeli agent doesn't play a double game with the East."

Heavy, isolated drops of rain began to fall, splattering at random on the platform.

"You could have saved yourself the effort of running me down," Mallory said. "I was going to look you up tomorrow."

"Business or friendship?"

"Both. I was hoping you might be able to give me a hand."

"What do you need?"

"A way out if the checkpoints are covered."

Steiner shook his head. "There isn't any."

"No tunnels? I know we don't have any, but I was hoping you . . ."

"Not anymore. If your man blows his cover and he can't come out through a checkpoint, he's had it."

A drop of rain struck Mallory's cheek, and he wiped away the wetness with the back of his hand. "I don't have a man for this one; I'm going in myself."

"*You* are? What the hell is Pendleton up to?"

"It's raining, Rolf."

Steiner expelled his breath with a hiss — whether in frustration or disgust, Mallory couldn't tell.

"Don't worry about it," Mallory said. "I'll make out."

After a moment of silence, Steiner said, "Just how desperate are you for an escape hatch?"

"I don't know."

Raindrops were falling with increasing frequency, and Steiner turned up the collar of his raincoat. "All right, I may have something for you," he said, "but I don't think you'll like it. Why don't we meet tomorrow — let's say at eleven at the Parkhaus Café in the Englischer Garten, and we can talk some more."

"That suits me."

They shook hands, and Steiner turned away and left the platform just as the clouds opened up and rain descended in a torrent. Mallory stayed where he was for a few moments longer, watching the pelting rain crush the flowers atop the East German barrier.

Mallory squinted against the sunlight reflecting off the deep green water of the river Spree, which meandered along the edge of Berlin's Tiergarten park. He stepped off the gravel path running along the river and moved into the shade of the willows lining the bank. A sight-seeing boat glided by, its wake barely rippling the water's glassy surface, and the tour guide's monologue drifted across to Mallory from the boat's muted loudspeakers, mingling with the chirping of birds in the dry, still air.

Mallory had come early for his meeting with Steiner, hoping that a slow walk along the Spree would clear his head. He had expected to sleep through the night, but instead he had tossed restlessly until, exhausted, he had finally drifted off shortly before dawn. It wasn't simple nervousness that had kept him awake, but a vague uneasiness that had little to do with the obvious risks of the operation. Mallory couldn't escape the feeling that Pendleton had not leveled with him, that he was a pawn in a game he didn't understand.

The feeling had been growing ever since he had arrived in Berlin, but though he had gone over his talks with Pendleton time and time again, he could not pinpoint precisely what it was that bothered him. Pendleton's cat's-paw, Ryder had called him, but even Ryder had accepted the CI chief's motives at face value.

Mallory glanced at his watch and saw that it was time to go. He walked back onto the path and followed a turn off to the left, which led away from the river toward the Englischer Garten. The air was heavy with the scent of freshly mown grass on the manicured park lawns and the shifting fragrances from the beds of brilliant flowers planted beside the path.

A small wooden sign pointed the way to the Parkhaus Café, and as he approached he heard the soft strains of piano music coming from the Parkhaus, which was screened from his view by a thick stand of trees. The café's white metal tables and chairs were set in the open and shaded by white and blue beach umbrellas. The effect was intended to be gay, but the dazzling white in the bright sunlight only intensified the dull ache behind Mallory's eyes.

Steiner sat at the table farthest from the little café building. Three tables away, two matronly Berlin hausfraus divided their time between eating ice cream and feeding crumbs to a flock of tiny birds fluttering around them. The other tables were deserted.

In the light, Steiner looked considerably older. His close-cropped, bristly hair was completely gray and shading to white at the temples, but age had not softened his wiry body; if anything, he looked even tougher than Mallory remembered. His eyes were slitted against the sun, reminding Mallory of how he had looked the first time Mallory had seen him, in the courtyard of Gestapo headquarters.

As Mallory sat down, Steiner signaled the waitress, who was idling by the rear entrance to the café's kitchen. "I took the liberty of ordering your coffee in advance," Steiner said. "A double order, of course," he added with a smile.

"I can use it. I didn't sleep worth a damn last night."

The waitress came over with a cup and a pot of coffee. "It is especially hot," she said, "just as the Herr ordered."

"Thank you," Mallory said, pouring himself a cup.

"When are you going in?" Steiner asked when the waitress was out of earshot.

Mallory sipped the coffee. "Tomorrow, on a one-day tourist card. I should be out again by evening."

"Is this going to make trouble for me, Richard?"

"Only if I have to use your escape route. Then some shit may fly in your direction."

"I'm good at ducking. What about you?"

"I'm expendable."

Steiner frowned and poured some fresh beer from a bottle into his glass, taking time to choose his words. "The SSD is very good these days — very professional — and you have not operated here for fifteen years."

Mallory smiled wryly. "Are you afraid that I'm past it?"

"I just don't want you to underestimate the opposition," Steiner said seriously.

"Have I ever?"

"No, but you have been away a long time."

Mallory shrugged. "The turf may change, but the principles don't. I haven't exactly been in retirement all these years, you know."

"You never took a desk job?"

"It was never offered."

Steiner nodded; there was no need for comment.

"I was a little surprised to learn you were still in Berlin," Mallory said.

198 –

"I managed to avoid a transfer to a headquarters desk at Pullach. That may be one of the reasons I survived the shake-up after the Felfe affair. Now I suspect that Berlin is my fief until I retire. You know, in some ways we've benfited from the cold shoulder the Company has given us since Felfe. It's forced us to stand on our own feet. We even have our own giant computer now."

"Terrific."

Steiner smiled. "Well, you can't fight progress."

Mallory drained his cup and immediately refilled it. As always, the coffee stimulated his desire for a smoke, and he took out his cigarettes. "What's your reading on Hollis's operation?"

"Discreet, efficient, and apparently very productive."

"Too productive?"

Steiner did not answer immediately. "Perhaps."

Mallory lit a cigarette. "Are they being fed chicken feed?"

"Let's just say that they seem to be much more successful in obtaining detailed information from the East than we have been."

"And what about Bradford's Black Ops Section?"

"Again I would say, discreet and efficient."

"No slipups."

Steiner nodded. "None. Bradford seems competent, and perhaps he's lucky as well."

"Yes, if you believe in luck," Mallory said, turning to watch the women who were still feeding the birds.

After a moment, Steiner said, "What's bothering you, Richard?"

"Hollis and Bradford are too confident for my taste, and to a certain extent I'm going to have to depend on them."

Steiner shook his head. "Maybe the SSD has been taking them for a ride, and maybe not, but that's not what's really worrying you. That's not why you asked about an escape route. For some reason, you don't trust your own people. Why not?"

"I'm just trying to hedge my bets a little, Rolf, that's all. Do you have something for me or not?"

Steiner sighed. "The quick answer is no, but I'll let you judge for yourself," he said, signaling the waitress for the check. "What we have is in the Bernauerstrasse."

The East-West border ran straight down the middle of the Bernauerstrasse. When the Russians had first sealed off East Berlin, the apartment houses on the East Berlin half of the street had formed part of the barrier; but after dozens of East Germans had escaped by jumping from the roofs into the nets of West Berlin firemen, the apartments had been razed and replaced by the double wall and death strip.

Steiner led Mallory across the street to walk beside the outer wall down the long slope of the Bernauerstrasse. Technically they were in East Berlin, and the few feet of earth between the sidewalk and the concrete wall was overgrown with weeds and dry, untended grass. Faded placards on rusting signposts still warned that this was the limit of the French Sector. The wall was covered with graffiti, and one message in particular caught Mallory's eye: *And for this, too, we thank you, Führer.*

Although it was midday and the streets running into the Bernauerstrasse pulsed with life, the border street itself was strangely still. The modern apartments lining the West Berlin side of the street were as quiet as if they were vacant. Only occasionally did a car drive by, breaking the silence with the dry rattle of its tires on the cobblestones.

Steiner stopped at a wooden observation platform next to the wall. Fastened to one of its supports was a small sign encircled by a black wreath, marking the spot where an East Berliner had died trying to escape. *Erika Braun, aged 19, August 5, 1963.*

"Let's go up," Steiner said. "You can see from the platform what I want to show you."

By day, the radically altered skyline of East Berlin was immediately apparent. A construction boom that was still in progress had followed the sealing of the border, and the belated rebuilding of East Berlin was proceeding at a furious pace. The spindly towers of construction derricks covered the city like a sparse, steel forest.

Beyond the Wall were block upon block of new apartments, their old German architecture contrasting with the postwar style of the West Berlin apartments facing them. The central district, however, was being rebuilt in modern fashion. Glass-walled hotels, office complexes, theaters, and exhibition halls had risen from the rubble, and in their midst the sun glinted on the futuristic East Berlin Radio Tower, the symbol of the new city.

From the platform, Mallory had an excellent view of the inner wall and the death strip, which ran in a straight line for half a mile before making a right-angle bend at the bottom of the Bernauerstrasse. The square, concrete guard towers built at intervals along the inner wall were as silently menacing in the daylight as they had been at night.

From around the distant bend in the Wall came the soft stutter of a small-bore engine, and a moment later two Vopos riding a motorcycle and sidecar appeared and drove up the asphalt road that ran along the inner wall. All along the death strip, the men in the towers were backed up by motorized and foot patrols between the walls, and at night by dogs as well.

Steiner and Mallory were in plain sight of the guards in the nearest tower, two hundred yards away, and Steiner made no overt gesture as he directed Mallory's attention to an old, red-brick church diagonally across from them. The church's facade had become an integral part of the Wall, with the inner concrete wall abutting it on both sides. The sculptured image of Christ on the Cross, mounted on the church tower, gazed mournfully down on the death strip.

"You can see that the street beside the church runs right up to the Wall," Steiner said. "You can approach to within fifty yards of the Wall without challenge, but if you come closer you are likely to be confronted by a Vopo. The church, however, blocks the view of the street from the nearest guard tower, and the Vopos don't patrol that street in pairs. It should be possible to overpower the street guard and reach the Wall."

"And then what?" Mallory said. It was clear why the street was lightly patrolled. Even if a man could get over the electrified fence, as soon as he climbed the Wall he would come into view of the guard tower, and there was no chance at all of making it across the death strip.

"Notice the construction site on our side of the Bernauerstrasse, opposite the church," Steiner said.

Seventy-five yards down the Bernauerstrasse, on the West Berlin side, the foundation for an apartment building had been laid, and in the center of the site stood a derrick eight stories high, with a long, horizontal, cable-braced boom near the top. Mallory saw immediately that if the boom were rotated, it would extend across the street and overhang the death strip.

"The idea," Steiner continued, "is to drop a construction bucket on the end of a cable into the street beside the church. It would have to be at night, when the guards would not be able to see the boom swinging toward the Wall. My men would be in the operator's cab at the top of the derrick, where they would have a clear view of the street beside the church. There would be no prearranged time; they would simply watch and wait — through the night, or several nights in succession, if necessary."

Mallory was studying the derrick. "The boom isn't long enough to span the distance between the two walls," he said.

Steiner smiled thinly. "Yes, I know. The derrick has been modified so that the boom can be rotated at a high rate of speed. If the bucket is released at precisely the right moment as the boom swings, the bucket's momentum will carry it across the necessary distance as it falls. That's the theory, at any rate. Of course it's never been tried, and if the bucket fell short, or went wide of the street, there wouldn't be a second try. The Vopos react very quickly."

Mallory shook his head slowly. "Who dreamed this up?"

"A man very much like your Mr. Bradford. I let him amuse himself with projects like this to keep him out of trouble. It might work, of course, but . . ."

Mallory nodded and turned to look out over the death strip. "I get the point; I'll pass."

"I could still give you the edge you're looking for," Steiner said. "We have reliable safe houses over there. If you do get into trouble, we could get you out through a checkpoint as soon as the heat died down."

"I know," Mallory said.

"There wouldn't be any strings attached."

"I know that, too."

"Then why haven't you asked?"

"I appreciate the offer, Rolf, but I can't accept. If I get tripped up, I don't want some poor, unsuspecting bastard to take the fall with me."

17

MALLORY went in shortly before noon the following day. Rather than crossing on foot at Checkpoint Charlie, he rode the S-Bahn into East Berlin. Owned and operated by the East Germans, the S-Bahn served both halves of the divided city, a dingy, rusting elevated train line snaking through East and West Berlin. He boarded at the Zoo station, a few blocks from his hotel.

The East German ownership of the S-Bahn was apparent even as Mallory bought his ticket. The surly, middle-aged woman in the ticket booth had the dull, listless eyes and doughy, gray-white flesh produced by an unbalanced, starchy diet. The ticket itself evinced the poverty of the DDR. It was made of a cheap, low-quality cardboard that Mallory could have crumbled into dust with his fingers.

Mallory walked through the empty station and climbed the dirty stairs to the platform, where less than a dozen passengers were waiting. Despite the infrequent use of the S-Bahn by West Berliners, the platform was littered with cigarette butts, and Mallory guessed that it had not been swept for at least a month. The midday sunlight was gray and dim by the time it filtered through the dirty window glass in the shedlike platform enclosure.

The passengers waited in subdued silence. No one glanced at his watch or went to the edge of the platform to look out along the rusting, weed-infested tracks for a first glimpse of an oncoming train. Everyone expected delay, and no one was in a hurry to cross into the East. Out of habit Mallory lit a cigarette, but he smoked perfunctorily, without really tasting the tobacco.

Mallory was into his second cigarette when a nearly empty train finally rattled into the station. He chose a car at random and settled himself on one of its uncomfortable wooden benches. The only other passengers were two women and a teenage girl. Judging by their clothes, they were West Berliners, and Mallory assumed they were going across to visit relatives. He shifted in his seat, trying to find a comfortable position, and finally turned sideways so that the hard, unnatural curve of the wooden backrest no longer pressed into his kidneys.

As the train pulled out of the station, he felt his nervousness begin to ebb. It was not too late to turn back, but mentally he was committed; the time for second thoughts had passed. The role Pendleton had given him to play was cut and dried, and if he was walking into a trap, there was little he could do about it. He looked at his watch; in a little over three hours he would know. As that moment approached, he knew, the comforting fatalism would desert him, but until it did, he could relax and run on automatic.

He stared out the window and let his mind slide into neutral. The train made three more short stops at stations in West Berlin and then crossed the Spree into the Eastern Zone. Below the elevated tracks, a guard tower slid by. Beyond it the Wall stretched away into the distance. The tracks curved to the right and ran parallel to the Wall for a time, passing through a section of East Berlin that was as yet untouched by the rebuilding program. The old, dilapidated apartment buildings and vacant lots reminded Mallory of the slums in the Bronx.

As the train turned away from the Wall toward the city's center, the new East Berlin came into view. In the distance the lance-shaped East Berlin Radio Tower jutted against the sky, supporting a spherically enclosed observation platform high above the earth. The effect was of a giant billiard ball skewered by a huge pool cue.

The train slowed and pulled into the Friedrichstrasse station, where all passengers entering East Berlin had to pass through the border control. The station had originally been built to accommodate thousands of rush-hour commuters, and as Mallory got off the train he was struck by the eerie quiet of the virtually deserted platforms. He looked back down the track the way they had come, back toward West Berlin. At the far end of the station, on a catwalk suspended high above the platforms, uniformed guards stood watch over the tracks.

The sun's yellow glare streaming in through the station's glassed wall at the guards' backs rendered them as black silhouettes, silently threatening, their peaked officer's caps, breeches, and jackboots evoking in Mallory sharp, bitter memories of other German guards at other railway stations. Here, that dark past was not dead; the political ideology had changed, but the ruthless efficiency of a police state lived on.

There were no signs directing passengers to the border control, but no signs were necessary. There was only one exit from the platform, and Mallory joined the other passengers descending the staircase to ground level. Despite the infrequency of train arrivals from West Berlin and the small number of passengers on each train, the processing of passengers through the border control was so slow that a crowd of more than fifty people had formed on the stairs, prevented by a gray-uniformed Vopo from entering the customs holding room, which was filled to capacity.

Mallory took his place in line and settled down to wait. Ten minutes passed, and then twenty, and gradually the line behind Mallory lengthened. At last the guard at the bottom of the stairs stepped aside and allowed the crowd to proceed to the holding room. The passengers filed down a short corridor and into an unpleasant room with yellow-tiled walls, harshly lit by fluorescent ceiling lamps. They were greeted by the heat and smell that the previous crowd had left behind.

At the back of the room were six narrow, electronically operated doors that were opened at intervals to allow individuals through for processing. Signs in German above the doors indicated which were to be used by West Germans and which were reserved for foreigners, and there was much milling about as the tourists who could not read German endeavored to get themselves into the proper lines.

The ventilation was inadequate, and as the temperature rose the people began to sweat, their faces glistening in the fluorescent glare. "Jesus Christ," a fat American in a flowered sport shirt standing behind Mallory growled to his wife. "This is a mess. I thought the Germans were organized."

"They certainly aren't set up for tourists," his wife agreed. "You'd think they'd try harder. After all, they need the foreign currency."

The couple was right, Mallory thought; the East Germans were not set up for tourists, and they did need the Western currency. But the Americans were wrong in thinking that the East Germans were inefficient, and Mallory wondered how the couple could possibly have missed the point. They weren't visiting just another foreign country; they were seeking admittance to a gigantic prison.

Forty-five minutes passed before Mallory's turn came. The automatic door in front of him swung open to reveal a short, narrow, brightly lit passageway no wider than a man's shoulders and sealed at the other end by another electronic door. Mallory turned sideways, edged through the door, and came face to face with a Vopo staring at him from behind a thick glass panel. Angled mirrors behind Mallory's feet and above his head gave the Vopo a clear view of the rear of his body.

The door closed automatically, trapping him in the closetlike space until the Vopo chose to release him. Mallory slipped his passport and a five-mark visa fee through a slot in the glass panel. The Vopo, a pimply young man barely out of his teens, said nothing; there was not even a pretense of courtesy.

He silently scrutinized each page of Mallory's passport and then lifted his unsmiling eyes to compare Mallory's face with the passport photo, feature by feature. When he had completed his examination, he dropped his eyes again, and Mallory assumed he was consulting a name list below Mallory's line of vision. Finally the Vopo slipped a one-day visa card into the passport and wordlessly returned the passport through the panel slot. The exit door clicked open, and Mallory sidled through the doorway and stepped into the customs hall.

Again there were no direction signs, but there was only one path that could be followed. The first stop was a booth where each visitor was required to exchange a minimum of twenty-five West German marks for twenty-five East German marks, a larcenous exchange rate. The East German currency had to be spent in East Berlin or left behind when the traveler came out. Behind the exchange booth were the inspection counters, where luggage and handbags were scrupulously checked for contraband and illegal literature.

There were no routine body searches, and since Mallory carried no luggage, he was quickly cleared. In less than five minutes he was on the street outside the station. Aside from delays, getting into East Berlin was easy; getting out again was another matter.

Mallory checked his watch, turned, and walked north up the Friedrichstrasse, away from the city's center. He had two hours to kill before the rendezvous — plenty of time to walk and to watch his back. The surveillance check would be simply a matter of routine, for he had no reason to believe the SSD had picked him up; spotting an unidentified agent was virtually impossible. If it was a trap, they would be waiting for him at Alex.

A half block from the S-Bahn station, the Friedrichstrasse crossed over the Spree. Mallory stopped in the center of the bridge, leaned casually against the stone balustrade, and looked out over the river, squinting against the glare of the sunlight on the blue-gray water. Occasionally he glanced back the way he had come, or to his right, up the Friedrichstrasse.

It was immediately clear to him that discreet surveillance was still difficult in East Berlin; there was too little cover for pursuers. Traffic was light everywhere in the city, and there were remarkably few people on the streets. A deserted, dusty streetcar trundled over the bridge, followed minutes later by an equally empty bus.

Mallory straightened up and walked on. Beyond the bridge, on the right, rose the ten-story administration building of the Soviet Railway, and a great sign on its side bore one of the few advertisements to be seen in East Berlin:

BERLIN TO MOSCOW IN COMFORTABLE CARS
INTERESTING AND PUNCTUAL

The need for the come-on struck Mallory as pathetic, considering that travel in the opposite direction was impossible.

As Mallory continued north, the city rapidly became residential. Reconstructed apartments had taken the place of the rubble and the gutted shells of bombed-out buildings that he remembered from fifteen years earlier, but the atmosphere was still depressing. Even the newest buildings had a dingy, neglected look, with stucco flaking off the facades and paint peeling from the windowsills and doors.

Some of the apartment buildings housed obscure government agencies, and these buildings were the most seriously neglected, with grass growing out from under the eaves and in the silt that had collected in the gutters. Here and there were small, state-owned grocery stores, a drugstore, or an occasional cheap restaurant. The signs above the stores were uniformly faded and dirty, and the window displays had a drab, halfhearted look; there was no incentive to attract customers.

In contrast to West Berlin, which sparkled with bright flowers, lush trees, and strips of well-tended lawn, no real attempt had been made to relieve the gray and brown drabness of residential East Berlin. A flower box beneath an apartment window was a rare sight, and trees were few and far between, most of them hardly more than saplings. The occasional patches of grass were dried out and untrimmed.

But most depressing of all was the lifeless silence that overlay the district, a silence that was somehow different from the peaceful quiet of a West Berlin suburb. It reminded Mallory of the silence in wartime Paris — the subdued quiet of a defeated, occupied city. The absence of people on the streets puzzled him.

It had been this way in the fifties, too, but then the city had still been in ruins and the deserted streets had not seemed as strange.

He passed a small, one-story elementary school. It was modern and not very different from a school one might see in the United States — if one overlooked the flaking paint and the three-foot-high letters glued to the windows, which proclaimed: THE STRONGER SOCIALISM, THE SURER THE PEACE. Where were the children now? There should have been at least a few playing in the streets. Had everyone taken the punctual, interesting trip to Moscow?

By the time Mallory reached the Wilhelm-Pieckstrasse and turned to follow it in an easterly direction, he was sure he wasn't being followed. Mallory walked on at a leisurely pace, heading toward the Brunnenstrasse. He was following a long U-shaped route that would eventually bring him back to the city's center and to Alexanderplatz. The combination of bright sunlight and cool, dry air made walking a pleasure, and for minutes at a time he could almost forget why he was here.

When Mallory reached the intersection with the Brunnen-strasse, he checked his watch again. He still had time to kill, so he crossed the street to a small park plaza on the corner and sat down on a bench in the shade of an old apartment house. The plaza was clean, but here, too, the grass was burnt and uncut. The apartment house was occupied by yet another government subagency, and on the wall facing the plaza was a sign urging citizens to do one good deed each day for socialism and peace; but below the official sign someone had painted a more down-to-earth message: TEEN SEX.

Mallory stretched out his legs and settled back to let time slip away, watching the occasional passerby. The lower standard of living was apparent in the people's clothing, but the most striking difference was the absence of makeup on the faces of the women and teenage girls. This missing aspect of Western influence, Mallory decided, was no loss.

Mallory had carefully selected his own clothes in a cheap secondhand store in West Berlin the previous day. His lightweight slacks and shirt, as well as his shoes, were cut in a neutral European style, and he had gone to a barber to shorten his hair along the sides. He would not stand out in an East Berlin crowd.

Fifteen minutes passed, then a half hour, and gradually Mallory's muscles began to tense, first in his stomach and then in his legs. Nervousness was returning sooner than he had expected. He stood up and stretched, trying to release the unnatural stiffness in his body, but it was no use; the easy part was over. He looked at his watch and verified that it was time to move on. If he started out now, he would reach Alex thirty minutes before the scheduled rendezvous, and that was how he wanted it.

His lips twitched into a slight, nervous smile as he thought of how Bradford with the black mind would react to this trashing of tradecraft. He would be appalled. Bradford would walk up to the fountain in the middle of Alex at precisely fifteen hundred hours, just the way they ran the drills in Baltimore. He would play it by the book because he had absorbed his training as gospel — as Mallory had once done in the SOE training school on the shore of a lonely Scottish loch. To Bradford, tradecraft was sacred and betrayal was only a word.

Nowhere was the contrast between the new East Berlin and the old more dramatic than in the square mile of ultramodern urban construction surrounding the soaring Radio Tower, the city's major tourist attraction. Shining, glass-walled buildings reached toward the sky, reflecting light into the great, sun-drenched square surrounding the tower. The square swarmed with East European tourists, and here, at least, was life and laughter.

Stretching away from the tower base was a long, curving line of tourists waiting patiently in the sun to ride an elevator up to the tower's observation platform, where they could squander their cash in the restaurant in the sky. Mallory paused near the base of the tower and tilted back his head to look up at the needlelike peak. White clouds drifting across the sky made it seem as if the tower itself were moving, and Mallory experienced a momentary sense of vertigo.

A giggling group of twelve-year-old Polish girls wearing the gray uniform of the Young Pioneers trooped by, heading for the Neptune Fountain beyond the tower. They were grinning in anticipation of joining the children who were dangling their bare feet in the water cascading in tiers from the fountain into a wide rectangular reflecting pool.

As Mallory looked about him, he was reminded of some other place he had once seen, but at first he couldn't think where. Taken individually, the buildings surrounding the huge square were like buildings one might see in the heart of any modern city, yet the total effect was somehow off-key. Then he made the connection: Disney World.

He was standing in the middle of a fake city, built entirely for show and designed to impress tourists, with the tower playing the role of the fairy castle in Disney's Magic Kingdom. It was a magnet for sightseers, visible from miles away. Berliners did not come to the city center to work; tourists came here to be entertained and impressed by empty architecture.

The new hotels were for tourists, the restaurants and cafés were for tourists, the shops were for tourists; and the brand-new, towering apartments were reserved for the Party elite. This was a city center without real commerce, where land could be squandered for gigantic public squares and broad avenues many times wider than was necessary for the pitiful trickle of traffic.

For Mallory these thoughts were fleeting and of no consequence. He wiped away the patina of sweat that had formed on his brow and walked toward the S-Bahn trestle, which divided the square surrounding the Radio Tower from Alex. He paused in the shade beneath the trestle and gazed out across Alexanderplatz, looking . . . for what? The SSD was unlikely to oblige him by tipping its hand.

Once the focal point for all Berlin, Alexanderplatz was another great square, an expanse of concrete framed on three sides by newly completed skyscrapers and buildings still under construction. The purpose of one of the buildings was ironic; it housed the official travel agency of the Deutsche Demokratische Republik. On the far side of Alex, across from where Mallory stood, was the new thirty-three-story Hotel Stadt Berlin. On its roof was a huge sign proclaiming: BERLIN, CAPITAL OF THE DDR, GREETS ITS

GUESTS. In the center of the square was the circular fountain where Mallory was to meet Martin.

If they were waiting for him, he thought, they would be in place by now. Men could be watching through field glasses from behind any one of a thousand windows overlooking Alex, and others would be mingling with the tourists milling about on the sunbaked concrete, or sitting on the park benches set at intervals along the square's perimeter. What had he expected to gain by arriving early? What did he really expect to see? Logic had told him it was useless to come early, but his instinct had overruled his head. But what now?

There was no point in remaining where he was. If he was to catch the scent of a trap, he would have to move in closer. Diagonally across the square was a café, close to the fountain. Anyone keeping watch on the fountain might well take a window table inside. Mallory stepped out of the shade and walked across the square toward the café.

As he walked past the fountain, a sudden chill rippled over his spine, as if he could feel someone watching him, and he cursed himself for letting his imagination take hold. Even if they were waiting, there was no way they could identify him. The sun was hot on his shoulders and on the back of his neck, yet his hands were ice-cold. *Why the jitters, Mallory? For Christ's sake, you're supposed to be an old hand.*

As he walked into the café he had to pause for a moment to let his eyes adjust to the dim light. The smoke-laden air was hot and stuffy, and Mallory wondered why the windows were closed. Despite the crowds outside, the café was half empty, and Mallory chose a vacant table at the back of the room. He wasn't interested in watching the fountain; he wanted to study the people inside.

A hunched, sour-faced waiter appeared and handed him a menu. The prices on the menu explained why so few people were in the café. The waiter didn't bother to wipe away the crumbs and coffee spills left behind by previous customers.

"A pilsner, please," Mallory said to the man in German.

The waiter grunted, snatched away the menu, and departed.

Mallory looked again at his watch. He had fifteen minutes. He took out his cigarettes. His fingers were stiff and awkward as he fumbled with his matches. Was he afraid of an SSD trap and a stretch in an East German jail, or was it something else entirely? He lit his cigarette and was reasonably satisfied with the steadiness of his hand.

To Mallory's surprise, the waiter returned immediately with the beer and Mallory paid him at once; he didn't want to have to wait for a check. The beer was too warm and somewhat bitter, but it slaked his thirst. He leaned back in his chair and began his check of the window tables. *All right, hotshot, let's see if you can make the SSD spotter — if there's one here. Maybe he'll be wearing a badge.* At the window table nearest the entrance sat a pair of East Berlin teenagers, smoking and working at a worldly, sophisticated look. The girl was managing it, but the boy was trying too hard.

At the next table, two middle-aged, overweight women were daintily devouring *Erdbeerkuchen,* their eyes fixed on their plates with single-minded intensity. Mallory looked away and then did a double take; the pair looked like the women he had seen in the Parkhaus Café the day before. But when he looked at them again, he saw that the similarity was only slight. His imagination was working overtime again. *Face it, Mallory, this is pointless. Just settle back, finish this crummy beer, and then go out to the damned fountain and see what happens. That's what they're paying you for.*

Instead, he looked at the patrons at another table: tourists, East European. They were watching a group of youngsters in the square outside unfurling a hand-lettered banner above the entrance to the subway. AMERICANS OUT OF VIETNAM, it demanded in English. *What will you do if you spot a ringer — cut and run? What will you tell Pendleton — that you bolted because you thought some character looked fishy?*

Mallory took another deep drag on his cigarette and looked at his hands. They were still steady. He was tense, but in control. Seven minutes to go. It wasn't just simple fear that was making him nervous, he realized. It was the feeling again that Pendleton had not leveled with him.

Mallory shifted his gaze to the right and something on the periphery of his vision made him look toward a table by the window in the far corner of the room. The table had been screened by people sitting in Mallory's line of sight, but now they were leaving. Mallory's breath caught in his throat as he saw the figure seated in the corner, and his cheeks flushed, only to be drained of color an instant later, like furnace-red steel plunged into icy water.

Mallory knew he had walked into a trap.

18

Twenty-six years had wrought little change in the features of the woman seated at the corner table, and Mallory's memory of the girl he'd called Marie leapt across the gap of time like lightning, taking his breath away. Her blond hair was darker now, and she wore it longer, swept back and pinned behind her head, revealing streaks of gray above her temples. Her thin figure had filled out, but she was still slim, and although there were lines at the corners of her eyes and around her mouth, the years had not taken the beauty from her face.

It seemed to Mallory that he had been staring at her, unable to tear his eyes away, for a very long time, but only seconds had passed. He shifted in his seat, turning away from her, and slowly, deliberately ground out his cigarette, trying to absorb the shock. Her face still hovered in his mind's eye, but it was her face as he had seen it on that final day in Paris — pale and withdrawn, the haunting, lovely face of betrayal.

Now Mallory knew why Lessard had never found her. Marie was German. She had not been a collaborator; she had been an Abwehr penetration agent. And now, Mallory was sure, she worked for the SSD. Mallory swallowed the bitter taste of bile in his throat. She was still plying her trade, he thought grimly, still baiting traps. Only this time, luck was on his side.

He stood up, amazed at his steadiness, and walked casually

toward the café entrance, keeping his back to her. He still had time to get clear of Alex before the rendezvous time, with perhaps a minute or two to spare. She had not recognized him, but there was no reason why she should have. They couldn't know who was coming to meet with Martin, and as Steiner had told him, he looked quite different with a mustache and without glasses. Luck, pure luck.

Outside, he turned left and walked away from the café, keeping to the edge of the square out of Marie's line of sight. Others were undoubtedly keeping watch, but only she could recognize him. Mallory suppressed the urge to hurry and maintained a pace consistent with the people around him.

He'd thought she was dead. He'd had no proof, but Lessard had believed so, and Mallory had accepted it as fact. It had helped him to bury the past. Eventually even the dreams had stopped coming. Now it came rushing back as if Paris had been yesterday: the fierce passion that had turned to aching hatred. With an effort of will he wrenched his thoughts away from her and focused on escape. Later there would be time enough to feel and to think. Later, perhaps, there would be a reckoning.

He passed beneath the S-Bahn trestle and walked into the square surrounding the Radio Tower, putting Alex behind him. He was in the clear, and more minutes would pass before they were sure no one was coming. Even then they would do nothing; they couldn't guess that he had tumbled to the setup. He had nothing to fear from the border control.

So it had been a simple SSD burn, after all. Pendleton had been too clever, too averse to the obvious. Max, the realist, had seen it. So much for mystical instinct, for the vague feeling that Pendleton was using him for an obscure purpose. He, too, had been unwilling to accept the obvious.

He skirted the square and doubled back toward the Friedrichstrasse station; his visa required him to leave East Berlin the same way he had come in. He walked more quickly now. Though he told himself there was no risk, he didn't want to remain in the East one minute more than necessary.

An hour later, Mallory crossed into West Berlin. He got off at the first stop and went to a public telephone. His first priority was to stop the pickup team from going in. He was running on automatic, repressing the emotions seething within him. He dialed the number of the special line to Hollis and received a musical tone in response, followed by a woman's voice speaking in German. "I am sorry, but the number you have dialed is no longer in service."

"Simon," Mallory said.

"Hold the line, please," the woman said, switching to English.

In the ten seconds it took for Hollis to come on the line, Mallory changed his mind about what he would say. He had made the SSD surveillance, and he could close the book on Martin right now. But he was no longer willing to do so — not yet.

"Simon?"

"Yes. It was a washout. Tell the quarterback not to send receivers downfield."

"I see. Any changes in the game plan?"

"No," Mallory said. "Advise Sam."

"Will do," Hollis replied, and there was a click as the line went dead.

Mallory hung up and took a deep breath, resisting the riptide of anger that had begun to tear at his control. He compressed his lips, inserted another coin in the phone, and called a number Steiner had given him the day before. No, the book was not yet closed, and he was going to need help that Hollis couldn't give him.

"Continental Insurance," a receptionist answered.

"I'd like to speak to Herr Heinz."

"One moment, please."

Rolf Steiner came on the line. "Heinz here."

"I'm back," Mallory said, knowing Steiner would recognize his voice.

"Good," Steiner said, and Mallory heard a genuine note of relief in his voice. "Was the trip a success?"

"I'm afraid not. I'd like to talk with you about acquiring additional insurance, and I need some information."

"Do you remember the place where we met in the old days?"

"Yes."

"Meet me there in an hour."

"I'll be there," Mallory said, but after he hung up he added softly in English, "you son of a bitch."

The quiet, tree-shaded beer garden on a corner near Berlin's Free University had expanded in the fifteen years Mallory had been away, but it was still very much a local establishment. White metal tables and chairs were arranged in an open courtyard of fine, white gravel and surrounded by a thick hedge, which screened the patrons from the street. This was suburban West Berlin, graced by stately trees and lush with flowers and greenery, and undisturbed by traffic noise.

Mallory took a table in the corner of the courtyard and ordered two beers. By the time the waiter returned with the mugs, Steiner had appeared. He shook hands with Mallory, sat down, and immediately lifted his mug.

"It's been a thirsty day. *Prosit,* Richard."

"*Pros't.*" Mallory took a swallow of beer and then set the mug down with elaborate care, as if he were afraid that he might smash it against the table. "We were friends for a very long time," he said, and he could hear the ice in his own voice.

Steiner frowned slightly. *"Were?"*

Mallory could feel his pulse beating against his temple. "I saw her today, Rolf."

For a moment Steiner did not understand, but then his face slipped into an expressionless mask and his eyes turned watchful.

Mallory nodded grimly. "She was your agent once; you must have known where she had gone. You've known all along that she was working for the SSD."

Mallory's gaze locked with Steiner's, but Steiner's hard eyes didn't waver. "Yes, I knew," Steiner said levelly. "I only saw her once after the war — shortly after I returned to Berlin. Much later I learned that she had married a former Abwehr officer who was working for the SSD. He brought her in."

"Why didn't you tell me," Mallory said hoarsely, his throat constricted with anger.

"You were my friend, Richard, and I owe you — but not that much."

"Owe me? What the hell are you talking about?"

"I have not forgotten what you did for me when I returned with Ingrid from Switzerland and could find no work," Steiner said. "I know Gehlen would never have taken me on, had it not been for you. He preferred old SD and Gestapo men to Abwehr officers who were tied to the July 20 Plot. We, the 'backstabbers,' were the villains, not Hitler, whom we sought to destroy. But Gehlen was the Company's creature, and your recommendation got me the job. Still, there are limits to any debt."

"Damn it, you owed me nothing!"

"Then I have chosen my words badly," Steiner responded coolly. "I should have said that there are limits to friendship. I had other loyalties, as well."

"To Marie? If that's her name."

"Yes, to Marie. She did not deserve Mueller's fate."

Mallory did not respond, and Steiner smiled grimly. "Did you think I didn't know? The hit had all the earmarks of an *Action* liquidation, and it was not difficult for me to make the connection. Lessard was still with French Intelligence at the time, and he was running *Action*'s operations in this country."

Steiner paused, but still Mallory did not react, and he returned Steiner's gaze impassively.

"It was very neatly done, as I remember," Steiner said. "Mueller simply climbed into his private plane one day for a flight across the Alps and never returned. Tell me, Richard, did one of Lessard's technicians alter Mueller's altimeter, or did you do the job yourself?"

"It only required a screwdriver."

"Yes, I thought so. In some ways you are a very direct man;

vengeance once removed wouldn't satisfy you, would it? I remember the look on your face the day you discovered Mueller was working for your people in Frankfurt. You'd been trying to trace him for years, but he'd been too close — practically under your nose. Three days later he was dead.

"Mueller deserved killing, but Marie did not. She did a job she hated because we were at war and she thought it was her duty. Her father was a diplomat in Paris, and Marie grew up in France. Yet she was German, and when the Abwehr sought her help she reluctantly agreed. She was risking her life for her country — just as you were — but I knew you could never see it that way. You would have found a way to get to her. That look I spoke of — I can see it in your eyes now."

"Christ," Mallory breathed aloud. He picked up his mug and swallowed some beer to relieve the dryness in his throat.

Steiner, as addicted as Mallory to nicotine, brought out his cigarettes, took one for himself and gave one to Mallory. "What happened over there?" he said, lighting Mallory's cigarette.

"The bitch nearly nailed me again," Mallory said. "That's what happened."

"Are you going to lay it out for me, or not?"

Mallory exhaled a long stream of smoke. The edge was coming off his anger, and he was glad. Steiner was not a friend he wanted to lose. "If you promise not to laugh," he said.

"Have I ever?" Steiner said, and some of the hardness left his eyes.

"Frequently, as I recall," Mallory said. "You were right: this op was Pendleton's baby. I was to meet an SSD defector who claimed he knew the identity of a KGB sleeper at Langley, and if he checked out, I was to get his wife across the border for him. He was supposed to come out on his own. He insisted on meeting with a Company case officer, not a contract agent. It was an SSD setup a child could have spotted, but Pendleton went for the bait. So did I, for that matter."

"And?"

"I showed up early and spotted Marie waiting for the sucker. She never saw me, and I got out fast. End of story."

Steiner had not yet lit the cigarette he held in his hand. Now he did so, and he smoked for a few moments in silence. "You didn't try to make the contact?"

"No. And I don't step in front of moving buses, either."

"Then you don't really know it was a setup."

Mallory's lips twisted into the semblance of a smile. "Are you suggesting she was sitting there by coincidence?"

Steiner shook his head. "There's another possibility, you know — one that would immediately occur to anyone but you."

"What?"

"That Marie is your defector."

Mallory laughed harshly. "You're right; it didn't occur to me."

"This is not Paris, 1944," Steiner said pointedly, "and Marie is not an agent. She has been a CI analyst for the last ten years, and she has nothing whatsoever to do with SSD operations. There is no reason why she should be involved in such a setup. None."

Mallory started to respond, but then he hesitated. Martin was supposed to be a man, but Martin had been cagey from the start. And the escape plan had been set up to extract a woman. "Are you guessing, Rolf, or do you know?"

"I only know she's not in Operations. And if she's in deep with their CI staff, she might have known in advance that they were about to pick up the Israeli agent. She could have been the one who tipped him off."

Mallory struggled to readjust, to think clearly. Steiner was right: only he would have immediately assumed that Marie was part of a trap. "Would she leave her husband?"

"He died two years ago."

Mallory raised his eyebrows. "You kept tabs on her?"

"Not really. You know what blew Felfe — his incredibly detailed information on SSD personnel. No one could figure out how he did it. Well, it turned out to be surprisingly accurate, and we've managed to keep it reasonably up-to-date."

"Any children?"

"No."

"Then why can't she get herself out?"

"Don't be thick," Steiner snapped. "You've seen the border

control. Unless she had access to the Documents Section, she's no better off than the man in the street."

"But how the hell could she possibly know about a KGB sleeper?"

"She couldn't," Stiener said flatly. "Neither could anyone else in the SSD — as Pendleton damned well knows. Still, he sent you in to find out, didn't he?"

Mallory took another sip of beer. It was a warm night, and the beer was going flat, but he was too preoccupied to notice. He drank the beer simply because it was in front of him. "Pendleton thinks this is a KGB ploy. Would Marie go out on a limb for the Russians?"

"I don't really know. I don't think so, but I don't know. As I told you, I only saw her once after the war. She would seem an odd choice for them, no matter how you look at it. Maybe she's on her own, Richard. Maybe she just wants out."

"Maybe," Mallory said tonelessly and fell silent.

"Well?" Steiner prodded. "What are you going to do?"

"I don't have much choice, do I? I'll have to go back in. There was a backup contact scheduled for tomorrow in case one of us didn't show."

"Will your people okay it?"

"I'm on my own. They only know that today's meeting was a washout. I kept the details to myself."

"I see," Steiner said grimly. "You did intend to go after her."

"Maybe."

"And now?"

"I told you: I don't have much choice. I'll have to go in and check her out. But I'm not going to play by the rules unless I have to — and that's up to you, Rolf. Can you give me Marie's address?"

Steiner did not respond immediately. "What makes you think I have it? I didn't say our files were that complete."

"If you tell me you don't have it, you don't," Mallory said and waited.

"I have her address," Steiner said finally. "Why do you want it?"

"I'll go in early and hope to find her in her apartment. I don't want to go to that rendezvous unless I have to."

"You're still worried about an SSD setup."

"Let's just say I'd feel better having an edge — now more than ever."

"I'll have to think about it."

Mallory nodded. "And while you're thinking, I'll ask for a little more. I'd like an American passport with a new I.D. photo. I'm going to ditch the mustache and switch to glasses."

Steiner frowned. "You could get that from Hollis."

"Humor me, Rolf."

Steiner took out a notebook, scribbled an address, tore out the page and handed it to Mallory. "Be there at eight this evening. We've just started using the place, so I doubt that the opposition has it locked in."

"What about Marie's address?"

"I told you I'd think about it. If I decide to let you have it, you'll get it when you pick up the passport."

"If she's our defector, Rolf, I'll bring her out. That's what I'm being paid to do."

"And if she isn't?"

"Then I'll just have to play it by ear," Mallory said quietly, his eyes locking with Steiner's. An observer watching them at that moment would not have guessed they were friends. "How are you going to bet, Rolf? If she's pure as the driven snow, neither one of us has a thing to worry about. Not a thing."

Mallory walked up to the entrance of a gray stucco building in the Kantstrasse at precisely eight P.M. He buzzed the top floor, and a moment later the electronic lock clicked open. He pushed open the ripple-glass door and stepped into the darkened vestibule, fumbling for the light switch on the wall. He found it and flooded the hallway and stairs with yellow light. A directory on the wall listed the small businesses housed in the building. Eberhardt Travel was on the fifth floor.

He ignored the claustrophobically small elevator on his right and trudged up the stairs. The scrape of his footsteps sounded unnaturally loud in the deserted building. The fake marble veneer on the steps and the brass railing extended only to the second floor. From that point on, the steps were bare concrete and the railing was painted steel. The BND budget, Mallory decided, must have been shrinking.

By the time he reached the fifth floor he was winded, and he paused to catch his breath before knocking on the gaudy aquamarine door to Eberhardt Travel. An automatic timer switched off the stairwell light as Mallory knocked, and he waited in the darkness rather than try to find another switch.

The door opened to reveal a slim, dark-haired woman in her late thirties. She peered at Mallory's face, which was only dimly illuminated by the light behind her, and nodded. "Let's make this quick," she said. "I have a date tonight."

Mallory followed her through the company's small offices to a cubicle in the rear, where a camera and floodlights were set up. "Sit on the stool," the woman commanded. "That's it. Look this way — good. Hold it." The shutter clicked, and the woman pulled the film pack from the back of the camera. "I trust you can speak English," she said. "This will be an American passport."

"Yes, I speak the language."

"I can see that you've recently shaved off a mustache. The skin is too white. It won't show on the photograph, but you should do something about it."

"I know."

"Wait here," the woman said. "I'll be back shortly."

She disappeared into another room and closed the door. Mallory looked at his watch, guessing that it would take her thirty minutes. He would have liked to find a chair more comfortable than the stool on which he was sitting, but he doubted that the woman would take kindly to his wandering about the place and she probably had the ears of a cat.

She was back in twenty minutes.

Mallory accepted the passport from her and opened it to check the craftsmanship.

"It's perfect," the woman snapped impatiently, but Mallory ignored her and checked it over carefully, page by page.

When he was through he looked up and tried a conciliatory smile. "You're right," he said. "It's perfect."

"I have something else for you," she said, producing a slip of paper. "Read it now. You can't take the paper with you."

On the paper was written: *Fr. Marie Eisen, Frankfurter Allee 125, Lichtenberg*. Mallory committed it to memory, nodded, and stood up.

"So, our business is finished," the woman said curtly and quickly ushered Mallory to the door. As he left the building, he looked up and saw that the lights on the fifth floor had already gone out.

Again and again, Mallory rearranged the pieces of the puzzle in his mind, but they refused to fit together to form a coherent pattern. He lay on his back and stared out the hotel window at the pink glow of Berlin's lights suffusing the night sky. It was midnight and the city had quieted; the hiss and rumble of traffic along the Ku'damm had died away, and the last train of the night had rattled over the S-Bahn tracks behind the Kempinski. There was nothing to keep Mallory awake but his own thoughts chasing each other through his head.

An SSD setup was still the best fit to the facts, a simple ploy to burn a case officer. Suck him in and nail him on camera for the mass media: a low-budget, zero-risk propaganda coup. Pendleton had rejected the idea out of hand, but his arguments had lost their force with Mallory. He was no longer ensnared in the tangled web of Pendleton's reasoning. Yet Steiner had insisted that Marie would not be involved in such an operation, and Mallory had no reason to doubt him.

The same objection could be raised if Martin was a creation of the KGB, as Pendleton believed. Surely the KGB would choose someone more plausible than Marie to play the role: an SSD officer who had worked in Moscow, an officer of higher rank and greater responsibility.

Steiner's suggestion that Marie was acting for herself made no more sense. It wasn't credible that she should know of a KGB mole in the Company, even if one existed. If Marie was Martin,

Mallory failed to see how she could expect to con the case officer she had demanded to meet.

Yet she had been at Alex, and Mallory rejected coincidence. Coincidence was possible but dangerous to accept. Marie was involved; she had to be. And Pendleton had chosen Mallory, of all people — a man she could recognize — to go in after Martin. Was that coincidence?

The old feeling had returned, stronger than before, the feeling that Pendleton was playing a game Mallory didn't understand. Yet it seemed impossible that Pendleton could know of his connection to Marie, or that the knowledge could serve Pendleton's purpose, however obscure. Nothing about the op made sense.

Mallory closed his eyes as he yielded to sleep, and he knew that the op itself was no longer important to him. He wasn't going back in as Pendleton's cat's-paw; he was going back for himself.

Steiner had known. That was probably why he'd given Mallory the address; he had known that, one way or another, Mallory would find a way to reach her. Mallory didn't know what he would do when he confronted her. He only knew that he had to go back.

Mallory crossed into East Berlin on the S-Bahn the next morning, and he cleared the border control without incident. It was another bright, clear day, but Mallory was not attuned to the weather as he walked down the Friedrichstrasse, past Unter den Linden, toward the city's center; he was intent on watching his back. Today it was imperative that he avoid being followed, no matter how unlikely the possibility might be.

A half block before the intersection with the Leipzigerstrasse was a U-Bahn station, and he descended into the subway for the first leg of the run out to District Lichtenberg. The eerie, non-functional feel of the city was evident here, too, in the nearly empty subway station. A train glided into the station on rubberized wheels, the stale wind of its passage ruffling Mallory's hair.

He did not board with the other passengers, and the train pulled away, leaving Mallory alone on the platform. He was able to memorize the faces of the few people who joined him on the platform before the next train arrived, and when he got off two stops down the line, he was certain that none of them had gotten off with him.

Satisfied, he boarded the next train that came along. He settled into a seat and tried to relax. Two teenage girls across the aisle were watching him, but with no real curiosity, and they looked away when he met their eyes. Absently he noted again how much prettier the girls looked without makeup.

At the Alexanderplatz U-Bahn station, Mallory got off to transfer to the line that ran out under the Karl Marx Allee to Lichtenberg. His footsteps echoed hollowly in the underground transfer area, which, like the Friedrichstrasse S-Bahn station, had been constructed to accommodate thousands of commuters. Two young boys were roller-skating with abandon across the virtually deserted expanse of concrete, and for them, at least, the underutilized subway system was a boon.

As Mallory walked onto the platform for the train to Lichtenberg, his muscles began to tense. The mechanics of the border crossing and the exercise of elementary tradecraft had been enough to occupy his mind, but those were behind him now. This was not the nervousness of yesterday. Mallory was still wary of a trap, but that danger now seemed only incidental to the strange mixture of dread and desire with which he looked forward to seeing Marie.

As he waited for the train, he tried to distract himself by reading the propaganda posters on the sea-green tile walls, which were mounted in frames originally intended for advertisements. In place of invitations to capture life on Agfa film, to bank one's money in the Sparkasse or to join the Marlboro Man in a smoke, there were demands for the United States to end its imperialistic aggression in Vietnam, to get out of Europe, and to end the arms race. It made dismal reading, and it failed to distract Mallory's thoughts.

He saw her face in his mind's eye, but again it was the face of the girl, not of the woman he had seen in the café. Twenty-six years had passed — longer than they had been alive when they'd been together in Paris; they were not the same people. He was chasing a phantom. Why couldn't he let it go?

Mallory emerged from the subway where the Karl Marx Allee became the Frankfurter Allee, a broad avenue extending radially from the city's center. Up and down the street new apartment buildings were being erected at a rate comparable to that which West Berlin had seen two decades earlier. Mallory checked his bearings against the street map he carried and walked west, noting the numbers on the buildings that were occupied. They were modern, solidly built structures without a trace of Soviet influence, and their brand-new, colorful facades shone in the sunlight.

Marie's apartment building stood alone at the end of a block, a rectangular, glass and concrete tower set back from the street. Enough room had been left on the street corner to construct a brick plaza with a small fountain surrounded by park benches, and the building's entrance opened onto this plaza. Two small children were playing by the fountain, laughing as they splashed their hands in the sparkling water.

Mallory passed by the building on the opposite side of the street, heading for a telephone booth he had spotted two blocks farther west along the Frankfurter Allee. As he approached the booth, he saw that one of its dusty glass walls was broken, and for a moment he thought the booth had been vandalized. But the phone was intact, and the telephone directory was in its place. He found Marie's name without difficulty, lifted the receiver, waited for the tone, inserted a twenty-pfennig coin, and dialed.

On the third ring a woman answered, but Mallory could not be certain it was Marie. Suddenly he felt short of breath, and he had to pause before speaking. "I'd like to speak with Herr Uwe Seitz, please," Mallory said.

"You must have the wrong number. Herr Seitz does not live here." The timbre of her voice was lower, huskier than he remembered, but still the voice struck a chord deep within him and he knew with certainty that it was Marie's. Unconsciously his hand tightened on the receiver until his knuckles showed white.

"I'm sorry to have disturbed you," Mallory managed to say and hung up. Slowly he unlocked his fingers from the receiver, pushed open the door and stepped out of the booth. He took a deep breath and massaged the back of his neck, trying to relieve its stiffness. His fingers were cold.

He could still walk away, he thought; he could forget Pendleton and the op, and walk away. But as he looked down the block toward Marie's apartment, he could feel something unraveling inside him, and he knew that he no longer had the will to think through his actions. He had to see her.

The children playing by the fountain glanced at Mallory as he sat down on a bench facing the apartment and then returned to their game, apparently satisfied that he was harmless. They were clearly brother and sister. The girl, of kindergarten age, was patiently teaching her younger brother how to splash water for maximum effect.

Mallory leaned back on the bench, crossed his legs, and looked casually toward the apartment. Through the wide glass windows at the building's entrance Mallory could see a desk and someone moving behind it. The porter. He'd forgotten about the damned East Berlin porters! They were everywhere, and invariably they were SSD informers. Mallory grimaced. Forgetting such details was a bad sign.

The door at the entrance opened, and a young woman emerged and walked toward the fountain, calling out to the children. They paid no attention to her, forcing her to come to them. Mallory immediately saw that the children resembled her. They had her blond, curly hair and round, widely spaced blue eyes. She glanced at Mallory as she came near, perhaps wary of a stranger sitting beside her children, and Mallory gave her his best Sunday-morning smile. If he was lucky, the woman could get him past the porter.

"A beautiful morning," he said, just loudly enough to force a response.

"Yes, it is," the children's mother answered perfunctorily, picking up her boy.

"Frau Eisen told me this was a very pleasant place to live, and I must agree," Mallory said. The young woman recognized the name, and her expression became less distant. Mallory quickly followed up. "May I say that your handsome children are extraordinarily well-behaved." The compliment had no basis in fact, and it came out in a more stilted fashion than Mallory had intended, but it worked just the same.

"Thank you," the woman said, smiling for the first time. "*Komm, Spätzchen*," she said to the little girl, who acknowledged her mother's presence at last and turned away from the fountain. "We're late. You must get properly dressed now."

Mallory rose from the bench. "You didn't happen to see Frau Eisen on the stairs, by any chance?" Mallory said, looking at his watch. "I'm afraid we're late, too."

"No, I didn't," the woman replied, shifting the boy onto her hip and reaching down with her free arm to take her little girl's hand.

As she turned and walked back toward the apartment, Mallory casually fell into step beside her. "Perhaps I'd better see what's keeping her," he said with a faint sigh. "How old are your children?"

"Five and three," the woman answered.

"You must be very proud of them; they are very bright."

The woman beamed, and Mallory knew he'd struck pay dirt. "Yes, yes, they are — I mean, we are quite proud of them. My husband thinks we should enroll Greta in a special school."

Mallory nodded seriously and said, "Absolutely. I couldn't agree more."

From that point on, Mallory only needed to nod or to smile to keep the woman talking about her children. At the entrance, he opened the door for her and the children and followed in their wake past the gray-haired, stoop-shouldered porter behind the desk, who, on the basis of the young woman's smiling chatter, assumed that Mallory was an acquaintance.

The woman's apartment was on the second floor. Mallory said good-bye to her and continued up the stairs, checking the nameplates on the apartment doors on each landing. On the fifth floor were two apartments. The white enameled door to Mallory's right bore the name he was looking for: Marie Eisen.

The climb had overtaxed his smoker's lungs, and he waited a few moments to recover. The stairwell was brightly illuminated by daylight coming in through panes of frosted glass in the outer wall, but the glass was cleverly shaded from direct sunlight and the air in the stairwell was cool. Mallory waited in the silent stairwell until his breathing slowed. Then he reached out a cold hand and pressed the doorbell.

19

"**D**on't cry out, or I'll kill you," Mallory said softly.

Marie's eyes went wide with shock as she recognized him. "Richard!" she gasped.

Her lips parted again, but no sound emerged as she stood frozen in the doorway. As Mallory moved toward her, Marie's hand fell away from the door handle, and she retreated uncertainly, reaching behind her, as if seeking support. Mallory stepped into the apartment and closed the door behind him.

His eyes darted around the room. A single cigarette burned in an ashtray on a coffee table in front of the living room sofa. To the right of the sofa was an open doorway through which Mallory could see into the bedroom. To his left was a dining alcove and the door to the kitchen., Classical music played softly from a radio on a bookshelf in one corner, but otherwise there was no sound. Marie was alone.

His eyes returned to her. She wore a white, sleeveless blouse and a straight, dark blue skirt that accentuated her trim figure. In her low-heeled shoes she stood a half inch shorter than Mallory. She was looking at him with wide eyes, her breasts rising and falling in an uneven rhythm.

Haltingly she reached out and touched his face, as if to verify his presence. "Richard," she whispered, saying his name just as she had so many years ago. Her eyes glistened as her fingers traced the ridge of scar tissue above his right eye.

He might have reacted differently had her beauty faded with the years, had her green eyes lost their power to beguile, but too much of the girl remained in the woman before him — the girl he had loved too deeply to forgive. "You can save the tears," Mallory said harshly. "It stopped hurting a long time ago."

Marie flinched as if he'd struck her. Her already pale face turned a shade whiter, and her voice shook as she spoke. "Do you still hate me so much, then?"

"What did you expect?" Mallory said, his voice grating out the words.

"Expect?" Marie said tearfully. "I don't — I . . . My God, Richard, I never expected to see you again. How did you find me? Why are you here?"

"I'm the one you were waiting for at Alex yesterday," Mallory said.

"You? . . ."

Mallory saw understanding come into Marie's eyes. She blinked back her tears and walked unsteadily to the sofa and sat down, clasping her hands about her knees in the same rigid pose Mallory had seen once before — in the stationmaster's office in the Gare Saint-Lazare.

Mallory went to the wide plate-glass window overlooking the Frankfurter Allee and closed the translucent drapes, blocking the view into the apartment from the building across the street. Even with the drapes closed, the living room remained bright and cheerful, mocking its occupants.

"How did Pendleton know it was I who contacted him?" Marie said in a small, brittle voice.

"He didn't," Mallory said, barely registering this confirmation that Marie and Martin were one and the same.

Marie appeared not to have understood him. "And why did he send you?" she asked, her voice rising. "And if you hated me so, why did you come?"

"I came because it's my job," Mallory said woodenly. "I didn't

234 –

know it would be you. Pendleton didn't know it would be you."

Marie shook her head. "I don't understand," she said distractedly, brushing back a strand of golden hair that had fallen across her eyes.

"I was at Alex yesterday," Mallory said. "I came early, and I saw you."

Marie looked at him in confusion. "You were there? . . . But why didn't you? . . ." Suddenly her eyes filled with tears again. "You came early because you suspected a trap," she said bitterly, "and when you saw me there you were sure of it. Weren't you? Weren't you!"

"Yes, you bitch!"

"Then why did you come back, Richard?" she cried, balling her hands into fists. "Why did you change your mind?"

"I'm not sure I have," Mallory said coldly.

"You mean you still think I . . ." Marie shook her head slowly, and then her control dissolved. Her shoulders sagged and she sank back against the sofa, as if the weight of her own slight body was suddenly too much to support. She closed her eyes, and tears slid out from beneath her long, dark lashes and rolled down her cheeks.

Mallory slowly advanced on her, driven forward by the drumbeat of his hammering pulse. He saw her misery, but he did not believe in it. He had believed in her once — utterly — and it had nearly killed him. He, more than anyone, knew how good an actress she could be. She had encouraged his love and used it with deliberate cunning, pretending to love him in return.

Her face was averted, her lips slightly parted, and her breasts rose and fell provocatively beneath her light, clinging blouse. Mallory felt a sudden surge of desire, and he recoiled from it in unreasoning anger. If she was bait for a trap, he would kill her.

Marie turned her head and looked up at him, and Mallory was sure that she knew what was in his mind. Yet she didn't move, she didn't speak. For seconds that seemed like hours their eyes remained locked together. Then a shudder passed through Mallory and he stepped back, his arms hanging slackly at his sides.

He felt a weakness and a sense of release akin to the breaking of a fever. He couldn't sustain his anger; in spite of everything he still loved her.

Marie was looking at him with questioning eyes, her white teeth biting into her lower lip in the way Mallory remembered so clearly. "Don't you understand, Richard?" she said huskily. "I loved you. We were enemies, but I loved you."

Mallory's throat constricted, and he didn't try to speak. Wordlessly he held out his hand, and when she took it he drew her up from the sofa. He felt her tremble as he took her in his arms, but for a moment she resisted his embrace. "I didn't betray you to the Gestapo," she said in a choked voice, tears streaming down her cheeks. "I couldn't have. I loved you too much — as I still love you."

Strands of hair clung wetly to her cheeks, and Mallory gently brushed them away. "I just never thought it was possible," he said hoarsely, "I never really believed you could love me."

He kissed her then, and she pressed against him, yielding to him with fierce passion. For an instant he thought again of where he was and why he was here, of the danger and of the need to ask questions, but the joy flooding through him, washing away the years of bitterness and hatred, swept away these thoughts, too . . .

They lay together on Marie's bed, their arms about each other, drowsy, contented, and for the moment unwilling to shatter with words the illusion that they were removed and safe from the world outside. Marie's lips and cheeks were lightly flushed and her eyes were puffy from crying, giving her face a soft, warm, vulnerable look. Mallory ran his hand lightly over her hair.

"I'm going gray," Marie said huskily. "I should have dyed my hair long ago."

Mallory shook his head. "I like you the way you are. I *love* you the way you are," he said and kissed her tenderly.

"I didn't care until now," she said, unconsciously running her fingers over the places around her mouth and on her neck where she knew wrinkles had formed.

236 –

"Don't," Mallory said, placing his hand over hers. "You are as beautiful as ever, Marie. To me, you will always be."

"So many years wasted," Marie sighed. "So many years . . ."

"We'll make up for it."

"Do you mean that?" she asked.

"Of course. Why shouldn't I?"

"But . . ." she said, hesitating and unconsciously biting her lower lip. "Are you not married?"

Mallory laughed softly. "A little late to be asking, isn't it?"

Marie frowned and pulled away from him, looking at him with serious eyes. "But *are* you married?"

Mallory shook his head.

"Why not?" Marie said, and Mallory laughed again at the half-accusing tone in her voice, which seemed to say that a man of his age had a duty to be married.

"I don't know. It just didn't happen, that's all."

Marie came close again and rested her head on his chest. She wore no perfume, and the scent of her hair and of her body was just as he remembered. "I'm glad," she said. Then she lifted her head again, cocked it to one side and smiled crookedly. "It's so *strange* talking with you in German."

"Well, French is out. I'm too rusty."

"It doesn't matter. It just seems strange, that's all."

Mallory was looking past her toward a framed photograph on the nightstand beside the bed. "The man in the picture," he said. "Was he your husband?" The picture showed a blond, broad-faced man in his early forties with mild eyes and a relaxed, good-humored smile.

"Yes. His name was Jürgen. He died in a car crash two years ago."

"I know. Rolf Steiner told me."

"*Ach, der Steiner,*" Marie said, lifting her head. "So he kept track of me . . . That is how you knew where to find me!"

Mallory nodded and then his eyes clouded. "He could have told me about you years ago. He should have; it might have saved us those wasted years. He didn't want me to find you. He was afraid . . ."

Marie again touched the scar tissue above Mallory's eye, and she shook her head slowly. "Are you so sure he was wrong?"

Marie was looking at him intently. He knew what she was thinking, and he shook his head. "I could never have hurt you, Marie."

"But maybe Steiner didn't know that. He must have wanted to protect me. That is the way he is. You thought I was older, but I was only nineteen when we were together in Paris. When Steiner took over as my control, he was upset to find I was so young, and I think he felt guilty about using me. When you were captured, he used that as an excuse to transfer me back to Germany. We met once in Berlin after the war, and he tried to persuade me to come to the West. He still felt protective toward me."

"Why did you stay in the East?"

Marie sighed. "My father was still alive then, and our home was in Leipzig. He wanted to live out the end of his life there, and he had no one left but me. That was one of the reasons I stayed. The others are not as easily explained. Later, I met Jürgen . . . and, well . . ."

"What was your husband like?" Mallory said into the silence, and instantly regretted the question. He didn't really want to know.

"I think you would have liked him," she said.

"Did he bring you into the SSD?" Mallory said. A hard edge had crept into his voice, but if Marie noticed, she ignored it.

"Yes. He had been an Abwehr staff officer in Berlin, and a job with the SSD was considered a bit of luck in those first years after the war. Our only child died shortly after he was born, and Jürgen brought me into the SSD soon afterward — to give me something to occupy my mind. I needed that very much."

"You never tried to have more children?"

Marie shook her head. "Our son died of an inherited defect — from Jürgen's side — and Jürgen was unwilling to try again. I . . . Well, that's in the past."

Marie rested her head on Mallory's chest again and he held

238 –

her close, and for a long time they lay together without speaking. Mallory knew he should be asking different questions entirely, that he should be planning the next move for them both, but second by second, minute by minute, he kept putting it off, unwilling to break the spell that held the world at bay. Just a little longer, he thought, just a little longer . . .

"Why didn't you become an engineer?" Marie asked. "I thought that's what you wanted to be."

"I tried it for two years, but it didn't take. I couldn't settle down. I joined CIA in '47."

"You say that as if you regret it."

Mallory shrugged slightly, finding the gesture awkward while lying on his back with his arm around Marie. "For a long time the work suited me well enough, and it's a little late for regrets now. And it's my work that brought me here today. I don't regret that."

Mallory raised his head to kiss Marie, but he knew the spell was broken, and from the slight stiffening of her body he knew that she realized it too. He lifted his arm and glanced at his watch. It was almost noon. There were still six hours before the pickup — a surfeit of time, unless there were problems Mallory didn't know about.

Marie slipped out of his arms, and in unspoken understanding they got out of bed and started to dress.

"Will you take me across today?" Marie asked in an unconsciously hushed voice.

"Yes. The pickup is arranged for eighteen hundred hours in front of the Hotel Stadt Berlin."

"Will you be coming with me?"

The touch of anxiety he heard in her voice took Mallory aback, roughly reminding him that, for her, intelligence work was desk work. She was no longer the girl who had coolly operated in Paris. "I'll stick around to see that you get off safely," he said, "but then I'll go back the way I came in — on a one-day tourist card."

Mallory bent down to tie his shoelaces, and it gave him an excuse not to look at her as he asked the question he had been putting off. It had to be asked, but he didn't want to have to look at her. "Did you contact Pendleton on your own, Marie, or is this part of an SSD setup?"

Marie did not respond, and her silence forced him to look up at her. She was standing very still, her hands still on the top button of her blouse. "How could you make love to me if you thought that was possible?" she said in a small voice.

Mallory straightened up. "Because it didn't make any difference, damn it. I wanted you and nothing else mattered. Nothing! It still makes no difference. I just have to know."

Marie surprised him then by smiling, and she came across to kiss him. It was a soft, lingering kiss. "I love you, *chéri*," she said in French. "I love you." Then she smiled again and shook her head. Switching back to German, she said, "You can stop worrying, my suspicious man. There in no trap, just me."

Her gently mocking tone nettled Mallory, but the flash of annoyance he felt was as much an aftereffect of the brief moment of tension as it was a result of her playful mockery. "Who wouldn't be suspicious, Marie? Why the hell did you demand to meet with a case officer? You must know that we don't work that way."

Marie frowned slightly and took a half step back, her hands still resting lightly on Mallory's shoulders. "But I —"

"And how did you expect to con him?" Mallory continued. "You're lucky Pendleton picked me. How the hell would you have sold some stranger on your KGB sleeper?"

"I didn't insist on a case officer!" Marie protested, her frown deepening. "As for my information, I can see why you wouldn't want —"

"Wait, back up," Mallory broke in. "What do you mean, you didn't insist on a case officer?"

"I just asked Pendleton to get me out of East Berlin, and he agreed to send in an agent to bring me out — an agent I was supposed to meet yesterday at Alex. What is it, Richard? What's wrong?"

"I'm not sure," Mallory said slowly, feeling an uneasiness akin to the sensation just before a violent summer storm, when the barometer plummets and for a moment the oppressive air is deathly still. "Maybe nothing. Pendleton has been playing games, and I can't figure out why . . . He told me that you had insisted on meeting with a case officer. Why would he do that? That's what made the whole deal smell so fishy . . . Hell, Max was sure it was an SSD setup . . ."

"Max? Not — Max Ryder."

"Yes," Mallory said distractedly, fumbling for the cigarettes in his pocket as he tried to understand what Pendleton was after. "Max was the one who . . ." And then Marie's words slid through the tangle of questions in Mallory's mind and penetrated his consciousness. In France she had known Ryder only as Max; she had not known his surname. He looked at her, a cigarette halfway to his lips.

She was staring at him with uncomprehending eyes, and once again her face was deathly pale. "My God," she said, her voice barely above a whisper. "Didn't he believe me?"

"Who, Pendleton? Believe what?"

"Max Ryder!" Marie cried. "Don't you understand? Didn't Pendleton tell you? Max Ryder is a Soviet agent!"

20

"MAX will make sure we don't get out of here alive," Marie said breathlessly.

Mallory blinked and stifled the laugh that Marie's accusation had nearly surprised out of him. He would have laughed had he not heard the edge of hysteria in Marie's voice. He reached out and took hold of her hands. They were ice-cold. "Are you saying that you sent Pendleton a message informing him that Max Ryder is a KGB mole?"

"Yes! What's happening, Richard?"

Mallory's lips compressed into a hard, angry line. "Pendleton's gone round the bend, that's what's happened," he said grimly. "But it doesn't matter. I'm getting you out of here today."

"But Max *knows!*" Marie said with a quick, involuntary look in the direction of the front door, as if she expected to hear someone pounding on it at any second. "Whatever escape you've arranged will be cut off. They'll never let us get out!"

Mallory tightened his grip on her hands. "Listen to me, Marie. I don't know why you think that Max is a Soviet agent, but he's no more a KGB mole than I am. Believe me, I'll have you out before the sun goes —"

"Damn it!" Marie cried in frustration. She wrenched her hands free and struck Mallory hard on the chest with her fist. "You listen to *me!* Max is a KGB mole. He was a Soviet agent even when you worked with him in Paris. I'm not imagining it; I have proof!"

"All right," Mallory said quickly, anxious to calm her down. "You can tell me what you have." It was just to calm her down, he told himself, but from a dark corner of his mind, doubt slithered out like a snake. "Let's go into the living room, sit down, and have this out. Even if what you say is true, we're safe here for the moment. I'm the only one who knows you're Martin, and if I'd been followed here, they would have raided us by now."

Marie nodded stiffly, and he took her by the arm, led her into the living room, and sat beside her on the couch. He gave her a cigarette and lit it. She inhaled too quickly and coughed, but then the ritual of smoking began to steady her, and her breathing slowed and her expression became less tense.

"I found out about Max six months ago," she said, making a deliberate effort to keep her voice level. "It was pure chance. I was called upon to fill in as a tempoary instructor for new recruits learning the rudiments of counterintelligence. I was given material used by the regular instructor to illustrate counterintelligence techniques that have been used by the SSD and by other services in the past.

"Apparently my predecessor had a sardonic sense of humor, for he had culled old Abwehr and SD files in our possession for cases in which Soviet agents operating in Germany and in occupied territory during the war had been exposed by radio intercepts. All of these were GRU agents. All through the war, the GRU maintained rigid radio schedules with its agents, and this made it child's play for our DF units to locate the transmitters."

Although Marie was looking at Mallory, she was too intent on what she was saying to notice the brief flicker in his eyes as she said "our DF units."

"The case histories he had gathered were complete and detailed," she continued, "even down to the decoded texts of the intercepted transmissions. One case involved the interception of transmissions from Paris to Moscow on three consecutive nights. They were very brief, but because the operator transmitted at precisely the same time each night, the transmitter was located.

– 243

"The coordinates of the transmitter were given to the SD rather than to the Abwehr, and there was a delay in setting up a raid. The Gestapo raided the building where the transmitter was located the next morning — on March 29, 1944. It's not a date I could forget."

Nor could Mallory. "It's coincidence," he said, with a single, sharp shake of his head. "It must be." But an imperceptible shiver rippled up his spine.

"No, Richard. I had nothing to do with the raid that caught Roland that morning. It came as a complete surprise to us — and it was triggered by a radio fix on an illegal transmitter. That much, I've always known; but until I read the case history, I had assumed that Max had been in contact with London."

"No, not London," Mallory said half to himself, remembering. "While we were in Paris we had one-way contact only . . ." But again he shook his head vehemently. "There has to be another explanation. What was the text of those messages? Were they decoded?"

Marie nodded. "Yes, but months later, because no code keys were found in the raid. During the war, the GRU depended almost exclusively on radio communication with its agents, but replacing damaged radios was always difficult. This agent was to deliver a replacement radio to a GRU cell in Paris, but his first message reported failure to make contact with the cell. The last two messages repeated this and requested further instructions . . . You remember about Max and the radio . . ."

Mallory remembered. He remembered Ryder's stubborn insistence on bringing the radio with them to Paris — despite the risk, despite the fact that they would not need it. Mallory was looking directly at Marie but not seeing her. "I can't believe . . . He was m-my friend," he said, not realizing that he had lapsed into English. "I *know* Max; it's just not possible . . ."

But Mallory knew it was, even as he denied it. In the shadow world in which he'd chosen to live, it was possible. Even as he tried to deny the possibility, Mallory found himself wondering what excuse Ryder would have used to explain the loss of their radio, if he had succeeded in contacting the Soviet agents; and

Mallory realized that he had already accepted the possibility as fact.

Marie was right; it fitted. It fitted in every detail, and it explained something that had always puzzled Mallory: how Ryder, who had seemed almost addicted to danger during the war, had managed to settle into the administrative mold. Ryder had never left the danger behind. Every day he had walked the tightrope of the double agent.

In the space of seconds Mallory's world had been turned inside out. For twenty-six years, he realized, he had been looking at the photographic negative of reality, seeing black as white and white as black. Marie had not betrayed them; it had been Ryder's determination to maintain radio contact with his Soviet control that had killed Stebbings and corroded Mallory's life. *Max, you were my friend . . .*

He felt Marie's hand on his arm, and his eyes snapped back into focus. Betrayal had been a fact of life for too many years for it to throw him off balance for long — a balance necessary for survival. Dismay, bitterness — they were a luxury he couldn't afford now.

Click, click, click. The pieces of the puzzle he had been unable to solve snapped into place. At last he understood Pendleton's game. *Pendleton, you bastard. You dirty son of a bitch!* It was simple — so deviously simple.

"How did you know that Max worked for CIA?" Mallory asked Marie. It didn't really matter, but asking her to fill in the details would give him more time to think.

"I've known it for years," Marie said, much calmer now that Mallory believed her. "Some of us were put through a KGB training course, and one day they put on a slide show with close-up photographs of CIA desk officers. I suppose it was meant to show off KGB prowess. One of those pictures was of Max, and of course I recognized him.

"When I read that case history and realized that Max must still be a Soviet agent, I saw a chance to use the information to get to the West. Ever since Jürgen died I've wanted to leave, but without help it wasn't possible. It took me months to work out a way to pass a message directly to Pendleton. I was terrified that Max might get wind of it otherwise . . . And now Max does know — Why, Richard? What's happening?"

A side window of the living room was open slightly and a child's musical laughter drifted faintly up from the street below. The drapes before the window billowed gently in response to a momentary breeze.

"It's a trap, Marie, but not for us — and that's why we can still make it out. Pendleton has set a trap for Max, and we're the bait."

It took only a fraction of a second for Marie to absorb what Mallory had said, and the question that had started to form on her lips died stillborn. She turned and stabbed out her cigarette, and when she looked back at Mallory her green eyes glittered coldly in anger. "Pendleton sent you in as a guinea pig — to see what Max would do."

Mallory nodded. "The details don't matter, but he needed me as an excuse to draw Max into this." The nonsense about a case officer and the reasons Pendleton had given for wanting Mallory had been pure invention. Only one truth remained: Mallory was expendable — and so was Marie.

"But why?" Marie said. "All he had to do was to get me out. I had proof."

Mallory smiled grimly. "'Pendleton wants his own proof; it's the only kind he trusts. If Max takes the bait, Pendleton will have it."

"Will Max take the bait?"

"I don't know. He must be a cool one to have lasted all these years. He doesn't know about you, and there's no reason for him to believe someone in the SSD could blow him. He might just sit tight."

"But you don't believe he will."

Mallory shook his head. "Pendleton's trap is fur-lined, Marie. The crazy story he fed us makes the whole thing look like an SSD setup to burn a case officer, and Max will think he can sabotage the operation with no risk to himself. It would be simple enough to arrange: the moment I meet with Martin in Alex, a flying squad jumps us — before we have a chance to talk to each

246 –

other. Martin is hauled off and disappears permanently. Eventually I'm released, having been led to believe that I fell into an SSD trap. Pendelton is embarrassed and Ryder is in the clear. Simple and neat."

Mallory's lips twisted into the crooked semblance of a smile. "Max might not want to do it to me — particularly since he can't know that Martin is a real danger to him — but I think he will. I think he has."

"Then Max does know about the pickup arranged for today," Marie said, a catch in her voice betraying the nervousness that was reasserting itself. She was fighting against it, Mallory knew; maintaining her composure was the only way left to her to help him.

Mallory nodded. "He knows, and we'll have to assume that we can't use it." The strains of classical music from the radio were no more than a soft background, but Mallory was suddenly aware that the music was getting on his nerves, which were stretched taut. "Can we turn the radio off?" he said.

Marie got up quickly and crossed the room to switch off the radio. She had not put on her shoes, and she moved silently, with a lithe, almost animal grace. How like a cat she was, Mallory thought. Just watching her stirred him deeply, and he knew that he couldn't stand losing her again. He would get her out or die trying.

"I can't bring you out today, Marie," he said as she returned and sat down close beside him.

She leaned toward him and kissed him. "I know."

"You won't have to wait long, and you should be safe enough. I'm the only one who knows you're Martin. As soon as I'm across, I'll go to Steiner; he'll get you out. Just wait for him to contact you."

"What will you do about Max?"

"Nothing," Mallory said firmly. "I'm going to leave Pendelton in the dark until Steiner pulls you out. I don't trust that devious bastard . . ." He abruptly took hold of Marie's hand and squeezed it reproachfully. "Why, for God's sake, didn't you go to Steiner in the first place, Marie? He could have gotten you out."

Marie shook her head in a quick, defensive gesture. "I'm not sure . . . I mean it's a little difficult to explain. I said that I had wanted to leave ever since Jürgen died, and that's true, but it wasn't that definite, you know. I didn't wake up each morning and say to myself, 'I must find a way to flee to the West.' The idea was just in the back of my mind.

"You must understand, Richard . . . I have a job, a routine, friends. I wasn't desperate to defect. But then, suddenly, I learned about Max. I had information an agent would risk his life for, and I thought, 'This is my chance; the Americans will get me out.' Once I started thinking about it, one step led to another. I never really considered alternatives, but even if I had, I don't think I would have asked Steiner to take risks for the sake of friendship."

Mallory sighed and ran his hand gently over her hair. "Well, you won't be trading on friendship now," he said. "The BND will jump at the chance to get you out. After the way the Company has rubbed their noses in the Felfe affair, Rolf's superiors would sell their souls to expose a Soviet agent in Langley."

Marie glanced nervously at her watch, and then she looked at Mallory, her eyes moving restlessly over his face, as if she were trying to memorize each detail. "You'd better go now, Richard. The sooner the better . . ." Mallory heard her sharp intake of breath as another thought struck her. "But *can* you get back now? Max must have given them your description and your cover."

"They'll be looking for a man without glasses and with a mustache," Mallory said. "And I'm carrying a passport Max knows nothing about. But I don't think it matters. I've got a hunch they don't have the checkpoints covered — at least not now. I doubt that the Soviets have alerted the SSD. They will handle this themselves with a small team and play it very close to the vest. Very close. Remember, they have no real reason to believe that Martin knows about Max — and every reason to doubt it.

"They have too much invested in Ryder to risk blowing his cover themselves, and they worry about leaks in the SSD as much as we worry about the BND. If Pendleton should pick up vibrations of something unusual afoot over here, he might realize they'd been tipped off and Max would automatically become a prime suspect.

"And they won't think they need the SSD; they have an ace in the hole: the meeting at Alex. If Max took the bait, they were there yesterday and they'll be there again today. My leaving early must have shaken them up a bit, but what the hell could they do?"

"Then go now," Marie said, with a quick, nervous gesture of dismissal. "Don't just sit here, talking."

Mallory reached out and smoothed away the small, vertical frown lines that had formed between Marie's dark eyebrows. Then he leaned back against the sofa in a deliberately casual manner, simulating a calm he didn't feel. "I still have a few hours to kill," he said, shaking a cigarette loose from the pack with one hand and inserting it in the corner of his mouth. "I'm going to show up at Alex this afternoon."

"No, Richard," Marie implored. "If you're right about the border control, you can get out now without trouble."

"*I* could get out, but what about you? What would I tell Pendleton — that I lost my nerve and didn't make the rendezvous? He might buy it, but Max wouldn't; he knows me too well. Max would know something was wrong, and he'd pull the ejection lever. They must have his escape route primed."

"Then tell Pendleton that you went to Alex and Martin didn't appear."

Mallory had started shaking his head impatiently even before she had finished the sentence. "It wouldn't work. Max would learn from his Soviet contact that I hadn't showed, and then he'd really know something was wrong. He'd bolt for certain. If Max pulls the plug, the KGB will come down on the SSD like a ton of bricks. Your CI people will throw a security net over SSD personnel that a fly couldn't crawl through. There's no telling when we could get you out. If it were only a question of waiting, it wouldn't matter, but the cross-checking would begin. Maybe they wouldn't pick up the connection between you and Max, but I wouldn't want to bet on it. The KGB would be out for blood."

"If you told Pendleton what actually happened," Marie persisted, "he could figure out a way to handle Max. You should go now, before —"

"I'm not taking the chance," Mallory said sharply, his own nervousness spilling out as anger. "Pendleton wants the agent-in-place; he won't give a damn about you!" He took the unlit cigarette from his mouth and tossed it into the ashtray.

"Look," he said, forcing his voice back to normal. "If I show up at Alex and stand around in plain sight, waiting for a contact that never comes, they'll assume it's a washout. Even if they're suspicious, they can't pick me up if they think Martin is still out there running around loose, still capable of contacting Pendleton. It could tip their hand and blow Max sky-high. They'll have to let me go back.

"I'll tell Pendleton that Martin never made contact, and Max's friends will confirm it, so he'll sit tight — long enough to get you out. I'll have to slip Max a plausible story to explain why I left Alex early yesterday; he won't ask, of course, but he'll know about it and I don't want him to have unanswered questions."

Marie had taken his hand and was holding it tightly. She nodded slowly when he stopped speaking, but she had turned away from him and he wasn't sure she'd been listening. "Did Lessard survive the war?" she asked softly.

"Yes, he survived," Mallory said, wondering why she was thinking again of the war.

"I'm glad he wasn't killed," Marie said, and her voice was so low that Mallory barely understood. "I wish . . ."

She turned toward him, her eyes brimming with tears. "You haven't changed, Richard. You shouldn't have come back for me that day in Paris, but you did. You shouldn't have tried to bluff your way past the Gestapo in the railway station, but you did."

Tears broke loose and rolled slowly down her cheeks, and she angrily wiped them away. "Can you imagine how I felt when they took you? I loved you, Richard, and I thought you were going to die because of me. And now — now you are doing it again. You know you should leave now, before the meeting time, but you won't because of me, and I . . ."

"Marie — this isn't Paris; the danger isn't the same. Even if

I'm wrong and they take me, it will only mean a jail term — and a short one at that. There will be an exchange —"

"No!" Marie burst out, with a violent shake of her head. "Not even that — not because of me. Not again."

For the first time Mallory realized that their last day in Paris must have been burned into her memory, as it had been into his. He reached up and took her face between his hands, holding her eyes with his. "Listen to me, Marie," he said fiercely, willing her to believe him. "We're going to make it — both of us. Do you believe me? Do you?"

"Yes," she said huskily. "Yes, Richard, I believe you." But her eyes did not echo her words.

She pulled back slightly, and as Mallory released her she stood up. She looked at him gravely for a moment and then slowly slipped the wedding band from her finger and placed it on the coffee table. She held out her hands to Mallory and he rose from the couch. Silently she led him into the bedroom.

Mallory bought an S-Bahn ticket inside the Friedrichstrasse station and went outside again and around to the glass-walled annex at the rear of the station, where west-bound passengers had to pass through the border control. It was three-thirty in the afternoon, and although the sun was well past its zenith the weather had turned muggy and Mallory was sweating. A dull, yellow haze hung over the city.

Mallory had approached the fountain in Alexanderplatz at precisely three P.M. He had gone through the motions of the pre-scribed ritual, and then he had waited for a full fifteen minutes beside the fountain, with sweat beading his forehead and running down over his ribs in rivulets beneath his loose cotton shirt. When the fifteen minutes was up, he had left Alexanderplatz and walked to the Friedrichstrasse station. He had not detected any signs of surveillance, but that didn't comfort him. He expected the KGB team to be first-rate — if the team was there at all. Only after he cleared the border control would he be able to relax.

The interior of the annex was surprisingly cool, and he had arrived at the checkpoint at an opportune time; very few passengers were waiting to be processed. The young Vopo who was the first to check his passport actually smiled as he opened it to the identity photograph and compared Mallory's face with the picture. There was nothing careless about the check, however. The Vopo held the passport in his outstretched arm right next to Mallory's head, and his eyes clicked back and forth between Mallory's face and the picture for a full ten seconds.

Mallory had left his East German money with Marie, and as he carried no baggage and had nothing to declare, he swiftly cleared the baggage control. After a short wait he was admitted to one of the claustrophobic closets where he had to face another Vopo and sweat out the final passport check. He cleared it without difficulty, and as the electronic door opened to release him, he breathed an inaudible sigh of relief.

He had believed what he had told Marie — that a KGB team would have no choice but to let him go when Martin failed to appear — but the belief had not been a certainty. Only now was he sure that he had been right. It was also possible that Ryder had not taken the bait. A man who had survived so many years under Pendleton's nose was not the sort to panic.

Mallory trudged up the grimy concrete stairs to the upper level and walked out onto the platform. The nearly empty train to West Berlin stood waiting, its doors open. From the catwalk high above the tracks the silent, watchful guards looked down on the train. Christ, he thought, why had Max thrown in his lot with the Russians? It was impossible for Mallory to understand. Was it solely for the sake of intrigue, or was there an ideological passion buried deep inside Ryder, which Mallory had never glimpsed?

Mallory entered the nearest car and sat down on one of the hard, wooden benches. He pushed up his glasses and rubbed his eyes tiredly. In a few more minutes the train would pull out and he would be home free. God, how he hated leaving Marie behind, but there was no other way; and Steiner would get her out as quickly as anyone could. Mallory settled back and closed his eyes.

They would make up for the lost years. Marrying a defector would probably finish him with the Company, but he was ready to quit anyhow. He didn't care what he did, or where they lived, as long as they were together . . . Mallory felt a superstitious pang, and with a slight, self-deprecating smile he knocked softly on the wooden seat with his fist; he wasn't over the border yet. Lessard would have approved: "A man needs luck . . ."

Mallory heard a passenger come up the aisle and slide into a seat opposite him. He knew it was a man from the weight of his step and the scent of his tobacco. The man sighed heavily and cleared his throat, and Mallory opened his eyes.

"Hello, old friend," said Viktor Kurov.

21

MALLORY's throat constricted in a sudden spasm. *Marie!* Had they taken Marie? For a moment he didn't trust himself to speak, but his only outward reaction was a brief flicker in his eyes. Only he could feel his stomach muscles tighten into a knot, or hear the rushing sound in his ears.

"Hello, Viktor," Mallory said coolly. "Traveling west, are you?"

Kurov smiled crookedly and shook his great head. "I'm afraid not," he said.

Mallory nodded casually, forcing himself to appear composed. The response was automatic, a matter of form, but he knew he couldn't bluff his way past Kurov. Moscow had chosen well; they had sent in a man who knew Mallory as well as anyone could know an opponent.

Kurov was wearing a sport shirt with a flat, open collar that made his neck seem even shorter than it was. With his great head, set low on powerful shoulders, and his thick, barrel-chested body, he looked like a Russian bear in human form.

"I trust you'll allow us to proceed with discretion," Kurov said.

Mallory managed to shrug, but even that small movement required effort, as if gravity had suddenly increased threefold — weighing him down, suffocating him. "There really isn't anyplace to run, is there, Viktor?"

Kurov stood up. "We'd better go now; we're holding up the train."

Mallory didn't move. "You have no reason to detain me," he said quietly. None of the other passengers in the car were taking any notice of them. "My passport is in order and I had a valid one-day visa, and if you've been on my tail, you know I've made no contacts. Don't m-make a fool of yourself, Viktor."

Kurov's thick, bushy eyebrows drew together to form a continuous line across the bridge of his nose. "Come," he said curtly and turned away. Mallory rose from his seat, steadied himself, and followed Kurov out of the car.

Mallory didn't see Kurov give a signal, but as soon as they left the train, the car doors closed and the train pulled slowly out of the station. The platform was empty, and Mallory had no difficulty spotting the three Russians Kurov had brought with him: one man at each end of the train, and the third near the platform exit. The KGB hoods who had been covering the ends of the train hurried toward them.

Mallory fell into step beside Kurov as they walked toward the exit stairs; there was no point in hanging back. "Why did you leave it till the last minute?" Mallory said coldly. "I didn't think you were the cat-and-mouse type."

Kurov shrugged. "Sooner, later — what difference does it make in the end?"

"None," Mallory said.

They started down the stairs side by side, with the three hoods following close behind. Mallory wiped away the sweat beading his forehead, and Kurov pretended not to notice.

At the bottom of the stairs, Kurov skirted the small group of passengers awaiting processing by the border control, flashed his I.D. at a succession of Vopos, and led Mallory through a side passage that bypassed the customs hall. They left the station through an exit reserved for the military.

A Russian-made limousine awaited them at the curb. Kurov opened the rear door, gestured Mallory inside, and climbed into the rear seat beside him. The three KGB men remained on the sidewalk. "Lichtenberg," Kurov said to the Russian corporal at the wheel.

"Does that mean SSD Headquarters?" Mallory asked as the car pulled away from the curb.

Kurov nodded. "Germans make efficient jailers."

They rode in silence as the driver followed a zigzag route through side streets that skirted the city's center. When they reached the Karl Marx Allee, the driver turned west toward Lichtenberg. Kurov sat with his hands resting on his heavy thighs, looking straight ahead, his breath whistling softly in his nostrils. Mallory gazed bleakly out the window at the rundown apartments along the Karl Marx Allee. The Karl Marx Allee — formerly the Stalin Allee — had been the first avenue to be rebuilt in East Berlin, and now the cheaply built, Soviet-style block apartments that lined the streets were visibly decaying.

"Your system s-stinks, Viktor," Mallory said, bitterness grating inside him like dry sand. "You know that, don't you?"

Kurov ponderously turned his head to look in the direction of Mallory's gaze and shrugged. "For myself, I always preferred Berlin as a rubble heap," he said in his deep, gravelly voice. He took out a box of black Turkish cigarettes and handed one to Mallory. "Have a smoke, Richard; it may take the sting out of losing."

Mallory looked sharply at Kurov as the Russian gave him a light. Mallory coughed on the first drag, but he continued to smoke, oblivious to the harshness of the tobacco. Kurov's last remark just didn't ring true; it was out of character. Kurov didn't crow over his victories.

With a surge of hope Mallory realized that Kurov was bluffing; the Russian didn't know whether he'd won or lost, and he was trying to find out. It could only mean that Kurov had arrested him on a hunch — that he didn't know about Marie.

"You'd better have one yourself," Mallory said, laying the

groundwork for his own bluff, "because you should never have picked me up."

SSD Headquarters was not secreted in a remote area away from the city, nor was it surrounded by a security zone. Just off the Frankfurterstrasse and not far from Marie's apartment, the headquarters complex covered two square blocks in the midst of the Lichtenberg residential district. Had it not been for the gray-uniformed Vopos standing at fifty-yard intervals along the street in front of the massive, thirteen-story office buildings, one might have assumed the complex housed a conventional government bureau.

At the rear of SSD Headquarters, however, any illusion of a routine bureaucracy was shattered. As the Russian corporal turned left off the Frankfurterstrasse and drove up a narrow street behind the complex, the view of the office buildings was blocked by guard towers and a high concrete wall running beside the sidewalk. Closed-circuit TV cameras mounted on the wall were trained on the street. As the car moved slowly up the street, Vopos popped into view above the wall like jack-in-the-boxes.

The corporal turned into a driveway, stopped the car in front of a gateway in the wall, and sounded the horn. Immediately the gateway's heavy doors swung open, and the car passed into the cobblestoned courtyard of what had once been a municipal prison. The prison was now part of the SSD complex.

Kurov got out of the car and walked across the courtyard to meet a uniformed East German coming toward them. The German's jackboots shone in the sun, and the creases in his jodhpurs were razor sharp. Erect, self-possessed, and half a head taller than Kurov, he was a commanding figure, but even from a distance it was clear that Kurov was the one giving the orders.

Mallory let his eyes drift. The Vopos stationed along the guard wall were staring curiously at him. They were just boys, and compared to them he was an old man, but that was all right, he thought. Age was his advantage — age and having been there before. Twenty-six years had brought him full circle, from German prison to German prison — twenty-six years and Pendleton.

Pendleton, you bastard, where were you in that war? — high and dry in London, learning to play his games. And he was still high and dry, still playing with other people's lives. At least Max had put his own life on the line . . .

But most of Mallory's bitter anger was directed at himself, born of the fear that they would take Marie. Had he not returned to Alex, he might have made it out, but instead he'd walked into Kurov's arms. They might not yet know about Marie, but if he made another mistake, or if they broke him, she would pay the price.

Mallory shivered. In East Germany, the punishment for high treason was death by guillotine.

The muscles along the sides of Mallory's jaw worked as he silently ground his teeth. He wouldn't let the bastards break him, and he wouldn't make a mistake. He would hang on . . .

But if they used drugs . . .

With a conscious effort Mallory forced himself to relax. They couldn't go too far — not if they needed him as an exhange for Ryder. Max was finished. If the Russians didn't know that yet, they would soon.

A pink-cheeked Vopo approached the car and opened Mallory's door. The Russian corporal, slouched behind the wheel, paid no attention. "You will come with me," the Vopo said in schoolbook English. Mallory glanced toward the spot where Kurov and the East German officer had been standing, but they had disappeared.

Kurov conducted Mallory's first interrogation himself. The Russian sat at a small wooden table in the center of a ten-foot-square, windowless cubicle lit by a circular fluorescent ceiling lamp. There was no one-way observation glass, but TV cameras could have been hidden in the ventilation ducts in the upper corners of the room, and Mallory had no doubt that the interview was being recorded.

Mallory's Vopo escort left him alone with Kurov, who gestured for Mallory to sit on a low stool beside the table. The molded

258 –

plastic chair in which Kurov sat appeared to be only slightly more comfortable.

"You may smoke," Kurov said, indicating the pack of East German cigarettes on the table. Mallory's cigarettes had been taken from him, but Mallory ignored the offer and Kurov shrugged.

"So," Kurov said, drawing out the word. "I would have preferred to have met you again under more pleasant circumstances, but such is life." He looked at Mallory, as if he expected a response, but when he received none he continued. "I am familiar with your background, Richard — very familiar with it — and I know what you went through in the war. I don't imagine you would easily succumb to pressure, or to clever tricks, and I myself am no expert in interrogation. So — no games."

"All right," Mallory said. "No games. Then why don't you stop making an ass of yourself and simply let me go?"

Kurov smiled and wagged a thick finger at Mallory. "You always were able to make me laugh, Richard, but now is not the time for jokes," he said and turned off the smile. "Now it is time for you to answer my questions. It will save us both a great deal of trouble."

"Okay," Mallory said. He shifted on the stool, trying to find a comfortable position. The white paint on the cubicle's walls had only recently dried, and Mallory found the lingering paint smell faintly nauseating.

"One hour ago, Max Ryder was arrested at his home," Kurov said. Again Mallory did not respond, and Kurov raised his eyebrows theatrically. "That information does not appear to surprise you."

"I told you in the car that it was a mistake to pick me up."

"And how do you know I am telling you the truth?" Kurov said. "How do you know I haven't just tricked you into an admission?"

Mallory shrugged and started to lean back, forgetting for a moment that he was on a stool. "It makes no difference. The moment you picked me up, Viktor, you blew Max's cover. Unless he pulled the plug before you arrested me, he's dead meat."

Mallory did not expect a visible reaction from Kurov, and he

— 259

got none. "Max Ryder was your friend," Kurov said. "How long have you known he was in our service?"

"I didn't know for certain until you nailed me this afternoon. I was the bait. Pendleton dangled me, and you people bit. Finis."

"Perhaps you would care to amplify that," Kurov said.

"No, I don't think I would," Mallory said with a slight smile.

"Do so anyway," Kurov said mildly.

They weren't really fencing, just going through the motions. Now that Kurov had seen what tack Mallory was taking, he could largely anticipate Mallory's answers. And he wouldn't believe them. He couldn't, for to do so would be to admit to a fatal error in judgment. Still, in one respect, Mallory had not fully committed himself.

He was tempted to pretend that Pendleton had invented Martin, but he decided to stick as close to the truth as possible. Let the possibility that Martin didn't exist occur to Kurov. The hesitation lasted no more than a half second.

"Pendleton sent me in to bring out an SSD defector who claimed to have proof that Ryder was a mole," Mallory said, "but he never showed."

"How could an SSD officer discover the identity of a KGB mole?"

Mallory shrugged. "I have no idea."

"You didn't know this defector's identity?"

"Pendleton didn't tell me, and I didn't need to know," Mallory said with an air of satisfaction. "It didn't matter, you see. I was just bait. Pendleton tapped me for the job simply as an excuse to bring in Ryder, and then he sat back to see what you people would do. You should have let me go, Viktor. Max Ryder would still be a free man."

"And you were willing to act as bait?" Kurov said, cocking one heavy eyebrow. On his face it was an unintentionally comic gesture.

"Does that surprise you?" Mallory said.

Kurov didn't answer. After a moment of silence he said, "And now you expect to be exchanged."

Mallory nodded.

"What if your Mr. Pendleton leaves you holding the bag?

There are those in your organization who have a pronounced vindictive streak. Can you be sure Ryder will not contract a fatal cold?"

"Pendleton will make the exchange," Mallory said, and the certainty in his voice was real. Pendleton, forever suspicious, would have no choice. Already, Mallory was sure, Pendleton would be wondering if the KGB had turned the tables on him — had tricked him into going after an innocent man. Max, who had beaten the lie detector for years, would maintain his innocence to the end, and only the exchange could give Pendleton the final, irrefutable proof that would satisfy him.

"Why did you leave Alexanderplatz early that first day?" Kurov said. "Why didn't you wait to meet with your Martin?"

"Maybe I got nervous. It happens to the best of us."

Kurov dismissed the explanation with a sarcastic smile. "And why do you think Martin failed to appear on the second day?"

"Maybe he spotted you and your hoods clomping around Alex," Mallory answered. "Or maybe he just got nervous — like I did the first day."

"And perhaps there is no Martin," Kurov said.

Mallory shrugged. "It's possible. Pendleton may not have been playing straight with me." He paused and put on a deliberate smile. "The fact is, it doesn't matter," he said. "Either way, Viktor, you're in deep shit."

Kurov watched his own image flicker and die on the TV monitor in the office of Colonel Walter Steglitz, chief of SSD Counterintelligence. Kurov reached out and switched off the video recorder, which was set up on a table beside the colonel's desk. Night had fallen, and the lights of Berlin's skyline were visible through the office windows on the top floor of the SSD's principal office building.

Steglitz sat behind a mahogany desk with his swivel chair pushed back far enough to allow him to sit with his legs crossed. Even while he was seated, his spine was as straight as if he were standing to attention. This stiff military posture apparently required no effort on his part, for his expression and manner indicated that he was completely relaxed. "Well?" Steglitz inquired in a carefully neutral tone. "How much of his story do you believe?"

"Some," Kurov said, continuing to stare at the blank TV screen, his heavy eyebrows drawn together in a frown. "Not very much."

Kurov sat in a leather armchair in front of Steglitz's desk. He and Steglitz were conversing in English, for Steglitz's Russian was not fluent and Kurov refused to speak German.

"Do you think there *is* a defector to be found?" Steglitz asked.

Kurov's frown deepened as he looked over at Steglitz. "That's why I'm sitting here in your fancy office, Colonel," he growled.

Everything about the SSD colonel annoyed Kurov: his clipped, precise speech, his ramrod-stiff bearing, his pencil mustache. The same characteristics in an Englishman would simply have amused Kurov, but Steglitz was German.

Steglitz smiled thinly. "Yes, well, it's a pity you people did not see fit to bring us into this affair at an earlier stage. We could have had Mallory under continuous surveillance, and we would undoubtedly know considerably more than we do now."

"Good. Now that you've got that off your chest," Kurov said, "we can get down to business."

Steglitz propped his elbows on his chair's armrests, steepled his long, manicured fingers, and looked Kurov directly in the eye. "I think there is a little more to be said first, Comrade Kurov," Steglitz said, emphasizing the "Comrade" with dry irony. "As the American put it so succinctly, you are in deep shit. I would like to remind you that I am not the one who dropped you into it. Like it or not, we are on the same side."

That drew a laugh from Kurov, an explosive, rasping laugh from deep within his barrel chest. "All right, *Comrade*," he said, "point taken. What do you make of the affair?"

"The possibility that an SSD officer should learn of a KGB mole in Washington is remote, to say the least," Steglitz said. "The external facts, as we know them, suggest that the mysterious Martin does not exist. Twice Mallory appeared at the supposed rendezvous, and twice there was no contact. Yet as soon as you detained Mallory, your agent in Washington was arrested. Mallory was clearly bait for a trap."

"Tell me something, Colonel," Kurov said, studying the tips of his blunt fingers. "If you had been in my place, would you have arrested Mallory?"

"No," Steglitz said without hesitation. "There was no contact, no reason to justify the risk in arresting him."

"Precisely," Kurov said, and he smiled, revealing his chipped, tobacco-stained teeth. "I grant you that Mallory was bait, but the Americans could not possibly have expected us to detain Mallory unless he made contact. Without a defector, there could be no trap."

Steglitz pursed his lips and drummed lightly on the desktop with his fingers. Finally he said, "Why *did* you arrest Mallory?"

"Because I thought contact had been made," Kurov said, tapping the side of his nose with a thick forefinger. "I could smell it."

Steglitz arched his eyebrows, but made no comment. He waited to see if Kurov would explain himself.

Kurov let the German wait. He had arrested Mallory on instinct, knowing he was risking his career, but he had been sent to Berlin because he knew Mallory, and risk had never frightened Kurov.

Mallory's early arrival at Alexanderplatz on the first day had been unorthodox, but it hadn't surprised Kurov. The alarm bells had started ringing only when Mallory had left without trying to make contact. Yet Kurov's man in the café had seen nothing that could explain Mallory's sudden departure, and Kurov had no choice but to let him go.

But on the second day, Mallory's behavior had forced Kurov's hand. Mallory had walked into Alexanderplatz on time and in the open, and as Kurov had watched him standing at the fountain, Kurov had suddenly felt that he was watching a show put on for his benefit. As the minutes had ticked by, the feeling had grown. Mallory's patient wait at the fountain was too pat, too obvious, when considered against his circumspect arrival and abrupt departure the day before.

Kurov had put off the final decision as long as possible, but in the end instinct had won out over caution; he had not been able to let Mallory take that train.

Neither the arrest of Max Ryder nor Mallory's glib story had changed Kurov's mind; he was still convinced that contact had been made. But he was not inclined to try to put his intuition into words. Let Steglitz do his own thinking. Kurov didn't have to answer to the SSD.

"My reasons for arresting Mallory don't matter now," Kurov said. "Our job is to uncover the defector."

Steglitz regarded Kurov coolly and said nothing.

"You still don't believe in Martin, do you, Colonel," Kurov said.

"Not entirely, but I can hardly ignore the possibility."

"I want more," Kurov said. "I want maximum effort."

"No doubt," Steglitz said dryly.

Kurov's eyes narrowed, but he kept his temper; he needed the German's cooperation. "How did Mallory strike you? What you saw of him on the tape."

"As self-possessed as one could expect under the circumstances. I would say he even appeared relaxed."

"Yes. Just what you'd expect if he had the operation behind him — if he could just sit back and await an exchange. After all, if he doesn't know Martin's identity, or if Martin doesn't exist, there is nothing for him to hide."

Steglitz nodded and waited for Kurov to make his point. He didn't like Kurov any more than the Russian liked him, but he didn't underestimate him. Kurov's argument that a trap without a defector was no trap at all had already convinced Steglitz that there probably was a defector to be found, but playing the skeptic forced Kurov into sharing more of what he knew. Steglitz would work with the Russian, not for him.

"Mallory was lying," Kurov said. "He had his answers ready before he came into the interrogation room."

"How can you be certain?"

"Because Mallory stammers. It isn't a heavy stammer, but it's always there. Yet he didn't stammer when he answered my questions — not once. He had those answers rehearsed, and I can think of only one thing he could be interested in hiding: Martin's identity."

"All right," Steglitz said. "I suggest we put him through the wringer."

"You can go to work on him at once," Kurov said, satisfied that Steglitz was now fully willing to cooperate, "but remember that we need him in one piece for the exchange. No permanent physical damage, and soft drugs only."

Steglitz shrugged. "If you insist."

"I insist. In the meantime, I want your CI staff to earn their keep."

Steglitz nodded. "We've already begun the obvious cross-checks on our people — officers who've worked in joint operations with the KGB, men who've trained in Moscow, that sort of thing. But I don't hold out hope for a quick result. Only a fluke could have exposed a deep-cover KGB mole to one of our people."

"I assume that Martin is still with us — that all SSD personnel are accounted for."

"Yes. And Border Control will be given a special checklist with descriptions and photographs of all SSD officers. Martin will find it difficult to leave without help, but if the Americans are still in contact with him, I can't make any guarantees. Putting the entire staff under surveillance is not practical."

Kurov shrugged. "If Martin escapes, at least you'll be rid of the rotten apple. As a matter of fact, it wouldn't hurt to let word of Mallory's arrest leak out. Maybe we can frighten Martin into trying to cross the border on his own."

Steglitz smiled wryly. Kurov's only real concern was to prove Martin's existence; he wouldn't lose sleep if Martin escaped.

"There's another angle your people could work on," Kurov said. "They should look for possible past connections between SSD personnel and Mallory himself. If he saw Martin and recognized him that first day, it could explain why he left early and how he managed to make contact later."

"*If* he made contact."

"Work on it, Colonel," Kurov said coldly.

"We will," Steglitz replied evenly. "Mallory operated in Berlin for five years, and we can try cross correlations from that angle; but if you're right, Mallory himself has the key. We should pry it loose."

"Moscow is sending out a specialist. He should be here tomorrow to give your interrogators a hand."

"And if Mallory doesn't crack?"

· "Ultimately Moscow may give me the authority to push harder. If it were up to me . . ."

Steglitz smiled thinly. "You'd pump him full of every drug we have."

"Maybe," Kurov replied absently, and Steglitz could see that he was following another line of thought. "But it's not up to me," Kurov said, standing up with a heavy grunt of fatigue. "If we can't force him to talk, I'll just have to try to persuade him."

Having dropped that cryptic remark, Kurov bade Steglitz good night and walked to the door. As he left, he turned back to Steglitz and said, "One thing is absolutely certain, Colonel: Mallory knows who Martin is. I'd bet my career on it."

The door closed behind Kurov and Steglitz nodded gravely. "You already have, Comrade," he said to the empty room. "You already have."

22

THE blade of the guillotine gleamed malevolently in the dull electric light suffusing the death chamber. A green, sliding curtain hung from an aluminum frame surrounding the guillotine, but the curtain was open and the razor-sharp steel irresistibly drew Mallory's gaze, holding it in morbid fascination. He had imagined a guillotine to be much larger, with the blade falling from a great height, but this was small enough to be portable, and its compact efficiency made it seem even more horrible. This guillotine was not a relic from the French Revolution; it was a modern instrument of death, and it was about to be used.

For one terrible instant, as Mallory had been led into the chamber, he had thought that the guillotine had been prepared for him, but then his prison guard had pushed him across the narrow room to stand against the stone wall and he had realized that he was to be a witness to an execution. But whose? Why was he here?

Without explanation, Mallory had been awakened in his cell an hour before dawn and had been driven through East Berlin's dark, silent streets to a prison on the outskirts of the city. Neither his escort in the car nor the prison guards who had taken charge of him had answered his questions. The Vopo standing beside him now was staring blankly into space, a look of boredom on his dull-witted face, and Mallory knew that it would be useless to ask him anything.

They were not alone in the cellar room. A squat, middle-aged man in a black civilian suit was fiddling with the guillotine's release mechanism. Apparently satisfied, he turned to examine the leather straps attached to the guillotine's short, narrow bed. Finally he adjusted the position of the galvanized tub into which the severed head would drop. With nothing more to do, he turned toward the door, clasped his blunt-fingered hands behind his back, and waited. Mallory didn't need to be told that this nondescript man, who looked like a grocer dressed for a funeral, was the executioner.

But who was about to die? Mallory could not even guess why he was being forced to witness an execution, but he sensed that Kurov was behind it. Mallory hadn't seen the crafty Russian since the day of his arrest; so far, Kurov had left him in the hands of SSD interrogators and a KGB ringer from Moscow. They were good, but predictable, and Mallory had had no difficulty sticking to his original story. He had stuck to it and waited — waited for Kurov to go to work on him. Kurov was out on a limb, and unless Moscow pulled him off the case, he wouldn't give up.

Had it been four days or five? Mallory had tried to use his meals to keep track of time, but they could easily have deceived him and exhaustion had dulled his mind. Some drugs had been used, but Mallory had been able to resist their effect. The interrogators had relied primarily on sleep deprivation in their efforts to break him down. They had given him only enough sleep to keep him alive. Sleep. How long had they allowed him to sleep this last time? An hour? Two hours?

Mallory was standing against the stone wall with his knees locked to keep himself upright. The floor seemed to be rocking slowly beneath his feet, like the deck of a ship wallowing in a gentle swell. They hadn't let him smoke either, but after a few days his need for sleep had eclipsed his craving for nicotine. He closed his aching, red-rimmed eyes; the inside of his inflamed eyelids burned.

Mallory grunted as the guard beside him struck him in the ribs to bring him awake. He blinked and his eyes watered, blurring the image of the guillotine's blade. The blade became two blades as his eyes slipped out of focus, but Mallory made no attempt to suppress the double vision. Why couldn't he stare at something else — at the floor, or the wall — anything but that gleaming blade.

He heard footsteps in the corridor outside, and a second black-suited civilian entered, carrying towels and a bucket of soapy water in which a sponge floated. The man set the bucket down beside the guillotine, said something to his colleague in a voice too low for Mallory to hear, and then he, too, turned toward the door, clasped his hands behind his back, and waited. The two men were strikingly similar in appearance, and Mallory wondered if they were brothers — brother executioners. He found himself staring at their hands. Their hands were scrupulously clean and very white.

The clang of a bolt being thrown back resounded at the far end of the corridor leading to the death chamber, followed by the sound of a heavy door opening. The blankly somber expressions of the executioners did not change, but Mallory's guard stiffened and his face lost its look of boredom. Heavy footsteps echoed in the corridor, approaching at a measured, formal pace, and as they drew closer Mallory heard the dry, shuffling slip of soft-soled slippers on the concrete floor — the dragging steps of the condemned.

The condemned was a woman. She was escorted by a male guard and a prison matron, and they brought her straight into the chamber without ceremony. There was no final scene on the threshold — no request for last words, no formal reading of a death sentence, no priest reading from a Bible. The woman hung back as she caught sight of the thing before her, and the matron had to pull her through the doorway.

The condemned woman was no longer young, and her long hair, which had been pinned up in back to expose the nape of her neck, was gray. She wore a blue prison smock and slippers.

Her dark eyes were locked on the guillotine and they glowed feverishly in her chalk-white face. Her bloodless lips were parted, and Mallory could hear the hiss of her breath in her throat.

No one spoke. The executioners stepped forward in unison, pinned the woman's arms to her sides, swept up her frail body, and laid her facedown on the guillotine's bed. Swiftly they trussed her with the straps, and as one of the men locked in her neck beneath the waiting blade, his companion drew the curtain to block the witnesses' view of the guillotine. But the curtain couldn't block sound.

In the final seconds, the woman's control broke and a desperate, moaning wail filled the chamber, rising abruptly to a shriek an instant before the blade fell. The dull thump of the blade was followed by a brief, soft, liquid splatter, and then there was silence.

Mallory awoke suddenly, his neck and chest slick with sweat. For a moment he thought he'd had a nightmare, but then his mind cleared and he knew that the execution had been real. Gingerly he rubbed his eyes. The eyelids were still inflamed and his head ached dully, but he could tell that they had allowed him several hours of sleep. Why? Why had they broken the relentless rhythm of interrogation to have him witness an execution?

"You look terrible," a voice said close by, and Mallory started. Viktor Kurov was standing against the opposite wall of the cell three paces away. Mallory swung his legs over the edge of the bunk and sat up. Kurov stepped forward and handed Mallory his glasses. As Mallory slipped them on, he saw that a plate of stew and a tin cup of water had been set on the floor just inside the cell door. Ignoring Kurov, Mallory got up, drank the water, and then went to the corner to urinate into the toilet. Still ignoring Kurov, he returned to the bunk and sat down. After days of not smoking he could smell the tobacco odor clinging to the Russian's clothes.

Kurov came over and sat down on the bunk beside Mallory, hiking up his baggy, East European trousers so that a strip of thick, hairy calf showed between the cuffs and socks. Tufts of matted chest hair poked out from under the open neck of his shirt.

Kurov took out his Turkish cigarettes and handed one to Mallory, who snatched it and looked to Kurov for a light. "You really have a craving, don't you," Kurov said as he struck a wooden match and lit the cigarette. "It's a pity it's not strong enough to make you talk."

Mallory sucked in the smoke, luxuriating in the tingling relief that instantly permeated his lungs. "I've talked and talked and talked, Viktor," he said, the smoke coming out with the words. "I just don't have what you want."

Kurov smiled and nodded. "You're very good, you know. Even some of your interrogators are beginning to wonder if you might not be telling them the truth. They don't know what a good poker player you are."

Mallory said nothing. He just continued to smoke, ignoring the dizziness that accompanied the rush of nicotine into his system.

"I'm afraid that conventional methods simply won't work with you," Kurov said.

Mallory shook his head. "I'm more b-brittle than you think."

Kurov laughed, a quick, explosive, barking laugh. "Are you? Are you, indeed."

Mallory leaned back against the cell wall and shook his head tiredly. "All right, have it your own way," he said, dragging on his cigarette. "I'm a man of steel."

Kurov lit a cigarette for himself and shifted around to look at Mallory. His dark, glittering eyes were slitted against the smoke drifting up from the cigarette, which dangled from the corner of his mouth. "I arranged for you to witness that macabre ritual this morning," he said.

"Was that supposed to frighten me?"

"No — not directly. The woman was executed for high treason. She was a BND agent working in the DDR Ministry of Defense. I wanted you to see firsthand what will happen to your Martin if we are forced to find him ourselves."

Mallory looked steadily at Kurov. *"C'est la guerre,"* Mallory said coldly.

Kurov smiled his crooked smile. "Very good — very professional," he said, nodding with mock approval. "But I wonder if you mean it."

Kurov stood up, walked away from the bunk, and turned back to face Mallory. "You know why we haven't taken the gloves off, I suppose. We need you for the exchange. And there is also the fact that you are a case officer, not a contract agent; going too far with you might set a dangerous precedent — unwritten rules and all that."

The Russian shoved his hands into the pockets of his trousers and jingled some coins. "It's all right for Moscow to handle this with kid gloves. Their main interest now is in getting Ryder back, and I doubt that they really believe in Martin's existence. Nevertheless, they'll have great fun rubbing the Germans' noses in the affair. It's a perfect excuse to curb the independence of the SSD — and of the other Warsaw Pact services, as well. But I need Martin. I need him to prove that I wasn't a fool to arrest you."

"We all have our little problems," Mallory said and waited tensely for Kurov's punch line.

Kurov sighed heavily. "Yes, but I intend to solve mine, Richard — with or without Moscow's approval . . . Do you follow?"

"You're going to take the gloves off on your own, before they pull you off the case," Mallory said, surprised that he could sound so cool, so uncaring. "Will it be drugs, or does your taste run to electrodes on the testicles?"

"Drugs, my friend. The risky ones — the ones that work."

Mallory dropped his cigarette onto the concrete floor and ground it under his heel, his foot slipping inside his shoe, from which the laces had been removed. "You'll be wasting your time, Viktor. I don't have what you want."

"I think you do," Kurov said, walking to where the plate of stew had been left on the floor. "In fact I have a theory about you and the mysterious Martin." He bent down, picked up the plate, sniffed, and wrinkled his nose in distaste. "I not only think you know Martin," he said, removing his cigarette from the corner of his mouth and tapping the ash into the stew. "I think you know him personally. I think you care what happens to him." Kurov set the plate back on the floor. "That's why I had you watch that woman die this morning."

"Sure, Viktor," Mallory said. "I'm a very caring person, and I have a half dozen personal friends in the SSD."

Kurov smiled. "It does sound ridiculous, doesn't it. I don't even understand it myself. Still, it would explain two puzzling aspects of this affair. First of all, if you knew Martin, you could have spotted him at Alexanderplatz that first day. That would explain how you made contact without our knowledge."

"You're the only one who's puzzled," Mallory said. "You just can't admit that there was no contact — that you blew Ryder out of the water all by yourself."

Kurov ignored the comment and continued. "And if you knew Martin personally, it might also explain why you made the mistake of returning to Alexanderplatz instead of clearing out while you had the chance."

"Nobody's perfect," Mallory said dryly, but his nerves were stretched taut. Kurov was striking perilously close to the mark.

"No, not perfect," Kurov said, "but you are a very careful operator, Richard. It was a mistake you shouldn't have made. Something threw you off that day — something or someone. I think it was your Martin."

Mallory bent down and picked up his crushed cigarette butt to cover his difficulty in swallowing. His throat had gone dry. "You know what I think, Viktor," he said, deftly flipping the butt into the open toilet, "I think you're past it. One of us made a mistake that day, but it wasn't me."

Kurov shrugged, and the gesture seemed to merge his head completely with his thick shoulders. "It's just a theory, and to me it's of little value. I can't peddle theories, only facts. But if it *is* true, you may want to consider a proposition I have for you: If you don't force me to go against Moscow's orders, if you tell me who Martin is, I'll see to it that he gets a prison term instead of death. I still have the leverage to make the deal."

"Betray him to save him, is that it?" Mallory said hoarsely.

"And yourself. The drugs I'll use will open you up all right, but it will be like breaking an egg. Unless we're lucky, Richard, you'll never be the same again."

Slowly, deliberately, Mallory shook his head. "You're wasting your breath. I don't know who Martin is."

Kurov's eyes narrowed. "I'm not bluffing, Richard. Gamble on that and you'll lose everything."

But Mallory wasn't gambling. Kurov might be bluffing, or he might not, but it didn't matter; for Mallory there simply was no choice. In his own mind, there was nothing worse than betrayal. He couldn't bring himself to betray Marie, even to save her life.

"I'm not bluffing either," Mallory said grimly. If Kurov wanted Marie's name, he would have to tear it out of him.

Kurov looked hard at Mallory for several seconds and then called for the guard. "I'll give you twenty-four hours to think about it," he said as the warder opened the cell door. "If you care what happens to Martin, you'll accept my offer. There won't be another."

The door closed behind Kurov, and Mallory listened to the footsteps receding down the corridor. He heard the muffled sound of the cell-block door at the end of the passage opening and closing, and then there was silence.

But for Mallory the silence did not endure. Into its vacuum rushed sounds from within his own mind — sounds no less vivid for being memories. He heard Marie's soft voice almost as clearly as if she were in the cell with him, but a moment later her voice was drowned out by a woman's last, desperate scream and the thud of a guillotine's blade . . .

Mallory was asleep when Kurov returned, and he awakened with a start when the warder snapped open the slide of the door's observation slit. Mallory twisted his head around to see the Vopo peering through the slit at him. He fumbled for his glasses on the floor, slipped them on, and sat up as the guard unlocked the door. Kurov came into the cell.

"That was a short twenty-four hours," Mallory said, suppressing a shiver that passed through him. "Is Moscow getting impatient for results?"

Kurov shook his head. "There won't be any need for drugs now," he said. "I came to tell you." His gravelly voice sounded even rougher than usual, as if he'd gone without sleep, or had smoked too much, or both.

Mallory blinked and looked suspiciously at the Russian, unwilling to give way to relief. "Why not?"

"You've been dealt out of the game, Richard," Kurov said, and Mallory detected an uncharacteristic diffidence in his tone.

"What is that supposed to mean?"

"We both overlooked the obvious," Kurov said. "I focused on you, on ways to pressure you, and you resisted. We should have considered more carefully how Martin might react to your arrest. To protect Martin, you were willing to risk whatever we might do to you; but Martin . . . Martin was not willing."

"What's happened, Viktor?" Mallory said, his voice barely above a whisper.

"Three hours ago, Marie Eisen turned herself in to clear the way for your exchange."

23

THE exchange took place just after dawn on October 29, eighty-seven days after Mallory's arest. It was still dark as the black Agency limousine carrying Ryder to the border sped over the deserted, rain-slick Königstrasse, through the heavily forested outskirts of Berlin-Zehlendorf toward the Glienicker Bridge.

In the rear of the car, Max Ryder sat between Berlin Station's COS, Avery Hollis, and a taciturn, frosty-eyed army colonel representing Berlin's Military Command. Hollis and the colonel were silent and preoccupied. The car's scrambler-equipped transceiver was turned on, and it emitted a soft, steady hiss of static from its speaker. Ryder appeared to be dozing. The tick-tick-tick of the windshield wipers beat an out-of-synch counterpoint to Ryder's slow, rhythmic breathing.

The cloud-covered sky was shading from black to gray as the driver slowed for the final bend in the highway before they reached the old steel-girder bridge spanning the narrows of the Havel River, which ran along the southeastern border of West Berlin. As if sensing that they had arrived, Ryder opened his eyes, blinked twice, and yawned.

Ryder shifted in his seat, brushing against the army colonel's arm, and the colonel glanced at him with distaste. As the car neared the bridge, its headlights illuminated an army jeep drawn up in front of the barrier at the Western end of the bridge. Four

MPs climbed out of the jeep, the outlines of the rifles they carried visible beneath their ponchos.

The limousine's driver, an Agency man, halted the car beside the jeep, picked up an umbrella from the seat beside him, got out, and opened the door for the colonel. Hollis remained with Ryder in the car.

The lieutenant in charge of the MP detail stepped forward and saluted the colonel. "Dirkson, sir," he said, unable to keep the excitement out of his voice. "I haven't seen any activity over there yet, but it's almost dawn, sir."

"Yes, Lieutenant," the colonel drawled. "I know." He looked over at the MPs standing beside the jeep and shook his head. "I don't know what crazy bastard issued your men shoulder weapons, Lieutenant, but I want them unloaded and kept out of sight."

"Yes, sir."

The colonel stepped past the lieutenant and walked toward the two red-and-white-striped poles blocking the roadway. The Agency driver started to follow, holding the umbrella over the colonel's head, but the colonel stopped him. "Stay with the radio. I want to know as soon as Charlie comes through," he said and walked on alone to the barricade.

The real barrier was on the far side of the Glienicker Bridge, partly blocked from view by the arch of the bridge's span. On the opposite bank, on either side of the bridge, a steel fence shone under floodlights, and beyond the fence was the concrete Wall.

The colonel glanced at his watch, clasped his hands behind his back, spread his feet, and settled into parade rest to wait out the four minutes that remained until dawn. He stood alone, staring out across the bridge, ignoring the rain and oblivious to the stares of the West Berlin border police watching him from their shelter alongside the roadway. Silently he cursed the general who had given him this inglorious duty; he hated the very idea of letting a traitor go.

With the coming of dawn the floodlights across the river seemed to lose intensity, and as the horizon lightened, the outline of the distant terrain beyond the Wall began to emerge. But there was little color in the half-light, and the scene developed in shades of gray. The river, which flowed gently between wide lakes on either side of the narrows, remained black, its shimmering surface pocked by rain.

Precisely at dawn, soldiers came into view at the Eastern end of the bridge and ran up the flags of the DDR and of the Soviet Union on flagpoles bracketing the roadway. The Glienicker Bridge was the only Berlin checkpoint at which the Russian flag flew. As the colonel watched the Red banner being raised, he sucked his teeth in disgust. Patton had been right, he thought bitterly; they should have run the bastards out of Germany in '45.

Seconds after the colors were raised, a lone figure appeared, walked up to the waist-high steel fence that stretched across the roadway at the Eastern end of the bridge, and stood there, waiting. The colonel turned and gestured to the MP lieutenant, who responded at the double.

"Yes, sir?" the lieutenant said, slightly out of breath.

"Calm down, Lieutenant. This is no big deal."

"Yes, sir."

"Your presence here is for show only."

"What if someone on the other side starts shooting as our man is coming off the bridge, sir?"

"They won't, Lieutenant. This business is cut-and-dried. In any event, you are to do nothing unless I order it. Is that understood?"

"Yes, sir. But what if . . ."

"You do *nothing*, Lieutenant! And make sure your men understand, too."

"Yes, sir."

"All right. Ivan over there is probably getting impatient; I'd better go out to meet him."

Mallory stood between two Soviet army privates beside the roadway, watching Kurov and an American officer walking toward each other from opposite ends of the bridge. Mallory wore an oversized Russian military raincoat and a shapeless civilian hat he had been given. Raindrops dripped steadily from its brim.

It was not unseasonably cold, but after months of confinement the wet October morning chilled him, and every so often he shivered. He felt no sense of anticipation, only an empty, infinite weariness. His release meant nothing to him, nothing at all. Pendleton had won, and Kurov had won; he had lost everything.

When Mallory had arrived at the checkpoint, Kurov had spoken briefly with him, but already Mallory had forgotten what the Russian had said. It was the first time they had met since Kurov had brought him the news of Marie's surrender. Twice, a nameless Russian intelligence officer had interviewed him, but the questioning had been perfunctory. Mallory's repeated requests to see Marie had been ignored, and eventually he had stopped asking.

Mallory had not dissolved in despair, nor had he raged. He had not even wept for Marie during the endless days and nights of his confinement. He did not understand why. But the wound was there, deep within him; it would always be there.

Kurov and the American officer met at the center of the bridge, where the border had been unintentionally delineated by the workmen who had painted their respective halves of the bridge. Both crews had used olive-green paint, but the East Germans had used a lighter shade. Mallory saw Kurov exchange a few words with the American, and then both men signaled to their people for the exchange to proceed.

One of the Russian soldiers prodded Mallory forward and marched him through the gate in the low steel fence and out onto the bridge. Ryder and his escort approached from the opposite bank. As Mallory caught sight of Ryder, a part of him felt a momentary pity for the man who had been his friend. Ryder was not escaping; he was going into permanent exile, and exile to the Soviet Union would be punishment enough — however strong Ryder's political conviction might be.

The two pairs reached the center of the bridge simultaneously, and Mallory belatedly recognized Hollis as the man escorting Ryder.

"Hello, Richard," Ryder said with an odd half smile. He looked

— 279

pale and drawn, but he was dressed with his usual elegance, and his bearing was erect and outwardly self-assured. As always, Mallory thought, he carried on with style.

"Hello, Max."

"Is this our man?" the American colonel asked Hollis, and Hollis frowned uncertainly.

Mallory removed his hat and glasses, and Hollis's face cleared. "Yes, that's Mallory."

"All conditions have been met," Kurov said to Hollis. "Let us proceed."

"Wait one damned minute," the colonel snapped. "No one goes anywhere until we receive confirmation."

The colonel turned and looked back toward the cluster of MPs standing at the Western end of the bridge, and Mallory caught Ryder's eye. Ryder shrugged. Neither of them knew what the colonel was waiting for.

Ryder cleared his throat and said to Mallory, "I'd appreciate it if you'd look in on Karen when you get back. I think she could use the support."

"All right."

Mallory thought Ryder was about to say something more, but then Ryder gave the same half smile and looked away. No one spoke, and the six men continued to stand in the center of the Glienicker Bridge in a silent tableau.

Mallory noticed that Hollis was looking at him with undisguised admiration, and for a moment Mallory was taken aback; but then he understood. So this was how Pendleton had decided to play it, he thought. Mallory was to be the hero of the hour, the man who had risked capture to uncover a KGB sleeper. The credit for the operation would be Mallory's, to buy his silence. Tricking a case officer into acting as bait was not something Pendleton would want to advertise.

Mallory saw a civilian come to the Western end of the bridge and wave his arm.

"That's it," the colonel said, pulling an envelope from beneath his jacket and handing it to Ryder. "This contains a release signed by the Attorney General of the United States waiving prosecution — on the condition that you never again set foot in the United States or its Territories." The colonel paused, and his eyes narrowed. "If you do, you son of a bitch, we'll throw you in the slammer so fast your feet won't touch ground."

"I take your point, Colonel," Ryder said urbanely and took the envelope. He looked one last time at Ryder. "I'm sorry, Richard. I never meant to sell you out."

Mallory nodded tiredly. Ryder wouldn't know about Marie, and there seemed no point in telling him.

"Let's get the lead out," the colonel said impatiently.

Hollis reached out, clapped Mallory on the shoulder, and drew him across to the West, as Ryder stepped past him in the opposite direction.

Hollis was in an expansive mood, and Mallory let him talk. He sat in a soft leather chair in front of Hollis's desk, nodding occasionally when it seemed appropriate. Drained and uncaring, he was only half listening.

The COS had brought Mallory into the Station with no outright fanfare, but most of the Station's personnel had managed to get a look at him on the way to Hollis's office. There had been admiring smiles from the women and thumbs-up gestures from the men, but Mallory had not summoned the energy to smile in return. As soon as the office door had closed, Hollis had surprised him by offering him a bourbon, and Mallory now held the whiskey glass slackly in his left hand, his arm draped over the armrest.

"I knew you had what it takes the day you walked in here," Hollis was saying, and Mallory sensed that his words were not entirely insincere. Hollis had the administrator's gift; he could reverse his opinions as the wind shifted and convince himself that he had never thought otherwise. "I daresay," Hollis continued, "that nice things are going to happen to you."

There was no condescension in Hollis's voice. He was talking to Mallory as an equal, and Mallory deduced that a big promotion for him was in the wind. He lifted the glass in his hand and absently took another swallow of bourbon. He winced as it burned its way down his throat. Pendleton must have been laying it on with a trowel, Mallory reflected tiredly. Hollis was not only letting him booze it up in the Station, he had even gone to the trouble of finding out what Mallory drank.

"One day I'd like to get a blow-by-blow from you," Hollis said. "We were given a rough picture, of course, but the details are a bit vague."

"I'll bet," Mallory muttered.

"What was that?"

Mallory shook his head. "Nothing. You were saying?"

"That I'd like to get the details someday — when the dust settles a bit."

Mallory nodded, and Hollis beamed.

"I'd like to think we held up our end — even as bit players."

"You did fine," Mallory said thickly. The drink was hitting him hard, but that was all right; that was just fine.

"We weren't much help to you in the operation itself," Hollis said, "but we didn't do too badly in the exchange negotiations — if I do say so myself. The Russians insisted on keeping the talks at a low level, so I was called upon to deal for our side. You know how they are, never willing to call a spade a spade; they didn't want to admit that they were anxious to get their man back."

"Mmmh."

"Exactly. Well, that fellow at the bridge — Kurov is his name — did the talking for them. Quite a character. Fancies himself a tough customer, but oddly enough he blew his end of the deal."

Mallory had been staring at the glass in his hand, but now he looked up with a faint flicker of interest.

"That's right, he blew it. Practically the first thing he said to me when we had our initial meeting was that they wouldn't consider exchanging both you and the SSD defector for Ryder. He was quite belligerent about it." Hollis smiled and shook his head. "Hell, I hadn't heard anything about an SSD defector; my instructions were simply to trade Ryder for you. But Kurov let the cat out of the bag. As soon as he said that, I knew that the Russians thought we would ask for this defector as well, so naturally I dug in my heels. Why settle for half a loaf, eh? As I said, Kurov is an odd character. When we finally came to terms, he actually seemed satisfied; he never did realize he'd been had. You know, these KGB types are not always —"

"The terms," Mallory broke in hoarsely, his heart pounding. "What were the terms?"

"Didn't they tell you? That's what we were waiting for on the bridge — confirmation by radio that the East Germans had released the woman at Checkpoint Char— Mallory, are you feeling all right?"

"Where is she? I'd like to see her. I'd like to see her now."

"Sure, no problem. Bradford has her somewhere about the place. Some CI types came over from Langley to debrief her. But are you sure you're all right? You look a bit rocky."

Hollis stood in the doorway to the Station's interrogation room, breathing the air from the hallway rather than the stale, sweaty atmosphere that two hours of questioning had produced in the windowless, harshly lit room. Mallory and the East German woman stood in the center of the room, locked in a passionate embrace, but Hollis had recovered from his surprise and he was no longer looking at them. He was watching with amusement the peculiar expressions on the two fish-eyed men from Langley. It was the first time Hollis had ever seen CI types out of their depth.

Pendleton shifted his pipe from one corner of his mouth to the other, spilling ashes onto the Deputy Director of Operations' Moroccan leather sofa. The DDO didn't seem to mind. The pipe, the ashes, the worn tweed coat sagging on Pendleton's rounded shoulders, his overall shaggy appearance simply had to be accepted. With the exception of Pendleton, none of the DDO's immediate subordinates would have thought to enter his office without razor-sharp creases in their trousers or with haircuts over a week old, but Pendleton existed in a sphere all his own.

"I'm not sure we can bottle this up indefinitely," the DDO said. "Word of the exchange is bound to leak out. I'm a bit surprised we haven't seen a piece turn up in the *Times*."

Pendleton shrugged. "Let it ooze out, then. When the time comes, we can have a word with a few of the friendlies in the press. It shouldn't be too difficult to minimize Ryder's standing in the Company, and it can't do any harm to suggest that we were playing him back against the Soviets all along. Who's to say we weren't?"

The DDO smiled, his capped teeth dazzling white against his smoothly tanned skin. The tan was beginning to fade, and he had accordingly laid on a trip to the Caribbean. He liked to think of himself as a man's man, and he wouldn't stoop to sunlamps. "Good idea, Tom. I was thinking along the same lines myself. I'll need a sanitized report of this affair to pass upstairs for the Oversight Committee, though."

Pendleton nodded.

"Your man, Mallory, is due in from Berlin tomorrow, I understand. I want to —"

"Travis's man."

"What?"

"He's Travis's man. I simply borrowed him."

"Ah. Well, I signed a Special Citation for him this afternoon. He's a bit long in the tooth for a field man. Judging from his performance, I'd say it's high time he moved up. I understand you have some suggestions along that line."

"Yes, that was the idea," Pendleton said, sucking noisily on his pipe and tilting his head back to peer at the DDO through his horn-rimmed glasses, which had, as usual, slipped down on the bridge of his nose.

The DDO caught the drift immediately. "Second thoughts?"

"Well, let's not rush things."

The DDO frowned. "Why are you backpedaling? From what you told me, he sounds like a rough-cut jewel in the Company's crown. You aren't getting suspicious of *him*, for God's sake, are you, Tom?"

Pendleton laughed along with the DDO. When he took the trouble, he was an accomplished actor. He shook his head, drew a folded sheet of paper from the inside pocket of his jacket, and handed it to the DDO. It was Mallory's letter of resignation.

"This is dated before he took on this last assignment," the DDO said. "Do you think he still intends to resign?"

"Perhaps not, but I've had some second thoughts about over-looking the original intent. A promotion might persuade him to stay on, but I'm not sure it would be a good investment. He's a skilled officer, but he may be burned out. Perhaps we shouldn't block off a slot that a younger man could fill."

Again the DDO frowned, and there was some annoyance in his eyes. "We can't very well pull the rug out from under him at this point. It would be damned poor form."

"I'm not suggesting we pull the rug out — just that there is an alternative to promotion. A big bonus and a handsome pension might be a more appropriate reward."

The DDO shifted restlessly in his richly padded desk chair and looked again at Mallory's letter. "Are you sure about this?"

Pendleton removed his pipe from his mouth and stared at it for a moment. "No, not entirely. I just have some second thoughts, that's all."

"Damn it, Tom, make up your mind," the DDO snapped irritably, handing back Mallory's letter. "The man's done a hell of a job, and he's flying in tomorrow. I want your recommendation on my desk in the morning."

Pendleton nodded, uncoiled his long, thin body, and stood up. "You'll have it."

For a short time after Pendleton left the office, the DDO stared into middle distance, wondering if Pendleton might be losing his grip. It was not like Pendleton to be unsure of anything. It was a trivial matter, perhaps, but there were other small signs as well . . .

The DDO might have pondered the question of Pendleton a while longer, but he was distracted by some lint clinging to the sleeve of his dark blue blazer. By the time he finished removing the lint, his thoughts had wandered elsewhere.

Pendleton tilted the shade of his desk lamp away from him and leaned back in his chair with a barely audible sigh. He pushed up his glasses and slowly massaged his eyes. Long periods of reading were becoming impossible for him; his eyes couldn't take the strain. It was the eyestrain that stopped him, he told himself, not a diminishing power of concentration.

He rested his head against the back of his chair and let the stillness of the night soothe him. Though his soundproofed office was perpetually quiet and the heavy, lighttight curtains were always drawn, he knew without looking at a clock when it was night; he could feel the silence in the rest of the building and sense the darkness outside.

As always, his desktop was buried under piles of documents, but in a space he had cleared in the clutter of papers was the MARTIN file. The case was closed and he had won the game, yet a sense of satisfaction eluded him.

Absently Pendleton tapped the ashes from his pipe and restoked it. The dry scratch of the match he struck sounded unnaturally loud in the silent room. Why should he not be satisfied? He had laid his trap with care, and he had succeeded despite the unexpected, hidden links between Ryder, Mallory, and Martin.

Those links, which had been at the very heart of the affair, had not surfaced until the very end — links that had dragged one man down and raised another up. In that sense, nothing had changed, and it was this symmetry that disturbed Pendleton. The symmetry was only an abstraction, and yet . . .

Pendleton could not pinpoint the moment when a worm of doubt had begun to eat away inside him, the moment when the thought had first occurred to him that perhaps he was *meant* to be satisfied.

They had gotten very little from Ryder: the identification of his control in the Soviet embassy and of a Norwegian diplomat who had acted as cutout — useless information. Throughout the months of interrogations Ryder had maintained that he had worked all those years in isolation, that he knew of no other penetration agents.

That would be ideal, of course; but why should Ryder have achieved the perfect isolation that had eluded Philby and so many others? There were always connections from the past, inescapable bonds between men recruited into the Soviet service in their youth. Why should Ryder be an exception?

Bonds between men recruited in their youth . . . Mallory and Ryder had been friends for twenty-six years, and it was Ryder who had brought Mallory into the Company. Pendleton's lips twisted slowly into a wry smile. Paranoid. That's what the DDO would think. If Mallory were also a Soviet plant, the DDO would argue, the woman would have simply disappeared and Mallory would have returned to report no contact.

But Ryder would still have been damaged goods, never quite free of suspicion, Pendleton retorted in his own mind. Ryder would know that, and so would his KGB masters. How much cleverer it would be to write off Ryder and to move Mallory into position in his place. A symmetrical exchange.

Fatigue tugged at Pendleton's eyelids. It seemed as if he needed more sleep every night. But to sleep he needed to clear his mind of doubt. He took Mallory's letter of resignation from his jacket pocket and held it under the light. The letter itself argued against Pendleton's suspicions. A Soviet penetration agent would hardly resign. But Mallory, in fact, had not resigned. Not yet.

Pendleton shook his head and took out his pen. He was too tired to think through the endlessly branching possibilities; his mind demanded rest. He ripped a sheet from his memo pad, scrawled a note in his tight, spidery script, slipped it into a security envelope, and addressed the envelope to the DDO. It would reach the DDO's desk in the morning.

Accept Mallory's resignation, the note read.

Now, Pendleton was satisfied.